THE
SUMMER
SHE
VANISHED

Jessica Irena Smith is a glass artist from County Durham and has a BA in Glass & Ceramics and an MA in Glass, both from the University of Sunderland, where she was based at the National Glass Centre. Jessica's writing is inspired by many things, but she loves podcasts, especially true crime, which she listens to while cutting glass and loading kilns. In 2016, Jessica won a Northern Writers' Award; in 2017, she was awarded a TLC 'Free Read' by New Writing North; and in 2020, she was longlisted for Mslexia's Novel Competition. *The Summer She Vanished* is her debut novel.

THE
SUMMER
SHE
VANISHED

Jessica Irena Smith

HEADLINE

First published in 2023 by
HEADLINE PUBLISHING GROUP

1

Cataloguing in Publication Data is available from the British Library

ISBN 978 1 0354 0518 3

Typeset in 11/15.25 pt Adobe Garamond Pro by Jouve (UK), Milton Keynes

Printed and bound in Great Britain by Clays Ltd, Elcograf S.p.A.

Headline's policy is to use papers that are natural, renewable and recyclable
products and made from wood grown in well-managed forests and other
controlled sources. The logging and manufacturing processes are expected to
conform to the environmental regulations of the country of origin.

HEADLINE PUBLISHING GROUP
An Hachette UK Company
Carmelite House
50 Victoria Embankment
London EC4Y 0DZ

www.headline.co.uk
www.hachette.co.uk

To all those who've had the courage to speak out
And those yet to do so

Someone once described Boweridge as a waterlogged sponge, so soaked with secrets that at some point they start seeping out. The same, I've since discovered, can be said of families. Mine especially.

I

It was Uncle JJ who picked me up from the airport. Not my mom. Not even Bob. We passed the two-hour drive talking about everything and nothing, stopping once at a roadside service station for petrol – *gas*, Uncle JJ reminded me. The conversation was stilted, the awkwardness of two people who used to be close.

By the time we reached Boweridge, it was evening, but JJ insisted on detouring through the centre of town, for old times' sake. The last time I'd been home, just over two years ago, the first since I'd left for good, there'd been no time for sightseeing.

'You're kidding!' I exclaimed as we drove by Wally's Wafflehouse, thought of after-school visits with Lo – *one milkshake, two straws* – weekend breakfasts with JJ and Greg. 'Wally's is still going?'

'You betcha,' JJ replied with a smile.

We passed Neeley's Picture House, the tiny one-screen cinema – now the Boweridge Community Theatre – where Mr Neeley once patrolled the aisles, shining his flashlight on awkward first-date teens, making sure they weren't up to no good. We stopped at traffic lights on Main – 'Used to be just a lowly old stop sign,' JJ commented. 'Remember?' – where the only grocery store in town once stood. Now a Starbucks, one of two Boweridge had to offer these days, the payphone outside, from which Lo and I would prank-call school friends, was also long gone.

As we drove, the knot in my stomach, a clenched fist that had formed before I'd even set foot on the plane, began to ease. Things had changed over the years in Boweridge, that was for sure, but I was pleasantly surprised at how much remained the same, surprised that it felt weirdly comforting. There were good memories, I realised. It wasn't so much the town itself that plagued me, more the associations I had with it. Maybe I could do this after all.

The sun was low as we drew up outside the house, but the air still quivered with heat. I was about to get out the car when my uncle stopped me, placing a hand on my wrist.

'You don't have to do this, you know,' he said. 'Stay with her, I mean. Greg and I would be only too glad to have you.'

'Thanks, Uncle J,' I told him, 'really. But Mom would never forgive me. It's been a while.'

He nodded. 'Well, if it all gets too much, Mags . . .' He was the only one who called me Mags, had done for as long as I could remember. 'I mean it.'

'I know,' I said, and I did.

'We'll catch up for a coffee after the funeral,' he called over his shoulder as he jogged back to the car, having lugged my suitcase up to the porch. He waved his keys in the air and was gone, and when I turned, Bob was standing by the open door.

'You're early,' he greeted me. 'I'm sorry, your mom . . . we weren't expecting you till later. Here.' He grasped the handle of my enormous suitcase and hauled it over the stoop. 'Let me get that for you.'

The house was just as I remembered: cold, pristine, super-sized. Far too big for just two people. The huge front door swung shut behind us with an unnervingly quiet click. I remembered that, too.

'Is Mom around?' My voice echoed off the hardwood flooring.

'Oh yeah, course. But she's resting.' Bob had a year-round mahogany tan, but I could still see his cheeks flush. 'You know how she is,' he added. He dug his hands into his pockets and looked at the floor, rocking on his heels.

I nodded, unsure what to say. I knew exactly how Mom was. Even so, she could've at least made an effort. I mean, she hadn't seen me in two years.

The house was five beds, six baths, with a self-contained suite in the basement, my home for the next few days. I didn't think the basement was where Mom put her favourite guests – those she was keen to impress – but for me, it did just fine: a bedroom, en suite and small living area with a TV. Clean and tidy, if more dated than the rest of the house, and separate. It could be worse, I thought, fighting the urge to pick up the phone to Dad, or Em, or Tabby, back home in the UK.

'Can I fix you something to eat?' Bob asked, as he bumped my case down the basement stairs, me trailing behind.

His offer seemed genuine, but the thought of making small talk with my mom's husband, whom I barely knew, was more than I could take after a long day of travelling.

'Uh, thanks,' I said, 'but I'm pretty exhausted. Think I'll just shower, get an early night.'

We'd reached my room. Bob set my case down and stood awkwardly for a moment. 'Sure thing,' he said. 'Well, I'll be upstairs if you need anything. Goodnight.'

'Night. And thanks.'

As the door to my suite closed behind him, I flopped backwards onto the bed. When I'd booked my flight, I'd agonised about the minimum amount of time I could get away with. Two weeks, I'd decided in the end. Fourteen long days. They stretched before me like an eternity. Why on earth did I think I'd last that long? I was beginning to wish I'd taken Uncle JJ up on his offer, but I knew uprooting part way through my stay, abandoning my mother – again – would not go down well. That was Mom's thing, you see, people abandoning her: first Dad, then Em, then me.

On the bright side, a couple of weeks away could be just what I needed right now.

'And your supervisor's fine with it?' Em had asked when I phoned to tell her I'd booked my flight. 'Fine with you taking two weeks out?'

'It's not ideal,' I admitted, hoping my voice didn't betray anything, hoping Em wouldn't notice I'd swerved the question. Truth was, Simon didn't know. I hadn't told him, hadn't spoken to him at all, not since . . .

I couldn't think about that right now. I sighed, heaving myself to my feet to go shower, but I'd stood up too quickly, felt suddenly light-headed. I was cold, too, shivery, and had the beginnings of a headache. I decided to forgo the shower and get to bed.

In my limited experience, the one thing I've learned about McMansions is that despite outward appearances, their walls are often paper-thin. I wasn't quite sure what time it was, but I awoke to the sound of muffled voices somewhere upstairs – Mom and Bob – which became raised, punctuated by bursts of footsteps pacing back and forth on hardwood floors. A long silence followed and I must have drifted off, because the sound of a door slamming jolted me awake again. Outside, a car started, drove away.

The house began to settle around me, falling still once more.

A poor sleeper at the best of times, I lay tossing and turning. My phone sat next to the bed. The display read 3.30 a.m. Would it have adjusted automatically when I landed, or was it still on UK time? I wasn't sure. I felt for my watch, which I knew I'd changed, but despite my eyes having adjusted somewhat to the dark, I had to switch on the light to find it. I squinted in the brightness. Yes, a little after 3.30.

I did a quick scroll of my messages. Nothing interesting, bar one from my best friend, Tabby.

Hope you made it okay. Be thinking of you tomorrow. Call me when you get the chance. Tabs x

I'd reply later.

Next, I logged into my university email. I closed my eyes as the inbox loaded, not realising I was holding my breath until I opened them again and breathed a sigh of relief. Just admin emails and university circulars.

Fully awake now, not quite sure what to do, I got up and opened the bedroom door a crack, listening. From somewhere upstairs came the sound of a TV. I was about to close the door and go back to bed when I paused. In the darkness of the small living area, I could make out the shapes of furniture – sofa, coffee table, TV – but something else too. Boxes I hadn't noticed earlier. Two or three, at least, their dark shapes calling to me in the gloom. Funny. Mom detested clutter, especially on view, even in a spare room (God forbid a guest should see it).

I flicked on the light and padded over to them. There were actually four boxes, taped shut, but so full to bursting the tops bulged. I crouched down beside them, peeling yellowed, curling packing tape from the nearest, lifting the flap, peeking inside. Albums – photo albums, the dated faux-leather type with gold-tooled edging and dog-eared tracing paper sticking from between the pages. They must be Grandma Ida's.

I'd been surprised when Mom told me she'd been helping JJ clear their mom's house, even more so that she'd bring any of Grandma Ida's things home. Still, I could see her taking them, if only to deprive her brothers, could picture her breezing home, triumphant, Bob staggering behind under the weight of cardboard boxes. *Where'd you want 'em, honey?* he would have asked, smiling through gritted teeth. *How should I know?* Mom would have replied, a dismissive flick of her hand.

Just find somewhere – I don't know, the basement. They'd be out of the way down here.

Perhaps she even *wanted* me to find the boxes, I thought, settling myself cross-legged in front of them. If she did, I was walking right into her trap. I shook my head. *Stop overthinking things.*

The next three boxes, it turned out, contained little more than trinkets and knick-knacks: statues of Our Lady, rosaries, prayer cards. Grandma Ida's, for sure. Disappointed – I'd been hoping for something juicier – I returned to the box with the albums. I'd never really given much thought to Mom's past, I realised, as I began sifting through them. She never told stories of her childhood, nor did she have many photos round the house; just a handful of her and Bob looking glamorous on some exotic holiday or other, and a couple of Em: one from her university graduation, the other of her wedding, Mom centre-front of shot, obviously. The only picture she kept of me was an old middle-school photo from when I was about twelve or thirteen, just before I started high school, not long before I left. There were no graduation photos of me. Certainly no wedding pictures.

Under the albums lay stacks of loose photos of my mom and uncles at various stages of growing up, and Grandma Ida and Grandpa John too, in their younger days. Looking at them, it struck me how little I'd actually known my grandparents, though we'd lived just a few miles apart for the first fourteen years of my life. Grandma Ida had been as po-faced and pious-looking in her younger days as the old woman I remembered. She was the antithesis of my mother – never wore make-up or nice clothes, never glammed herself up. She'd apparently always looked pretty ancient too: the hairstyle that hadn't changed in decades (centre-parted, worn in a bun), the frumpy clothing. It astonished me how she'd managed to give birth to four such handsome, healthy-looking offspring.

As for Grandpa John, I was surprised to see photos of him looking relaxed and carefree. Happy, even. The man I remembered was stoic and silent, worn down by years of henpecking at the hands of Grandma Ida. He'd been a man of few words, though I always felt he'd tried with Em and me, giving us sweets and the odd bit of pocket money, but only when Grandma Ida's back was turned. 'Don't tell your grandma,' he'd say, before sloping off to dig the garden, or read the newspaper, or smoke a cigarette. I also knew he liked a drink. No one told me that as such, but I suppose children just sort of pick these things up – the knowing looks exchanged between grown-ups, the seemingly innocuous comments you don't quite understand but know have another meaning. I also remembered his smell, which to me seemed almost exotic: alcohol, cigarettes and peppermints.

I put the bundles of photos down and turned back to the albums, flipping open the cover of the topmost one. On the first page was a photo of the Larson siblings, veiled by a layer of tissue. I peeled it back. The photo was a colour shot with the unmistakable tones of the 1970s, that golden aura, a sort of overexposed, sunshiny hue.

There they stood in order of age: teenage Walter, William and John Junior, together with the baby of the family, my mom, Barbara, a beautiful little doll no more than nine or ten years old. They stood posed on a metal swing set, a lanky Walter leaning nonchalantly against the frame, William, JJ and Mom each seated on a swing. The hairstyles and the clothes! I couldn't help but smile: bell-bottoms (Walt and William) and too-tight shorts (Uncle JJ), pudding-basin haircuts (all the boys) and jam-jar spectacles (poor JJ again). Despite this, they were a good-looking bunch: blonde, blue-eyed, with goofy gap-toothed smiles, my mom sun-kissed and freckled, neat and tidy in her smocked dress and Mary-Janes, her brothers brown as berries.

What struck me most about the picture, though, was how happy they looked. Mom especially. I'd never seen her like this before, I realised – so carefree. It made me ache. She wasn't someone who was prone to smiling, not naturally. Yes, she'd smile when she met people, just as she would when she was trying to get her own way, batting her eyelashes, tilting her head at just the right angle. That was how she'd attracted Bob. That and her looks, I was certain of it. But spontaneous, genuine smiling? No, not my mom.

Unable to look at their beaming faces any longer, about to snap the album cover shut, I stopped, noticing that the thin white border – the type many older photos had – was missing on the right-hand side. I slipped the picture gently from its fixings and found that it had been folded, hiding three or four centimetres. Unfolding it carefully, I smoothed it out, and gasped. On the other side of the swing set from Uncle Walt, the two of them bookending the three youngsters in the middle, was a girl no more than sixteen or seventeen. She stood at a slight distance – not quite part of the gang – but resembled the others so much, Mom especially, that she couldn't *not* be related. But where Mom was petite, fragile-looking, this girl was long-limbed and tanned, with a sort of natural, wholesome beauty that not even my mom – with all her salon visits, her primping and her make-up – could compete with. The sort of lazy beauty she resented in others.

What struck me most, though, made the hair on my arms stand on end, was not how much the girl resembled the Larson siblings, but how much she looked like *me*. Her blonde hair was longer than mine, straighter too, centre-parted as seventies fashion dictated. But apart from that, we were almost identical: same features, same build, same skin tone. And those eyes, those dark brown eyes – *my* brown eyes – the only feature I didn't get from Mom.

I studied the image more closely. There was something else too, something not right. It wasn't just that my mom and her brothers were *physically* closer, arranged next to one another; it was more like there was an invisible barrier separating them from the girl, accentuated by the photo's stark white fold-line. It was the girl's expression that jarred most, though: sullen, unsmiling. Her head was slightly downcast, but her gaze was focused upwards, not *at* the camera, but straight through its lens. What was it, that look? Resentment? Hostility?

Fear?

I shook my head. I was reading too much into it, like I always did. Chasing shadows. Looking for a story where there wasn't one. Whoever she was, this girl, she was probably just a typical moody teenager. I was sure there must be a few photos of me from my teens where I looked like I'd rather be anywhere else. I flipped the picture over. *Summer 1972* was written on the back in faded blue ink. That would make my mom ten. I put the photo down and began to rake through the loose ones again, the other albums, too, determined to find the mystery girl. I flipped through photo after photo, page after page, but there was no trace of her, but for the occasional blank space in the albums – paler, ghost-like squares, flanked by empty photo corners.

Spaces where photos once lived.

I slept fitfully for the rest of the night and was wide awake again by 6 a.m. After lying for a while thinking about the mystery girl – convincing myself I'd blown the whole thing out of proportion, as happens in the small hours – I decided to get up.

Out in the basement hallway, the door opposite mine – the one to Bob's study – stood ajar. There was a light on inside, the sound of a TV playing softly.

I knocked gently and the door swung inward. 'Hello?'

'Maggie, hey,' exclaimed Bob from inside. Dressed in sweats and trainers, he was perched on the edge of his desk, hugging a coffee mug in his hands. 'Hope I didn't wake you?'

'Oh,' I said, unsure if he was referring to just now, or the commotion during the night. 'No. I couldn't sleep, that's all.'

'Me neither. Thought I'd go for an early-morning run before it gets too hot. Blow the cobwebs away, y'know?'

I looked around as he talked, trying not to be too obvious. The room was a mess. A little bit of rebellion on Bob's part, I guessed. The thought made me smile. Against one wall was the desk on which he perched; next to that a filing cabinet, a bag of golf clubs propped beside it. Against the other wall was a pull-out couch, bed made up, sheets rumpled.

'I sleep down here,' Bob said, following my gaze. 'Sometimes,' he added hastily, flushing. 'When I work late.'

I nodded weakly. 'Right . . .'

A few years Mom's senior, Bob had by all accounts had an extremely successful career. Something in finance. He'd been married once before, decades ago, way before Mom, but didn't have children. I imagined he must have been quite a catch: handsome, financially successful, no real baggage. I also imagined this wasn't how he'd envisaged his retirement. The sad thing was, just like Dad, I could tell Bob loved my mom. I also knew, just like with Dad, that sometimes love wasn't enough.

'It's been a rough time, these last few weeks,' he said. 'Losing your grandma, well, I guess you could say it's been a real turning point for your mom.'

'I get it,' I said, though I didn't. Not really. Mom and Grandma Ida had never been close. 'It's still her mother.'

I must have sounded as unconvinced as I felt, because Bob said, 'You know she's getting help? Actually seeing someone?'

'A psychologist?' I asked, surprised.

'Psychiatrist.'

'They put her on meds?'

Bob nodded.

'She actually taking them?'

He didn't respond, not right away, which was all the answer I needed. 'I count them sometimes, when she's not around,' he said. 'The tablets. Make sure there's the right number left.'

Do you also watch her twenty-four-seven, make sure she's not dumping them down the drain? I wanted to ask. *Do you drive her to her therapy sessions, accompany her inside? Sit in the waiting room till she's called?* If the answer to any of these questions was no, then I doubted Mom was taking her meds *or* attending therapy. I mean, why would she, when she was convinced it was everyone else who had the problem? Plus Mom lied. Lied for no reason. Lied about big stuff, little stuff. Lied in a way that normal people couldn't even begin to understand.

But Bob, I was quite sure, was already painfully aware of this.

He fidgeted, looked at the floor, and I felt so bad for him, wanted to tell him: *I feel your pain.* But I didn't think we had that kind of relationship, not yet, so instead, to change the subject, I said, 'Speaking of Grandma Ida, I found a photo.'

His expression brightened, more relief than anything. 'Oh yeah?'

'It was of the Larsons,' I told him. 'When they were kids. Walt, Bill, JJ, Mom. But there was this other girl, too. Long blonde hair. Bit older. Looked just like them. Like me. Do they have a cousin?'

'A cousin,' Bob repeated under his breath. He placed his mug on the desk, brushed at something invisible on the leg of his sweatpants. 'No, no cousin.'

'Well, do you know who she could be?'

His eyes snapped back to mine. 'You'd really have to ask your mom, Maggie.'

'Huh,' I laughed. 'Okay. 'Cos we both know how that'd go. Couldn't *you* just tell me what you know?'

'Look, sweetie, it's really not my place to say.' Bob had never called me sweetie before. He pushed off from his perch, leaving his coffee, and flicked off the TV. I thought he was going to walk out, but instead he turned to the filing cabinet. 'Your mom asked me to keep a bunch of stuff aside,' he said, his back to me. 'Separate from the rest.'

I was expecting another box, but instead he slid a large brown envelope from on top of the cabinet. He held it out, hesitated, then placed it on the desk.

'What is it?'

'Like I say, you'd really have to ask your mom.' He patted the envelope. 'Coffee's ready upstairs when you are. Switch the light off when you're done.' And he left the room.

The envelope was so tattered and full to bursting it looked ready to fall apart. It wasn't sealed, so I upended it, spilling the contents onto the desk. It was legal stuff mostly – property titles, insurance paperwork. Grandpa John's death certificate. Nothing unusual until I reached the birth certificates. There were four in total, one for each of the Larson children: Barbara, born 1962; John Junior, 1960; William, 1958; and finally eldest son Walter, 1956. No, wait. There was one more. *Five* birth certificates. I scanned the fifth, and there it was, filled out in neat cursive script: *Margaret Mary Larson, Feb 16 1955*.

I did a quick calculation. Seventeen. She'd have been seventeen in the photo. The eldest Larson sibling.

But why had I never heard of Margaret Mary Larson, and where was she now?

2

The funeral of Ida Joan Larson took place at St Augustine's church on 16 July 2019, the day after my return to the States. Mom emerged from her room that morning as if it hadn't been two years since we'd seen each other. She greeted me, cupping my face in her hands, 'Maggie, darling', stretched on tiptoe to kiss me on each cheek and I breathed her in, that ever-familiar smell: Chanel No. 5; a whiff of hairspray.

She was still beautiful, but she was thinner than ever, and I was secretly gratified to see up close the network of little lines framing her eyes, the sides of her mouth too.

She held my face a moment too long and smiled wanly. 'You look tired.'

I pulled away. 'Thanks, Mom.'

My eyes followed her as she fussed around the kitchen, and as I drank my coffee, tried to eat a piece of toast, I couldn't get the photograph out of my head. I considered asking her about it then and there. *What happened to her, Mom? To Margaret, your sister?* But something stopped the words from forming. Right now, before the funeral, was not the time.

*

Two black limos drove us to St Augustine's. Mom, Walt, Bill and JJ, with their respective partners, all but Greg, travelled in one; my cousins – Walt and Bill's children – and I in the other. The ride was sombre, owing more to the fact that I barely knew my uncles' off-spring than to the occasion. Though not dissimilar in age, my sister and I had seen very little of them growing up because they lived out of state. After the move to the UK, first Em's, then mine, we lost contact altogether.

To my dismay, as we climbed from the car I could see there was already a little gathering of mourners. Supported on either side by Bob and me, Mom was in her element, her knees buckling with each grief-stricken step, making the short walk from car to church feel like an eternity. Her head was bowed as we all but pulled her up the church steps, but I knew that from behind the dark lenses of her enormous Jackie O glasses, which dwarfed her gaunt face, she'd be stealing side-ways glances at the crowd. I wished *I'd* had the foresight to wear sunglasses, not because I planned on crying, but because it would have helped hide the embarrassment that must have been plain to see from my beet-red face. I'd never wanted more for the ground to open up and swallow me. I wondered if Bob felt the same.

My mom had a talent for stealing the spotlight. Years ago, when Em got engaged, she'd wanted a low-key wedding, maybe even to elope. But when Mom got wind of it, she kicked up such an almighty fuss that even from the other side of the Atlantic she made Em's life almost unbearable.

'Darling,' Mom said to me earnestly, during one of our rare phone conversations, 'this might be the only chance Mommy has to be mother of the bride.'

She had a point, so she got her way and somehow, from a distance, all but planned the wedding herself, everything from the venue to the band, table settings, my outfit – even Em's dress. When the big day arrived, it was as horrendous as we all expected. Her first trip to England, Mom arrived at the church in an outfit so ostentatious it was mortifying, and I spent much of the day trying to keep her and her then boyfriend (not Bob) separate from Dad and his new, much younger wife.

Before the ceremony, despite Mom not having seen Em in years, and though my sister had never looked more beautiful, the first thing Mom said was, 'Darling, what happened?'

Em, freshly laced into her wedding dress, looked blank. I shuffled uncomfortably. Here it comes, I thought, flinching.

'You gained weight,' Mom said, as though out of genuine concern.

Em's best friend, putting the finishing touches to my sister's make-up, stopped with her blusher brush mid-air, mouth half open. There was a moment's excruciating silence before my sister laughed, a small, tight sound.

'You're right, Mom,' she said. 'I did. It's been a few years.'

Not content with this, once proceedings were under way at the church, Mom became so overwhelmed that she had one of her fainting spells and had to be assisted out, guests and in-laws dancing attendance, finding her a chair, a glass of water, a cool place to recover.

Em, as only she could, shrugged the whole thing off.

'But she practically *ruined* your day,' I wailed afterwards, frustrated at her seeming indifference to the whole thing.

Em rolled her eyes. 'You know what she's like,' she said, which was what everyone said. 'It could've been much worse.'

I was surprised at the turnout for Grandma Ida's funeral. Most people who live to their late eighties find their friend numbers dwindling. Grandma Ida, I was sure, was not someone who'd had many friends to begin with; but as the priest reminded us, with the exception of the last two years, St Augustine's had been her church for decades, and many of the mourners in attendance were parishioners. He eulogised about Grandma Ida's life – 'devoted to God and her family'; her values (Catholic), her husband, 'whom she loved dearly' (I wasn't so sure), and the children she'd raised, who were 'all in attendance today'.

Not all, I thought. Margaret's not here.

I'd brought the photo with me, slipped it into my pocket before we left, as if I might need reminding what Margaret looked like. Before the service began, I'd scanned the congregation, hoping to see someone who looked like an older version of me, but from my seat in the first row of pews, sandwiched between Mom and JJ, it was hard to see without twisting round and drawing too much attention. It wasn't until we were filing out of church, making our way to the graveyard, that I got a better look.

At the back of the church, sitting in an otherwise empty pew, a man caught my eye. He stood out not just because he appeared to be alone, but because whilst everyone else was sidestepping from the rows of creaking pews, he remained seated, the order of service clasped in his hands. He was at least mid sixties I reckoned, with a sallow complexion, a moustache, and thinning grey hair. He wore a too-big black suit, collar open at the neck, tie askew. He looked up, and our eyes met for a beat too long before I looked away. When I dared to glance back, he was still staring. For no more than a few seconds I was swept along, lost in the bottleneck of mourners exiting the church, and by the time I looked over my shoulder again, the man was nowhere to be seen.

As the midday sun beat down and Grandma Ida's coffin was lowered into her grave, my mother wept and wailed, clutching at my arm with one hand, dabbing her eyes beneath her sunglasses with the other. Next to me, silent and stiff, stood Uncle JJ. From the corner of my eye, I saw a single tear slide down his face. I reached beside me, found his hand, and took it in mine.

*

Though closer to St Augustine's, the Larson home, where Grandma Ida had lived all her married life and raised her children, had sat empty for two years, so the wake was held at Mom and Bob's instead. Never one to pass up an opportunity to show off her beautiful house, Mom wafted among the guests like an ageing starlet in an episode of *Columbo*, the gracious hostess accepting condolences, making sure people's glasses were filled and that everyone had canapés.

For the most part, I managed to keep out of her way, but when our paths crossed in the company of guests, she'd say by way of introduction, 'This is my daughter, Maggie,' before lowering her voice and adding, 'Not the doctor, the other one.'

If anyone bothered to ask what exactly I did, Mom would give a sad smile and answer for me, 'Still a student, aren't you, Maggie darling?' in the tone one might use when confiding in someone that they have a terminal illness. I'd just stand, silently kicking myself for not being more assertive, for not adding that that was rich coming from a woman who'd made a vocation out of living off men, who hadn't worked since the age of eighteen, and that I was, in fact, doing a DPhil.

As I completed yet another circuit of the room – no sign of the man from the funeral – I weighed up whether I should raise Mom's sister with her later, one on one, or now, in the relative safety of company. As it happened, Mom made the decision for me: with guest numbers dwindling, she approached and, taking me by the elbow, steered me gently to one side.

'Darling,' she cooed, 'such a beautiful service, don't you think?' Then, before I could answer, she added, 'Just a shame Em couldn't make it. Then the whole family would've been together.'

'Not the *whole* family, Mom,' I blurted out, then wished I hadn't.

But Mom just tilted her head. 'Whatever do you mean?'

She sounded so genuinely puzzled that for a moment I doubted myself, but then I thought of the photos, how leaving them where I'd chance upon them was such a Mom thing to do. 'I found the boxes you left in the basement,' I explained – *game's up, Mom.* 'The albums. There was a girl. Margaret.' The photo burned in my pocket. 'Your sister.'

For a second Mom looked like I'd slapped her, but she quickly recovered herself, rebuilt her expression with one I knew well, one that told me the conversation was over. She made to leave and, the moment slipping from my grasp – *this could be my only chance!* – I reached out. 'Wait . . .'

Though I hadn't touched her, Mom stopped, rigid.

'What happened to her?' I asked, my whole body tense. 'To Margaret. I mean, I'm sorry, Mom, for bringing it up. But you *named* me after her.' Growing up, I'd hated my name. It was so unlike all the Ashleys and Briannas and Brittanys I'd gone to school with. So old-fashioned. 'You *did* name me after her, didn't you?'

Across the room, someone waved at Mom, gestured that they were leaving. Mom, still the consummate host, returned their smile, gestured back – *hang on one minute, I'll come see you out!* – then turned to me, her expression changing again in an instant.

'Margaret made a choice,' she said, her voice quiet but firm. Dangerous. I gripped my wine glass so tightly my knuckles blanched. 'She left this family over forty years ago.' And with that, Mom walked away.

I retreated to the garden, where a figure sat a little way off on a sunlounger by the pool. It was Uncle JJ, his expression caught somewhere between quizzical and concerned.

'Everything okay?' he called over.

The collar of his shirt was undone, sleeves rolled up, his black jacket and tie draped on the seat beside him. I opened my mouth to reply, closed it again.

'Rough day, huh?' He motioned at the lounger across from him as he lit a cigarette. 'Come, sit.'

The last time I'd been back in Boweridge, a little over two years ago, was after Grandpa John died. It was term-time, so a flying visit, and though we said we'd meet up, I hadn't seen JJ at all. He wasn't at Grandpa John's funeral. Wasn't welcome. Yesterday was the first time I'd seen him in years, and I'd been alarmed at how he'd aged, his once fair hair now grey, his tanned face lined and craggy.

'Thought you'd given up?' I nodded at the cigarette.

He raised an eyebrow, smiled. 'You and me both.'

For a few minutes we sat in silence, Uncle JJ puffing on his cigarette, blowing smoke from the side of his mouth.

'Was she like this when you were growing up?' I asked at last.

'Who? Your mom?' He laughed, took a drag.

He knew more than most what Mom could be like. Growing up, of all my uncles I'd been closest to JJ by miles. He and his partner, Greg, lived nearby, not so far from Mom and Bob's house now, in fact. Uncle JJ had been there for me in a way Mom hadn't, in a way she could never be, but even more so after she and Dad separated in '97. I was nine. A year later, Dad got a job offer he couldn't refuse from an archi-tect's firm in England. The pull of home was too much to resist, and he returned to the UK, sixteen years after leaving. Apart from my sister, who was seven years my senior and had her own life by then, my only constant was JJ and Greg. When Mom took to her bed for days on end, they'd pick me up from school, take me out at weekends, let me stay round theirs. They were, for a time, my parents.

Uncle JJ took another drag, exhaled. 'What set her off this time?'

'I asked about Margaret,' I said, studying his face, waiting for his reaction.

It took a second to register, and when it did, I was sure he'd shut the conversation down, just like Mom. But I didn't give him enough credit. JJ was nothing like Mom. Instead, he took his time, finished his cigarette, then reached down, grinding it out on the patio. I smiled to myself. Mom would've had kittens if she'd seen.

'What was it you wanted to know?'

I took the photo of the Larson siblings from my pocket and held it out. JJ took it, studied it. Sighed.

'What happened to her, Uncle J?' I asked. 'I mean, God, she'd be, what, sixty by now?'

'Sixty-four,' JJ said. 'Five years older than me, seven years older than your mom.'

Seven years, I thought. Seven years between Mom and her sister. The same difference as Em and me.

'But why does no one talk about her?'

JJ took a pack of cigarettes from his pocket, lit one, took a drag. 'It was Minna,' he said, exhaling. 'Her name was Minna.'

3

' "Minna was born in a snowstorm. It was the worst winter Boweridge had ever seen." ' JJ said it in an old-man voice, like he was recounting the start of a fairy tale. Then he laughed. 'That's how your Grandpa John told it, anyhow.'

We were in JJ's car, driving downtown. 'I dunno about you,' he'd said, after I'd asked about Margaret, 'but I think I've had just about enough of family for one day.' He'd smiled. 'Present company excepted, of course. What do you say we get outta here, let me show you something?' He'd finished his cigarette, and we'd left the wake via the garden gate, sneaking out like naughty teenagers.

'Minna was the eldest,' I said.

'Right, the firstborn. Then came Walt, Bill, yours truly, and finally your mom.'

'So where'd Minna come from? The name, I mean?'

'I guess that's down to Walt. Apparently, when he was little – like, *really* little – everyone thought he was trying to say Mama. Turned out he was trying to say Margaret – he doted on his big sister – 'cept it kinda came out like *Mi-ah* instead, just sorta stuck. "There's Scandinavian blood in the Larson veins." ' JJ used the old-man voice again.

'That was another thing your grandpa used to say, that in Sweden, the name Minna means love. Cute, huh?'

'So what happened to Minna?' I asked. 'She just upped and left?'

'Pretty much.' Uncle JJ switched on the indicator, turning into a quiet residential street. 'June '72. As for what happened to her . . .' he sighed, like he'd been through it all before, 'everyone's got their theories.'

'What's yours?'

'Honestly?' A slight shrug this time. JJ's eyes flicked to the mirror as he pulled in to the kerb. 'There's part of me believes the most popular theory, that she ran away, that she's out there somewhere living her life.'

'And the other part?'

He parked up, cut the engine. 'She was seventeen, for God's sakes. She vanished. People don't just do that.'

'People run away all the time,' I said, not entirely convinced.

He nodded. 'But stay away? That's different. Not make contact for decades? Cut all ties, start over?'

'Well, if she did run away, she must've had her reasons.'

'Oh, there were reasons all right,' JJ said, taking a pack of cigarettes from the cup holder, tucking them into his shirt pocket. 'Look. What you have to understand is that Minna was a free spirit, but she was troubled, too.'

'Troubled how?'

There was a shriek of laughter from outside – children playing in a sprinkler in the early-evening sun – and when I turned back, Uncle JJ was already out the car. I hurried after him.

The Larson family home was on the opposite side of town from Mom and Bob's, an area once known for being less affluent. Now pleasant-looking, well-kept, tree-lined, it was an up-and-coming neighbourhood. A mixture of clapboard and brick, the Larson residence was still quaint, though probably more down-at-heel than its neighbours would have liked, having been empty for two years and neglected for some time before that. The flaky picket fence leaned at a gravity-defying angle, and as I made my way up the flagstone path, I saw just how overgrown the garden had become. Though it had been years since I'd last visited, the same swing set still stood there, the one I recognised from the photo, now rusty and choked with weeds.

Uncle JJ paused on the porch, digging for his keys.

'You're putting the house up for sale?' I looked around at the weather-worn porch, the paint-chipped windowsills, the holes in the screen door.

JJ nodded, slid the key into the lock. 'Realtor's coming next week.' He pushed open the front door, dust dancing before us in shafts of light, and smiled wryly. 'Guess it's what you'd call a fixer-upper.'

He wasn't kidding. As my eyes adjusted to the gloom, I saw that the room we'd stepped into was empty – a far cry from the clutter I recalled from childhood visits – just dated, peeling wallpaper, greying net curtains, and a solitary wooden crucifix on one wall.

'Me and Greg've cleared most of it already,' Uncle JJ explained as he started upstairs. 'With a little help from your mom.' Another wry smile.

The irony of the fact that it was JJ who'd done most of the work wasn't lost on me. Prior to Grandma Ida's death, he hadn't set foot in the Larson home for decades; for different reasons, neither had I.

He stopped in front of me on the landing. 'The front bedroom was the girls'. Your mom and Minna's.'

I realised now that on our infrequent childhood visits, Em and I had never stayed the night at our grandparents', never even been upstairs. JJ held the door of the first room open and I stepped in. It was small and square, carpeted, with a single white metal bed frame on either wall, a bare bulb hanging from the ceiling. Apart from that, there was nothing except for one of those large blue IKEA bags.

Uncle JJ nodded at it. 'That stuff,' he said, 'it was Minna's. Your mom sure didn't want it, and I wasn't sure what to do with it. There's nothing valuable, but, well, it didn't seem right to throw it in the trash.' He cleared his throat. 'Anyhow, I'll leave you to it. Got some things to sort through in the other room.'

I barely heard him leave. I could only stare at the bag: all that was left of Minna. I kneeled and began sifting through it. It was school stuff mostly – report cards, exercise books, yearbooks. I picked up the most recent yearbook first. *St Thomas Aquinas Catholic High School for Girls, 1971*, the cover read. One year before Minna went missing. She would've been sixteen. The pages were filled with black-and-white head shots of teenage girls, looking old and young all at once, with braces, retro glasses and set hair. It didn't take long to find Minna. She stood out. Unlike her classmates, with their slightly Stepford looks, their beehives and perms – hangovers from the sixties – Minna was different. Not posed like her peers, there was something more understated about her – that inscrutable expression, the corners of her mouth slightly upturned. *Smile, Minna!* I imagined the photographer saying to her. And she did. Like she had a secret.

Next to each photo was a caption detailing students' roles and achievements, things like hall monitor, cafeteria supervisor, chess club champion, student council. *Larson, Margaret Mary*, Minna's read. *Library monitor, book club member, school paper journalist*. It didn't sound like the résumé of someone who was off the rails.

The rest of the yearbook was filled with pages detailing students' achievements, as well as the various clubs and activities the school ran. One such page, entitled *The St Thomas Aquinas Gazette*, featured a montage of photos depicting student members of the paper's 'press pack'. The largest photo, showing all the journalists, was captioned: *Students hard at work preparing the week's edition of the St Thomas Aquinas Gazette!* There were eight in total, Minna among them, sitting at desks, heads bowed in concentration. In another photo, a fair-haired young teacher appeared to be helping them, stooped over one of the desks, pencil in hand.

So Minna had been a student journalist. I felt the tug of an invisible cord linking us through generations. Before I'd left for the UK, in my first and only year of high school, *I'd* been a student journalist. My best friend, Lo, and I were the *Boweridge High Enquirer*'s only reporting duo, and in our short time together had co-authored a number of pieces. When we were younger, becoming writers had seemed like a realistic ambition. I wondered if that had been Minna's ambition too; wondered what Lo was up to these days.

I leafed through the rest of the yearbook. At the very back were profiles of the teaching staff; mostly nuns, but a couple of priests too.

I put the yearbook aside and began rifling through the rest of the box's contents. There were some school textbooks and old exercise books, one of which yielded a sepia Polaroid showing Minna with a teenage boy – a young man, really, tall and handsome, the square-jawed football-jock type, one arm slung nonchalantly around Minna's shoulder. He grinned confidently at the camera and Minna beamed up at him, one arm round his waist, the other hand resting against his chest, gazing at him so adoringly that I felt somehow I was intruding. At the bottom of the Polaroid, in a teenage hand and accented by love hearts, was written *Mike & Minna, May 1972*. One month later, she was gone.

I picked up the report cards. They dated from the summer term of 1972 and were somewhat worse for wear, paper yellowed, ink faded. Some of the comments were no more than illegible scrawl, but still I was able to get the gist of things. *Margaret often arrives late to class*, her maths teacher wrote. *She can be insolent and wilful, tells untruths, and has been given a number of detentions*, wrote another. *Margaret has been spoken to about the lies she tells . . . Margaret cannot be trusted to tell the truth . . . Margaret has a tendency to exaggerate. Margaret tells tall tales.*

Margaret lies.

Those two small words. A memory, vague, like a loose thread that if I only just tugged on . . . And then it hit me.

I was transported back two years, to the last time I was in Boweridge, for Grandpa John's funeral, and I'd visited Grandma Ida in her nursing home. She had dementia, so I was surprised when, at the sight of me, her eyes lit up in recognition. She remembers me, I thought. She reached out, took hold of my face between cold, trembling hands. Then, like a cloud passing over the sun, her expression darkened.

'Minna lies,' she said, ever so quietly, and squeezed my face tighter. '*Minna lies.*'

Though I'd no idea what she was on about at the time, there was something in the way she said it that stuck with me. I'd asked Mom about it, of course, but she simply shrugged it off. 'Maggie, darling,' she said, in a bored-sounding drawl. 'Your grandma's demented. She thinks Eisenhower's president.'

There was only one report in the pile different from the rest, not least because it referred to Minna, rather than Margaret. *Minna is a gifted student with a talent for writing*, it read. *She has a vivid imagination and a kind nature. She is bright and intelligent, though sometimes lacks concentration, and would benefit from applying herself more. She was, until last term, a valued member of the school newspaper. I'm hopeful she will return.*

The report was by Minna's English teacher, who was also apparently her form tutor, and was signed by a Sister Fran . . . something. Frances? Francesca? The faded writing was too hard to read.

I found Uncle JJ outside, sitting on the top step of the porch, soaking up the last of the evening sun and smoking another cigarette. He shuffled along and I sat down beside him, still clutching the 1971 yearbook.

'You said she was troubled.'

His eyes flicked to the book on my lap, then off into the distance. 'I did, huh?'

'What did you mean?'

'Just teenage angst, I guess.'

I was taken aback. When he'd mentioned it in the car, it had sounded like so much more. Still, I decided not to push it. 'So that summer,' I asked instead, 'what happened?'

'That's just it. Nothing.' He tapped his cigarette over the side of the steps. 'The summer she vanished was just like any other.' He shook his head, a wistful, faraway look in his eye. 'God, it was hot. Me, Walt and Bill spent all day every day outdoors, down at the lake mostly, playing on rope swings, climbing trees, making dens. Typical kid stuff.'

'And the day itself?'

'The day she upped and left? We'd stayed out past dark, your uncles and me. Missed our curfew. We were dusty as hell – that red dust, gets everywhere – covered head to toe.' He smiled at the memory. *Good times.* 'Guess we were expecting a hiding from Mom, but when we got home, she barely noticed us, so we snuck in, went straight to our rooms. Her and Dad seemed kinda distracted. Not worried, you know? Just, well, I don't know. Minna hadn't come home again.'

'She did that a lot?'

'No more than a night here or there,' JJ said. 'Always came back the next day.'

'Except this time.'

'Right. Not the next day, or the next.'

'Did they report her missing?'

'To the police? I guess. I mean, the cops showed up here, spoke to Mom and Dad. School was out, but they asked around her teachers, classmates too. In the end, I guess they just reckoned she'd run away.'

Classmates. It seemed an odd turn of phrase. Not *girlfriends*, or *friends.*

'And you've never tried to find her? You don't want to know what happened to her?'

'You have to remember, Mags, I was no more than twelve, thirteen at the time. I barely knew her. I've *not* known her far more years than I knew her.'

I was staggered. Growing up, I wasn't close to Em. The age gap had seen to that. Plus her move to the UK before mine. But I knew that if my sister went missing, if she'd simply upped and vanished with no apparent explanation, I'd have moved heaven and earth to find her.

'Look . . .' Uncle JJ flicked his cigarette, 'I know it sounds cold, but back then, I had my own shit going on. I'd just hit my teens, was struggling with being gay. Things are different now, even in Boweridge, but in those days, well – gay kid, small town, Catholic family. You can guess the rest.'

I had an idea. *What did Grandma Ida say when you told her you were gay?* I'd asked him once. *That I'd burn in hell*, he'd replied simply.

'I get it,' I said, 'I do. But since then. Aren't you curious? Don't you ever wonder what happened?'

'Sure.' JJ nodded, took a drag. 'But after she disappeared, Mom didn't like us talking about her. Guess we just got used to it. There're a lot of secrets in our family, Mags. A lot of skeletons. I learned long ago it's easier to let sleeping dogs lie.'

Secrets? Was he talking about himself? The fact that he didn't come out till he was almost thirty, though he'd been with Greg since his early twenties? That his mother had disowned him when he did, barred him from the family home, not spoken to him again, nor ever met his partner of more than thirty years?

Or was it something else?

'Secrets like what?' I asked.

'Huh.' He gave a bitter laugh. 'That's just it, they're secrets. They're not meant to be found out.'

'Is that what you meant about Minna being troubled?' I tried again. Before now, JJ had always seemed like such an open book.

'Listen, Mags.' He ground his cigarette out in an empty plant pot and got to his feet. 'You know me. I probably overexaggerated. Minna could be a bit rebellious, that's all. But aren't all teenagers? Christ,' he said with a shudder, laughing, 'I know I was.'

He held out a hand and I took it, letting him pull me from the step.

'And I guess she had a tendency to tell tall tales, too,' he said, 'but it wasn't much more than that.'

There it was again: *a tendency to tell tall tales.*

Margaret has been spoken to about the lies she tells . . . Margaret cannot be trusted to tell the truth . . . Margaret has a tendency to exaggerate.

Margaret lies.

Minna lies.

4

That night, after Uncle JJ dropped me home, I was sitting on my bed scrolling through my phone when a message pinged from Em.

How's it going? 😔 *Still alive? X*

I checked my watch. Not five in the UK yet. I tried ringing her.

'Did you know we had an aunt?' I asked when she picked up, the line between us crackling and echoey.

'A what? An aunt? What on earth are you on about?'

Like me, my sister had long since lost her American accent. Within a year of Dad leaving for the UK, Em had joined him; was a fully fledged Brit now, married, with two young children, a third on the way. When we learned that Grandma Ida had died, when our hearts sank at the thought that at least one of us would have to go back for her funeral, mine had sunk a little more. Being seven months pregnant was a pretty good excuse for not going, not one that I – single, childless – could trump. I'd scolded myself for thinking it convenient that Em had also been pregnant for Grandpa John's funeral, not attended that either.

'Maggie?' Em's voice came down the line. 'You still there?'

'Mom had an older sister.' I leaned back on the bed, twisting the phone cord on the ancient landline round my fingers. 'Minna.'

There was a pause, and I thought Em was taking a moment to

process what I'd told her, but then I heard her say in a muffled tone, 'No, Ben, sweetheart – put that down. Mummy's just cleaned it.' It was teatime back home. Not the best time to have called. 'Sorry, Maggie, you were saying – an aunt?'

I tried Dad next. 'Did you know Mom had an older sister?' was the first thing I said. There was silence on the line, and I wondered if he was still there. 'Dad?'

A sigh. 'You mean Minna. What did your mother tell you?'

'Nothing.'

'JJ?'

'Only that she went missing in '72.'

Dad hadn't met Mom until 1980. She was eighteen, a typist, he a dashing young architect at the same firm, six years her senior, fresh off the boat from England, a rising star in the world of architecture from a well-to-do family. He charmed her with his British accent and sophisticated ways. The fact that he was tall, dark and handsome didn't hurt either. All the girls in the office were after him, Mom said, but he chose her. I often wondered if he ever regretted it.

Dad was Mom's first real boyfriend. A whirlwind romance. They married within a month of meeting, late summer 1980. That it didn't last came as no surprise to anyone. The surprise was that Dad stuck it out for so long. I'd love to say they simply married too young, just grew apart, but it wouldn't have been true. It didn't stop me from telling people that, though, on the rare occasion it came up in conversation. That version was far simpler.

'I'm afraid I don't know much more than that,' Dad said. 'The impression I got was that Minna ran away, but it wasn't something openly discussed in the Larson house, or by your mother. In fact, they seemed to actively avoid the subject.'

Dad couldn't tell me much more, so I rang off in favour of Tabby, who was trying to FaceTime me.

'Bloody hell, you look awful!' she said, peering at me through the phone screen.

'Jeez,' I said, 'don't hold back.'

'Sorry.' She grimaced, and her face went all pixely. 'You just look tired. Must be the jet lag.'

Tabby was sitting on the sofa facing the window in her tiny dive of a London flat, the late-afternoon sun streaming in. She shifted, the stone set in the slim gold band on her left ring finger glinting in the light, and for a moment I felt a lump in my throat, like the one I'd felt when she first told me, the one that made my voice come out all squeaky when I'd said, 'Oh my God, congratulations!' when what I'd wanted to ask was, *Why?*

I had a sudden vision of us sitting on that very sofa every time one or other of us went through a break-up, of Tabby playfully barging me with her shoulder, reminding me of the pact we made that we'd never get married, that we'd end our days cat-lady spinsters together. I swallowed, inwardly blaming the jet lag, my fatigue, the headache that had nagged at me since yesterday . . .

'You okay?' Tabby asked, leaning in.

'Huh? Oh yeah, I've not been sleeping great, that's all.'

'So how was it? The funeral?'

I filled her in on everything, including my discovery.

'Minna lies about what?' she asked when I'd finished. 'What does that even mean?' She wrinkled her nose and for a moment her face was frozen in time. Bad connection.

'That's just it,' I said, relieved that finally someone was giving this the focus I thought it deserved. 'No one really says.'

'Shit,' said Tabby. 'Your mum's family's even more screwed up than you thought. Guess it's hardly surprising, though. I mean, your gran sounded like a pretty cold fish, and look at your mum. No offence,' she added quickly.

'None taken.' I laughed, though I couldn't help but feel stung. Tabby could be pretty forthright, especially when it came to my family. But what did I expect? I'd spent years complaining about Mom, could hardly object. 'I look like Minna, too,' I added, changing the subject. 'Even more than I look like Mom.'

'God, that's creepy.' Tabby's phone was balanced on the coffee table in front of her, lower down than she was, so her face wasn't always in shot. 'So what do you think happened to her? You really think she ran away?'

'To be honest, I've no idea. I don't know much about the circumstances yet. That's another thing people haven't exactly been forthcoming about. Apparently she had issues, though.'

'This might seem kind of obvs,' Tabby said, 'but have you tried googling her? Or looking on Facebook? If she's out there somewhere, it'd be hard not to have some kind of online presence.'

'You're right,' I said, 'I should try.'

'Come on.' She grinned. 'What's the worst that could happen?'

'But she mightn't even be using the same name. I mean, she'd be in her sixties now. She could've married, had children, could be anywhere.'

Tabby leaned forward to reply, but the screen froze again, this time for good. I waited a couple of minutes, then messaged her.

Dunno what happened. Connection pretty bad here. Will let you know what I find out about Minna. M x

Sighing, about to get up, I realised Tabby was right: I should at least google Minna. I'd been putting it off, afraid of what I might – or might not – discover, but there was no point resenting the Larsons for being so secretive without at least *trying* to do something myself. If I couldn't find Minna, well, that would be that. If I did find her and she didn't want to know, then likewise. But at least I'd have tried.

I got my laptop out and typed in *Margaret Larson*. I'd guessed it'd be a common name, though maybe, if she was still local, there'd be something. But other than some American journalist and a couple of LinkedIn profiles, nothing came up. Next I turned to Facebook, which, unsurprisingly, had hundreds of Margaret Larsons. I spent an hour or so trawling through them, discounting half on the grounds of age – too young, mostly – while the rest had either blank profile pictures or no information to show at all.

Maybe searching for Minna Larson would be more fruitful. Minna was, after all, the name she went by, and was certainly more uncommon. Or so I reckoned. I reopened Google, typed *Minna Larson* and hit enter. 258,000 results. Great. I sighed. There was a Swedish actress, a Minna Larsson, double S, born in the late nineteenth century. Other than that, there were a few Facebook profiles, mostly good-looking young Swedes, all with the same double S spelling. The name appeared on genealogy sites too, but again, nothing useful, nothing that made me think I'd found *my* Minna.

It was on the second page of the Google search results that I spotted something – a conversation thread in a Facebook group called 'Who killed Sister Fran?' My heart quickened. I clicked the link. Minna's name – if it *was* Minna – appeared to have come up in relation to a photo posted on the group's page: a black-and-white portrait of a good-looking young nun, kind-faced and smiling, wearing a habit and veil. The caption read: *40 years this year since Boweridge nun and beloved high school teacher Sister Francesca Pepitone was murdered, a murder that still remains unsolved.*

I scrolled down. Beneath the photo there were fifty-seven comments, some, it appeared, from people who had known Sister Fran – *She was my form teacher for a year at St Tom's* or *My fave teacher! Everyone loved her!* – others from complete strangers: *I've never met Sister Francesca, but she's in my thoughts every day.*

The last few looked like a conversation between four or five people, a string of rambling, typo-ridden messages, but interesting all the same:

> **Brad Mitchell** Hey, I didn't no Sis Fran personly but my ex was at St Tom's when she was killed. Anyone else hear the rumor about that minna Larson? Like that her dissapearnce was connected to the nuns death?

My heart skipped a beat. I scrolled further. The next comment, posted the same day, read:

> **Betty Adams nee Kelley** If you know something helpful you should go to the police if not BUTT OUT!!!

That comment had been liked more than all the others put together. The next comment read:

> **Randy T** Yeah I heard that too. There was a lotta dark shit goin on at that school. Looks like the nun was murdered to cover stuff up. Minna too if you ask me.

Two days later:

> **Tammy Samms** LOL ITS A LOAD OF BS. I WAS AT THAT SCHOOL SIX YEARS AND NEVER SAW NOTHING.

Then, a few hours later:

> **Deirdra Hinkle-Schroeder** Fckn armchair detectives.

> **Betty Adams nee Kelley** @DeirdraHinkle-Schroeder LOL!

I checked the date on the thread. 2012. My heart sank. The discussion was seven years old. But forty years since 2012 would make it 1972 when Sister Fran was killed. The same year Minna disappeared.

So who *was* this Sister Francesca? The name, the face, even, seemed familiar. Then I remembered: *Minna is a gifted student with a talent for writing.* Minna's English teacher. I scrabbled for the yearbook, flipping to the back few pages, and there she was: *Sister Francesca Pepitone.* Same smiling, dimpled face, same bright eyes.

I took a deep breath and clicked on the 'Write a comment' box underneath the photo.

Hi, my name's Maggie Elmore, I typed. *I think the Minna Larson you're talking about was my aunt. She went to St Thomas Aquinas High School and disappeared in 1972. If anyone's heard from her since, got any info on her or can shed any light on her disappearance, I'd be really grateful. Thanks.*

I closed the lid of my laptop, sat back and waited.

5

When I woke up, the first thing I did was log into Facebook to see if anyone had replied. Nothing. I slumped against the headboard. The original post had been from 2012, the comments seven years old. Maybe no one even checked the page any longer.

I logged into my uni account next and found an email from Simon. He'd tried calling me a handful of times in the days after – the last as I sat in departures, right before I boarded my flight, though he'd no idea I was even going – but I'd let them go to voicemail. The fact that he hadn't tried to contact me since had lulled me into a false sense of security. I'd assumed he'd given up. So when I saw his message nestled innocuously among the others – more admin emails, social invites, seminar and conference dates, deadline reminders – I had that sudden lurch of sickness, the one you get on a fairground ride when it drops at speed but your stomach's a beat behind. The subject was an old one – *Supervision next week* – and I swithered about opening it at all, hovering the mouse uncertainly before finally clicking it.

Maggie, we need to talk.
Simon

The brevity of it, the clinicalness, took me completely aback. He was acting like *I* was the one in trouble, which somehow incensed me more than if he'd sought to explain himself.

My hands shook with anger. I clicked the trash can, logged out.

There was no sign of Mom at breakfast, though Bob was at the table drinking coffee and reading the morning paper, wearing cream chinos and a polo shirt.

'Golf?' I asked, pouring myself a coffee, a residual shakiness to my hands.

'You bet,' he replied. 'You know I can get you a guest pass, right? For the country club. You could use the spa, get a treatment.'

'Um, thanks.' I wasn't really a spa type of person, had never had a treatment in my life. 'But I thought I might pop into town, visit the library.'

'They really do work you hard,' Bob said. 'I thought students got the summer off?'

I didn't bother telling him that postgrads didn't get the summer off, and that my supervisor had no idea I was currently on the other side of the world. It was easier to go along with it.

'I also wondered about hiring a car,' I added casually, leaning against the worktop, taking a sip of my coffee, eyeing him over the top of the mug. 'You know, to get around.'

'Sounds good,' Bob said. 'There's a rentals place on Main Street.'

'Oh?' I feigned surprise, but I already knew. I'd looked it up online. It was right across the road from Boweridge Police Department.

'I can run you down there if you like?' Bob offered. 'Be leaving in ten.'

I'd genuinely considered hiring a car. I didn't own one in the UK, didn't need to, but I'd had my driver's licence for years and apparently all I needed to hire one here was that and a credit card. Problem was, I'd never really liked driving, and the thought of doing it on the wrong side of the road I liked even less. But I didn't tell Bob this. When he dropped me off outside Art's Auto Rentals, he waited until I'd actually opened the door and gone inside before he drove away, even though I paused pointedly on the threshold to turn and wave at him. I was watching through the glass, my plan to hightail it back out onto Main Street as soon as his car had disappeared, when a chirpy voice made me jump.

'Welcome to Art's Auto Rentals!'

I turned to see a lady with big hair, late middle-aged, standing behind a counter at the back of the shop.

'How may I help you today?' she asked in a sing-song voice.

I decided it'd look weird to leave now. Reluctantly I approached the counter. 'I was wondering about hiring a car,' I said.

'Oh my gosh, your accent! It's just adorable! You're from England, right?'

'Thanks, uh, yeah.' I stepped closer to the counter. The woman's gaze fixed properly on me for the first time and her smile froze.

I tucked my hair behind my ear, shifted from foot to foot. 'You need my licence?' I asked.

My question seemed to snap her out of her trance. 'Licence and credit card,' she said with a nod. 'Yes.'

I pulled my purse from my bag, took my licence from my purse and slid it across the counter. The woman took it, peered closely at it through bright pink reading glasses. She turned it over, turned it back, glanced at me, at my photo on the card. 'You look just like someone I used to know,' she said, cocking her head. 'Someone I went to high school with.'

'Oh?'

She tapped the licence with a long crimson acrylic nail. 'But her name was Larson.'

'Larson's my mom's maiden name.'

'Your mom's Minna Larson?' She sounded surprised, yet like it made sense to her at the same time.

'Oh no. My mom was – is – Minna's younger sister,' I explained,

'Barbara Larson.' Then, seizing my chance, I asked innocently, 'You knew Minna well?'

The woman looked down at my licence again, started typing the details into her computer. 'No one knew Minna well,' she said. The atmosphere in the room changed. Though not unkind, there was something in her tone that told me I was missing something. 'She kept to herself, I guess is all, and then, well, you'll know . . . she ran away.'

'She disappeared,' I corrected. 'No one knows for sure that she left of her own accord.'

The woman shrugged – *same difference* – asked, 'Credit card?' a little too brightly, like we hadn't just been talking about my missing aunt.

Feeling increasingly uncomfortable, I reopened my purse, making a pretence of searching through it again. 'Credit card, credit card . . .' I stopped when I reached my one and only credit card, my fingers hovering over it. 'Shoot.' I looked up. 'You know what? I don't have my credit card with me. I'll have to come back.'

Before the woman could respond, I grabbed my licence from the counter and hurried out. I envisaged her watching me go, before picking up the phone, dialling her friends with those talon-like acrylics. *Remember Minna Larson? Uh-huh, yes, that's right, the runaway. You'll never guess who I ran into today. Looked just like her . . .*

This town. It was more small-minded and oppressive than I remembered.

It was mid morning, but already the sun was high, heat bouncing off the pavements, as I crossed a quiet Main Street. Main Street itself hadn't changed much since I'd left, though it appeared to have had something of a facelift. It was wide, with that all-American small-town look: neat and tidy, with olde-worlde lamp posts, shiny litter bins and well-filled plant pots, and freshly painted store fronts on the type of shops no one really needed since out-of-town malls and internet shopping. Aside from Art's Auto Rentals, there was a new

Starbucks, a drugstore, a dry cleaner's, an antique store – a *Closed for Vacation* sign in the window – a liquor store, a jeweller's, and an upmarket-looking thrift store. There was a post office and a doctor's, a veterinarian, a couple more coffee shops – independent ones – and a bakery; and in the centre of it all, smack-bang in the middle of Main Street, Boweridge Police Department, a modern two-storey glass-fronted building, a couple of police cruisers parked out front.

I'd come to the conclusion that morning that if I was going to find out what had happened to Minna, I needed to do things properly, and since Uncle JJ had said he thought Minna's disappearance had been reported to the police, Boweridge PD seemed the logical place to start.

I pushed open the heavy glass door and entered the air-conditioned lobby. There was a sort of waiting area, with an angular pleather couch and a couple of matching chairs that looked like they'd never been sat on. If anyone *had* sat on them, they'd have had a perfect view of the opposite wall, plastered with posters advertising local get-togethers and events – church fete on Saturday; Story Time at Stevenson Library on Wednesdays; Bower Cove Summer Camp! Coffee with a Cop on Tuesday mornings at Starbucks – along with friendly reminders not to leave dogs or children in hot cars, or valuables unattended, well, anywhere.

The man behind the reception desk looked barely old enough to have graduated school, never mind joined the police.

'Good morning, ma'am.'

He was pale, blonde and freckled, with spiky hair, a small moustache that looked like it had taken all his energy to muster, and the air of an overeager boy scout. He wore the sort of uniform you see in cop shows – navy trousers, pale blue short-sleeved shirt, and a cumbersome-looking belt housing, among other things, his holster and gun. He had a radio on his left shoulder, his shiny metal police badge pinned to his left chest. A smaller badge above his right shirt pocket read in capitals: *C. P. FEEHEY.*

'I'm trying to find information on my aunt,' I explained. 'She's missing.'

'You want to file a missing persons report?' he asked.

'I think one's already been filed.'

'She's been missing more than forty-eight hours?'

'Since 1972.' I could tell from the look on his face that I might as well have said 1872. He opened his mouth and it just sort of hung there. I stared at him, questioningly.

'Uh, your aunt's name?' he asked.

'Minna Larson.' I spelled it for him, emphasis on the O.

There was a door behind the reception desk and a wall of glass windows with slatted blinds looking into what appeared to be offices. Without another word, the young cop turned and disappeared through the door, and for a few minutes I just stood there. Eventually the door reopened and another man came out, followed closely by Officer Feehey. Unlike his younger counterpart, this man wore a suit, so I guessed he was more senior. When he moved, I could see his badge and gun at his hip, beneath his jacket. He was forties, maybe, with dark crew-cut hair and a deep tan. Good-looking, but with the attitude of someone who knew it.

'You asking about Minna Larson?' he asked.

There was an impatience about him, but still I felt a small spark of hope. Relief. 'You know Minna's case?'

'My father was on the force back in '72,' he replied. 'Everyone knew it.'

'So there is one?'

'One what?'

'A case? She was reported missing, hasn't turned up. So there must be one, right? Still open.'

'It's not quite as simple as that, ma'am.' His tone was patronising. It wouldn't have surprised me if he'd added, *You run along now, little lady, you hear me?*

But he didn't, and I'd no intention of running along, so I asked, 'Her case is closed, then?'

The young deputy shifted uncomfortably behind his superior, shuffling papers, pretending to tidy the desk.

'Look, Ms . . .' the older man said.

'Elmore,' I replied. 'I was told my aunt was reported missing, so there must be some kind of record, right?'

'Look,' he said again, 'runaways were a dime a dozen in those days.' There was something in his tone that made me shiver. 'Maybe a report was made,' he said, 'maybe it wasn't, but right now, we got active cases that need our attention. If there was anything new to report, your family would be the first to know.' Just then his mobile rang in his shirt pocket and he turned away to answer it. 'Detective Brennan. Uh-huh. Uh-huh. *Really?* No kidding . . .'

I decided it was pointless to wait around – I was never going to get anything useful out of this detective – so I turned and walked briskly to the door, almost colliding with a man who was pushing his way through it backwards, carrying a cardboard tray of coffees.

'Whoa, hey, sorry,' he said when he saw me, flattening himself against the door, holding it open for me. He was tall, dressed in jeans, a Boweridge PD baseball cap and, despite the heat outside, a hooded sweatshirt. I ducked past him, and as I did, he said, 'Wait, don't I know you?'

'I doubt it,' I said, brusquely. 'I'm not from here.'

He started to reply, but just then the detective called after me across the foyer. I looked up. He was still at the reception desk, phone to his ear, other hand covering the mouthpiece. 'Your aunt ran away, Ms Elmore,' he said. 'Everyone in town knows it.'

Not her family, I thought, the heavy glass door swinging shut behind me. I was back in the searing heat of Main Street.

Not all of them.

6

The Stevenson public library sat at the far end of Main Street, opposite the park. A well-maintained red-brick building with its name and the date, 1911, carved into the stonework above the arched door. I stepped into the cool lobby and approached the front desk.

'Welcome to Stevenson Library,' chirruped the middle-aged lady behind it. She was the very stereotype of a librarian – prim, cardigan-wearing, glasses round her neck on a string. *Mavis*, her name badge read. She looked like a Mavis.

'I'd like to see your newspaper archives from the seventies, please.'

Although I wasn't a member of the library, it turned out that with ID, I was entitled to a guest pass. Nevertheless, Mavis eyed me with the sort of suspicion with which one might regard a potential shop-lifter as I filled out the necessary form, then slid it and my ID across the desk to her.

'You can't withdraw books on a visitor pass,' she said, glasses on, head down, scanning the form.

'No problem.'

She stopped, looked up, peering at me over her glasses. 'Reason for visit?'

'Sorry?'

'You left it blank.' She tapped the form with her pen. 'Reason for visit?'

'Like I said, to use the archives.' There was a pause, as if she was waiting for more. 'I was hoping to find some newspaper stories on my aunt.'

'And your aunt is?'

None of your business, I wanted to say. 'She went missing in the seventies. I'm trying to track her down.'

Mavis narrowed her eyes. 'You mean Minna? Minna Larson? We went to high school together.'

Christ, I thought, are there any middle-aged women in this town who didn't go to school with my aunt? 'You knew her well?' I asked, against my better judgement. I remembered the car rentals lady, her response to the same question. I had a sinking feeling I knew where this was going.

'Everyone knew everyone back then,' Mavis said, 'but no, I didn't know your aunt well.'

'Do you know anything about her disappearance?'

'Only that she ran away, that no one was surprised. She was flighty like that.' Though I could hardly argue – I'd only just found out that Minna existed, had no idea if she was flighty – something in Mavis's tone, in what I felt she was implying, didn't sit well. I opened my mouth, about to protest, but she looked over my shoulder and called, 'Kimmy? Kimmy!'

A young girl, late teens, scurried over carrying an armful of books.

'Kimmy,' Mavis said. 'Show Ms . . .' she scanned my form again, 'Ms Elmore down to the archives.'

'Oh,' I said. 'That's really not necessary, thanks. If you can just point me in the right direction, I'll—'

'All guests using the facilities must be inducted,' Mavis interrupted. 'No exceptions.'

As we turned from the desk, I could feel her eyes boring into my back. Kimmy shot me a sympathetic smile.

'No one likes her,' she whispered, once we were out of earshot. 'Mavis, I mean.'

'You surprise me.'

She giggled. 'You're not from round here.'

'What gave it away?'

When I'd moved to live with Dad, desperate to fit in, leave my old life behind, my American accent was one of the first things I lost. I'd shed it like a snake sheds its skin.

'Wow,' Kimmy said, wide-eyed, when she asked me what I did and I told her, rather apologetically, that I was a student at Oxford. Psychology. 'That's pretty prestigious, right? It'd be a total dream to go to school there. I wanna do English? Or journalism. Like my cousin? She's a writer, lives in New York. She's, like, *so* talented.'

I smiled. Despite myself, I was warming to Kimmy. The way she talked nineteen-to-the-dozen, her boundless enthusiasm, reminded me of Tabby.

'What brings you to Boweridge?' she asked, interrupting my thoughts.

We were coming to the end of a corridor signed *Elevator*, our shoes squeaking on the shiny floor like trainers in a school gym.

'Oh,' I said, 'just visiting family. I grew up here.'

'Huh? What – here? Boweridge?'

'Uh huh.'

'But you sound so – so *British*.'

'Well, I've been in the UK over half my life now. And my dad's British too,' I added, 'so I guess it rubbed off on me.'

'So where'd you go to school? When you lived here, I mean?'

'McArthur Elementary and Middle.' We were waiting for the lift down to the basement. 'Then Boweridge High, but only for a year before I moved to—'

'Oh my God! Boweridge High? *I* go there. My cousin did too – the one in New York? *And* she went to McArthur. I mean, it was like, *for ever* ago,' she clarified, widening her eyes as though to emphasise just how long ago it actually was. 'Maybe you know her?'

How old did she think I was? 'What's her name?' I said, unconvinced.

'Lauren. Lo Ekhart?'

'Oh God, Lo. We were in the same class. So she's in New York? How is she?'

'Oh, she's great,' said Kimmy dreamily. The lift had finally arrived and we stepped inside. 'Loves it there. She must be, like, thirty now.'

Thirty-one, I thought.

'Actually,' Kimmy went on, 'she's home visiting my aunt – her mom – for a couple weeks. You should, like, meet up!'

'Oh,' I said quickly. 'It's been so long. I'm sure she'd barely remember me.'

The lift pinged – a welcome interruption – and we stepped out into an apparently deserted basement. It was not, Kimmy explained enthusiastically, as luxurious as the rest of the library, the upstairs, which was refurbished in 2011 to celebrate its centenary. Luckily, though, also in 2011 they'd begun transferring the archived copies of the *Boweridge Herald* onto microfilm, so I wouldn't have to trawl through hard copies the old-fashioned way, by hand.

I thanked her for her help and she left me to it, but not before insisting I give her my number to pass on to Lo.

Alone at last, I felt a sense of release. I was at home here, relaxed. Not like the police station. Here I wasn't reliant on what information people were willing to share with me. With a bit of digging, I felt sure I'd find some answers. There had to be something.

Having located the relevant reels, I made myself comfortable, loaded the first microfilm and began my search. I knew I was looking for articles from 1972, specifically the summer months, so I started from May of that year. The *Herald* painted an idyllic picture of seventies Boweridge, with very little crime. What there was seemed fairly petty, by today's standards at least: cookies stolen from a local old people's home; student high jinks TP'ing a neighbour's house.

For a while there was only the *whir-whir-whir* of film as I scrolled unsuccessfully through. Then something caught my eye. I reversed a little and stopped. The article was on the front page of the Monday 19 June edition. *Boweridge Nun Slain in Diner Parking Lot*, the headline read. I zoomed in.

Officers Search For Clues as Murder of
Popular Boweridge Nun Leaves Police Baffled

Police have launched a homicide investigation after the body of a young nun was discovered in a parking lot on the outskirts of town.

Sister Francesca Pepitone, 25, a local nun and popular teacher at St Thomas Aquinas Catholic High School, was found strangled to death outside Don's Diner at 11.15 p.m., Saturday night. Sister Francesca was identified by patrons, who say she entered the diner briefly around thirty-five minutes earlier that evening. Her car was found parked nearby, and police speculate she may have been meeting someone, though they've yet to confirm this.

Missing Necklace

According to sources, a crucifix Sister Francesca always wore was missing, leading police to believe the motive may have been robbery. 'We believe this to be a tragic case of wrong place, wrong time,' said Boweridge police chief Detective Jim Brennan, 'but would appeal to any witnesses, or anyone with information, to come forward.'

Accompanying the article was a black-and-white photo, the same one I'd seen in the yearbook and on the Sister Fran Facebook page, but grainier.

A week later, Monday 26 June:

No New Leads in Sister Fran Case, Says Police Chief

Nine days since the body of Boweridge nun and high school teacher Sister Francesca Pepitone, 25, was discovered in an out-of-town parking lot, and there are no new leads, police say.

'We believe Sister Francesca may have gone to the diner to meet someone that night, though we've not been able to establish who this person was,' said Boweridge police chief Detective Jim Brennan. 'However, based upon a necklace worn by the victim – a distinctive silver crucifix – which was not recovered from the scene, we believe that the motive for this homicide was robbery.'

No Link With Missing Boweridge Teen

My heart skipped a beat. I read on.

Police have also laid to rest rumors of a link between the Sister Francesca case and that of missing Boweridge teen Margaret 'Minna' Larson. Minna, 17, a student of Sister Francesca's at St Thomas Aquinas Catholic High School, was reported missing just one week after Sister Francesca's body was found, leading to local speculation that the two cases are connected.

'We are confident that there is no link between the murder of Sister Francesca Pepitone and the disappearance of Minna Larson,' Detective Brennan said. Described as 'troubled' by police, Minna was last seen by family on the evening of Thursday June 22, when she left home to visit a boyfriend. 'Minna Larson was reported missing on Saturday June 24, two days after she was last seen. At that time, she had on jean shorts, a white T-shirt, a plaid shirt tied round her waist, and tennis shoes,' Detective Brennan said. 'We are keeping an open mind, but at this stage, all evidence points to Minna having left of her own accord.' According to her family, Detective Brennan also said, Minna has run away from home before. Anyone with information should contact the Boweridge Police Department.

Unlike the article on Sister Fran, there was no photograph.

Could that really be right? Minna left of her own accord? Both the woman from the car rental and librarian Mavis had thought so. Even JJ seemed to think it was possible, though while he'd said Minna had stayed away from home the odd night here and there, he'd said nothing about a history of running away. But then he'd been so young at the time, maybe he didn't remember.

I kept going through the records. The following month, July, there was an article on page 2 of the *Herald*.

No Developments in Hunt for Murdered Nun's Killer

Police have admitted today that they are no further forward in the hunt for the killer of local nun, Sister Francesca Pepitone, found strangled to death in an out-of-town parking lot on June 17. Despite local speculation, they have also continued to deny there is any link between the popular high school teacher's murder and the disappearance just days later of one of her pupils, 17-year-old Minna Larson. A spokesperson for St Thomas Aquinas Catholic High School, currently on summer vacation, said that their prayers are with both families. 'We have faith that police are investigating most thoroughly the circumstances surrounding Sister Francesca's tragic death and Margaret Larson's disappearance, but they have assured us there is no link between the two,' said school principal Sister Patricia Kinkel. 'We understand that this is a difficult time for St Thomas Aquinas students, and we will provide support and guidance to those who need it on their return from summer vacation.'

I rubbed my eyes. How could they be so sure there was no connection? It seemed too coincidental that in a small town like Boweridge – a place with relatively low crime – two major incidents could occur so close together and not be connected.

I continued to trawl the papers for anything on Sister Fran or Minna, but the articles became fewer and further between, buried deeper in the *Herald*'s pages, and contained little more than rehashes of the original story: no new leads, no arrests. The cases, it seemed, had gone cold.

After finishing my research and printing copies of the newspaper articles, I made the mistake of checking my emails and found another from Simon.

Look, Maggie, can't we just talk about this? Like grown-ups?

He'd signed it *Si*, something he did when he wanted to come across as on his students' level, like he was one of us. Now it made my skin crawl.

After everything that morning, the idea of returning to Mom's, spending the rest of the day with her, was less than appealing, so I called Uncle JJ instead. He met me at the library and we ate a sandwich together in the park, before returning to the apartment he shared with Greg and their cat, an elderly, obese long-haired tabby called Dorothy.

Both JJ and Greg were lawyers – that was how they'd met, law school – but JJ was now retired and Greg semi-retired, working with student interns at a local Innocence Project. When Greg returned home that evening – the first time I'd seen him in years – we spent hours catching up. I didn't mention Minna, didn't tell them what I'd discovered, and for a while I was able to pretend it was just like old times.

But when Greg asked me how my DPhil was going and I dissembled, said something like, *Oh, you know* . . . then fell silent, he looked at me – *really* looked at me – and, as I squirmed under his gaze, asked, 'Is everything okay, Maggie?'

Where would I even begin? I wondered. So I told him everything was fine, I laughed, even, added something about the workload, the stress, the deadlines. Next year was my write-up, I said. I was dreading it. That much was true.

It was after 11p.m. when Uncle JJ dropped me home. On the doorstep, as I fumbled with the spare key Bob had given me, a car drove by, slowing almost to a stop at the end of the driveway, speeding up again once it had passed. A police cruiser, I was certain. Probably doing its nightly patrol.

The house was in darkness as I let myself in, went straight to the nearest window and peeped through the blind. The street lamps illuminated a deserted street: parked cars, a cat slinking by on the pavement. So why did I feel so uneasy? Why had a chill crept over me, made the hairs on the back of my neck stand on end?

There were no signs of life in the house either, not until I was tiptoeing my way across the kitchen to the basement stairs.

'Darling.' The voice from the gloom made me jump.

I turned to see Mom sitting by the window, silhouetted in the dim light.

'What are you doing in the dark?' I felt the wall for the light switch, flicked it on, saw the lipstick-smeared wine glass on the windowsill next to her, the almost empty bottle.

'You want to know about Minna.'

It wasn't a question. I hesitated. If Mom had been drinking, no good would come of it, but despite the little voice in my head – *don't do it!* – I slid the photo of the Larson siblings from my pocket.

Mom took the photo, stroked it tenderly with her thumb, but when she spoke, her voice was full of bitterness. 'Minna was always the centre of attention,' she said. 'She was the prettiest, the brightest, the most athletic. The best at everything.'

'If that's true, why does everyone think she ran away?'

She turned towards me, and I saw tear tracks down her cheeks, glinting in the half-light. She waved a hand, then turned away again. 'Because she was selfish, that's why.' Her words slurred.

'God, Mom, she was little more than a child. Kids don't just run away from home like that. Not without good reason.'

'Oh, there were reasons.'

'Like what?' I tried to keep my voice level. Hadn't Uncle JJ said something similar?'

'She'd steal stuff,' Mom said petulantly, like a five-year-old telling tales. 'My stuff, Walt's, Bill's, JJ's. All the time.'

'Okay,' I said, throwing up my hands. 'So she took your stuff.'

She shook her head in disgust, like I was missing the point. 'It was all the time. Like she couldn't help it. And she lied, too.'

Minna lies. Though I'd heard it before, read it in the school reports, coming from Mom it was pretty rich. 'Lied about *what*, Mom? Tell me.'

'Anything and everything,' she said. 'There was this one teacher, Sister Fran?'

My heart quickened. 'What about her?'

'She turned up dead, murdered. Minna told me she knew who'd done it, can you believe? But it wasn't just me – she told other people, too.'

'Who'd she say did it?'

'Huh.' Mom laughed mockingly. 'She didn't *say*. No, that wasn't Minna's style. She'd tell stories, stir the pot, then take a step back and watch.'

Who does that sound like? I thought. 'And it didn't cross anyone's mind to take her seriously?'

'Oh Maggie,' Mom said. 'Minna didn't know who killed Sister Fran. She just *said* she did to get attention. That's what she did, like the boy who cried wolf.'

'Don't you see?' I said, exasperated. 'The whole point about the boy who cried wolf was that he told the truth in the end! What if *Minna* was telling the truth? What if she knew who killed this Sister Fran and no one listened?'

'Well, we'll never know,' Mom said, sullenly. 'Because she left.'

'Christ, Mom, it's like you don't care.' I shook my head, turned to leave, turned back. 'Yet you named me after her. She must've meant *something* to you. Not even you would name a child after someone you hated.' I doubted myself as soon as I said it.

'That's just it,' Mom said quietly. 'I didn't hate Minna. I loved her. I loved her and she abandoned me.' She thrust the photo back at me, reached for the wine bottle.

'Should you even be drinking?'

She stopped dead, turned squarely to face me, and I resisted the urge to shrink back. 'Bob told you,' she said. 'I might've known.'

She dug in a pocket and pulled out a little plastic pill bottle, held it up, rattled it in front of me as though to illustrate: *full disclosure*. I had a sudden flashback: Mom slumped over the toilet bowl, me grasping the back of her head . . .

'Are you even taking them?' I asked, trying to banish the memory, something I'd managed relatively successfully until now. *Lock it all up and throw away the key, Maggie . . .*

Mom scoffed, reached for the wine glass, but there was nothing in it but dregs, and she was clumsy, poorly coordinated, almost knocked it over. I got there first, snatched it up, held it out of reach.

'Did he also tell you I'm seeing someone? A *psychiatrist*.' There was an edge of contempt to the word, though I couldn't tell if it was directed at the psychiatrist or Bob. 'Gave me an ultimatum.' Bob, then. 'Get help or I'm leaving.'

Good for Bob, I wanted to say, *didn't know he had it in him*. But instead I said, 'I think it's good, Mom. A positive step. If this' – I gestured with my hands – 'if it all stems from Minna, then maybe it can help you, help you to . . .' To what? Move on? Find closure? Heal? Become normal? All of the above?

'You think all *this* can be resolved by talking?' Mom threw up her hands, pills rattling. 'None of you understand – not you, not Bob, not Dr Kindler.'

'Then tell me, Mom,' I pleaded. 'Tell me about Minna's disappearance. What you know.'

'What I know?' She laughed again, but her eyes filled with tears. 'What I know is that the summer she vanished is a scar that never heals. What I know is that all people want to do is *pick, pick, pick*. Open up old wounds. Dr Kindler says I have to be honest with myself. She says in order to move on, I have to confront the memories.'

'She's right, Mom,' I said quietly. 'You have to confront your past, come to the realisation of what it did to you, how it shaped you, otherwise she can't help you.' I took a step closer, crouched down beside her, stopped short of taking her hand. 'So do it,' I urged, looking her right in the eye. 'Tell me about your sister, Mom. Tell me about Minna.'

7

Barbara, summer 1972

It was a Saturday the day Daddy took the photo. One week left, then school would be out for summer. Barbara sat on the porch in her best outfit, wishing they'd all hurry up. It had been Bill's idea – it was Bill's camera – but Daddy would take the picture, all the Larson siblings at once. Daddy said that getting them all together was like wrangling cats, so Barb had decided that until they were sorted, arranged as they should be – with her centre-front of shot, obviously – no more squabbling and fussing, she wouldn't take her place. After all, she didn't want to get her dress and shoes all in a mess. The yard was so dusty, what with it being the hottest summer and all, and although her outfit (a hand-me-down from a kindly neighbour) wasn't exactly new, it was new to her and so pretty it would be a shame to spoil it. So she continued to watch from the porch.

It was just then that the screen door crashed open and JJ, Barb's brother, the youngest of the boys, bounded out of the house so fast he almost fell over her.

'Hey, watch it!' Barb scolded, but JJ just ignored her, taking the porch steps in one go, running to join his two older brothers already at the swing set.

'Anyone seen Minna?' Daddy called, looking first to the boys, then at Barb, who hadn't budged from the porch.

'She was here a minute ago,' Bill said.

'She's not in the house.' That was JJ.

'Can we just get this over with?' asked Walt.

Walt was the second oldest, only a year younger than Minna, and when Bill had suggested the group photo, Walt had rolled his eyes. 'Do we have to?' Walt thought he was too cool for everything these days and Barb had felt a little sorry for Bill: he only wanted to test his new camera. Bill had been working Saturday mornings as bag boy at the new grocery store a few blocks away, all so he could buy his first camera. Barb only hoped he kept his eye on it, as things around the Larson home were wont to go missing. She'd spent much of that morning sulking, after her new cassette recorder – her pride and joy, which she'd saved her chore money for near a year to buy – had disappeared. She'd asked Minna if she'd seen it, of course, but Minna just laughed.

'What would I want with your cassette recorder, little Barb? It's for babies.'

Barb knew her cassette recorder wasn't for babies (it was so swell, it even had a little microphone so she could tape her favourite songs from the radio, ones by bands Mommy didn't like her listening to, like the Osmonds – Donny Osmond, what a dreamboat! – and the Jackson 5), but Minna's comment stung all the same. Minna said such hurtful things these days, which was why Barb was sure there was something wrong. That and the fact that Minna lied a lot – about big things and little things – so even though she *said* she hadn't taken Barb's cassette recorder, Barb wasn't sure she believed her. Minna's tales had gotten so bad that nowadays Barb had trouble telling whether anything her sister said was true.

'Can someone go find her?' Daddy meant Minna. Barb could tell he was growing impatient. It was hot. He had things to do.

'She's probably round back smoking a cigarette.' Walt snickered, and Barb glared at him.

'What's that?' Daddy said.

'Nothing.' All three boys snickered.

'I'll go,' Barb said quickly.

She hopped from her perch and scuttled down the porch steps and round the side, where she found Minna standing with her back to her at the corner of the house, a cigarette dangling between slender fingers.

'Hey, little Barb.' Minna turned and sniffed, and Barb wondered if she'd been crying. Minna cried ever so much these days.

'Daddy's ready to take the photo,' Barb told her. 'He doesn't want to wait much longer. He says that getting us all together is like wrangling cats.'

'Oh, little Barb, where do you get these things from?' Minna laughed and sighed all at once, then stubbed her cigarette out on the wall.

Minna had only started smoking cigarettes recently, but Barb had the feeling she didn't even like them, that she only really did it because her boyfriend smoked them too. Barb reached into the pocket of her new dress and pulled from it an unwrapped peppermint. Daddy had given it to her – he sucked on them to hide the smell of cigarettes that Mommy so hated – so it was covered in lint and fluff from his pocket as well as Barb's, though Minna took it all the same.

'Thanks, little Barb,' she said, and she ruffled Barb's hair, which both annoyed Barb – she'd spent a long time perfecting her hairstyle for the photo, then not moving her head lest she muss it all up – and made her glow with pride all at once.

Barb threaded her hot little hand into Minna's and together they made their way to the front yard, where the boys and Daddy were waiting.

'Finally!' said Walt, in his annoying way, as the girls rounded the porch.

'Do I look okay?' Minna whispered to Barb.

Barb looked up at her sister's face. Minna was tanned, and her long blonde hair shone in the afternoon sun – like the straw spun into gold in the fairy tale Barb liked but couldn't remember the name of – though she was thin, real thin, and tired-looking. There was still a trace of the black eye too, the one she'd come home with a few days ago, though she'd refused to say how it happened.

'You look just beautiful,' Barb said, and her big sister squeezed her hand.

Later that night, after Daddy had taken the photo, after supper was eaten and chores done and prayers said, Barb lay awake in the room she and her sister shared. Minna wasn't home yet. Barb thought about the day, how Daddy had finally lined them all up, fourteen-year-old Bill wailing, 'It's gotta be in order of age: Minna, Walt, me, JJ and Barb!' and how, much to Barb's dismay, Daddy had agreed (it was Bill's camera, after all). Then, in all the commotion, they found that Minna had wandered off again, and when at last they got her back, she just sort of stuck herself on the end of the line-up, the opposite end of the swing set from Walter, the opposite end from where, according to Bill, she should have been. Barb didn't mind, though: if she couldn't be in the middle of the picture, the next best place would be next to her big sister, the Larson girls together.

'Minna's in the wrong spot!' Bill had protested, and Walt had said – through gritted teeth, so Daddy wouldn't hear him – 'Just take the damn picture, will you?' and Daddy had just ignored Bill and let Minna be, and had shouted at them all to say *cheese!* Everyone did say *cheese!* (Barb had always thought it a funny thing to say, but it did the trick), everyone but Minna, who stood staring sullenly at the ground.

Barb could barely wait for the photograph to be developed, but Bill, who was planning to do it himself in a dark room he hadn't yet constructed (but which he planned, unbeknownst to Daddy, to construct in Daddy's tool shed), said she'd have to be patient. These things took time.

After the photo, when the chaos had died down, Barb thought she and Minna might spend some time together, just like they used to. Their brothers had scattered, escaping back down to the lake, where they spent most of their weekends, Daddy was still fussing with the camera, and Mommy had come outdoors to see what was taking so long (she needed Daddy to fix a leaking faucet). But before she knew it, Minna had slipped away. She'd probably gone to see that boyfriend of hers, Barb thought, with a pang of jealousy. It was weird, because although Barb disliked Minna's boyfriend, Mommy and Daddy didn't seem to mind him. Before, Mommy and Daddy argued about Minna all the time. Barb would sit at the top of the stairs, past her bedtime, and listen to them fight, though she was careful not to let them know that she was there. One night, Mommy told Daddy that Minna was going about things the right way to get a rep-u-ta-tion round town. Barb didn't know exactly what a rep-u-ta-tion was, but she knew from the way Mommy said it – and the way she talked about other girls' rep-u-ta-tions – that it wasn't a good thing. Barb had also heard Mommy call Minna terrible words, words that, had the same ones come out of Barb's mouth – or her brothers', though they were all potty-mouths when they knew their parents weren't listening – she was sure she'd have gotten a good spanking.

Lately, though, Mommy and Daddy hadn't been arguing quite so much, either with each other or with Minna. Barb knew she should be thankful, and she'd thought Minna should have been too, yet her sister seemed sadder than ever. Sometimes Barb wondered how Minna's boyfriend felt about this sad Minna.

Not that Minna was always sad. She had happy days now and then, days when, even though Barb knew she was hurting on the inside, she didn't show it on the outside. It was almost like having the old Minna back, and Barb loved the old Minna more than anything. The old Minna didn't mock her pebble collection like her brothers did (Barb only collected the pretty ones, ones that looked like they might've once been something else a very long time ago), but listened carefully as her little sister took her through each one, telling her exactly what she thought it might have been (*some fossilised sea creature! a mammoth tooth!*), or where it might have come from (*the desert! outer space!*). The old Minna made Barb pancakes while Mommy was visiting with the old lady up the street, the one Mommy didn't even like, though she visited with her all the same because she was an old lady and it was the Christian thing to do. The old Minna let Barb tell her all the things she'd learned at school that day, like her additions and subtractions and, sometimes, her multiplications, and on weekends from Sunday school, about Job and Joseph and Jacob or whoever else. The old Minna would roll her eyes and laugh at the things Barb told her, though not unkindly. The old Minna would say things like, 'Oh, little Barb, you're such a hoot', and, 'Oh, Barb, who told you that?' when her sister came out with facts like why moths fly at electric lights (they mistake them for the moon!); but really, deep down, Barb could tell Minna was impressed, and it made her feel so proud she could almost burst.

When Minna had eventually gotten home that night and slid into bed, she was crying again, and Barb felt her heart break. Barb thought it had been a good day, a happy one, but she must have been wrong.

Minna used to sing Barb to sleep, but now it was Barb who'd sing her sister to sleep. Without a sound, she slipped from her own bed, padded barefoot across the room and crawled into her sister's. Minna was facing the wall. She didn't move, though her body shook with silent sobs as Barb wrapped her little arms around her. These days, it was the only time she could bear to let Barb hug her properly. These days, the slightest touch made Minna flinch.

Barb stroked Minna's hair as she sang 'You Are My Sunshine'. It was one of the songs Minna used to sing to Barb when she was little. Littler than now. That and 'Hush, Little Baby'. When Barb was a toddler, though she could scarcely remember it, Minna, no more than eight or nine herself, would carry her around on her hip, just like she'd seen Mommy do with her brothers when they were babies. Even when Barb was getting too big to carry, Minna would pick her up. They'd dance together in the kitchen, Minna singing to Barb at the top of her lungs until Mommy said *enough*.

Now, they were so close, Barb hugging her sister so tight she could feel Minna's heartbeat. Or was it her own?

Barb continued to sing and Minna continued to cry until at last she fell asleep, but Barb knew that she'd keep on singing. She'd start over from the beginning, afraid that if she stopped, Minna would wake and begin crying again and the spell would be broken.

She knew this, for the same thing happened almost every night.

8

After Mom began telling me about Minna, the day the photo was taken, it had all come tumbling out. I didn't interrupt, just stood there perfectly still, listening, afraid that if I moved or coughed or said anything – breathed, even – she'd stop, and the moment would be gone for ever.

When she'd finished, she closed her eyes, and when she opened them, I'd asked her gently, 'Why was Minna crying all the time, Mom?'

She'd left me with so many unanswered questions, like why, for a start, she hadn't told me all this before. I was angry that she'd burdened me with it now, without warning – typical Mom – yet also angry that she hadn't told me sooner. If she had, things might have been different between us: the loss of a sister – for that was what it was – provided some explanation, if not an excuse, for her behaviour all these years.

'Mom?' I'd tried again. 'Why was Minna so upset all the time?'

But it was too late. She'd clammed up. She'd said too much and now regretted it, like drunk-texting an ex, professing your love for them at three in the morning. I'd admitted defeat, had slunk off to my room, where I lay awake again for most of the night. When morning eventually came and I checked my phone, I found a missed call from an unknown number. An unknown American number. My voicemail symbol was blinking.

'Hey, Maggie, it's Lo,' the message said. 'Heard you're in town. Would love to see you. Can we meet up? Uh, give me a call on this number, okay? Bye.'

A few hours later, I was cycling through the midday heat to Mainstreet's, the downtown bar Lo had suggested we meet at, which ironically wasn't even on Main Street. Boweridge had grown in the years since I left, so much so that it now had an area of town devoted entirely to nightlife, a trendy street of pubs, bars and eateries, where hipsters, students and young professionals mingled at all hours.

I arrived before Lo, too wired for coffee and in need of something to steady my nerves, so although I preferred red wine these days, I ordered myself a glass of white, because who drinks red when it's thirty degrees outside? (Who drinks red at all at one in the afternoon?) The tremor I'd noticed in my hands – lack of sleep, I'd decided; nothing to do with meeting Lo – required just enough alcohol to still it, not so much that it made it worse, so I only ordered a small glass, separate glass of ice on the side.

I'd just chosen a seat at a table in a quiet, dark corner, was plinking ice cubes into my wine with tiny silver tongs, when a voice behind me made me jump.

'Maggie?'

I turned in my seat, looked up. 'Lo? Oh my God, Lo!'

My plan had been to insist on buying her a drink, but there she was, looking cool, glass already in hand.

She must have seen the look on my face, for she said, almost apologetically, 'I grabbed a Coke on my way in.'

Coke. Of course. Like any normal person at lunchtime.

Lo's glance flicked to my wine. Mine did too, like I'd no idea how it had got there. 'I just grabbed a wine.'

She laughed politely. 'It's five o'clock somewhere, right?'

We didn't hug, but I got up from my seat, and after an awkward moment, we both sat down. There followed another awkward moment – neither of us knowing quite what to say – while Lo pulled the paper sheath off the tip of her straw, took a sip of Coke.

'I tried to find you on Facebook,' I said lamely.

'Oh.' She waved a hand. 'I don't really do the whole social media thing.'

'Me neither,' I said quickly, then, realising how stupid that sounded, added, 'I mean, I'm *on* Facebook, I'm just never *on* it, if you know what I mean.'

'Right.' She nodded politely.

God, I was such an idiot.

'Look,' I said, leaning back in my seat, trying to appear relaxed, feeling anything but. 'I feel really bad – about what happened, you know? How I left everything.'

Lo shrugged. 'It was a long time ago, Maggie.'

'Still. I should've told you I was leaving that summer – that I wasn't coming back. We were best friends. I guess I just cut all ties.'

'You did what you had to do.' That stung. 'It's water under the bridge.'

'New York obviously agrees with you,' I said. 'I mean, look at you – you look . . . great.'

I wasn't just saying it. The years had been kind to Lo. Everything about her that had once made her my dorky-looking best friend now made her beautiful. Her dark hair was long and glossy ('I discovered straighteners,' she said, laughing, when I commented on it), her clothes were expensive-looking but understated – that effortless New York chic – and she wore just the right amount of make-up. I felt suddenly self-conscious in my T-shirt and jeans, no make-up and less than perfect hair. After returning Lo's call, despite having the whole morning, I'd only just showered before heading out, had shoved my hair up in a messy bun – not the good kind – borrowed Bob's bike and cycled downtown, arriving at Mainstreet's sweating and stressed, cursing my decision not to hire a car or take up Bob's offer of a lift.

'You've not changed,' Lo said, and though it was said with no malice, I couldn't tell if it was a compliment. 'I mean,' she added, 'your accent has, but—'

'You're a writer?' I interrupted clumsily.

She looked surprised.

'Your cousin – Kimmy, is it? – she mentioned it.'

Lo smiled fondly. 'Ah, Kimmy. She makes it sound more glamorous than it is.' She pulled a face. 'I mean, yeah, I guess you could say I'm a writer – it's freelance, though, so I never really know where my next pay cheque's coming from. It's mostly fashion, too, not exactly the direction I wanted to go in, not *serious journalism*' – she made air quotes with her fingers – 'but I guess writing articles on neck messes and curated ears pays the bills. Just. And you?' she asked, clearly keen to change the subject. 'What're you up to these days?'

'Oh,' I said, pulling my best self-deprecating face, 'still studying.'

But for a slight raise of her eyebrows, Lo hid her surprise well. 'What subject?'

'Psychology?' It came out all squeaky, like a question. 'DPhil,' I added, trying to justify why, at the age of thirty-one, I wasn't settled in a job like any normal person. 'Third year.' I didn't mention I'd won a scholarship, that Dad wasn't paying for any of it, though people automatically assumed he was. 'I mean, I work a little on the side, too.'

'Oh?'

'Yeah, I'm a fit model. They fit clothes on me?' *Duh*, of course she knows what a fit model is – she's a fashion writer. But if she did know, she was too polite to say, instead nodding at me encouragingly: *go on*. 'It's not like proper modelling, I mean. It's for companies, designers.'

I'd had numerous jobs over the years. Most I didn't like, didn't stick at for more than a few months; some I got let go from, including the sandwich shop where I was fired for slamming the tops on the sandwiches with such force I left handprints in the bread. I'd dabbled in proper modelling in my younger years, after being scouted by an agency when I was eighteen, just started uni, but although the money was good at first, I wasn't quite tall enough for catwalk, or skinny enough for editorial. Plus, in model years I was now practically geriatric. But commercial fit modelling? That was different. All that was required was that I turn up and stand still while I was draped with fabric and stuck with pins – kind of like going to the hairdresser without the awkward chit-chat, the designers too engrossed in their work to talk to me, other than a *turn this way* here and a *turn that way* there. The pay wasn't bad either – enough that, with my scholarship, I didn't have to ask Dad for money – and though the work was sporadic, it suited me fine, given that undertaking any sort of job outside a DPhil was frowned upon.

There followed yet another awkward pause, during which Lo sipped earnestly at her Coke and I pretended to drink my wine, still kicking myself over my choice. I hadn't touched white wine since that night, though it had been Simon drinking it, not me. Now the mere smell of it turned my stomach.

'So, uh,' Lo said at last, 'I guess I should tell you why I really asked to meet with you.' She flushed, adding hastily, 'Not that I wasn't happy to catch up, but it was Kimmy, actually.'

'Kimmy?'

'She mentioned you were looking at newspaper articles, doing some digging into your aunt's disappearance?'

'Wait – you know about Minna?'

Lo nodded. 'A little. How much do *you* know about her?'

'Not a lot. Pretty much that she went missing when she was seventeen, never turned back up.'

'And St Tom's?'

'Sorry?'

'St Thomas Aquinas. Minna's old school.'

'Um . . .' I stopped, almost took a sip of wine, felt my stomach turn again. 'I read there was this teacher there, a nun – Sister Fran? I know that she was murdered – most of the stuff I dug up at the library was on her. Something about a robbery gone wrong?'

Lo leaned down and fished in her bag, pulled from it a piece of A4 paper, which she slid across the table to me.

'I think you should read this,' she said.

I took the paper – wrong way up – and turned it round. At its centre was a black-and-white image, a grainy photocopy of a newspaper article a few centimetres square. I leaned over it, peering at the text in the bar's dim light.

'It's from the *Boweridge Herald*,' Lo said. 'Nineteen sixty-eight.'

Sixty-eight. Four years before Minna disappeared. Four years before Sister Fran's murder.

Promising St Thomas Aquinas Student Dies in Railroad Tragedy, the headline blared.

I glanced up at Lo. 'I don't understand.'

'I'll explain,' she said, 'but read it first.'

The text was small and badly aligned, so I used my index finger as a guide as I began to read.

The tragic death of Boweridge student Susan Turner, 17, was suicide, local police said yesterday. According to family, Susan, a popular student at St Thomas Aquinas High School, was last seen by her parents on Saturday afternoon, when she left home to meet friends. But instead, police say, Susan traveled out of town, ending up on railroad tracks, where she was hit by a train a little after 9 p.m. that same night.

Police were called to the location of the tragedy by locals, alerted by the train's driver. Describing what he encountered as 'real bad', Officer Harris, first on scene, identified Susan from belongings, including her purse and wristwatch, which according to witnesses had been left stacked neatly by the side of the tracks. Her identity has since been confirmed by dental records.

Described by family as 'a loving daughter and sister' and 'the perfect student', police are still investigating what might have caused the popular honor roll student to take her own life, but say they are not looking for anyone else in connection with the teen's death.

I straightened up, Lo's eyes on me, expectant.

'You don't think it was suicide?' I asked.

'Oh, it was suicide all right.'

'Then I still don't understand.'

Lo fiddled with a cardboard beer mat. 'St Tom's closed in the nineties,' she began, 'lay empty for years after that. Then, about eleven, twelve years ago, when I was just starting out as a junior reporter at the *Herald*, it was announced that the old school site was to be developed.'

'Into what?'

'Luxury apartments.' She waved a hand. 'I know, I know. You're thinking, no big deal, right? Well, I was given the job of researching the site, writing a piece – purely to do with the history of it, the upcoming development. I decided to look through the *Herald*'s archives, see if there was anything interesting, good-news stories about the school – student wins award, successful alumni, local celeb opens school fete, that kind of thing.'

I touched the paper on the table between us. 'But instead you found this.'

She nodded glumly. 'Let's just say, when I began researching St Tom's, I fell down a whole different rabbit hole than the one I expected. A dark one.'

'Let me guess,' I said, finally taking a drink. I needed it. 'Susan Turner. You found out why she killed herself.'

9

'At first,' Lo explained, 'when I found that article, I didn't know anything about St Tom's. But there was something about Susan's story that just didn't seem to make any sense. Why would a straight-A student from a loving family – thinking of her future, applying to colleges – kill herself?'

I could only guess. Bullying? School pressures? Boyfriend troubles? Life could be hard for teenage girls.

Lo went on. 'I started digging, found . . .' She stopped, chewed her lip a moment. 'I found that Susan Turner was being abused.'

I gasped. 'For sure?'

Lo nodded. 'I tracked down her mom, interviewed her.'

'Her mom *knew*?' I asked, open-mouthed. 'Did she know who was doing it?'

Lo didn't reply, just dug in her bag again, this time pulling out her mobile. 'It's all on here.' She unlocked the screen, thrust it at me. 'Go ahead.'

Mainstreet's was surprisingly busy for a weekday afternoon, and while we weren't exactly shouting, we had to speak up to make ourselves heard. I didn't know if I wanted to listen to whatever was on Lo's phone, but even if I did, I wasn't sure the middle of a bar was the right place. Still, I felt I owed it to her, so against my better judgement, I reached out and took the phone.

'Wait a sec.' She handed me a set of tangled headphones. 'You'll need these.'

I plugged the headphones in, slid the buds into my ears, and pressed play. At first there was only static, followed by some clicking, then I could hear muffled voices. With the phone on the table in front of me, I covered my ears with my hands, pressing the headphones in harder, trying to block out the hubbub.

'Mrs Turner.' The voice, Lo's voice, clear now, was so sudden it made me jump. 'I was wondering if you could tell me about your daughter Susan again, please, like we discussed?'

'Everything?' This voice was female too, but older. Weary.

'Everything. If you don't mind. Pretend like we're not even recording.'

'Where shall I start?' There was uncertainty in the woman's voice.

'How about you start by telling me what she was like, if you could. What she was like as a daughter, a sister, a friend.'

There was the clink of something – a teacup, a water glass, maybe – then the other voice, Susan's mother, began.

'Susan was a good girl. A good student. Good daughter and sister. She was perfect, really – thoughtful, loving and caring, always helping out around the home. Her friends loved her too; teachers always said how bright she was, how conscientious and kind. She had a promising future ahead of her, so they all said. That's why it was such a shock that she . . . when . . .'

'How old was Susan, Mrs Turner?'

I could hear sniffing. The rustle of material. I imagined Lo reaching over to comfort her.

'When it happened? Seventeen. Just seventeen when she died.'

A pause, more clinking of glasses or teacups, something placed down near the microphone, moved again.

'And if you don't mind' – Lo's voice – 'I know it's painful to go over again, but can you tell me what happened the day Susan died?'

Mrs Turner cleared her throat. 'It was just an ordinary day. Susan had been working on her college applications. Everything seemed normal. But something had been troubling her.'

'You knew that? At the time?'

'Not so much. I guess not till afterwards, not till she did what she did. But yes, when I look back, I realise there was something wrong. Susan was a quiet girl, but those last few months she'd become real quiet. But that's how she was, you see. I guess you'd say she bottled things up. Nowadays they encourage people to talk about stuff, to *open up*' – she said those two words like there were air quotes around them – 'but back then, people didn't do that. At the time, we – her father and me – we put it down to stress at school. Exams, college applications. Susan was a perfectionist, put a lot of pressure on herself. We were always telling her to take time out, go see her friends . . .'

'And that's where you thought she was that last afternoon? Meeting friends.'

'That's what she told us, yes.'

'So when did you begin to worry?'

'Later that evening, when she hadn't come home. Susan didn't have a curfew – didn't need one. She was a sensible girl. Always home before dark.'

'So when it grew late, you called the police?'

'Didn't have to. They came to our door, told us Susan had been found.'

'Every parent's worst nightmare.'

A pause. 'Yes.'

'And if you don't mind, Mrs Turner, if it's not too much, can you tell me what had happened to Susan? I know we've been through this before, but for the tape?'

'We were told by police that she'd been found out of town. We don't know how she got there – she didn't drive; she hitched, they thought – but she'd travelled to the railroad tracks, laid right down on them. Waited. Can you imagine how desperate she must have felt to do that?' Her voice broke. 'Sorry,' she added.

'Don't apologise,' Lo said, 'I'm sorry to make you relive it.'

Another pause. 'It was dark. The train driver saw her in his headlights, but it was too late. He'd no hope of stopping . . .'

This time the pause felt endless.

'You mentioned earlier that you knew something was troubling Susan?'

No reply.

'This is a hard question to ask' – another pause, some shuffling sounds – 'but did you believe your daughter could have been suicidal?'

'Before? No. After?' A beat. 'Maybe. I don't know. We didn't want to believe it, but we knew from what the police told us – what the train driver said – that there was no one else involved. We were in shock. I guess we just accepted it. Our daughter, our beautiful Susan. She was gone.'

'But then something happened, Mrs Turner, isn't that right? Something that – and I hope you don't mind me saying this – erased any doubt in your minds about whether Susan took her own life?'

'Yes.' Mrs Turner's voice was faint. 'We received a letter from Susan. She'd mailed it the day she died. Her suicide note.'

There was some static, a noise like someone was shifting the tape recorder, repositioning it, then Lo again. 'I won't ask you to tell me exactly what was in the letter, Mrs Turner, not word for word. But if you wouldn't mind, can you outline what it was Susan wanted so badly to tell you? What you told me before?'

'She . . . she said that she loved us, all of us, but that . . . that she couldn't go on. I can remember every word by heart. I see them at night when I close my eyes, those letters on the page in her hand. Though I've never spoken them aloud.'

'I know this is hard, Mrs Turner, but did Susan's letter tell you why she felt she couldn't go on?'

'She said she was being . . . that someone at that school was . . . was doing things to her.'

'She was being sexually abused?'

No reply. I imagined Mrs Turner nodding.

'And – and I'm sorry, Mrs Turner, but I have to ask this – this was the first you'd heard of it?'

'Yes.'

'Did Susan say in the letter who it was who'd been abusing her?'

'Yes.' One word, more resolute than all the others. 'It was a priest. A priest at St Tom's, Susan's school. Father Todd Brennan. He took gym class there. Me and Susan's father, we stayed up all night the day we got that letter. My husband, well, he was so angry, it was all I could do to stop him going to Father Brennan himself, confronting him. He'd've killed him, I'm quite sure of that. The fact that I stopped him is something I've regretted ever since. I let my faith – in God, the Church, the justice system – guide me. That was my biggest mistake.'

'So what did you do instead?'

A shaky sigh. 'We went to the archdiocese. A decision I also lived to regret.'

'What did the archdiocese do?'

'Huh.' A bitter laugh. 'It's what they didn't do.'

'Meaning?'

'We met with the archbishop himself, placed our daughter's letter – her suicide note – on his desk, watched as he read it. The archbishop, he shook my husband's hand, consoled me as I wept, prayed with us for our daughter, for Susan. He promised us – promised! – the matter would be fully investigated, said he'd see to it personally, that we'd be kept informed at every step. He said Father Brennan would be dealt with.'

'And?'

'And we never heard from him again. We waited a few days, then weeks. Then we chased it, telephoned the archdiocese, but our calls went unreturned. We tried writing, of course, sent countless letters. We received a reply, eventually, a letter from the archbishop's secretary.'

'What did it say?'

'The archbishop denied ever having met with us.'

'What about the suicide note?'

'We left it with the archbishop that day, never saw it again.'

The tape ended. There was a loud *whoop* from somewhere over the other side of the bar, a shriek of raucous laughter, and suddenly I was back in the room. I'd been so lost in the tape, I'd forgotten where I was.

'Shit.' It was all I could think of to say.

'I know,' said Lo. 'Heavy stuff. But you know what the worst of it was? The Church refused to allow Susan – what was left of her – to be buried on consecrated ground. She'd taken her own life, a mortal sin in the eyes of the Catholic Church. It was such a slap in the face for the Turners. The final indignity.'

'Wasn't there anything her parents could do? Go to the police, the papers?'

Lo shrugged. 'They tried, but no one would listen. Everywhere they turned, doors were closed in their faces. Even with Susan's letter it would've been hard; without it, it was impossible – their word against the Church's. Jeannie – Mrs Turner – never got over it. Her husband, well, he died of cancer a few months after Susan's death, but everyone knew he really died of a broken heart.'

'God, that's so awful.'

She began to pick at the beer mat. 'Jeannie felt she'd let her daughter down, that her punishment was to live the rest of her life alone, tortured by guilt.'

'Did she have other children?'

'Yes, but they grew up, moved away. She hardly saw them, and when she did, they didn't want to talk about Susan.' Lo's eyes shone with tears. 'That poor woman suffered alone all these years. No one listened to her then, and no one's listening now.'

'*You* listened to her,' I said.

'No.' She shook her head, blinked away tears. 'I mean, I tried. But in the end, like everyone else, I let her down.'

'How?'

She stared at the table. She'd picked the beer mat to shreds, a tiny pile of confetti in its place. 'I knew when I wrote Susan's story that it wasn't the story my editor had asked for,' she said quietly. 'But I was sure he'd publish it. I mean, local schoolgirls abused by a Catholic priest?' She shoved her drink away, little pieces of cardboard scattering. 'I'd taken my time on the story, been thorough, made sure what I had was accurate. I'd asked around – spoken with people who'd known Susan, spoken with people who knew people – worked out dates, timelines. Everything checked out. I had hours of taped conversations.'

'So what happened?'

'My editor said he'd read it, asked to listen to the tapes. I gave him everything.'

'And?'

'And a couple of days later, he calls me into his office. He was pissed. *Really* pissed. Like, didn't I realise these were well-respected local figures I'd be libelling? Had I no idea of the consequences of a story like this, that I could get him sued? He told me to get rid of it, forget I'd ever started it. Then he took me off the piece, gave it to another junior, who, like a good cub reporter, wrote the story the *Herald* wanted – the one about the luxurious apartments being built on the site of St Tom's.'

'What did you do after that?'

'Nothing. I was nineteen, scared. I regret not standing up to my editor, sure, but I didn't know what else to do. I was at the beginning of my career and he acted like *I* was the one who'd done something wrong, like *I* was the one in trouble.'

I knew that feeling. 'What about the tapes?' I asked.

Lo shook her head. 'My editor kept them. I never saw them again. You know, when I was writing Susan's story, I learned there were people in Boweridge – adults – who knew what was going on at St Tom's but did nothing. Not just nothing – some of them actually protected Father Brennan. Turns out my editor was one of them.'

'Hang on, so if your editor kept the tapes, how . . .?'

'The one you just listened to? When I handed them over, I didn't realise there was still one in the Dictaphone. I'd been transcribing them, had forgotten it was there.' She gave the faintest smile. 'I backed it up after that, made a couple extra copies just in case.'

'And Jeannie? Did you see her again?'

Lo's smile fell and her eyes became tear-filled once more. 'I could barely face her after everything, but I knew I had to. She needed to hear it from me that the story wouldn't be running. So I went to see her one last time.'

'What did she say?'

'I was sure she was home – she rarely went out – but she didn't answer the door. I left a note explaining, telling her how sorry I was. I'd gained her trust, made promises I shouldn't have. She'd been so reluctant to talk when I first turned up and told her I was a journalist, that I was looking into Susan's story. She'd been burned so many times before. But I *persuaded* her, Maggie, persuaded her to talk, to go on the record. I promised we'd get justice for Susan, that Father Brennan would be made to pay.'

'You tried your best,' I said. 'I'm sure she'd have understood.'

'Well, I guess I'll never know.' Lo drew a deep, shaky breath. 'I left the *Herald* less than a month later, the day I read in the obituaries that Jeannie Turner had passed away. She was eighty-three, died of a massive stroke at home. Alone.'

'God, Lo, I'm so sorry.' I hesitated, not wanting to seem insensitive. 'But what's this got to do with Minna's disappearance? Sister Fran's murder? They happened four years after Susan's suicide. You think they're all connected somehow? That, what? St Tom's – Father Brennan – is the missing link?'

'I don't *think*,' Lo said emphatically, eyes shining. 'I *know*. I know,' she repeated, 'I just don't have proof. All roads lead back to St Tom's, with Father Brennan at the dark heart of it.'

10

There was a thunderstorm that night. I lay in bed listening to the rain, the rumbles of thunder growing closer until they were overhead, and wondered if Lo could be right. Could one man, a priest, be the common thread in all this? If he was, what did that even mean? Okay, so we could be pretty certain he was behind Susan Turner's abuse, the cause of her suicide, even. But Sister Fran's murder? Minna's disappearance? Other than a gut feeling, Lo admitted she had no proof. Like me, she'd only learned about Sister Fran and Minna through Facebook, knew little more about them than I did. The one thing she did know, though, was that there were other girls. She and Mrs Turner had touched on it in the tapes – the tapes that disappeared after Lo handed them to her editor. Lo said Mrs Turner had told her how, in the years since her daughter's death, people had come to her, confided in her about things Father Brennan had done to them. Things that made her toes curl. *You either knew or you didn't*, they all said. It was an open secret.

An open secret no one talked about.

The next day, I rose early and showered, then checked my emails and found a Facebook message. Sent during the small hours of the morning, it was from a complete stranger.

> Hello Maggie, I'm Gretchen Wood. I saw your post on the Sister Fran Facebook page and thought I should message you directly. I started the group a few years ago, after talk of a high school reunion. I was a pupil at St Tom's, the same form class as your aunt, Minna. There have always been rumors about what happened to Sister Fran and Minna, whether the two were connected. I don't know how much I can help you, or what you already know, but I wondered if you'd like to meet up?

Active 5 mins ago, it said under Gretchen's name. I seized my chance.

> Hi Gretchen, thanks for your message. It'd be great to meet up. I know very little about Minna or Sister Fran, but would love to know more. I'm visiting from the UK, here for another few days, but my schedule's pretty free, so let me know when/where would be good for you. Thanks.

I stared at the screen, willing something to happen. A few minutes passed and I was about to give up, go and get breakfast, when a message pinged.

> My house, 3 p.m.?

As I rode to Gretchen's on Bob's bike, it crossed my mind that this whole thing might be a hoax. I'd already done a little snooping on Gretchen's profile, like any self-respecting Facebook user messaged by a complete stranger, and it looked legit – she had a little over a hundred and fifty friends; her profile picture was a handsome-looking Labrador, her cover photo a panoramic sunset – but there were no photos of Gretchen herself, and everyone knows a fake Facebook profile is easily set up. What better guise than that of a seemingly benign middle-aged woman?

I arrived at the address at two minutes past three and, still wondering if I'd been catfished, was beginning to talk myself out of the whole thing as I reached for the doorbell. I'd almost decided to scurry back down the well-kept pathway, hop on Bob's bike and skedaddle, when the door opened. No going back now.

'Maggie?' asked the woman standing before me in the doorway.

The first thing I noticed about her was that she was pretty nondescript: medium height, slim, mid sixties. The second thing I noticed was that she was not so nondescript after all: her short hair was dyed an improbable shade of strawberry blonde, she had multiple piercings in each ear, and fingers full of rings.

'Gretchen?'

For a horrible moment I thought she was going in for a hug, but she must have seen me stiffen like a frightened cat and she reached for a slightly awkward handshake instead, smiled a warm, genuine smile. I felt myself relax.

'Come in,' she said.

She held the door wide, but before I could step inside, a huge Labrador – presumably the one from Gretchen's Facebook profile – shoved his way past her, tail thumping so vigorously it almost knocked me off my feet.

'Who's this?' I asked, laughing. The overexuberant, puppy-ish greeting notwithstanding, the dog's lumbering gait and salt-and-pepper muzzle made me realise he was getting on.

'This,' said Gretchen, giving the dog's butt a playful swat, 'is Brian.' She flattened herself to one side, allowing us both to pass. 'Gosh.' She watched me go with a shake of her head. 'I'm not great with faces, but even I can see you're so much like her.'

I knew without asking that she meant Minna. It was a weird

feeling. All my life people – strangers, even – had told me how much I looked like my mom. But here I was, for the third time in recent days, being compared to someone I'd never even met.

'I'm sorry,' Gretchen apologised. 'I've made you uncomfortable.'

'It's fine,' I insisted. I thought of the woman at Art's Autos, of librarian Mavis. Gretchen was the first person I'd met who'd showed a willingness to open up about Minna. I couldn't lose this opportunity. 'It's strange, that's all. I mean, I didn't even know of my aunt's existence till a few days ago.'

Now that we were inside, I saw that Gretchen wore shorts, a vest top, one of those loose-fitting light-knit cardigans – the waterfall type that my mom hated – and a pair of hideous bright green Crocs.

'Don't worry,' she said, gesturing at her footwear like she'd read my mind. 'I don't actually go out in them.' She winked at me. 'Unless you count the yard,' she added as I followed her through to the kitchen, the smell of fresh coffee brewing.

Gretchen's house – a decent-sized detached older property a couple of streets from where Lo used to live – was as eclectic as she was. *Lived in*, my mom would have called it with a shudder. Until I met Tabby, I'd always thought of that as a bad thing, but Tabby's house was lived in in a good way. It had stuff and clutter, dirty dishes by the sink, muddy trainers in the hallway. It had pets and people and noise (Tabby has four older brothers); the type of home that once would have made me feel on edge, but now made me feel at ease.

'So,' Gretchen said, reaching for two mugs from a high-up cupboard, 'you're looking into her disappearance.'

I nodded half-heartedly. 'Trying to. Not getting very far.' Truthfully, I was still torn. *A scar that never heals* was how Mom had described Minna's disappearance. Did I really want to reopen that old wound?

Gretchen, her back to me, nodded too. 'Coffee okay?' She set the mugs on the counter and, without waiting for an answer, asked, 'Milk? Sugar?'

'Black, thanks,' I told her.

She added milk to one of the mugs, stirred it thoughtfully. Then she set the teaspoon down by the sink, handed me my mug and picked up her own.

'I thought we'd chat in the basement,' she said, heading to a door across the far side of the kitchen. She opened it and started down the stairs, and I followed, mug in hand, Brian at my heels.

'So you know she went missing in '72?' Gretchen asked as we descended.

'That's about all I do know.' Not quite true, but almost.

At the bottom of the staircase, I looked around. The basement was spacious and open-plan, painted all white with bright strip lighting, not dark and dingy like I'd envisaged. Half the space was given over to storage – an artificial Christmas tree, packing cases, furniture, boxes of crockery, old toys that had probably belonged to Gretchen's now grown-up kids; the other half was an office-slash-den.

'I mentioned that Minna and I were at high school together?' Gretchen asked. 'Same form class?' She shifted a stack of papers from a tired-looking couch, gestured to me to sit down.

I nodded. 'My mom went there too, a few years later, though.'

I took a seat, Brian scrambling up beside me, aided by a boost to his rear from Gretchen ('Arthritis,' she told me, 'poor guy'), before she carried her coffee to the other side of the room and took a seat on an office swivel chair, next to a desk with a cumbersome-looking home computer occupying most of its surface.

'Well, I'm sure you'll already know this, but St Thomas Aquinas High School' – she said it grandly – 'St Tom's for short, was an all-girls Catholic school.'

I nodded again. I knew from Mom, though I'd never given it much thought.

Gretchen took her time, sipped her coffee, set it down on the edge of the desk. 'Minna and I were there late sixties, early seventies. I graduated in '73. Minna would've too, except, well . . .'

'What can you tell me about her?'

'Honestly?' Gretchen pulled an apologetic face. 'Not a whole lot.'

'But you were in the same form class for at least three years?'

There was that face again. 'I had a close group of friends . . .' She trailed off.

'Minna didn't, you mean?'

'It wasn't like we deliberately excluded her,' Gretchen explained, 'but I guess you could say your aunt was something of a loner. Some of the girls thought she came over aloof, like she thought she was better than the rest of us. I always thought there was something else, something I couldn't put my finger on.'

'But she must've had *some* friends?'

'Look, hun,' Gretchen picked up her mug, wrapped her fingers around it, rings clinking on ceramic, 'I'm afraid that Minna wasn't just not part of *my* friendship group, she wasn't really a part of any. Not at school, anyhow. I guess she just wasn't a girls' girl. But one night, I was at a bowling alley with some friends, and we spotted her with some guy.'

'Like a boyfriend?' Mom had mentioned a boyfriend, the one she was jealous of for taking up so much of Minna's time.

'A boyfriend. Name was Mike.'

Mike. I remembered the photo, the inscription with the hand-drawn love hearts: *Mike & Minna, May 1972.* It had to be him.

'Mike was a pupil at the local boys' Catholic school,' Gretchen said, 'but a year or two above. From what I know, he'd already graduated, worked for the family business. He smoked, played football, was handsome and cool. The sight of him and Minna together caused quite a stir, as you can imagine. She was the talk of the class for much of the next day.'

'Just as she was when she disappeared, I'm guessing.'

'School was out by that time, but yes.' Gretchen nodded. 'Funny thing was, the summer she vanished was much like any other. I've thought about it a lot since. Guess you could say it's kind of haunted me. Minna was our classmate, the girl everyone loved to talk about yet no one really knew.'

'Do *you* think she ran away?'

'That's certainly what most people thought; what the papers reported. Then there were the rumours.'

'Like what?'

'That she'd gotten pregnant.'

'By this Mike guy?'

Gretchen shrugged. 'I guess.'

'I suppose that would be a good enough reason for running away. Strict Catholic family, pregnant at seventeen . . .'

Gretchen hesitated, and I could sense her uncertainty.

'Go on,' I told her.

'The pregnancy,' she said. 'Well, that was just the start. Of the rumours, I mean.'

'There were more?'

She sighed. 'There's no easy way to say it, hun, but there was talk around town that your grandparents had something to do with it – that they made Minna have an illegal abortion and she died in the process.'

'God,' I gasped. 'I mean, that'd be horrendous. But it sounds unlikely, don't you think? How would you cover it up? What would you do with the body?'

'I don't disagree. But it didn't stop there. See, there were those who said that . . . well, that your grandpa killed Minna when he found out she was pregnant.'

Strangely, I felt almost relieved. Of all the theories – and I wasn't sure how likely any of them were – this seemed the least probable. The Grandpa John I knew was a quiet man. Lacklustre, maybe. Henpecked, definitely. But stone-cold killer? I wasn't so sure. I'd have been less surprised had Gretchen suggested that Grandma Ida had killed Minna. That I could just about see.

'Why would they think that?'

'So, like, two, three weeks before she vanished, not long before school was out, Minna was seen around with a black eye.'

I shivered. Mom had said something about a trace of a black eye, the day the photo was taken.

'Did anyone ask her how she got it?'

'Lots of people. But no one could get a straight answer; Minna never told the same story twice. I guess everyone reckoned she was covering for someone, that her father did it – for whatever reason.' Gretchen's grip around her mug tightened. 'The one thing they all agreed on was that she seemed to revel in the attention it got her. Wore it like a badge of honour.'

'O-kay,' I said, unsure. Why would anyone *enjoy* having a black eye? Then I thought of Mom, how she'd have acted, and doubt began to trickle in. 'And you believe that?'

'For what it's worth, no, I didn't – don't,' she corrected herself. 'You see, there was always something I saw in Minna that other people didn't seem to. They said she was a free spirit, but all I saw was a lost soul.'

I swallowed. 'So what do you think really happened?' The newspaper articles had said Sister Fran's murder was a robbery gone wrong. Minna disappeared days later, out of the blue. Just another runaway. On the surface, there appeared to be no link. But after what Mom had said, what Lo had told me . . . 'You think Minna's disappearance and Sister Fran's murder are connected.'

'I didn't.' Gretchen puffed out her cheeks. 'Not at first, anyhow. For many years, like most people, I figured Minna had just run away. It was no secret she wasn't happy at home.'

'But you found something out that made you change your mind.'

Gretchen hesitated. She put her mug down and drew the front of her cardigan closer together, and I wondered whether she was cold – the basement air con was pretty savage – or if it was a comfort thing. When at last she spoke, she said, 'One of my closest friends at St Tom's was a girl called Marcie. Marcie was bright and pretty, wore glasses, had freckles, lovely long red hair – kind of a geek, I guess, but then we all were.' She smiled at the memory. 'She was smaller than the rest of us, young-looking for her age, shy, too. She was the sixth of eleven siblings in a big ol' Catholic family. She was quieter than her brothers and sisters, typical middle child, you could say, content to stay in the background.' She sighed, picked up her mug again. 'I don't know, perhaps she didn't get as much attention from her parents as she might've done, but she'd done well at elementary school all the same, and, like Minna and me, won a scholarship to St Tom's. But what Marcie's family didn't realise – what none of us did – was that she'd caught the eye of an older male cousin. She was ten when the abuse began.'

Gretchen looked skyward for a second, drew breath.

'I'd stayed in touch with her all these years. We'd gone our separate ways – different colleges, settled down, had families. Marcie had a loving husband, successful career. We'd meet every year or so for a catch-up, sometimes for dinner, and in all that time she never told me. Then, I guess in like 2012, before I started the Facebook group, there was talk of a reunion – St Tom's class of '73. It was coming up forty years since we graduated. Me and Marcie met for lunch, got to talking about it, and that's when she broke down, told me everything.'

'About what her cousin was doing?'

Gretchen nodded. 'But her cousin, well, he was just the start.'

I had a horrible feeling I knew where this was going.

'Marcie and her family,' Gretchen continued, 'this cousin included, attended St Thomas Aquinas Catholic church, next door to the all-girls Catholic high school of the same name. The priest at the church, well, he just happened to teach gym class at the school.'

'Let me guess,' I said. 'Father Todd Brennan.'

Gretchen looked surprised. 'You know.'

'I know he was abusing girls at St Tom's,' I explained. 'I met an old school friend yesterday. She told me about another student, Susan Turner, who killed herself in '68, named Father Brennan in her suicide note.'

'I heard about Susan,' Gretchen said.

'So your friend Marcie,' I prompted. 'Father Brennan began abusing her too?'

'Yes. You see, Marcie's cousin, good Catholic boy that he was, was an altar boy at St Tom's church, took confession with Father Brennan every week. You can guess what he must've confessed.'

I swallowed. Father Brennan had chosen Marcie, singled her out because she was already vulnerable.

'So where does Sister Fran come into all of this?'

'Ah, Sister Fran.' Gretchen smiled, and despite the little crow's feet around her eyes deepening, I noticed how much younger it made her look. 'She was a favourite with the girls at school, so much fun, not like the other nuns – not strict, uptight. Of course, it helped that she was just a few years older than us, pretty, too, and she didn't always wear her habit either, so I guess she was more normal-looking, more accessible somehow, like, we could relate to her.' She shook her head sadly. 'She was so full of life.'

'You must've known her pretty well. Sister Fran was your form tutor, right?'

Gretchen nodded. 'She was so creative, loved singing and art. But it was her passion for literature that shone through most. She'd taken over the running of the student newspaper, started St Tom's first book club, too. I think it was that passion, you know, that love for her subject and students, that inspired me to become a teacher myself.'

I might've guessed Gretchen was a teacher. She had that demeanour, the laid-back, cool sort – firm but fair – loved, or at least respected, by her pupils.

'See, and I didn't know this at the time, but Marcie told me that before Sister Fran's death, she'd started asking questions.'

'About Father Brennan? Marcie told Sister Fran what he was doing to her?'

'Sister Fran spoke to Marcie, yes, but Marcie was too scared to tell her. She was afraid Father Brennan would find out, afraid her family would, too.'

'But you think Sister Fran found out from someone?' It wouldn't be surprising. Lo had said there were others.

'Maybe she found out from someone, maybe she put two and two together. Either way, she'd been asking around, speaking to girls she suspected Father Brennan was targeting – for want of a better word.'

'Does Marcie know who? Which girls Sister Fran spoke to?'

'Not for sure. Not all of them. But – and there's no easy way to tell you this, Maggie – Minna was one of them.'

'Minna was being abused?' I asked in a small voice.

'It certainly looks that way.'

It shouldn't have come as a surprise, yet it hit me like a ton of bricks. How had I been so blind, especially after what I'd learned about Minna – the crying all the time, the acting out? What Lo had told me. *There were other girls.* Had Lo suspected Minna was one of them? And if Lo had figured it out, who else had? I thought back to my childhood. Though Mom had barely seemed to like me and Em most of the time, she was nevertheless fiercely protective of us. As a child, I'd simply seen it as yet another example of her controlling nature, but now I couldn't help but wonder: was it more than that? Had *Mom* known about the abuse? Had she, in her own weird, over-bearing way, been trying to protect me and Em?

But if Mom knew about the abuse, then surely Grandpa John and Grandma Ida would have too. Would Minna have told them? Tried to tell them?

Was this what people meant when they said *Minna lies*?

But Minna hadn't being lying, not about the abuse – not if Susan and Marcie were to be believed, if Lo and Gretchen were right. I thought of Mom's words, what she'd told me about Sister Fran's mur-der: *Minna told me she knew who'd done it . . . But it wasn't just me – she told other people too.*

And if Minna hadn't been lying about the abuse, I wondered, what else hadn't she lied about?

II

After Gretchen's revelation, which really shouldn't have come as a revelation at all, a silence fell between us, one that seemed to stretch for ever.

'So,' I said at last, Gretchen regarding me with such intense sympathy I had to look away, 'you think Sister Fran was murdered because of what she uncovered at St Tom's? That she was threatening to tell? Expose Father Brennan?'

'Right,' said Gretchen. 'But all I had was theory and suspicion. So I set up the Facebook page. Guess I hoped social media would stir up interest in the case, bring it to the attention of a whole new generation of Boweridgians, jog the memories of old ones. I mean, forty years had passed – you'd think after all that time people would be willing to talk.'

'And did they?'

'Yes and no. People came forward, but a lot of what they told me was hearsay. We're talking second-, third-hand information – stuff that might've had a grain of truth to it, but impossible to be sure. A few leads felt promising, but none came to anything. I'd trace them back to their source, only to find either the person had died or didn't want to talk. I had a lot on my plate back then, too – my husband was sick, passed away the following year; the kids were still back and forth;

I hadn't retired from teaching – and it all became too much. I wasn't able to update the Facebook page as regularly as I'd have liked, or spend as much time investigating. I guess it just kinda fizzled out. People lost interest.'

'So,' I said, 'what *do* you know for sure about Sister Fran's murder?' I was beginning to wonder if Gretchen knew any more than I did.

'Well,' she began, but at that moment, the doorbell rang from upstairs. 'Ah,' she said, rising from her chair, 'right on cue. That'll be our guest.'

I must have looked puzzled.

'When I told Ted I'd messaged you,' Gretchen explained, 'said you wanted to find out about Minna—'

'I'm sorry?' I said, more confused. 'Ted?'

'Ted,' Gretchen repeated. 'The detective I want you to meet.'

'Wait.' I stood. 'You invited a cop?'

'I didn't mention him?' She waved at me to sit back down. 'Ted's a good cop, honey. You'll see. He knows Sister Fran's case better than anyone. He's . . .' She broke off as the bell rang again. 'Well, he can tell you himself.'

Gretchen disappeared upstairs, and, feeling more than a little uneasy, I perched stiffly on the edge of the sofa, listened to the muffled voices, footsteps, the door closing, laughter. Beside me, Brian took advantage of the extra space and stretched out, his big head lolling behind my back. The warmth was comforting. A few moments later, there came footsteps on the basement stairs.

I'd been expecting some uniformed older man, possibly in his sixties, the stereotypical paunchy, balding, doughnut-eating policeman. The man who followed Gretchen into the room was anything but. He was young, I guessed around the same age as me, and tall, dressed in jeans and a T-shirt. He wore a navy Boweridge PD baseball cap and was carrying a cardboard box. With a vigour that surprised me, Brian leaped from the sofa and made a beeline for Gretchen's guest, tail thumping side to side. The man dropped the box and kneeled to greet him, chucking him under the chin, ruffling his golden fur playfully, wrinkling his face in mock-protest as Brian licked it so enthusiastically he almost knocked his cap off.

Gretchen cleared her throat.

'Oh, hey, sorry.' There was something alarmingly familiar about those words, that voice.

The man got to his feet, dusting himself down, and our eyes met, a look of recognition lighting up his face. *Shit.* I felt my ears burn red. *Coffee Guy, the one I'd almost collided with at the police station.*

'Maggie,' Gretchen said, oblivious, 'meet Detective Ted Hoppy. Ted, this is Maggie, the young lady I was telling you about.'

'Actually,' Ted said, 'Maggie and I have already met. In fact . . .' he turned to me, smiling, 'we go way back, don't we, Maggie?'

'You do?' Gretchen looked simultaneously surprised and pleased.

I hugged my arms across my middle, mumbled, 'We kind of bumped into each other at the police department the other day.'

'You did?' Gretchen, grinning ear to ear, looked at Ted.

'We did,' he confirmed, his smile annoyingly mischievous. 'I think Maggie here thought I was trying to get her number. I go, "Don't I know you?", and she's all, "I doubt it."'

'No I didn't,' I protested weakly.

Gretchen and Ted laughed. I felt the heat from my ears spread to my face.

'Seriously, though,' said Ted, 'I realised after you left where I know you from. My sister Jen? She went to school with you.'

There'd been two Jens in my class at McArthur, Jen P and Jen H, Jen Parker and Jen . . . 'You're Jen Hoppy's brother?'

'Yeah,' Ted said. 'Except she's not a Hoppy any more, got married last year.'

Though I wasn't exactly not friends with Jen H, we hadn't been especially close. All I remembered about her was that she was quiet. Nice. I'd been to a couple of her birthday parties, vaguely remembered a brother there, recalled some of the other girls giggling every time he spoke. Now that I came to think of it, I was sure he was called Ted. He was older, a tall, skinny kid . . .

'You were the grade above,' I said.

'Two.'

'Well,' interrupted Gretchen, putting me out of my misery. 'This is all very nice, but shall we get started?'

'Gretchen tells me you're Minna Larson's niece?' Ted helped himself to a chair, planted it opposite me, the other side of the desk from Gretchen's. 'You're trying to find out what happened to her?'

'I guess,' I said. I still found it hard to fully commit. Part of me was afraid where it might lead; the other part was afraid it might lead nowhere at all. 'You've got information on her case?'

'Some,' he said, 'but more on Sister Fran's.'

'I'd assumed they weren't active,' I said. 'Minna's case, at least, from what the detective at the station told me.'

'They aren't,' Ted told me. 'Not officially.' Brian had forsaken the comfort of the sofa in favour of the floor, draped himself across Ted's feet.

'Still,' Gretchen said, 'Ted can probably tell you more than anyone.'

'All thanks to this lady.' He jerked a thumb at her. 'I'd never even heard of Sister Fran and Minna's cases till a few years ago. Word had gotten round about the Sister Fran Facebook group down at the precinct. There were a few cops – old-schoolers, you know the type – who weren't too happy about it being raked up after all this time.'

'But the cases are over forty years old,' I said. 'There must be more recent ones you could look at. Why the interest in theirs?'

A fleeting look passed between Gretchen and Ted, and I felt like I was missing something.

'Ted's grandpa,' Gretchen told me, 'was Detective Ronald Hoppy. Ron worked the Sister Fran case back in '72, looked into Minna's disappearance as well.'

'My dad was on the force,' Ted explained. '*His* dad – Grandpa Ron – before him.'

As he spoke, Gretchen dug in the box Ted had brought, handed me a black-and-white photo of Ted's grandpa, a young Ronald Hoppy. From the 1960s, I guessed, it was a shoulders-up portrait – the kind you see lining precinct walls in American cop shows – Ron looking proud in his police cap and badge, a sort of handsome matinee idol. His hair was styled differently from Ted's, his eyes set a little closer together, jaw a little softer, but still, I could see the likeness.

'Around the time I first saw Gretchen's Facebook page,' Ted said, 'I'm having dinner at my parents', talking about the case – what Dad knows – and Mom's like, "You should have a look through your Grandpa's stuff." Turns out Grandpa'd kept all his notes from his time on the force.'

'Cops are allowed to do that?'

He shrugged. 'You'd be surprised.' He leaned forward, lifted the peak of his cap and rubbed his brow, and it struck me how unassumingly good-looking he was, if tall, dark and handsome was your thing (I told myself hastily it wasn't). 'After Grandpa passed, Dad ended up with 'em.' He pulled his cap back down. 'They'd been sitting in my parents' garage ever since – boxes and boxes – almost twenty years just layin' there waiting for me to come along.'

'So,' I said. 'What can you tell me about Sister Fran?'

'The whole story?' Ted sat back. 'It was June 17, the day she died,' he began. 'A Saturday. From what we know, at twenty after nine that evening, Sister Fran left the convent and drove to Don's Diner.'

'I read that the police thought she was meeting someone?'

'Right,' he agreed. 'Why else would she travel alone to a diner on the outskirts of town, late at night? But who she was meeting wasn't the only mystery.'

'Meaning?' I asked.

'Meaning the drive from convent to diner should've taken no more than a half-hour. Sister Fran should've gotten there around nine fifty p.m.'

'But she didn't?'

'Nope. Witnesses didn't place her there till twenty before eleven that night. There was a missing fifty minutes in her timeline.'

'You know for sure?'

'Yup. See, Grandpa was on duty that evening, first on scene. He was the one spoke with the witnesses. They swore she entered the diner at ten forty, then left again. Her body was found at eleven fifteen, meaning—'

'Meaning she was murdered some time in that thirty-five-minute window,' I filled in. 'Did anyone at the diner speak to her?'

'Nope. According to witnesses, she rushed in and rushed out. Not a word.'

'But they knew who she was? I mean, they identified her afterwards, right?'

'Right. Don, the diner's owner, and his son, Dewey – also there that night – both knew her. Don's daughter – Dewey's sister – was a student at St Tom's.'

'And after Sister Fran left the diner, no one heard or saw anything until she was found in the car park – parking lot – later?'

'Mm-hmm.' Ted gave a firm nod. 'Nothing. Not till quarter after eleven, thirty-five minutes after she'd entered: one of the regulars discovered her body there as he was leaving.'

'Were there any obvious clues?' I asked. 'Anything that stood out as – I don't know – out of the ordinary?'

'You mean aside from the fact that the vic was a nun, at an

out-of-town diner late at night?' He shook his head. 'Nothing *I* could find. Sister Fran wasn't wearing her habit that night, but I guess it wasn't all that unusual for her to go out and about in *normal clothing*.' He made bunny ears with his fingers. 'The order she belonged to didn't routinely wear habits. By all accounts, she was pretty independent. Sure, she lived at a convent, but she had a car, a job . . .'

'And she hadn't told anyone where she was going that night, who she was meeting?'

Ted shook his head. 'Not that Grandpa could ascertain. He checked her purse, pocket book, car, but there were no clues.'

'And I guess your grandpa spoke to friends, family – people she worked with?'

'It was summer vacation, but he spoke with as many of the St Tom's staff as he could – it's all in his notes. None of them could shed any light either. The one thing that kept coming up, though, was that pretty much everyone thought something was up with Sister Fran in the weeks before her death.'

'Up like how?'

'Like she had stuff on her mind, something bothering her maybe, but it was all a bit vague.'

'And her convent?'

'The impression I got – that Grandpa Ron had gotten – was that if they did know anything, they weren't telling.'

I felt a prickle of irritation. 'What could they have to hide?'

Ted shrugged. 'Good question. Grandpa Ron spoke to a young nun there, a Sister Joy Greenway, Sister Fran's roommate. She said that in the weeks leading up to the murder, Sister Fran had been getting letters in the mail, but whether or not that was related . . .'

Gretchen had disappeared upstairs and returned with a jug of iced tea. Empty coffee mugs pushed aside, she poured three glasses and handed them round, ice cubes clinking.

'So,' I said, taking a sip, sweet and cold, a sudden blast from childhood, 'the letters. Who were they from?'

'That's just it.' Ted took a drink too. 'They never found out. All Sister Joy knew was that they were hand-addressed.' He picked up a notebook from the box he'd brought, began to flip through it one-handed until he found what he was looking for. 'That they were "in a woman's writing, she thought" . . .' he peered closer, ' "but couldn't be sure". Grandpa searched Sister Fran's room at the convent, but the letters weren't there, so it looks like someone disposed of them, possibly Sister Fran herself.'

'I was going through some old newspaper articles,' I said, 'and it seemed at the time police thought the motive for Sister Fran's murder might have been robbery.'

'Uh-huh.' Ted nodded.

'But you mentioned her purse, her pocket book.'

'Yup.' He nodded some more, steepled his fingers together. 'Both were found at the scene that night, right by her body. Car keys too. She didn't have a lot of money – I mean, she was a nun, right? – but what she did have was there. Purse didn't look like it had even been gone through.'

'So *you* don't think the motive was robbery?'

'No. Grandpa Ron didn't either.'

'But what about her crucifix?' I asked. 'The one the newspapers mentioned.'

'Her crucifix,' Ted repeated, 'yes. Sister Fran's dad ID'd her body, asked about it. It wasn't valuable, more sentimental – her parents gave her it when she took her vows. She always wore it, apparently.'

'Could she have lost it that night, like if there'd been a struggle?'

'Not according to the medical examiner's report. There would've been marks – distinctive ones – if it had been torn from her neck.'

'Maybe it just came loose?' I tried. 'Fell off?'

'Maybe,' Ted said, but I could tell he was unconvinced. 'Even so, Grandpa and a deputy searched the lot that night with a fine-toothed comb. It wasn't there.'

'So if she wasn't wearing it and it wasn't subsequently found, then the most probable explanation is that the killer must've taken it.' I stopped, considered. It seemed a lot of trouble to go to – unfastening a fiddly little catch from a dead woman's neck – for a modest piece of jewellery. 'But if the motive wasn't robbery . . .'

Ted tilted his head, looked at me.

'What?' I shifted in my seat. 'Whoever killed Sister Fran took it as, like, a trophy?'

'Think about it.' Ted said. 'It's gotta be a possibility, right?'

'But that's what serial killers do.' I looked from Ted to Gretchen, then back at Ted. 'Take trophies from their victims. You think Sister Fran was murdered by a serial killer?'

'No,' Ted said quickly, 'I don't. Neither did Grandpa. But you know *how* she was killed, right?'

I swallowed. 'Only what I read in the papers. She was strangled.'

He put his glass down. 'She'd been struck from behind first, most likely using a rock found at the scene. The head wound probably wasn't enough to make her lose consciousness, but it would have been enough to disable her – cause her to fall to the ground.'

'Any defensive wounds? Signs of sexual assault?'

'No signs of sexual assault, thank God. Some defensive wounds – which also suggested she'd been conscious – though perhaps not as many as she might've had if she hadn't been struck first. She was probably pretty dazed. Her hands were grazed, like she'd held them out to break her fall; her knees, too, and there was dirt and grit stuck to her pant legs – palms of her hands too – from where she'd landed on the gravel.'

'Then, as she lay there, she was strangled,' I finished. So that was what Ted was getting at. 'It was personal,' I said. 'Strangulation. Sister Fran knew her killer.'

'Right,' Ted agreed. 'Grandpa Ron always thought so too. I mean, squeezing the very life out of someone . . .' He motioned with his hands, like he was wringing someone's neck. 'It's physically hard work. You gotta be angry, enraged – you're looking that person right in the eye the whole time. Yeah, I'd say it was personal.'

I shivered, trying to shake the image he'd just conjured. He grimaced apologetically.

'Did they ever account for the missing fifty minutes, or find out who Sister Fran was supposed to have been meeting that night?'

Ted shook his head.

'So there were never any suspects?'

'A couple, I guess, but nothing concrete. As for motive,' he sighed, 'little more than hearsay, speculation.'

That didn't surprise me. It sounded like hearsay and speculation were what Boweridge did best. 'Any of it worth mentioning?'

'Well, there'd been a rumour going round St Tom's that Sister Fran was romantically involved with a young priest, Father Gil Griffin. Father Gil taught English at the local boys' Catholic high school.'

'There was never any proof the rumours were true,' Gretchen piped up. 'But Father Gil and Sister Fran were only human. The path they'd chosen could be a lonely one, plus they were both young, good-looking . . .'

'Apparently,' said Ted, 'in the weeks before Sister Fran's death, the rumours had gotten so bad she was called in front of the principal of St Tom's, forced to deny them.'

'And did she?'

'According to Grandpa's notes, yes. She told the principal their relationship was purely platonic. I guess that put a pin in it for a while, but when news of her murder broke, well, the rumour mill went into over-drive again.'

'There was all kinds of stuff going round,' Gretchen said. 'Like Sister Fran and Father Gil were planning on running away together, but Sister Fran got cold feet, told Gil she couldn't go through with it, so he killed her.'

'And don't forget the rumour that she was pregnant,' Ted added, 'and that when Father Gil found out, he killed her to protect himself, avoid a scandal.'

'*Was* she pregnant?' I asked.

Ted shook his head firmly. 'That was one rumour the medical examiner was able to disprove unequivocally: Sister Fran was not pregnant at the time of her death, nor had she ever been.'

Not – I'd bet from what I'd learned – that it would make much difference to the Boweridge rumour mill.

'Did your grandpa ever suspect this Father Gil?' I asked Ted.

'It's hard to say for sure . . .' he sat back, rubbed his chin, 'but no, I don't think so. Number one, Father Gil had an alibi for the night Sister Fran was killed: he was at home with three, four other priests. And number two, according to Grandpa's notes – though granted, this isn't exactly evidence – after Sister Fran was murdered, Father Gil was a broken man. It was obvious that his feelings for her had been genuine, more than a friend. He loved her.'

'People kill for love all the time,' I said. 'Crimes of passion.'

'You're right,' said Ted. 'But the evidence just didn't stack up.'

'So who does that leave?' I asked. 'And how's it all connected to Minna?'

'Ah,' Gretchen chipped in, 'this is where it gets interesting.'

'So,' Ted continued, 'a week after Sister Fran's murder, Grandpa takes a phone call at the precinct about a missing seventeen-year-old.'

'Minna.'

'Minna. He made the connection straight away: Minna was a student at St Tom's; Sister Fran was her teacher. So while I guess her disappearance didn't necessarily ring alarm bells – it was summer vacation; Minna had been known to go AWOL every now and then – he decided to look into it all the same.'

'Do you know who made the call?'

'Let's see.' He consulted his grandpa's notebook again. 'Says here it was John Larson, Minna's father.'

Grandpa John. After JJ's shrugged *I guess* reply when I'd asked him if it was the Larsons who'd reported Minna missing, I couldn't help but feel relieved. So Minna's parents had cared something for her after all.

'According to Grandpa's notes,' Ted went on, 'by the time they made the call, your grandparents hadn't seen Minna in two days.'

'Did they say much?'

'Not really, only that she'd left Thursday evening to visit a boyfriend, hadn't returned. Seemed your grandma was more concerned about the fuss Minna was causing, what the neighbours might think, rather than the fact her daughter was missing.'

'Sounds like my family all right,' I said, almost under my breath. 'Did your grandpa have any theories about what might have happened to her?'

'On the face of it, there was nothing to suggest anything sinister. But if there's one thing I know about Grandpa Ron, he never took stuff at face value. Appearances count for a lot in Boweridge, but they can sure be deceiving.'

'So what did he do?'

'He asked around, spoke to Minna's boyfriend, her teachers, a handful of students.' *Students*. There it was again, like when JJ had said *classmates*. Not *friends*, *girlfriends*. 'Minna's boyfriend, Mike, confirmed your grandparents' story: Minna was supposed to visit with him the night she vanished, but didn't show. Her teachers were pretty tight-lipped – Grandpa got the impression they'd rather say nothing than speak ill of her – and as for the students, the only useful thing he learned was that before Minna's disappearance, she'd been telling people she knew who murdered Sister Fran.'

I thought again of what Mom said: *Minna told me she knew who'd done it, can you believe?* 'Did she tell anyone who she thought it was?'

'No – or if she did, no one was admitting it, so there wasn't anything much Grandpa Ron could do. Without evidence, it was all hearsay.'

'So the cases just went cold?'

'Well, it looked that way. Minna's at least. But, like, around that time too, some guy called the precinct, asked to speak to someone on the Sister Fran case.' Ted leaned forward. 'Said he had information on the murdered nun. This guy, Leland Eavers, owned properties – apartments, condos – and he *swore* that for the last few weeks he'd been renting an apartment to Sister Fran.'

'Huh? I thought she lived at the convent?'

'She did.'

'So why would she be renting an apartment?'

Ted shrugged. 'Eavers had no idea.'

I frowned. Nothing seemed to fit. 'Where was this apartment?'

'I'm not sure exactly, somewhere over the east side.'

'The *east* side? Isn't that . . .?'

'The wrong side of the tracks? Yeah. That's the weird thing. This guy's usual tenants were drifters – petty cons, people down on their luck – not nuns from convents the other side of town.'

'But witnesses get things wrong all the time, don't they?' I didn't doubt this Eavers believed his own story, but it just seemed too far-fetched. 'The landlord could've been mistaken. Maybe the woman who rented the apartment just looked like Sister Fran.' Or maybe he was one of those weirdos who liked to insert themselves into investigations, I thought. But I decided to keep that opinion to myself. 'I mean, the photo in the *Herald* was pretty grainy,' I pointed out. 'Would it really have been possible for him to be a hundred per cent sure from that?'

'Maybe.' Ted sucked in a breath. 'Maybe not. But that wasn't all. Eavers also told Grandpa Ron that after Sister Fran's murder, he never saw his tenant again. One hell of a coincidence, right?'

A chill passed over me. 'So what did your grandpa do?'

'He felt he was on to something, for sure. Felt he had enough to take it to his boss, anyhow.'

'And?'

'And they buried it.'

'Huh? Why?'

Ted made a *pffit* sound, shared a knowing look with Gretchen. 'Maybe it was because they had a pretty good idea who was responsible for Sister Fran's death in the first place. Or at least Grandpa Ron did.'

'What? If they had a suspect, why was no one ever arrested, charged?'

'Two reasons,' Ted said grimly. 'First, the chief suspect had a rock-solid alibi. Second, because of who that chief suspect actually was.'

'Don't tell me,' I said. 'Father Todd Brennan.'

'The one and only,' Ted confirmed. 'St Tom's priest, high school gym teacher and Sister Fran's colleague, who, it was known unofficially was molesting girls at the school.'

'So,' I said, 'like Gretchen, you think Sister Fran had found out somehow. That she was threatening to expose Father Brennan.'

'Pretty much, yeah.'

'But even if Father Brennan had an alibi, surely he at least warranted looking into, given his motive?'

'You'd think, wouldn't you?' Ted agreed, stretching back. Brian stirred at his feet.

'You think he was being protected. Because he was a priest.' I thought of Lo's editor. It wouldn't have been the first time.

'That's definitely a part of it,' Ted said, 'but there was another element at play, a third reason why Father Brennan was so untouchable.'

'Which was?'

'Grandpa's boss and Boweridge's police chief was one Detective Jim Brennan.' Ted paused for a beat. I hardly dared breathe. 'Father Todd Brennan's brother.'

12

My head was spinning. Jim Brennan, the detective from the newspaper articles, Boweridge's police chief, was Father Brennan's brother. How hadn't I made the connection?

'Do *you* think Sister Fran and Minna's cases are connected?' I asked Ted at last.

He shrugged half-heartedly. 'Small town, murdered nun,' he said. 'Murdered nun who happens to be the teacher of a teen. A teen who goes missing days later, after apparently telling people she knew who murdered her teacher. Go figure.'

'And Father Brennan,' I said, 'is he still alive? I mean, he'd be pretty old by now . . .'

'He was late thirties when all this was going on,' Gretchen said, 'so he'd be mid eighties by now.' She looked at Ted for confirmation. He nodded. 'As far as we know,' she continued, 'he is still alive. There's certainly no record of his death. But as for his whereabouts, well . . .' she took a deep breath, 'that's another question entirely.'

'But how can someone just disappear?' I asked. 'There must be some kind of record of where priests end up, even once they've retired?'

'You would think,' Gretchen agreed. 'But for some reason – I think we can guess why – with Father Brennan it's not so straightforward.'

I turned to Ted. 'Can't you look him up on some database?'

Ted removed his cap, held it out in front of him like he was waiting for spare change. 'Already tried, but I have to be careful at the precinct that no one thinks I'm snooping around where I shouldn't. There's rules about that kind of stuff, not to mention that the Brennans have dominated the force for decades. It'd be more than my career's worth getting caught digging up dirt on them in their own back yard. You see, I'm not the only one from a long line in law enforcement. The detective you spoke to down at the precinct? That's Jim Brennan's grandson.'

'Jesus,' I whispered. No wonder Ted's hands were tied. 'So do you know anything about Father Brennan's last known whereabouts?'

'We know he stayed in Boweridge a few years after the Sister Fran thing, left around 1980. Then, according to the archdiocese's register, he was put on indefinite sick leave some time in the late nineties.'

'If he went on sick leave in the nineties,' I said, 'and he's not resurfaced since, there's gotta be a possibility he's no longer alive?'

Gretchen and Ted exchanged looks, the kind that said *do you wanna tell her or should I?*

'What?'

'After leaving Boweridge, Father Brennan served in multiple parishes over the next couple decades. He moved around a whole bunch. Or, to put it more accurately . . .' Ted paused for effect, 'he was moved around.'

I remembered an article I'd read a few years ago revealing that the Catholic Church moved problem priests – those with a history of sexual offending – from parish to parish; how the term 'sick leave' was a euphemism used for those priests placed on leave of absence. 'The Church knew.' I shook my head, still not quite able to believe it. 'They knew all that time, yet did nothing.'

'Oh, not *nothing*,' Gretchen said. 'They protected him.'

I should have guessed. Lo had said as much. Susan Turner's parents had gone to the archdiocese in '68. The Church had known about Father Brennan then and had done nothing. How many more families had tried to report him, I wondered, both before and since? How many more priests had they protected?

'And his brother?' I swallowed. 'The police chief? Where's he?'

'Jim Brennan was a few years older than Todd,' Gretchen said. 'He retired in the nineties, died, what . . .' she looked at Ted, 'ten years ago?'

'And before you ask,' Ted added, voice dripping with cynicism, 'he retired without a stain on his character. Detective Jim Brennan was a much-respected, much-decorated member of Boweridge law enforcement. He was golfing buddies with the DA, right up till the end.'

It was evening by the time I left Gretchen's.

'Ted'll run you home,' she said.

'Thanks,' I replied, 'but it's fine. I borrowed a bike.'

'You don't want to be cycling in this heat, honey. He'll throw the bike in the back of his truck, save you the trouble.'

'Yeah, no problem,' Ted said. He was gathering his things – the box, his car keys. 'I'm going that direction anyhow.'

And so I gratefully accepted.

Ted's car turned out to be one of those huge, shiny trucks, the gas-guzzling type that makes you feel dwarfed no matter how tall you are, the type that would've seemed exotic to most Brits a few years ago but is now commonplace on the UK's roads and can usually be found straddling two parking spaces in supermarket car parks. From an environmental standpoint, I wanted to disapprove, but the early-evening sun was still hot, so I was just glad to be in a vehicle with air conditioning. I buckled my seat belt, watching in the passenger-side wing mirror as Ted loaded my bike, then hugged Gretchen, a doleful Brian looking on.

'Long day, huh?' he said, climbing into the driver's seat.

I leaned back against the headrest, closed my eyes for a second. 'You could say that.' I felt drained.

'So you're determined to get to the bottom of this?' he asked; then, throwing me an exaggerated look of suspicion, 'Hey, you're not one of those true-crime buffs, are you?'

I laughed. 'Psychology student, actually. And I don't know about determined. Guess I'm just curious.' I didn't mention that it was a relief to have something to focus on while I was here, to get me out the house, stop me thinking about everything back in the UK. It felt good to be distracted.

Ted laughed too. 'Makes sense.'

I'd expected the drive back to be awkward, but it wasn't. We talked, and I filled him in on what Lo had told me about Susan Turner. Like Gretchen, Ted had heard about Susan through the grapevine, but he hadn't known about the suicide note naming Father Brennan, nor did he know of the archdiocese's involvement. It didn't surprise him, though.

'Do you know if there were other allegations against Father Brennan?' I asked him. 'Anything official?'

'Nothing,' said Ted, jaw set tight. 'Not on record, anyhow. But that doesn't mean there weren't others, girls who tried to report him. Boweridge has a way of squashing stuff it doesn't want to come out, sweeping it under the rug. That goes for the police department, too. What you have to understand is the hold the Church had – has – over towns like this.'

'Is there really nothing to be done? You can't take it further now?' We'd slowed to a stop at a traffic light. 'There are cold-case units, aren't there?'

He laughed, though not unkindly. 'There has to be new evidence to reopen a case.'

'But what about Susan Turner? Her suicide note? That's new evidence. She *named* Father Brennan, for God's sake.'

'You said yourself,' Ted replied as we set off again, 'the note's gone. Without it, it never existed. Besides,' he added, 'there's a statute of limitations on sex crimes. Even if more people did come forward, it'd most likely be too late.'

We drove in silence for a bit, Ted watching the road ahead, me staring out the window at neat rows of houses on leafy suburban streets, family SUVs parked outside; moms wrangling pre-school-aged children; middle-aged joggers out for evening runs. Everything so familiar, yet so alien all at once. *Jamais vu*, the French call it.

'You ever been to the site?' Ted asked suddenly. He adjusted the car's visor, pulled his cap lower against the sun.

'Sorry?'

'The site. Don's Diner. You know, where Sister Fran's body was found.'

I shook my head, no.

There was a pause, then he asked, 'You fancy going? Now?'

'What, *now* now?' I hesitated.

'Don't worry.' He laughed. 'I'm not asking you on a date.'

Don's Diner was now DeeDee's Ice Cream Parlor, a single-storey prefab-looking building on a small lot, nestled somewhat incongruously – like it had been plonked there, dropped from the sky – in the middle of a little row of houses on an otherwise unremarkable street. The building itself was painted colourful pastel shades. On the pavement outside stood a large, anthropomorphic ice cream cone, with big googly eyes and gloved hands, one wielding a spoon, the other frozen in the act of waving.

When we first pulled up across the street, I didn't even realise we'd arrived. I'd no idea what Don's Diner looked like in '72, so had no frame of reference for what it might look like now, but even if I had, I doubt it would have helped.

'In those days,' Ted explained, meaning back in the seventies, 'this was the edge of town. There was nothing much here. I mean, there was a gas station a mile or so down the road that way,' he pointed, 'some houses about a half a mile the other, but apart from that, nothing but farmland and highway.'

'So all this,' I waved a hand, 'wouldn't have been here?'

He gave a shake of his head. 'Nuh-uh. It was just the diner, the lot out back, then, I guess, scrubland all the way till you hit the highway. All this land has been built on since. Highway got re-routed years ago, around the time everything happened.'

We climbed from the truck and crossed the quiet street. The ice cream parlour was closed, its slatted blinds shut, so I couldn't even get a glimpse inside. It was hard to imagine the place as anything other than it was now, certainly not a remote road off a dark highway, trucks thundering past in the distance.

On one side of the ice cream parlour, between it and the neighbouring house, was a tarmacked strip of land with parking for a few cars, and a sign that read *DeeDee's Patrons Only*. At the end of the car park, running past the back of DeeDee's, was a high wall and a row of giant wheelie bins. No large gravel lot with room for eighteen-wheelers, no scrubland. Just the rooftops of new-build houses peeping from the top of the wall.

'It's kind of hard to envisage what it looked like,' I told Ted.

'What you need is photos.'

He crossed back to the truck and I followed, climbed in. He opened the back door, rummaged around in his cardboard box, then climbed back into the driver's seat.

'Take a look at these,' he said, handing me a folder with *Diner Stuff* scrawled across the front in black Sharpie.

I opened it and slid out the contents: photos mostly, black-and-white ones, A4 blow-ups, but some papers too.

'I don't know about you, but I'd love a coffee,' Ted announced.

It was too hot for coffee and too late for caffeine, but I nodded in agreement, already lost in the photos, so Ted left me in the truck with the windows rolled down and walked to the strip mall on the next block, in search of a Wendy's or a Taco Bell, or whatever else.

The first photos in the bundle were of Don's Diner itself, from various angles, some aerial views, but all exterior. There was one front-on shot, taken from the exact spot, I guessed, where I was currently sitting. I held the photo up, compared the facade of Don's Diner to that of DeeDee's. It appeared that the shell of the building remained the same: wall-to-wall windows facing onto the street, broken only by the door in the middle. Apart from that, little was recognisable. It was hard to square this brightly coloured reincarnation – offering *$2 Sunday Sundaes!* and *Free Ice Cream for Under-5s and Seniors!* – with its monochrome seventies counterpart.

The aerial views gave more context and a sense of scale, painting the scene pretty much as Ted had described: a rectangular building sitting front and centre of a large, squarish parking lot, which appeared to be accessible from the road either side of the diner. If I'd been expecting a neat tarmacked area with painted lines marking out parking spaces, I'd have been mistaken. It was little more than a gravelly lot, bordered on three sides – right, left and back – by scrubby-looking trees and bushes; beyond that, at the top edge of the photo, what looked like the edge of the highway.

I wasn't sure when the photo had been taken – it was daylight, so not the night of the murder – but paper-clipped to it was a page from a notebook, with a hand-drawn map of the same area. Though the drawing was rough and clearly not to scale, it gave more detail than the photo: the cartographer – Ted's grandpa, I guessed – had marked where everything vital was located the night of the crime. Don's Diner was a rectangle at the centre bottom of the diagram, the parking lot a rough square surrounding it, bordered on three sides by trees and foliage denoted by curly scribbles. More rectangles marked out the rough locations of various cars, seven in total, presumably parked in the lot that night, each annotated with its owner's name. Six of the cars were depicted as being parked fairly close together, a small cluster – *Don*, *Joe*, *Joe*, *Earl*, *Burt* and *Lonnie*; the seventh, parked a little way from the rest in a far corner of the lot, was labelled *Sister Francesca*. Some distance from the car itself, towards the back of the lot and closest to Burt's car, was an *X*. The hair on my arms prickled. *X marks the spot.* Though it wasn't annotated, it was clear what it must be depicting: the location of Sister Fran's body. I wondered which of the patrons had had the misfortune of finding her.

There were other photos in the bundle too, probably also taken in the days following the murder. Shot in daylight, they showed the back of the diner and the lot, though other than the sheer scale of the area – I reminded myself that this was a car park built to take articulated lorries – there was nothing especially noteworthy. One thing I did notice, though, was the lack of lighting: no street lamps – why would there be? – so on a dark night, the only light would have been that which escaped from the back of the diner (the photos showed a back door, presumably leading to the kitchen, and a couple of high-up windows). The other thing that struck me was how easy it would have been to come and go from the parking lot unseen. By foot, in the dark, one could probably go completely unnoticed. By car – with the lot accessible from either side of the diner, depending on which direction you approached from – the most anyone inside the building would have seen, if they were even paying attention, would have been a brief sweep of headlights as the car turned out or in.

It was a remote, desolate location. In summer, I imagined, the lot would lie dusty and dry, as it had the night Sister Fran's body was found; in winter, it would become a puddly quagmire – at times snow-covered. Not, I thought with a shudder, a particularly nice place to spend your last waking moments at any time of year . . .

I leaped a mile when Ted opened the driver's-side door.

'Sorry. Didn't mean to startle you. I got coffees,' he said, climbing in, laden with takeout bags, 'and food.'

I wasn't usually a fast-food kind of girl, but I was so hungry I'd have eaten almost anything. For a few minutes we said nothing, just ate – nachos, tacos, fries ('I didn't know what you liked, so I just got a bit of everything') – staring out the window.

'So?' Ted said, when we'd finished. 'What d'you think?'

I wiped my hands on a paper napkin. I barely knew where to start, felt suddenly overwhelmed at the amount of information, the notes and diagrams and photos, the newspaper articles and the tape of Jeannie. Everything I'd learned over the past couple of days.

'I think I was crazy to come here.'

'*Here* here, or home, Boweridge?'

'Either. Both. I don't know. I suppose just how crazy I am believing there's any hope of finding Minna. I mean, look at this.' I gestured at the street, the ice cream parlour. Ted looked confused. 'It's been over forty years. Everything's changed. There's nothing left. Nothing use-ful, anyway. What possible hope is there of finding out what really happened – to Sister Fran *or* Minna?'

'The hardest cases are always the ones most worth solving. That's what Grandpa Ron used to say. And with fresh eyes on the evidence, you never know. You might spot something we missed.'

We sat in silence for a few more minutes.

'You and Gretchen are kind of an unlikely duo,' I said at last.

'Well,' Ted smiled, 'she's real smart. Plus she's like a dog with a bone when she gets going. You'll see.'

'I guess it's just where to start,' I said. 'I mean, I want to find out what happened to Minna more than anything. But there's just so much *stuff*, you know? I feel like we've got the corners of a jigsaw puzzle, nothing in between. What if at the end of it all we're no further forward? What if all we're left with is more questions?'

Ted didn't speak, just sucked on his soda straw – he'd got Cokes as well as coffees – and stared into the distance. He'd been so generous with his time and I must have seemed so ungrateful, I worried I'd offended him. But then he put his Coke down, rested his arm on the open window. 'You asked me why I was so interested in their cases – Minna's and Sister Fran's.'

I nodded, remembered the look that had passed between him and Gretchen.

'My answer . . .' He stared straight ahead, avoiding my eye, certainly easier sitting side by side. 'Well, I wasn't entirely honest with you. I didn't lie – everything I told you was true – I just didn't tell you everything.'

'Oh?' It came out so quietly I wasn't even sure Ted heard.

'My grandpa retired from the force in '95,' he continued. 'That same year, he and my grandma moved to a smallholding 'bout an hour's drive from Boweridge. It was nothing fancy – some land, couple of pigs, goats, a few chickens. One day, my grandma goes back to Boweridge overnight to visit with friends. When she returns the next morning, Grandpa Ron's nowhere to be found. His truck's there, the animals are waiting to be fed. She knows something's wrong. So she calls my dad and he goes straight out, searches the property.' Here Ted stopped, picked up his Coke, took a sip. 'It didn't take them long,' he said, looking down. 'They found him in one of the outhouses. Gunshot wound to the head.'

'My God.' I imagined the scene, some ramshackle old barn, a few tools scattered about, perhaps a gun rack or open cabinet, the once matinee-idol-handsome Ron Hoppy lying on the wooden floor, eyes open, staring upwards, a pool of blood – so dark it looked black – slowly spreading outwards from beneath his head . . .

'They ruled it an accident,' Ted said. 'Said he'd been cleaning his gun, that it must've gone off, that he would've died instantly.'

'And you believe that?'

He shrugged, sighed, crossed his arms. 'It happens,' he said. 'All the time. But not to someone like Grandpa. He'd grown up around guns, was a forty-year force veteran, fanatical about gun safety.'

'But if it wasn't an accident . . .'

'Grandpa struggled after he retired,' Ted said. 'Adjusting to civilian life wasn't easy. I've seen it over the years myself as a cop, families refusing to believe what's right in front of them, no matter the evidence . . . I just didn't want to be blind to it, you know?'

'So you think he killed himself?'

'Grandpa was a good cop, solved a lot of cases. But it's the unsolved ones that stick with you. Leave their mark. It was no different for Grandpa. He became obsessed by them, tormented even – Minna's and Sister Fran's most of all. I was only nine when he died, so I didn't know all this at the time, but seventeen years later, when I found out about Gretchen's Facebook group, started looking into both cases, my dad told me that not only did Grandpa Ron work the original investigations, he'd begun reinvestigating them after he retired. Weeks before he died.'

'*Re*investigating them. Like, officially?'

'No. Not officially. But according to Dad, Grandpa had been going through all the stuff he'd kept.' Ted jerked his head towards the box in the back. 'So I guess what I'm trying to say is, that's the answer to your question – why I'm so interested in Sister Fran and Minna. If I can find out what happened to them – cases that haunted my grandpa for so long – it's like I'm honouring him somehow, doing him justice, you know?'

I did.

'I've come to terms with the fact that I may never find out what happened to Grandpa Ron – how he really died, and why – and I guess I'm okay with that. But you can still get answers, Maggie. There's a chance you can find out what happened to your aunt. The clues are out there, we just have to find them.'

We. Did he mean him and me? Him, me and Gretchen? Whatever he meant, it was kind of comforting.

'So I guess what I'm also trying to say, as cheesy as it sounds . . .' he laughed, and I was relieved to see him smile again, 'is don't give up. If Grandpa Ron thought there was something worth investigating over twenty years after it happened, then it's sure as hell worth investigating after over forty. We'll have to keep it on the down-low at the precinct, of course, but if I can help in any way, unofficially . . .'

I nodded. But if Ted's grandpa had failed to get the bottom of the mystery at the time, had died in the process of reinvestigating it over two decades later, what hope did we have?

13

Late that night, back at Mom and Bob's, I sat cross-legged on my bed, the contents of Ronald Hoppy's box spread around me like a patch-work quilt.

'Take them,' Ted had insisted when he dropped me home that night after our detour to Don's Diner. 'Have a look through.'

'Are you sure?' I wasn't. It was his grandpa's precious material; all that remained of Sister Fran and Minna's cases.

'I trust you,' he said.

We were sitting in Ted's truck, a few houses down from Mom and Bob's. I'd asked him to drop me there, like awkward high schoolers after a first date.

'Besides,' he said, 'it'd be good to get your take on it all.'

We'd climbed from the truck and Ted had lifted out my bike. He'd offered to carry the box to the door, but I'd grabbed it from him, said, 'I can manage,' which came out snippier than I'd meant, so I'd added, 'Thanks, though.'

'No problem.' He'd smiled, watched me on my wobbly way as I wheeled my bike alongside me, the box balanced precariously on its seat.

*

In my basement room, I'd carefully removed the box's contents bundle by bundle, all the while replaying what Ted had told me. It was hard to shake. Though he hadn't said it in so many words, the more I thought about it, the more I wondered if he was hinting that there was more to his grandpa's death. Was it really just a tragic accident, as had been ruled, or had it been suicide – a man in despair, struggling at the loss of his job, his identity? Or was the truth something altogether darker? Had someone discovered Ron was reinvestigating Sister Fran and Minna's cases? Were they worried the retired cop would dig something up, bring attention to cases that by that time were over twenty years cold? Ted had said himself that Boweridge had a way of squashing stuff it didn't want coming to light. But did that mean murder? Maybe. But maybe I was overthinking things again. After all, though Gretchen had certainly faced obstacles in her hunt for the truth – people no longer alive, unwilling to talk – she'd never mentioned feeling threatened, in fear of her life.

I felt so rattled by it all that in the end I FaceTimed Tabby, filled her in on everything, but in true Tabby style, she was more interested in Ted than anything else.

'Wait, what?' she asked excitedly when I told her about him. 'A detective? Our age? Is he fit?'

'*Tabs*,' I said, frustrated, 'that's not the point.'

'Oh my God, that means he is.'

I rolled my eyes. 'Whatever.'

'Just don't be all, you know . . .'

'What?'

'All, like, stand-offish. I mean,' she added, 'you're a great catch, Maggie. You're clever, gorgeous. And I suppose you're sort of funny too. Don't scare him off, that's all.'

'Christ, Tabs,' I said, exasperated though trying not to smile. 'I'm looking for my aunt, not a husband.'

'Seriously, though.' Her change in tone made my stomach sink. Tabby didn't get serious all that often, so when she did, I knew she meant business. 'You don't have to do this, you know.'

'Do what?' I was trying to sound casual, but it came out prickly.

'The whole detective thing – whatever it is you're trying to prove.'

'And what exactly am I trying to prove?'

'I don't know. That you're different from your mum, your grandma,' she said. 'That there are women in your family who aren't screwed up.'

'Jeez, thanks.'

'I didn't mean it like that. It's just you've been looking for answers for – well – as long as I've known you. Does it ever occur to you that whatever it is you're looking for might not exist? It's not too late to admit that, to stop looking.'

'Is that what you'd do?' I shot back. 'Give up?'

But of course it was a question she'd never really have to consider. Troubled missing aunt you've never heard of? No. Tabby's family was far too normal for that.

'I'm sorry, Maggie,' she said. 'I'm just worried you might not like what you find, that you'll end up getting hurt. There'd be no shame in accepting that,' she added gently, 'in coming home.'

She was right, I realised, there would be no shame in throwing in the towel, cutting my trip short. It wasn't like I was spending quality time with Mom. She was right, too, that if I kept digging, I might not like what I uncovered. But she was wrong about it not being too late. I was already too invested. A new email from Simon had seen to that.

You didn't tell me you were out of the country. I had to find out from someone else. May I remind you that as your supervisor, I have a right to know? You're aware you have a deadline?

I'd gone to my drafts folder, opened the email I'd written to the head of department, the one that began, *It is with regret that I must make a formal complaint against my supervisor*, but hadn't had the nerve to send. I'd written it when I got home that night, redrafted it a couple of times, not read it again since.

It wasn't like I could compare our situations – what had happened to Minna was far worse than anything Simon had done – so it's hard to explain why, after all my ambivalence, that one short email was the tipping point. But as I'd hovered my mouse over the send button on my draft email, I realised there was something connecting Minna and me, something more than genetics, stronger than our shared looks and interests. I had the power to do something about Simon. I could still speak up, press send on that email. The difference was I hadn't. Not yet. But if what I'd learned was true, Minna *had* spoken up – tried to, at least. But no one had listened. *Minna lies*, they'd all said. All except Sister Fran, who, if Lo and Gretchen and Ted were right, paid with her life. So that was why, I'd decided, I had to get to the bottom of all this – at least do my best – for Minna, for Sister Fran. For Susan and Mrs Turner.

For all the other girls.

So now here I was, surrounded by everything that was known about Sister Fran's murder, about Minna's disappearance – everything documented by Ronald Hoppy, anyhow – determined to find answers.

I began with Minna, flipping to the relevant pages in Ron's notebook. Each entry was dated, so easy enough to find, his writing old-fashioned-looking and surprisingly neat. The entries were fairly short and mostly in note form; sometimes bullet-pointed, sometimes with brief updates added afterwards in the margins, with little asides – extra questions, things needing double-checking – noted in brackets. The first entry concerning Minna was dated 24 June 1972, the date she was reported missing.

06.24.72. Attended Larson residence approx 18:06, Sat June 24, re missing teen. Call came from father, John Larson. Mother, Ida Larson, also present. Parents not seen daughter, Margaret 'Minna' Larson, 17, since eve of 06.22. Also present younger sibs John Larson Junior, 12, Barbara Larson, 10. Parents not too concerned (Mrs L more worried about what neighbors might think; does most of the talking). Minna left 2 days ago, Thurs eve (exact time unsure – parents didn't see her leave), to visit with boyfriend Mike Freleng (19?). Would have walked to Freleng residence, says Mom (check for witnesses on route?). Larsons have contacted Freleng, who states Minna didn't show. No known reason for disappearance. No other known friends/girlfriends/contacts she might be with. Mom says Minna takes off every now and then, never for more than 24 hours. Parents unsure what she was wearing last. Had Mom check daughter's bedroom: thinks may be change of clothes missing, can't be sure. While at residence, son Walter, 16, arrived home. States his rucksack missing: Minna may have taken it? Spoke to John Junior (JJ) and Barbara separately. JJ unable to give any useful info. 10 y.o. Barbara saw sister leave Thurs eve, approx 19:00 hours: Minna not carrying rucksack/bag when she left & seemed normal. Barbara said Minna wearing jean shorts, white tee w/ plaid shirt round waist, & tennis shoes.

So Mom was the last person to see Minna. The last *known* person. It was Mom who'd confirmed what time Minna left that night, who'd given a description of what she'd been wearing. She'd also claimed Minna wasn't carrying a bag when she left, which, if true, appeared to put paid to any runaway rumours. I couldn't help but wonder how reliable her version of events would have been, though. The Mom I grew up with told lies for the sake of it. Would she have been more or less reliable aged ten? And did it even matter? What difference would it really make if what she'd told Ron Hoppy was accurate or not?

I read on.

06.24.72. Visited Freleng residence approx 21:25. Spoke with boy-friend, Mike Freleng, 19. Lives with mother, Mary-Ann Freleng, also present. Mike confirms Mr & Mrs Larson's story: Minna due to visit Thurs eve, 7ish ('she was usually late') to hang out, watch a movie (fits with Barbara's account of time sister left). Didn't show. Mike unconcerned at time – assumed Minna changed mind or been grounded ('parents could be pretty strict') – but cut up about it now. Not seen or heard from her since. Mrs Freleng home with son that night, confirms Minna didn't show.

Alongside this entry, a note had been added in the margin: Speak to neighbor Mr Maher?

Then, a couple of days later, an update:

06.26.72. Visited Maher residence, directly across street from Fre-lengs'. Mr Maher was on his porch Thurs June 22, approx 18:00 to 22.00 hours. Porch has clear view of Freleng porch and front door. Mr Maher states would ('absolutely, a hundred per cent') have seen Larson girl if she arrived at and entered the Freleng property during this time.

So according to Hoppy's notes, everything was pretty much as Ted had said: Minna had left home on the Thursday evening to walk to her boyfriend Mike's house, but never showed up. Whether of her own volition or someone else's, it seemed she'd disappeared sometime after 7 p.m. that Thursday, somewhere on the route between the Larson and Freleng homes.

I skimmed through the rest of the notebook, but information on Minna was pretty scant. A few days after Ron Hoppy's visits to the Larson and Freleng homes, he'd walked the route between the two houses himself, around the same time in the evening as Minna would have done. He'd canvassed properties en route, but days had passed: with school out for summer and the weather hot, although there'd been plenty of children out playing on the 22nd, no one could really remember what they were doing around 7 p.m. that Thursday, an evening much like any other. There were a few *I guess*es, *I might've*s, and *I could've*s, when Ron asked if they'd seen a young girl pass by that evening, but nothing certain. It was a route Minna walked to visit her boyfriend regularly, so even if someone had seen her, who knew for certain if it was really the day in question?

Apart from that, the only other information was some notes Hoppy had made following chats – so short they could hardly be termed interviews – with some of Minna's teachers and peers at St Tom's. The teachers, all nuns, had had little to add to what he already knew. They'd seemed cagey, reluctant to discuss their student at all. Minna's classmates, those who claimed they'd spoken to her in the days before her disappearance and said that she'd been going round saying she knew who'd killed Sister Fran, changed their stories, denied having heard anything directly from Minna herself, or said they'd dismissed her claims out of hand. They'd shrugged, said they 'never took what Minna said seriously' when Hoppy asked why they hadn't come forward sooner, said she was 'known to exaggerate, make up stories'. 'It's just what she does,' they'd added.

Minna lies, Ron Hoppy had written in his notebook, underlining the words several times, as though emphasising just how much he'd come to hear that refrain.

I closed the notebook and put it aside. From what I'd learned so far, there were only two potential scenarios: either Minna had left home that night, or she hadn't. But if she hadn't left home, and some terrible fate had befallen her at the hands of her parents, why did they bother to report her missing at all? True, Grandpa John and Grandma Ida didn't seem overly concerned by their missing daughter, according to Ron Hoppy's notes, but if they *did* have something to hide, why not at least wait longer to report it, buy themselves more time? It was the summer holidays, after all. Other than Mike, Minna had no real friends who'd miss her. They could have waited till school was back before anyone else even realised she was gone. And then there was the fact that my mom had been the last to see Minna that night, had backed up Grandpa John and Grandma Ida's story: Minna left the house around 7 p.m. and never returned.

That left the second scenario: Minna did leave home that night, but something happened to her after she left. Perhaps she set off for her boyfriend's, but for reasons unknown went somewhere else entirely – the runaway theory; or perhaps something more sinister happened to her – she was picked up, abducted, on the way.

I exhaled and leaned back on the bed, surveying the piles of papers around me. There was definitely less to go on with Minna, but if the two cases *were* connected, I supposed it didn't really matter: find out what happened to one, I told myself, and I'd find out what happened to the other.

Unravel the forty-year-old mystery behind a high school English teacher's murder, and I'd unravel the mystery behind my aunt's disappearance.

14

There was plenty of information on Sister Fran's case in Ronald Hoppy's box. No actual evidence, as such – no bloodied rock, no samples cut from clothing or personal effects, no fingernail scrapings (did they even do that back then?) – just good old-fashioned photos, papers and, of course, Ron's notebook. I flicked back a few pages from the entries on Minna to those on Sister Fran.

06.17.72. Attended Don's Diner approx 23:40 hours. Female vic, mid 20s?, deceased in parking lot. Lying face up. Initial obs: bruising to neck/throat, petechial hemorrhaging, some defensive wounds. Poss strangulation? Blood in hair, on ground next to head (poss head wound?). Clothing undisturbed. Purse, keys etc. found at scene. Diner owner and driver's license identify deceased as Sister Francesca Pepitone (not wearing habit/veil). Searched immediate area, secured scene, talked to witnesses while waiting for back-up.

The following page listed the witnesses present at the diner that night:

Donald 'Don' Hinkle, 42, diner owner
Dewey Hinkle, 19, Don's son

Joseph 'Joe' Pelley, 60, patron
Joseph 'Old Joe' Botich, 79, patron
Earl Armentrout, 67, patron
Burton 'Burt' Ackerman, 64, patron
Lonnie Greeson, 49, cook

With the exception of the cook, Lonnie, who'd been in the kitchen, they all told the same story: Sister Fran entered the diner at 10.40 p.m., scanned the place quickly, then left again straight away. 'It was like she was looking for someone, expecting them to be there already,' Don Hinkle had told Detective Hoppy. 'Then, when she didn't see 'em, she left.' Although she wasn't wearing her habit and veil, Don and Dewey had recognised her immediately: 'Daughter's a student at St Tom's,' Don had explained. 'Sister Fran was her favourite teacher.'

It wasn't until thirty-five minutes later, at 11.15 p.m., that Burt Ackerman discovered Sister Fran's lifeless body in the car park as he was leaving. 'Was so dark,' he'd said, 'almost tripped over her.' He ran back to the diner, shouted at Don to call the police. Though still a good drive away, Detective Ronald Hoppy had been closest to the scene, so was first to attend.

I put the notebook down and turned to the crime-scene photos. I'd never seen a dead body before, only photos of corpses on true-crime documentaries with the victims' faces – and any more gruesome details – obscured. Though the photos of Sister Fran were one step removed from seeing it in the flesh, they were shocking enough to make me recoil, graphic enough to make me feel a little ashamed, like a voyeur rubbernecking at a terrible car crash.

I skimmed through the photos as quickly as I felt I could get away with. There were close-ups of the body and ones of the whole scene, but all depicted a female figure lying on her back in the gravelled parking lot. Her hair was tied back, though a few strands had come loose, her head tilted upwards at an awkward, unnatural-looking angle. Her few belongings, presumably dropped either when she fell or during the struggle, were scattered about her. I imagined being struck from behind, falling, hitting the ground. I imagined putting a hand to my head, confused, in pain, scrabbling around in the dirt, trying to get up but only managing to turn myself over. I imagined the fear and desperation, wondered if Sister Fran had had time to see it coming, whether she'd seen her killer as he bore down upon her, met his eyes as his hands met her throat, or if she'd been too dazed from the blow to her head to be aware of what was going on (I hoped the latter). Most of all, I wondered if she'd recognised her killer, if he – or she – had been the person she'd gone to meet. I wondered if she'd had time to pray.

Despite everything, though, she looked remarkably peaceful, eyes closed like she was only asleep. I imagined, with a shudder, Detective Hoppy lifting each eyelid, checking for signs of life, finding none; wondered how many bodies he'd come across in his career, how many more were still to come . . .

I turned the photos over so I didn't have to look at them any longer, and picked up the ME's report, a printed form filled in by hand. As well as the date and approximate time of death, the decedent's name, date of birth and next of kin (her parents, Albie and Edith Pepitone), it stated that the cause of death was probable strangulation, and noted abrasions to the palms of the hands and the knees, some defensive wounds to the hands and wrists, contusions to the neck and the back of the head, and petechial haemorrhaging.

The attached autopsy report confirmed that Sister Fran's death was consistent with asphyxia as a result of homicidal strangulation, and noted a fractured hyoid bone. Also attached was a list of Sister Fran's clothing and belongings: purse, containing driving licence, pocket book and a small amount of cash; car key, found next to her body; and the clothes she'd been wearing that night – underwear, socks, sneakers, pants and shirt.

No jewellery. No crucifix.

I flicked through the rest of the notebook and papers looking for anything on potential suspects, but other than Father Brennan (referred to in Hoppy's notes as FB), there were none. Aside from the odd reference to Father Brennan in the course of Hoppy's conversations with witnesses, though – a *check FB's whereabouts* here, or *ask about FB* there – there wasn't a lot on him either. I guessed Ron would have been careful not to write too much down about Father Brennan; what he did document, he'd no doubt have kept close to his chest. The one thing he had done, however, was to draw up a timeline for the night of the murder, which included details of Father Brennan's alibi:

21:20 Sister Francesca leaves convent after evening prayer.

21:50 Time Sister Francesca should have arrived at Don's Diner – drive from convent to diner around 30 mins.

22:27 FB receives phone call (phone records confirm) at presbytery (25 min drive from Don's) from parishioner's family. FB leaves presbytery immediately, travels to dying parishioner's home, couple mins' drive away.

22:30 FB arrives at parishioner's home (confirmed).

22:40 Time Sister Francesca entered diner (confirmed), 50 mins later than should have. Where was she for missing 50 mins??

23:15 Sister Francesca's body found in Don's parking lot. Call placed to police from diner.

23:40 Arrived at Don's, secured scene.

05:30 (approx) FB leaves parishioner's home. Wasn't out of family's sight between 22:30 hours and approx 05:00 hours (confirmed).

My heart sank. Even though Ted had told me Father Brennan had a cast-iron alibi, I hadn't wanted to believe it. I was hoping he might have been mistaken, that there may have been room for doubt. But if Ron's timeline was correct, and there was no reason to believe it wasn't, there was simply no way Father Brennan could have murdered Sister Fran: at the time she was killed, he was a twenty-five-minute drive away surrounded by witnesses. If he *had* murdered her, the dying parishioner's family would either have had to be mistaken about the events of that night, or lying. That, or the diner owner and his patrons. Despite everything I'd heard about Boweridge being a town in the stranglehold of the Catholic Church, the likelihood of all these witnesses lying to protect a murderous priest – perhaps more so managing to keep that secret all these years – seemed pretty remote. It did cross my mind, however, that Father Brennan's alibi was perhaps too convenient. Could he have had someone else murder Sister Fran for him – a hit man? – while he was on the other side of town, secure in the knowledge that he had an unshakeable alibi?

Somewhat deflated, I continued my trawl, flicking through the rest of the notebook, finding notes on a short interview with Sister Fran's convent roommate, Sister Joy Greenway, who according to Ron had appeared nervous and on edge.

Sister Joy states Sister Francesca left convent on 06.17 at 19:20 hours, after evening prayer (finishes 19:15 every night). Didn't know she was going to Don's Diner ('no idea why she was going there or who she'd be meeting, no'). Said Sister Francesca had been receiving 'mysterious' letters in mail in weeks before death, acting like 'there was something on her mind'. Sister Joy has no knowledge of letters' contents ('didn't ask, didn't want to pry'), doesn't know who they were from (in 'a woman's writing', she thought, but 'couldn't be sure'). States she and Sister Francesca cordial ('I liked her'), though not close friends. Claims no knowledge of relationship between Sister Francesca and Father Gil Griffin (or FB). Sister Joy and Sister Francesca shared v small room at convent. Searched room (bed, bedding, bed frame, air vent, behind closet, drawers etc.) but no letters.

A note added in the margin alongside the last sentence stated: *Search of Sister Fran's car 06.17.72 also negative.*

Why would Sister Joy be on edge? I wondered. Did she have something to hide? Then I reminded myself that her roommate had just been murdered. Surely that would be enough to make anyone jumpy, especially with a killer still at large.

I turned the page. Slipped between the next two was a folded piece of paper. I opened it out, revealing a sheet of continuous form paper – that old-fashioned printer paper that comes in reams, the thin stuff with perforated strips and holes punched down either side. It took a second before I realised that what I was looking at was a transcript of a phone call.

DRH (Detective Ronald Hoppy) Detective Hoppy.

LE (Leland Eavers) Oh yeah, hi, Detective. You, uh, you the one working the nun's case?

DRH That's right, Mr . . .? I'm sorry, Dispatch didn't give me your name.

LE Leland Eavers. I rent apartments, the east side of town?

DRH What can I do for you, Mr Eavers? You wanted to speak to someone regarding the Sister Francesca homicide case?

LE Um, right, yeah. I rented an apartment to her, last few weeks.

DRH You what? I'm sorry, you rented an apartment to her?

LE Uh-huh, yeah, that's right. That nun from the news.

DRH All right.

LE 'Cept, see, I didn't know it was her, right? Didn't know she was a nun. She didn't wear all that nun get-up when I seen her, you know, the whaddya-call-it . . .

DRH Habit?

LE Yeah, right. Habit.

DRH So let me get this straight, Mr Eavers. You're saying that for the last few weeks, you've been renting an apartment to Sister Francesca Pepitone?

LE Right. Right. I mean, like I say, I didn't know it at the time, that she was a nun. Not till after she was murdered.

DRH Okay. So who did you think she was? If you didn't know it was Sister Francesca. What name did she go by?

LE See, that's just it, Detective. I never knew her name. She never told me, y'know? The people who rent from me, they don't always give names. When they do, it ain't always their real name, you know what I'm sayin'? [Laughs]

DRH I understand, yes.

LE I don't ask too many questions, right? They don't tell me, I don't ask.

DRH I get it, Mr Eavers, yes. But if you didn't know your tenant was Sister Francesca, didn't know her name, how'd you find out?

LE It was after, when I seen it in the news, few days later. Her picture was in the paper. I recognised her, says to my son, Travis, I says, hey, Trav, that's the lady been renting the apartment 'bove the Wash 'n' Go. [Inaudible]

DRH You speak to her much, this tenant, Sister Francesca?

LE Not really. Not since she moved in. But that was late at night, so, uh, I wasn't hanging around. Just gave her the keys. Look, Detective, she was a good tenant, paid her rent on time, kept to herself.

DRH And she was still living there June 17? You know that's when
     she was murdered, right?

LE Uh-huh, yeah, said it in the papers. Far as I know, she was still
     there.

DRH Far as you know? So her stuff's still there now? She must've
     had clothes, belongings, things she moved in with?

LE Yeah, she did, but, see, that's just it. That's how I know for sure
     it was her, see?

DRH Excuse me?

LE So, um, a few days ago – a day, two, maybe [inaudible], after she
     was murdered, before I seen it in the news – someone cleared her
     apartment. I goes round there after I seen her picture in the
     papers, but she'd gone. Place was empty.

DRH Okay.

LE But that's not the weirdest thing, right? Weirdest thing is, who-
     ever cleared the apartment leaves the keys, plus enough rent to
     pay up till the end of the next month. Cash, in an envelope.

This was the phone call from the landlord Ted had mentioned. It
was hard to tell from the transcript if Ronald Hoppy believed him or
not, but – I put the transcript down, flicked forward a few pages in
Hoppy's notebook – I could see he'd subsequently made a trip to the
apartment himself, checked it out, met with Leland Eavers. Though
Hoppy hadn't learned anything new, Eavers had stuck by his story. By
that time, though, his mystery tenant – if she *had* been Sister Fran –
was long gone, no trace of her left.

I put the notebook down, stretched and yawned. I was exhausted.
I'd make the next items – three photographs, paper-clipped together –
the last for the night.

The first photo was of a young nun I recognised as Sister Fran,
because it was a larger version of the black-and-white one from the

newspaper articles, the yearbook and Facebook. Despite the formality of it – a shoulders-up, portrait-type shot in habit and veil – Sister Fran was smiling a warm smile, cheeks dimpled, eyes shining. What I hadn't noticed in the other copies was the small silver crucifix round her neck – the one, I guessed, given to her by her parents. The second photo was similar, but a dog-collar-wearing portrait of a priest. He was young – early to mid twenties, about Sister Fran's age – and handsome in a slightly geeky way, with the smile of someone eager but a little unsure. I turned the picture over. *Father Gil Griffin* was written on the back. So this was Sister Fran's possible love interest.

The third photo, the only colour shot, was more candid. Taken outdoors, it showed another priest leaning against some railings smoking a cigarette, a guitar propped by his side. He looked older – thirties, maybe – and cut a striking figure, tall and lean, with dark hair, fair skin and bright blue eyes. Although he wasn't conventionally handsome, there was something about him – a coolness, an air of swagger, a stance that suggested confidence, self-assurance. *Father Todd Brennan* read the back of the photo. I shuddered. Had I not known what I did and were it not for the dog collar, Father Brennan might have been a 1970s pop star, one all the girls would have swooned over.

I put the photos back, packed everything away, then jotted down a few questions.

It was after 1 a.m. when I finished and my phone pinged with a Facebook notification: a friend request from Ted Hoppy. I accepted, then did the obligatory snoop, but Ted's profile was pretty bare: born '86 (two years older than me), with only 'Boweridge PD' listed under 'Work and education'. No relationship status, no cover photo, just a grainy scanned-in profile picture of what I guessed was him as a child, with a girl I recognised as his sister, Jen. I'd just clicked on 'Albums', was about to start trawling through the rest of his photos, when a message popped up in the bottom corner of the screen, making me jump.

Ted Hoppy: You get a chance to look through Grandpa's stuff yet?

I blushed, feeling like I'd been caught red-handed.

Maggie Elmore: A good chunk of it, yeah (there's a lot!). Got a couple of questions, though.

Ted Hoppy: Go ahead, shoot . . .

Maggie Elmore: Could someone have murdered Sister Fran for Father Brennan?

Maggie Elmore: Like a hit man?

Ted Hoppy: Possibly. I'm pretty sure it's something my grandpa would've considered, but no names ever came up. It would've been in his notes if they had done.

Maggie Elmore: Was he ever looked at as a suspect in Minna's case?

Ted Hoppy: Father Brennan? Not officially.

There it was again: *not officially.* I watched the undulating dots as Ted continued to type.

Ted Hoppy: It was never known for sure that anything actually happened to Minna, so it was never really looked at like a crime had been committed. How do you check out alibis when you don't know exactly what or when something occurred?

There was a pause while I considered.

Ted Hoppy: You said a couple questions? You got more?

Maggie Elmore: Oh, right. More. Gretchen said the missing 50 mins in Sister Fran's timeline that night was never accounted for?

Ted Hoppy: Sure wasn't. There's nothing in Grandpa's notes suggests it was anyhow. Nothing subsequently either.

Maggie Elmore: Okay. But how could your grandpa be so sure that the witnesses got it right? Timings-wise, I mean?

Maggie Elmore: How could the witnesses at the diner be so sure what time Sister Fran arrived, and how was it known exactly what time she left the convent to travel there? If one or both lots of witnesses got it wrong, there might be no missing window of time at all. Surely it's a possibility?

Ted Hoppy: Right. I wondered that myself at first, but it's all in Grandpa Ron's notes. Somewhere. See, only Sister Joy knew that Sister Fran had gone out that evening, but she was sure of the time. She and Sister Fran were together at evening prayer, which ran until the same time every night. Sister Fran snuck out pretty much straight after it finished, so 9.20 ish. The witnesses at the diner were certain of the time she entered that night 'cos of the new highway.

Maggie Elmore: ???

Ted Hoppy: Don's Diner got most of its trade from truckers, plus the handful of regulars, locals mainly, who were there the night Sister Fran died. A month or so before she was murdered, a new highway had opened, diverting traffic and killing Don's trade. Don swore he knew the exact time Sister Fran entered the diner 'cos he'd decided to close the kitchen for the night, send the cook home early. It'd been an especially quiet night. He said he'd just checked the time when the door flew open and in she came. The other diners and his son backed him up.

Maggie Elmore: I guess that's pretty concrete.

Ted Hoppy: As concrete as you can get in these circumstances.

For a moment there was nothing, then . . .

Ted Hoppy: Funny you should mention the timeline thing, though. Dad said Grandpa always thought there were 4 questions he needed answers to. Where Sister Fran was in the missing 50 minutes was one of them.

Maggie Elmore: And the other 3?

Ted Hoppy: Who she was meeting that night . . .

I waited, watching the row of undulating dots.

Ted Hoppy: Who wrote the letters she'd been receiving . . .

There was a pause that went on for more than a minute. I typed:

Maggie Elmore: And the fourth?

Ted Hoppy: Sorry, had to take a call on my cell!

Ted Hoppy: Where's Sister Fran's crucifix? Answer any or all of those questions and I think we'd find ourselves a killer.

I couldn't disagree.

But after forty years, was it possible to find answers to those questions, and if we did, would they also lead us to Minna?

15

According to its website, in 2016 Boweridge Country Club was named one of the top one hundred country clubs in the US. I was already familiar with what the club looked like, having viewed the expansive photo gallery online that morning, but I still gawped as Gretchen drove us up the imposing driveway and it came into view at the top of the hill. The clubhouse, set amid immaculate landscaped borders out front and a sprawling lush green golf course out back, was almost cartoonish, its stone cladding and timber frame like something from *The Flintstones*.

I'd woken ridiculously early that morning and lain in bed googling names that had cropped up in the course of Ron Hoppy's investigations. In an admittedly scattergun approach, I'd begun with Sister Fran's convent roommate, Sister Joy Greenway, but had no luck. Tracking people down from so long ago wasn't going to be easy, especially those with no online presence. What I needed was someone who *did* have an online presence – and that was when it came to me: I needed someone who not only had an online presence but had been close to both cases at the time, without being directly involved.

Hopping from my bed, I dug the copies I'd printed of the *Herald* newspaper articles from my suitcase. When I'd read them, I hadn't noticed who'd written them – whether the same journalist had penned them all – so I climbed back into bed and fanned the crumpled sheets out in front of me. There, on each piece, almost unnoticeable under the articles' headlines, were the words: *By IRIS HILLENBERG*. Pushing the papers aside, I grabbed my laptop and googled her. I'd hoped there might be a few leads for her, but it turned out there were thousands. Since cutting her teeth at the *Boweridge Herald* in the seventies, Iris Hillenberg had gone on to have an illustrious career. A feminist investigative journalist, now in her late seventies, according to the internet, she'd won numerous awards and worked for some of the US's best-known publications, but the most recent articles I could find – penned for *The New Yorker* – were now a couple of years old. Maybe she'd retired?

I clicked on the image search results next, revealing a striking-looking older lady, strong-featured, with slicked-back silver hair, heavy-framed glasses and a slash of red lipstick. There was a mix of portrait-style shots along with ones showing Iris at various functions and awards with the great and the good, the Obamas, Ronan Farrow, Gloria Steinem and Ruth Bader Ginsburg among them.

I was still scrolling a few minutes later when I spied a familiar face that made me stop. Wait. What? I scrolled back up and squinted at the screen, hardly able to believe what I was seeing. I clicked the photo to enlarge it. There, pictured with Iris Hillenberg, smiling, arms round each other, was Lo. The link beneath the photo led me to a 2014 article from the News & Events section of the UC Berkeley Graduate School of Journalism website:

UC Berkeley Alum Lo Ekhart Collects Her Coveted Hillenberg Student Award

Recent UC Berkeley journalism master's graduate Lo Ekhart said today she was 'beyond thrilled' to have been presented with her

Hillenberg Student Award by Iris Hillenberg at last night's ceremony. 'Iris and I actually started out in the same small town, same
newspaper,' Ekhart said, adding that she was 'surprised and hum-
bled' to win the award, and that 'Having Iris present me with it was
such an honor – the cherry on the cake.'

As part of her award, Ekhart, who's moving to New York next
month to pursue a journalism internship, also wins a package of
mentoring.

Speaking at the awards ceremony last night, Hillenberg
described Ekhart as a 'talented student journalist who presented a
strong body of work and has a bright future ahead of her. Her writing spoke to me in a way no one else's did.'

So my old friend Lo knew Iris Hillenberg. Sort of. I thought of Lo's
words when we'd parted that afternoon at Mainstreet's: *If there's anything you need from me, Maggie, anything at all, call me.* I grabbed my
mobile from the bedside and composed a text.

Hey Lo, it was so lovely catching up with you the other day after so long!

Too cheery, I thought when I read it back. Plus the exclamation
mark looked desperate. I deleted it, began again.

Great to see you the other day, I wrote instead, and hit send.

Then, before I could talk myself out of it, I kept typing.

BTW, you know Iris Hillenberg?

I tapped send again, watched the little delivery confirmation ticks
appear, then almost died when I realised how early it still was: ten to
six. Crap. I could only hope Lo kept her phone on silent during the
night.

I checked my mobile obsessively for the rest of the morning and had
almost given up hope of Lo replying until Gretchen and I were pulling
into the country club car park and my phone finally beeped.

Great to see you too. Yeah, wouldn't say I know Iris, but sort of. We met when I was doing my MA, before I moved to NY. Her first job was at the Boweridge Herald, you know? Small world, right?

Uncomfortably small, I thought.

Then, a few seconds later, another text.

Why?

I thought a moment, then typed:

She wrote stories on Sister Fran and Minna back in '72. Look, you've been more than helpful enough already and I know this is a big ask, but is there any chance you could put me in touch with her, like by phone, email?

'So you know what you're doing?' Gretchen interrupted as she manoeuvred into a parking space and cut the engine.

'I think so.' I muted my phone, slipped it into my bag.

"Cos you know we only get one shot at this?'

I swallowed. This whole thing had been Gretchen's idea. I'd have been lying if I said I was entirely convinced. It had all begun when I phoned her that morning after my googling session.

'Do you know where Sister Fran's convent roommate is these days?' I'd asked.

'Sister Joy?' Gretchen was eating breakfast when I called. I could hear the clink of a teaspoon in her coffee mug, could sense her holding the phone between her ear and chin as she poured her cereal, could almost see her sceptical eyebrow raise. 'She didn't seem to know so much.'

'I think she knew more than she was letting on,' I'd said, taking a seat at Mom and Bob's breakfast bar, pouring my own coffee. 'You ever speak to her?'

'No, but then as far as I know, Joy hasn't spoken to anyone about Sister Fran since Ron Hoppy. I think she still lives in Boweridge, though, so she shouldn't be hard to find.'

'There's still a convent here?'

'A convent, no. Sister Joy left the order after Sister Fran's murder. Got married soon after.'

'You're kidding?' It made sense, though, explained why I'd been unable to find any trace of her online. Sister Joy Greenway no longer existed, yet maybe there was still a chance of finding her.

'Nope. We were both members of Boweridge Country Club.'

I almost choked on my coffee. 'You're a member of Boweridge Country Club?' That was Bob's country club, the same one he'd offered me a guest pass for.

'*Was*,' Gretchen said. 'Not any more. Captained the ladies' golf team there for a while, actually.'

I had trouble imaging Gretchen being part of *any* club, let alone captaining a ladies' anything. I couldn't see her drinking from bone-china teacups – as, perhaps unfairly, I imagined those type of ladies did – or sticking to a dress code or becoming involved with the petty bureaucracy and in-fighting that usually went hand in hand with such roles.

'Problem is,' she said, 'I never really knew Joy. All I know is her surname's no longer Greenway, but I'll be darned if I can remember her married name.'

'So we know she still lives in Boweridge, but we don't know where, or what her surname is?' My renewed hope was rapidly diminishing.

Gretchen had known Joy's husband's name – Randy – but an internet search for *Randy and Joy, Boweridge* yielded nothing. Ted was at work, but we decided it would be too risky – and also unfair – to ask him to look Joy up for us on police time, so after I innocently mentioned that I could get my hands on a country club guest pass, Gretchen had hatched a plan.

After we'd hung up, I'd sought Bob out in his basement office. 'Hey, Bob. The guest pass for the country club. Does the offer still stand?'

*

Gretchen and I sat in her ancient rust-bucket of a Volvo – parked conspicuously amongst the Range Rovers and BMWs, windows rolled wide – having gone over the plan one more time. I'd made more of an effort with my hair that morning, had even put some make-up on, yet still felt thoroughly out of place as I climbed from the car – glancing back uncertainly at Gretchen, who, still in the driver's seat, gave me the thumbs-up and mouthed, 'Two minutes!' – and crunched up the gravel pathway to the clubhouse.

The main door, with its American flag flying high over the apex of the porch, swooshed open as I approached. If the outside of the clubhouse was Flintstone-esque, the inside was a cross between an alpine ski chalet and a bougie celebrity mansion. Everything was wood, leather or gilded; a large deer-antler chandelier hung from the lobby's high ceiling. Mahogany-mounted brass wall plaques directed members to the Bar & Deck, Dining Room and Spa & Swimming Pool; in the middle of the spacious lobby, an empty lounge area housed a chesterfield-style leather sofa and matching wingback armchairs, and a central coffee table adorned with stepped piles of newspapers and glossy home and golfing magazines.

Trying my best to look like I belonged, whatever that meant, as I drew nearer the front desk – all the while mentally rehearsing my lines – I glanced at the wall clock above: 10.30 a.m. Bang on time, according to Gretchen: the lull before the lunchtime rush, when only one member of staff would be working reception.

Sure enough, a young girl stood behind the front desk. She was good-looking, sleek and tanned, wearing a white polo shirt embroidered with the club's insignia, and a name badge: *Brianna*. She smiled at me as I approached.

'Welcome to Boweridge Country Club. How can we help you today?'

'Uh,' I said, like a complete idiot, 'I'm in town for a few days, and my mom's husband . . .' – the term sounded oddly formal – 'well, he said you did, like, a visitor's pass? That you could add me to his membership for a few days?'

Brianna smiled, revealing perfectly straight, white, all-American teeth. 'Absolutely we can help you with that. I just need your stepdad's name.'

Stepdad. I'd never really thought of Bob as my step-anything. 'Bob,' I told her, 'Bob Rodgers. With a D.'

She adjusted her flat-screen computer monitor, began to type. 'R-O-*D*-G-E-R-S?'

'Uh, yeah.' I stole a glance back at the entrance. No sign of Gretchen. Yet.

'Would that be Bob or Robert?'

'Sorry?'

'Bob, or Robert?' She smiled. 'Your stepdad.'

I hesitated. I'd only ever known Bob as Bob, but surely he'd be listed as Robert for formal stuff. But why did it even matter? And God, if I couldn't even get through this portion of the plan without coming across as shady, when I wasn't even doing anything wrong – *yet* – what hope was there for the rest of it? I screwed my face up apologetically.

'No sweat,' Brianna said. 'We'll try both.' Her fingers clacked on the keyboard again before she gave a satisfied nod. 'Here we are.' She rummaged on her desk. 'Okaaaay, so if you could just fill this out . . .' she handed me a form and a pen, 'you'll be good to go. Then I can get someone to give you the tour.'

I turned the paper round slowly, made a pretence of reading it, buying more time. Where on earth was Gretchen? We'd agreed she'd give me a couple of minutes' head start, but it must've been at least—

I spun around as the main doors opened and Gretchen burst in like a hurricane, flying across the lobby towards us.

Without even glancing at me – I had to step aside or risk being barrelled out of her way – she said, 'Excuse me? Excuse me!' and flapped her hands at Brianna. 'You must come with me at once.'

She was out of breath, I noticed. Nice touch.

Brianna, though startled, remained a picture of composure.

'I'll be with you in just one moment,' she told Gretchen, then, turning back to me, she smiled apologetically, a smile that might have been accompanied by an eye roll had she not been so professional.

But Gretchen was undeterred: whereas my acting skills could only have been described as awkward as hell, she was a complete natural.

'You don't understand,' she panted, fully embracing her role. 'It's an . . . an emergency. In the parking lot.'

I was beginning to think her shortness of breath was real, that she'd run all the way from the car. Either way, I had to hand it to her: she was killing it.

Unsure, Brianna looked from me to Gretchen, then back to me.

'Oh, don't mind me,' I told her.

She hesitated, about to reach for the phone on the desk. Quickly I put out my hand, touched her gently on the wrist.

'Go,' I said. *Go, but don't log out.*

She nodded, hesitated again, but this time Gretchen reached over the counter, grabbed the poor girl by the arm.

'Quickly,' she said. '*Now.*'

'I'm so sorry,' Brianna apologised. 'I'll just be a moment.'

And with that, she zipped round the front of the desk and allowed herself to be led outside.

I craned my neck, watching until they were out of sight, then, realising I had limited time, sprang into action. I did a quick sweep of the lobby – left, right, no one around – then scooted behind the reception desk. *Act natural*, I repeated in my head. *Don't blow it.*

I grabbed the mouse, exhaling with relief when I saw the computer was still logged in. I cleared the screen of Bob's details, then, as fast as

I could, began to type, my hands shaking so badly I had to do it one-fingered. *Joy Randy*, I entered into the search box, before hitting return. The computer thought for a moment, then ... Nothing. *No search results*. Shit. I wiped my sweaty palms down the front of my trousers and returned them to the keyboard. *Keep calm*, I told myself. *You planned for this*. I cleared the screen once more, re-opened the search box, and typed *Joy Randall*, but just as I hit return for the second time, an elderly man in golfing attire appeared, crossing the lobby.

I'd chosen my outfit carefully that morning: it had to be acceptable under country club dress code (no thong sandals or swimwear, no short-shorts or miniskirts, no hats indoors – other than in the pro shop – and only collared shirts for men), but also had to fit in on the other side of the desk – *this* side. The only suitable clothes I had were the plain white shirt and black trousers I'd worn for Grandma Ida's funeral – more office attire than country club receptionist – though they must have done the trick, for the old man – liver-spotted and as tanned as the chesterfield, his age anywhere between seventy-five and ninety-five – glanced in my direction and raised a hand in greeting as he passed. I smiled back, nodded, felt sick. I wasn't cut out for this undercover stuff. Apparently not noticing anything amiss, he disappeared out the other side of the lobby and I glanced back down at the computer screen. *One search result*: Mr Randall Snelling and Mrs Joy Snelling. *Bingo!* So Sister Joy Greenway was now Mrs Joy Snelling. On the screen before me was information on the Snellings' membership type (platinum), how long they'd been members (since '97), as well as dinner reservation records and tee times.

And beneath all that, their home telephone number and address.

16

I hung around at the country club long enough to complete my guest registration and get my tour. After hastily snapping a picture of Joy Snelling's contact details with my phone, I'd cleared the computer screen, then slipped back to the other side of the reception desk and finished filling out my guest pass form. Brianna returned a minute later, breathless and flustered, smoothing her hair, though giving nothing away.

'So sorry to have kept you waiting,' she'd apologised.

'No problem.' I didn't ask what had happened in the parking lot, and she didn't tell.

Back outside, I slid into the passenger seat of Gretchen's Volvo and breathed a sigh of relief.

'You get it?' Gretchen asked casually, like I'd been to the store for milk.

I showed her the photo.

'Way to go!' She high-fived me over the centre console.

'Well it looks like we're on a roll,' I said, holding my phone back up so she could see the text that had just come through from Lo:

I can do better than that. I've just called Iris. She's happy to meet.

*

Lo looked as effortlessly stylish as she had at Mainstreet's (I was hoping, somehow, she might not), while I, who hadn't had time to stop home and change, once again felt acutely self-conscious. She side-eyed me as I climbed into her car, taking in my trouser-and-shirt combo – I must've looked fresh from a shift waiting tables – but, typical Lo, was too polite to say anything. En route, she filled me in on Iris, how she'd recently moved back to Boweridge after retiring, and in return, I told her everything I'd learned since we last met.

Iris Hillenberg lived in Boweridge's newest gated retirement community, in the picturesque outskirts of town. Quite why an educated, cultured lady – one who'd lived all over the US – would retire to Boweridge escaped me. What she wanted with a place whose architecture bordered on Disney-esque I couldn't tell either, and as we pulled through the gates I could see Lo was wondering the same. *Paradise Springs Retirement Community*, the sign announced, and beneath it, *Enhancing the Lives of Boweridge's Senior Citizens.*

Once inside, Paradise Springs wasn't as bad as I'd feared, though it was still a bit Stepford for my taste, too much like an upmarket holiday complex. Quaint, clean and well-maintained, it was set in lush green grounds with handsome trees and colourful flower beds, ornamental ponds and miniature waterfalls flowing with turquoise water.

We parked up and found Iris's second-floor apartment easily. Now almost eighty, Iris walked with a stick, though she seemed to use it almost as much for prodding and pointing as for mobility. More handsome than beautiful, she was surprisingly tall and, dressed all in black, cut a striking figure, her short silver hair styled differently than in the photos I'd seen – a severe centre parting and a stump of a ponytail – though the signature heavy-framed glasses and streak of red lipstick remained the same.

With a large balcony overlooking the lake at the centre of the complex, the apartment was spacious and light, filled with an eclectic assortment of antique furniture that would have looked more at home in an Upper East Side New York apartment than a modern development. There were books, too, everywhere, and where bookcases weren't lining the walls, framed photos hung, many of them originals of those I'd seen online, an impressive catalogue of Iris's lifetime in journalism.

Considering that Lo and I had virtually doorstepped her, Iris was remarkably unfazed. After shaking my hand, air-kissing Lo and catching up on her New York news, she gestured for us to make ourselves comfortable in her beautiful living room.

'Lo tells me you're interested in the Sister Fran case?' she said, seating herself in an armchair, pushing her glasses up her nose, fixing me straight in the eye.

'Sort of.' I'd taken my cue from Lo, sat down beside her on a sofa across from Iris, a coffee table between us. 'But I guess more Minna's. Minna Larson? I'm her niece.'

Iris nodded. 'You look so much like her,' she said, 'though I only ever saw her in photos.'

Iris had made tea and Lo did the honours. 'Maggie's trying to find out what happened to Minna,' she explained.

'I never met her,' I said, taking a sip of too-hot tea. 'I mean, obviously – I didn't even know she existed till this week. But I read your articles.' I placed my teacup down, careful to use a coaster. 'I got the impression you felt the two cases were linked.'

'It sometimes felt like I was the only one who did,' Iris replied. She had a faraway look, like she was elsewhere in time. 'But there was a detective – Hoppy. He thought they were connected too – I was certain – though he never said so.'

'So what can you tell me about Minna?'

'Not so much,' said Iris, through a heavy sigh. 'The summer she vanished, I'd just moved here. I'd started working at the *Herald*, had been given a job in classifieds.'

'I thought you were a reporter?'

She shook her head. 'I applied for reporter, didn't get it. So instead I took calls, wrote ads, but reality was, I was little more than a glorified tea girl. A tea girl' – she tutted, flicked a hand in distaste – 'in my thirties! I had an Ivy League education, but I'd made the mistake of marrying young, was recently divorced, so I'd moved to Boweridge to start afresh. Problem was, I was a woman.'

'But you were ultimately assigned their stories,' I said. 'Sister Fran and Minna's. How'd that come about?'

'Sheer luck,' Iris said. 'It all started that Saturday night. I was home alone when the phone rang – my editor at the *Herald*. Rumours were coming in: dead nun, parking lot outside of town. The guy who'd usually cover the story – Boweridge's resident crime reporter – was sick. It was the weekend, late; everyone else had families, children . . . I was the only schmuck willing to go, not that I had much choice. "Get yourself down there," he said. "Find out what's going on." I knew I'd only been given the story because no one else was available, but I was eager to prove my worth, so I jumped in my car, drove to the diner.'

'You were actually at the scene that night?'

'Sure, yes. I'd never been to anything like it before. It was a big deal for the time – maybe not for a city, but crime was low in Boweridge, and homicides, well . . .'

'Did you see anything? Speak to anyone?'

Iris made a face. 'By the time I got there, the scene was taped off, body removed, witnesses sent home. There was the cop I mentioned, Ronald Hoppy, but he wasn't exactly forthcoming. The police trusted news reporters about as much as news reporters trusted police. Cause of death wasn't known yet – not officially – but I sensed from the start there was something more to it than a robbery.'

'So what did you do?'

'I went back to the newsroom.' She took a sip of tea. 'It was early

Sunday morning. The body hadn't been formally identified – identity hadn't been released, anyhow – but you know Boweridge: news travels fast. Place was abuzz, newsroom phone ringing off the hook. I heard from a number of sources that the victim was a young nun by the name of Sister Francesca Pepitone.'

'Did you interview anyone who knew her?' Lo asked.

'Not her family,' Iris said, 'not interviews. But I went to Sister Fran's convent, spoke to some of the sisters and the Mother Superior, Reverend Mother Loretta Byrne. A cold fish. Didn't like her one bit.'

'She didn't tell you anything?'

'Nothing useful, but as I was leaving, this young nun scurries up to me, says her name's Sister Joy.' At the mention of Sister Joy, I sat up straighter, glanced at Lo. Her ears pricked up too.

'Joy Greenway?' I asked.

Iris nodded. 'She was a timid thing, would only speak off the record, but with a little coaxing, she told me she was sure Sister Fran had discovered – or come to learn of – something; that this thing, whatever it was, had been on her mind in the weeks preceding her death.'

Hadn't Ron Hoppy's notes said something similar? Lo and I exchanged another glance.

'She also said,' Iris went on, 'that someone had been writing to Sister Fran in the weeks before she died.'

Those letters again. 'Did she say who?' I asked, hoping that if Joy *had* known, she'd have been more likely to confide in another female than a cop.

'No. All she could say was that the letters were handwritten – the envelopes at least. That's all she ever saw.'

My heart sank. We were no further forward.

'But,' Iris added, holding up a finger, 'I always sensed she knew more; that there was something she wasn't telling me. She seemed anxious, skittish, like she was afraid, though of what – or whom – I didn't know.'

Something else that fitted with Hoppy's notes.

'Then,' Iris continued, 'a week after Sister Fran's murder, Minna disappears. When the reports first started coming in, no one took much notice – they wrote her off as a troubled teen, a rebellious runaway with an older boyfriend and a tendency to go AWOL. Everyone expected she'd turn up.'

'But she didn't,' Lo said.

'Right,' Iris agreed. 'And when I found out Minna just happened to attend St Tom's, that Sister Fran just happened to be her teacher . . .'

'So your editor let you have that story too?'

She shrugged. 'No one else wanted it. Far as they were concerned, there wasn't one. I mean, missing teen? Summer vacation?' She made a *pffft* sound, flicked a hand like before. ' "No story there," they all said. "Just another runaway." '

'But you didn't think so?'

Iris tutted. Obviously not. 'Girl's teacher had been murdered a few days before. There wasn't much to go on, but still, I convinced my fathead of an editor I should go speak with Minna's family. He came round to the idea pretty quickly, pretended like it had been his in the first place.' She gave a faint eye roll. ' "The female touch will be better," he said. "They'll be more likely to open up to you." '

'And did they?'

'In a word, no. Your grandma . . .' Iris looked at me almost apologetically, 'well, she was plain old defensive, mistrustful; your grandpa barely said two words the whole time I was there, deferred to your grandma when I asked him anything. The only thing I learned was that Sister Fran had been Minna's form tutor and English teacher – that the pair got on well – but apart from that . . .' She shrugged again, sipped her tea.

'Did you speak to anyone else?' I asked.

'Some of the other teachers – nuns, mostly – a few girls from school . . .'

'Any priests?'

Iris smiled wryly. 'I never spoke with Father Brennan, if that's what you mean.'

So she knew. 'What did the sisters tell you? The girls?'

'About Sister Fran? Everyone spoke very highly of her. Of Minna? Not so much. At best, they said she was a loner; at worst, she was unreliable, attention-seeking.'

'Attention-seeking?'

'Yes. They said she'd exaggerate, stretch the truth, make stuff up to get attention.'

Minna lies. There it was again. 'Did they say how, exactly?'

'A couple weeks before school was out, Minna had shown up to class with a black eye. Apparently when people asked about it, she hadn't told the same story twice: one minute she said she'd walked into a door, the next she'd been hit in the eye with a baseball, or punched by the jealous girlfriend of some guy who was sweet on her. One thing everyone agreed on, though, was – whatever the truth – it was like she thrived on the drama. But that wasn't all,' Iris continued. 'In the days before she vanished – the days after Sister Fran's murder – Minna had apparently been telling people she knew who killed Sister Fran. She said she'd the evidence to prove it.'

'My mom mentioned that Minna had been saying that,' I admitted. 'Did you ever find out who she thought it was? Or what evidence she had?'

Iris shook her head. 'It was like a game of telephone: someone heard it from someone who'd heard it from someone. I'd track a source down, but they'd deny having heard it, or told it, or said they'd heard it from someone else entirely. No one would admit to Minna telling them first-hand, let alone go on record.'

'So like the cases, the stories died?'

'I guess,' she said. 'Weeks passed with no breaks. It was like the police weren't trying. I did my best to keep the stories alive, but with no new leads, my editor wouldn't waste column inches. You have to remember,' she added, 'all this happened around the same time Watergate broke. There was little appetite for small-town news, and Boweridge moved on. It's not a town that likes to dwell on unpleasantness. Not its own, anyhow.'

'I'm starting to get that,' I said.

'Ah, but you see, not everyone was so keen to forget.' She unwrapped her hands from her teacup, set it down. Her fingers were long and slender, I noticed, with large, bony knuckles. 'A year afterwards – a year to the day since Sister Fran's murder – came the first letter. Anonymous, typewritten.'

I sat forward. 'You received a letter? What did it say?'

'See for yourself.' She dug in her pocket and produced a folded piece of paper.

I took it from her outstretched hand and opened it. But for the date, June 17 1973, it contained just two simple sentences, typed by typewriter, set starkly in the middle of the page:

Minna didn't lie.
Father Brennan killed Sister Fran.

I passed it to Lo, watched her face change as she read it, then turned to Iris. 'Do you know who wrote it?'

Iris gave a single shake of her head. 'All I know is it was mailed from out of town.'

'What did you do with it?' Lo asked, refolding the letter and passing it back.

'I wrote another article, of course, a sort of anniversary piece, connecting the two cases, though without mentioning the letter.' Iris held it as she spoke, running her long nails along the crease, sharpening the fold line. 'Two days later, after the article ran, I was called into my editor's office. He told me in no uncertain terms to drop the story. It was a year on, he said. People didn't want to be reminded of what had happened.'

'Didn't you show him the letter?' I asked.

'Of course,' she replied indignantly, 'but it made no difference. You see, what I didn't find out till later was that the morning the article ran, my editor took a call from Boweridge PD. I don't know who it was from, or what was said, but I can take a pretty good guess.'

'The police chief,' I said. 'Father Brennan's brother, Jim Brennan.'

Iris didn't answer. Didn't need to. For a moment we just sat in silence, before suddenly, something occurred to me.

'You said the first? The *first* letter. There was another?'

'Huh.' She laughed. 'You could say that.' She rose stiffly from her chair and crossed to a mahogany bureau. Opening a drawer, she took something from it. Another letter? No, a wad of paper.

'So the following year, exactly one year since the first letter, I get this.' She slipped another folded piece of paper from an envelope and held it out, but before we'd had time to inspect it, she plucked out another. The stack was not a wad of papers, but a pile of white envelopes. She dropped them onto the coffee table with a *whump*, an avalanche cascading every which way.

Lo and I looked at each other open-mouthed, then up at Iris, and down at the table.

'Go on,' Iris said, with a prod of her finger.

Gingerly I picked an envelope at random from the pile, like an audience member at a magic show. *Pick a card, any card.* It was addressed to Iris care of the *Baltimore Sun*. I slipped the paper from inside, unfolded it.

The year was different – 1984 – but the letter's date and month were the same as the first, 17 June, as was the content:

Minna didn't lie.
Father Brennan killed Sister Fran.

I couldn't quite get my head around what I was seeing. I picked up another envelope, and another, and another. So did Lo. But for the year, and sometimes the envelope's typewritten address, each contained the same message:

Minna didn't lie.
Father Brennan killed Sister Fran.

Minna didn't lie. The words rang inside my head.

Iris sat back down. 'Every year, no matter where I've been in the world, the letters have come,' she said quietly. 'Every year, on – or close enough to – the anniversary of Sister Fran's death, another arrives.'

I was barely listening. I was gathering envelopes, stacking them in a pile, counting in my head. Calculating . . . *Forty-three, forty-four, forty-five . . .*

I stopped. 'Including the one you've got' – I nodded at Iris, the original now balanced on the arm of her chair – 'that's forty-six. Only forty-six.'

Lo furrowed her brow. 'Meaning?'

'One a year since '73,' I said, looking straight at Iris, 'including this year, that'd be forty-seven.'

Iris smiled. 'Smart girl.'

'Huh?' said Lo. 'There's one missing?'

'Same time every year since 1973, a letter's arrived,' Iris said coolly, watching my face. 'Every year, that is, but '79.'

So what happened in 1979?

17

Could the letters to Iris have been written by some kook, desperately trying to insert themselves into the investigation? If it had just been one letter, two even, then perhaps. But every year except one, on the same date, for over four decades? Seeking Iris out, finding her address in whatever city, was a lot of trouble to go to for a hoax. And why send the letters to Iris at all? Why not send them to the *Boweridge Herald*, or the police? Maybe the letter-writer didn't trust either. And if the writer was so sure Minna hadn't lied – Father Brennan *did* kill Sister Fran – could they prove it? Given his alibi, it was a pretty bold accusation. But perhaps the writer didn't mean the statement literally; rather that Father Brennan was somehow responsible for Sister Fran's death.

However many times I went over it all, I kept coming back to what people had said – Mom, Minna's classmates – that Minna claimed she knew who'd murdered Sister Fran.

Could it be Minna who'd been sending the letters all along? Was she out there somewhere, alive?

After we left Iris's, Lo dropped me back at Gretchen's, and for a few minutes we just sat in her car, engine idling, windows wound down.

The air smelled of summer – not British summers, but the US

kind, ones I remembered from my early teens. Lo and I would go downtown to the drugstore, paint our nails with the tester pots of nail varnish, each one a different colour, until the clerk threw us out. Then, giggling, nails still tacky, we'd cycle down to the lake, leave our bikes on the shore and sit at the end of the jetty, faces to the sun, me brown as a berry, Lo burning until either she tanned or all her freckles joined together – whichever came first.

I'd missed all this, I realised, missed Lo, and as I looked over at her now, we were suddenly thirteen again, side by side on the dock. I'd been so desperate to get away, to join Dad and Em in the UK, leave Mom and her drama behind, that I'd blocked it all out, even the good bits, like the lake, and Lo, and putting the world to rights. Talking about boys we liked, girls we didn't, complaining about our parents, my feet trailing the water, Lo's dangling above, our toenails painted matching shades of scarlet, two rows of shiny cherries glinting in the sun . . .

A bee buzzed at the open window and I was back in Lo's car again, and she was looking at me, half smiling, half concerned. 'It really is good to see you,' I blurted out. 'I mean, I'm sorry. Again. For everything. I just wish I'd kept in touch.'

'Me too.' She nodded, and I wondered if her memories of those days were as fond as mine. 'It's never too late to come back, you know, Maggie. To come home.'

Tabby had said something similar. But here, Boweridge, wasn't my home. Not any more. Still, I nodded weakly, swallowed the lump in my throat, blinked back tears. Lo looked away, let me collect myself.

'At some point, Maggie,' she said at last, 'you've got to stop punishing yourself. You've always been like that – unable to let things go.'

Had I? All the same, I nodded glumly again.

'But that's how I know,' Lo continued, 'that you won't give up. That you'll get to the bottom of what happened to Sister Fran. To Minna.

In a way I couldn't with Susan. I stopped digging when I shouldn't have. You don't need to make the same mistake.'

At that moment, Ted's truck pulled up behind us in the drive, and on impulse, I reached out, hugged Lo tight. She squeezed me back; then, catching sight of Ted climbing out, said, 'Go. But promise you'll let me know what happens with the cases. I'm here another few weeks, so we'll try meet up before you leave.'

I nodded. 'I'd like that. And Lo? Thanks. For everything.'

Ted and I met Gretchen in her doorway, and we followed her round the side of the house to the yard. We sat on wooden lawn chairs in the only patch of shade, Brian snoozing nearby in the sun, and I filled them both in on the meeting with Iris.

'Maybe whoever was sending them didn't have an address for Iris in '79?' Ted suggested, after I'd explained about the anonymous letters.

'I thought of that,' I said, 'but Iris moved to Baltimore in '76, was there till '85. She had the same address for nine years. Whoever was sending the letters mailed them there from '76 through '84, except for '79. Why not '79?'

'It might've just gotten lost in the mail?' Gretchen swatted at a bug that landed on her arm.

'Maybe,' I said. Somehow I didn't think so.

'Whatever,' Ted said, 'there's no mention of the letters in Grandpa's notes. Iris can't have taken them to the police.'

'She didn't trust them,' I explained. 'No offence.'

'None taken.' Ted half smiled. 'Don't blame her.'

We sat for a few minutes in comfortable silence, listening to children playing in neighbouring gardens, the sound of sprinklers whirring, distant lawnmowers. Gretchen had made lemonade, and I watched beads of condensation race each other down the outside of my glass, pooling on the wooden table beneath.

Just the idea of this trip had filled me with dread – the funeral, the weeks with Mom – but the reality, I realised, wasn't so bad. Maybe it was seeing JJ and Greg again; my heart-to-heart with Lo. Or maybe it was just being here, now, in this garden, with Gretchen and Ted, relative strangers, united in a common cause. Whatever it was, it was weird, because despite the weight of what I'd discovered, despite everything I'd learned about Minna, about Sister Fran, somehow I felt lighter, like a weight had been *lifted*. For the first time in a long time, I felt I had purpose and direction, something to focus on – something other than my past life here, my present life in the UK. I felt more in control than I'd felt for a while.

'Maybe,' said Ted eventually, leaning back, stretching his legs, 'we shouldn't be looking so much at *who* wrote the letters, more *why* their writer's so convinced Father Brennan is responsible. He had an alibi, after all.'

The sun was lower now. I shielded my eyes with my hand, peering between him and Gretchen through the glare, and realised I'd never have the words to express how grateful I was for them being so invested in my search for answers. But it was their search too.

'So what next?' He interlaced his hands behind his head.

'Well,' Gretchen said, 'I gave Sister Joy a call – or Mrs Joy Snelling, as she is now. Maggie's got a coffee date with her tomorrow morning.'

'I do?' This was the first I'd heard of it. I shot Gretchen a half-exasperated, half-amused look.

Ted sat forward. 'Hang on, you tracked her down?'

'Yeah,' said Gretchen. 'Maggie and I took a trip to the country club this morning. Turns out we make quite the team: I distracted the receptionist while Maggie accessed the computer system and got the Snellings' contact details.'

Ted put his head in his hands. '*Please* tell me you're kidding?'

'Nope.' Gretchen grinned. Over in his patch of sun, Brian opened one eye lazily, lifted his head, flopped back down again.

'Christ, Gretch,' Ted said. 'What if you'd gotten caught?'

'Oh, stop being such a Debbie Downer,' she chided. 'What's the worst could've happened? It's a country club, not the Pentagon.'

He shook his head. 'Unbelievable.'

'Look,' I said quickly, suppressing a laugh. 'We're sorry, aren't we, Gretchen?'

Gretchen shrugged, opening her mouth to say something, which instinct told me wasn't going to be an apology.

'But Ted,' I added quickly, 'both Iris and your grandpa thought Sister Joy knew more than she was letting on. We needed to track her down.'

'Okay,' said Ted, still shaking his head, 'okay. Look, I gotta get going, I'm due on shift, but Gretchen . . .' he rose, scooping his keys and phone up, 'no more dragging Maggie into your crazy schemes, okay? And Maggie, how about I come with you tomorrow, see what we can find out *above board*?' He gave Gretchen a pointed look, reducing us both to laughter.

Ted picked me up the following morning after his night shift and we drove to Joy Snelling's. It seemed Joy had moved up in the world since abandoning her vows, and now lived in one of the most affluent areas of Boweridge in a house so big it put Mom and Bob's to shame.

'Come in, come in!' she greeted us at the door, so friendly and laid-back – no trace of the timid young nun – that I wondered if Ronald Hoppy and Iris Hillenberg had it all wrong.

The Snellings' living room was pristine, like something from the pages of an interiors magazine, and when offered something to drink, I was too afraid to ask for anything other than water. Ted, by contrast, was completely relaxed. 'Coffee, please,' he said.

The three of us settled on two of the largest, plushest, creamest sofas I'd ever seen – me and Ted on one, Joy opposite on the other. Our sofa faced French windows, a backlit Joy framed by the view over a stunning landscaped garden. At seventy-two – the same age Sister Fran would have been had she lived – she was as polished and immaculate as her home, dressed in expensive loungewear (the sort not made for lounging in at all), with the kind of bouffant hair I'd only ever seen in old episodes of *Murder, She Wrote*. I studied her as she chit-chatted. She'd been married for decades, she told us, had three grown children and seven grandchildren. If I'd met her in the street, I'd have had her pegged as the wife of a congressman, the sort of lady who lunched regularly with the wives of her husband's friends; hosted events like a pro, did a little light charity work. I would not have looked at her and thought *nun*. Even *ex-nun*. The only trace of her former vocation was her frequent use of the word *blessed*, and the small diamond-set crucifix she wore around her neck that every now and then she'd touch her hand to.

She had been blessed with a wonderful husband and life, she told us; blessed with her amazing children and beautiful grandchildren; blessed with their lovely home. Hadn't we been blessed by this lovely weather for my visit? she asked as the housekeeper brought our drinks, mine in a weighty crystal tumbler so expensive-looking I was afraid to touch it.

'The lady who phoned,' she said. 'Gretchen, was it? She said something about one of you looking for an aunt?'

I raised a hand. 'That's me.'

'Maggie is Minna Larson's niece,' Ted explained.

'Minna Larson?' Joy looked confused. 'Wasn't she the runaway?'

There it was again. *Runaway*. The term made my skin prickle. Why was everyone in this town so quick to dismiss Minna's disappearance?

'That's what everyone thought,' I said. 'But she never turned up.

But it's actually your convent roommate we came here to ask you about. Sister Fran?'

For the first time, Joy's smile faltered. 'Like I told your friend when she called, that was all such a long time ago. I'm not sure I'll remember much.'

She looked anxious, and I wondered if I'd been the one who was mistaken, if the chirpy, confident exterior was all an act – one she'd had years to perfect – the timid young nun lurking beneath the surface after all.

'If you could just tell us what you *do* remember,' Ted said kindly, 'that's all we'd ask.'

'We think Sister Fran and my aunt's cases might be linked,' I added.

On the table between us was a wooden box, which Joy picked up and opened. 'After your friend called,' she said, 'I dug these out.' She took out a string of rosary beads and a couple of photos, the first of which she handed to Ted. 'This is all I have left from back then.'

Ted looked the first photo over, passed it to me.

'This is you?' I asked. Joy nodded.

It was a black-and-white portrait shot similar to the one I'd seen so many times of Sister Fran, but it was hard to reconcile this young woman – dressed in habit and veil, gazing into the distance in quiet contemplation – with the lady now sitting before us. Though I recognised the eyes and the round apple cheeks, it struck me how very different Joy looked in the photo; not just because she was younger and slimmer then, but because her hair – such a distinctive part of anybody, but particularly a woman – was covered.

'And here,' she said, a diamond tennis bracelet glinting on her wrist as she handed Ted the second photo. 'That's me.' She pointed to a figure at one end of the picture. 'Then Sister Clodagh, Sister Eleanor, Sister Evelyn-Marie . . .' She worked her way along the line, tapping each nun with a French-manicured nail. 'And this . . .' her tone changed, 'this is Sister Fran.'

Ted passed me the photo and I peered at the group of nuns, all habits and veils; among them the figure Joy had identified as herself and the figure I knew as Sister Fran – smiling, attractive, fresh-faced. So young.

I looked up. 'You left the order after Sister Fran's death?'

Joy nodded. 'Not right away. But soon after. I wouldn't say that what happened to her was my reason for leaving, not exactly. But I guess you could say it made my decision easier. Nothing was the same after she died.'

I knew from Hoppy's notes that Joy and Sister Fran hadn't exactly been bosom buddies, so I wondered if it wasn't a little odd that Sister Fran's death would have had such an impact on Joy's life.

'It must've been hard, losing someone you were close to,' I tried.

'Who said we were close?' asked Joy. 'Don't get me wrong, her death was a terrible, terrible tragedy. And yes, I liked her very much.' She met my gaze, smiled a little too brightly. 'But we weren't close.'

'But you were roommates,' Ted said, head tilted, enquiring, not accusing. 'You must've gotten to know each other, living in such close quarters?'

'Barely,' Joy said. 'I'd say we were more acquaintances than friends.' Something about her answer felt a bit too prepared, like the kind given by beauty queens in pageants. 'You have to understand' – she gave what sounded like a sigh of regret – 'we didn't room together all that long before, well . . .'

'Were you surprised when you learned Sister Fran had been found all the way out at Don's Diner?' I asked.

Joy flinched. 'In what sense?' Her voice was perfectly even, but there was something prickly about her tone, something not even she, with all her curves and soft edges, could disguise.

'I think what we were wondering,' Ted qualified, 'is if it was usual for sisters to be out so late, to be wearing' – he made bunny ears with his fingers – '*normal* clothing? We were told your order didn't always wear habits?'

Whatever it was about him worked its magic: Joy laughed, her whole face softened, and suddenly I could see the young nun in the photos. 'It may surprise you,' she said, and I could have sworn she gave a small wink, 'but yes, it wasn't all that unusual.'

'For sisters to wear normal clothing, or to be out at night?' I asked.

She took a sip of her drink, considered. 'Both, I guess. Going out, not so much – especially late – but it happened. And don't forget Sister Fran had a car. Wearing her' – she put down her glass, made air quotes of her own – '*own* clothes was not uncommon at all. You're right about our order: the habits, the veils you see in the photos – I guess you have to think of them as more formal attire.'

I thought back to the photos of Sister Fran. I'd only ever seen her in her habit, hair covered, so it was hard to imagine what she looked like without.

'I guess that's what her girls loved so much about her,' Joy said.

'The students at St Tom's, you mean?'

She nodded. She had a habit of looking at Ted even when she was answering my questions. 'Sister Fran was young – younger than a lot of the sisters who taught there. She was pretty, too, vivacious. Not as uptight – I guess you could say – as the older sisters. The girls related to her.'

For someone who hadn't been all that close to her roommate, Joy sure seemed to know a lot about her. 'Did she ever talk about any of her students by name?' I asked.

Joy's brow furrowed. 'Not that I recall.'

Ted put his coffee down. 'She never mentioned Minna?'

'No.' Joy shook her head, picked her glass up again, smiled. 'But then, as I say, we weren't close. Sister Fran worked long hours, so other than sleeping in the same room, we really didn't see all that much of each other. Not in a social sense, anyhow.'

'Did she have friends, people she did see socially?' Ted asked.

'She was close to her parents,' Joy said. 'An only child. She visited with them regularly.'

'And Father Gil?' I asked.

A short pause, a blink. Joy was still smiling, but it no longer reached her eyes. 'What about him?'

'They were good friends?'

'Sister Fran and Gil?'

'Yes.'

She blinked again, rapidly, machine-gun fire. 'I guess, yes.'

'More than friends?'

Joy placed her drink down, picked it up again. 'Shouldn't you be asking Gil all this?'

'We'd love to,' said Ted. 'Are you in touch with him?'

'No,' she said abruptly. 'He left soon after . . .' She waved a hand. 'It was all just too much for him. We didn't keep in touch. I've no idea where he is now.'

'So *did* you think Sister Fran and Father Gil were more than just good friends?'

'Not that I was aware, no.' Joy was no longer smiling, wasn't even pretending. 'But I don't see what all this has got to do with—'

'Hey, we're sorry,' Ted said, holding up his hands. He looked to me for backup.

'We don't mean to pry,' I agreed. I stopped, rethought. 'I mean, we *do* mean to pry, but only because we're trying to find out what happened. To Sister Fran *and* my aunt.'

Joy sagged. 'No,' she said, looking at me properly for the first time, '*I'm* sorry. It's just that it's been so long and it was such a horrible,

horrible time. Sometimes I question what I remember, what I know – what I thought I knew. I guess it's just easier to forget.'

'So that night,' I began tentatively, 'the night Sister Fran . . .' I didn't need to finish. 'You've no idea who she was meeting at the diner?'

Joy gave a shake of her head, looked down. 'No one knew. The police – a Detective Hoppy, I think – asked me at the time. It was all such a mystery.'

Before we'd arrived, we'd decided not to mention that Ted was a cop, lest Joy would be reluctant to speak to us. We'd also decided that, should it come up, we wouldn't mention that he was Ronald Hoppy's grandson either.

'This Detective Hoppy,' he said. 'Do you remember exactly what he asked you? What you told him?'

Joy wrung her hands as she spoke. 'I remember . . .' Her eyes flicked upwards, and I recalled something I'd read about people who are lying looking up and to the right, and those telling the truth looking up and left – something to do with how the brain works recalling memories. Or was it the other way round? 'I remember,' Joy said again, 'he wanted to know if there'd been anything troubling Sister Fran, if she had any enemies – anyone who might wish her harm. It struck me as an odd thing to ask.'

'Why's that?' asked Ted.

'Because she was a nun, of course,' Joy said, as though the very question somehow besmirched Sister Fran's good name. 'Everyone loved her. She didn't have an enemy in the world.'

'What about Father Brennan?' I asked.

Joy stiffened.

'You knew him?'

'Knew *of* him,' she said warily.

'What did you know?'

'That he had a temper.'

'You witnessed it?'

'Not personally. But I knew others who did. Boweridge was a small place back then.'

'We heard there was some kind of bad blood between him and Sister Fran,' I said. 'Did she mention anything?'

'No,' Joy replied; then, more cautiously, 'Well, not really. I knew she didn't like him, that's all.'

'You *did* mention to Detective Hoppy that you thought something had been troubling Sister Fran,' Ted said, 'in the weeks leading up to her death.'

Joy looked surprised.

'Could it have been something to do with Father Brennan?' I asked gently.

A clock somewhere began to chime, and Joy jumped like she'd been shot. I shifted in my seat.

'Troubling,' Joy repeated, pursing her lips, thinking. 'Troubling's the wrong word. I think I said preoccupied, maybe, like something was on her mind.'

'You also mentioned some letters Sister Fran had been receiving?'

'Why, yes,' Joy said. There was that surprise again. Was she surprised we knew about them, or was it because she'd forgotten all about them, only to be reminded after all these years? 'Yes, I did. She'd been getting letters in the mail.'

'Letters from whom? About what?'

'Oh, nothing bad or unpleasant,' she said, adding hastily, 'I mean, I don't think so, though I never saw their contents.'

'Then how can you be sure?'

'Only because when she started receiving them, she seemed happier than she had in a while.'

My pulse quickened. This shone a whole new light on things. Could they have been from Father Gil? I wondered. Love letters?

'You've no idea who they were from?' I asked.

'Oh no.' Joy shook her head disapprovingly. 'I never pried.'

'Not even a little?' Ted asked. 'You shared a room with her, right? Would've only been natural that she might leave things lying around, that you might—'

'No!' Joy cut in, perhaps more bluntly than she'd intended, for her face flushed. 'No. All I ever saw were the envelopes. I told the police that at the time.'

'But you saw the handwriting,' I said. This we already knew.

'Mm-hmm,' she said, calmer. 'A woman's, that much I was sure of.'

My heart sank. Of course, I remembered now. Hoppy's notes said as much at the time: a woman's handwriting. So most likely not love letters, unless there was another angle we hadn't considered. There followed an awkward silence and I wondered if our time was up, but suddenly Joy leaned forward. 'Look,' she said. 'What I told the police at the time . . .' She dropped her gaze, staring at her hands clasped in her lap.

Ted and I exchanged glances. 'Yes?' I said, half afraid she'd clam up again.

A single tear ran down her cheek. She looked up at Ted, then me, and I saw fear in her eyes. 'It wasn't that I didn't tell the truth,' she said in a small voice.

I nodded encouragingly. Ted did too.

'Just that, well, I . . .' she sniffed, 'I left something out. It was written on the envelope, you see. You have to understand, I wasn't snooping.'

'Of course not,' I assured her, shooting Ted another look. The air felt fragile, like it could shatter at any second. 'But you saw something. On the envelope. Something you never told the police?'

'The *back* of the envelope.' Again Joy paused, and the silence seemed to swell until it filled the room.

'An address,' she said at last, exhaling. 'I saw a return address.'

18

I didn't plan on snooping, it just sort of happened. After Joy told us about the return address she'd seen on the envelopes, the one she'd remembered all these years, she'd written it on a piece of paper, unable to disguise the tremor in her hand. I'd watched her, something niggling at me, though I wasn't sure what.

'May I use your bathroom, please?' I asked when she'd finished.

Joy directed me to a cloakroom, where I'd splashed my face with cold water, gathering my thoughts, trying to work out what was bothering me. Back out in the hallway, I'd intended to rejoin Ted and Joy, but as I gazed upon the smiling Snelling family portraits lining the walls – children, grandchildren, pets; weddings, christenings, Christmases – that was when it struck me: Joy had claimed she wasn't in touch with Father Gil, didn't know where he was, but had referred to him as Gil, not Father Gil. Wasn't that a little odd?

About halfway down the hall was a Chippendale-esque telephone table with a twee Victorian-style phone, the type with a rotary dial and clunky handset. In the front of the table was a drawer. I sidled up to it, slid the drawer open, then paused, holding my breath. What was I doing? I stood listening. From one end of the hallway, through a part-open door, came kitchen sounds: the clinking of dishes, a radio playing softly. Joy's housekeeper, probably. From the other end, the living room end, I could hear the low, indistinct sound of Joy and Ted talking.

I turned back to the drawer. It held all the usual bumph – leaflets, pens, loose paper clips, business cards, and a leather-bound address book, which I picked up and began to leaf through. One way or the other, this would settle my mind. I flicked through the alphabetised pages until I reached the Gs, began tracing my finger down the names, past *Gaarder, Gabelman* and *Gackowski*; *Geller, Glatt* and *Goldberg*, and there it was: *Griffin. Gil Griffin.* A telephone number and Florida address. I took out my phone and snapped a quick picture, just as voices came from further down the hallway and Ted and Joy emerged from the living room. I froze. Joy, luckily, had her back to me, and though Ted's eyes widened ever so slightly on seeing me, he gave nothing away, continuing to engage Joy in conversation while I, quickly and quietly, slipped the address book back and the drawer shut.

I cleared my throat.

Joy turned and Ted looked up, like he'd only just seen me. 'There she is,' he exclaimed.

'We were getting worried about you,' Joy said.

'Sorry.' I held up my mobile, still in my hand. 'Had to take a call,' I lied.

'Gretchen's becoming a bad influence on you,' Ted said. 'Or maybe it's the other way round. Tell me you weren't doing what I think you were doing.'

We were back in his truck, his attention half on me, half on his sat nav, into which he was programming the address Joy had given us.

'And what exactly did you think I was doing?' I asked innocently.

He glanced sideways at me. 'Snooping.'

I buckled my seat belt. 'Joy lied to us,' I said, self-righteous.

'No she didn't.' Ted fastened his seat belt too. 'She just didn't tell us about the return address straight away.'

'I don't mean that.' I passed him my phone, showed him the photo of the address book.

'Gil Griffin,' Ted read aloud.

'At the very least, she's in touch with someone she claimed she wasn't – she's got his phone number, his address.'

'So she has his contact details.' He shrugged. 'Doesn't mean she lied. She might've genuinely forgotten she had them; they mightn't even be current. You tried the number?'

I nodded, sighed. I'd dialled as we'd climbed into the truck. 'Went straight to one of these auto messages,' I admitted. *The number you have called is not available. Please try again later.* Not even a voicemail.

'Look,' Ted said, 'we'll keep going, but one thing at a time. Right now . . .' he fired up the sat nav, started the engine, 'let's concentrate on finding this address.'

The address Joy had given us was a good distance away on the east side of town, and when the sat nav announced our arrival, we found our destination was a small apartment above a laundrette in a run-down street of shops. A narrow alleyway ran along the side of the building, the apartment itself accessed by a fire-escape-style external metal stairwell. We parked across the road and rolled the windows down. It was unbearably hot.

'I'll go,' Ted announced. 'Check it out first.'

I snorted. 'What? And take all the credit? No way.'

He laughed. We exited the truck and crossed the empty street, standing for a moment at the bottom of the stairs looking up before beginning our climb. At the top was a metal platform, weeds springing between it and the wall. The door to the apartment itself was flimsy-looking, as though one firm kick would have opened it. There was some kind of entry-phone buzzer, which Ted reached out and – typical man – pressed more times than was really necessary. It made a harsh, tinny sound, like it was ringing into an empty apartment. No signs of life. The heat was searing. I tugged at the neck of my T-shirt. Ted reached out, rang once more, then tried the door, but contrary to appearances it didn't budge.

Unfazed, he turned. 'Right,' he said, 'let's try downstairs.'

24/7 Laundromat read the flickering neon sign in the window. As we stepped through the open door, the laundrette, with all its dryers blowing out warm air, was even hotter than outside. At the far end, a woman stood behind a counter, in front of a curtain separating the main shop from the back. On the counter top in front of her was a dog – one of those small, hairless types – and as we drew closer, I could have sworn she was squeezing spots on its back. She stopped, watching us with what could only be described as deep suspicion.

'Hey,' said Ted. 'You the owner?'

I hovered uncomfortably at his side; the few customers there were turning to stare. I wondered if we really looked so very out of place.

'Who's asking?'

'We've just got a couple questions, is all,' Ted continued, unperturbed. 'So is the owner about or not?'

'Nope.'

I squirmed, but Ted just smiled.

'How about the apartment upstairs?' he asked. 'Know who owns it?'

The woman narrowed her eyes. 'Why'd you wanna know?'

'Look,' said Ted, 'you know who owns it or not?'

The woman held his stare defiantly. 'Nuh-uh. Now, if you're not here to wash shit, stop wasting my time.'

She lifted the dog down from the counter and it trotted off out of sight, into the back room. The woman continued to glare at us, one hand on her hip for added sass, then turned her back pointedly.

'Couldn't you just have – I don't know – shown her your police badge?' I asked Ted, once we were back in the relative safety of his truck.

'I don't think that would've endeared me to her,' he said. 'Besides, don't forget, I'm here *unofficially*.' He winked.

'So what now? We come back another day?'

'Not so fast,' Ted said. 'We do what any good cops would do.'

'Which is?' I asked, dreading the answer.

'We wait.'

19

While Ted fetched coffees from a rather questionable-looking café, I tried Father Gil's number again, with no luck, then called Gretchen, summarised what we'd learned from Joy and gave her the number to keep trying. Ted returned with our drinks, and we sat watching a steady stream of customers come and go from the laundrette.

'So your mom never talked about her sister, huh?' Ted was looking out the window of the truck, his arm resting on the sill.

'No,' I said, picking at my polystyrene cup. 'Their relationship sounded pretty complicated.'

Ted nodded, sipping his coffee. 'You don't come back to Boweridge much, then?'

'Not if I can help it,' I said without thinking, then winced at his expression.

He nodded some more. 'I get it.'

'That came out all wrong,' I said, trying to explain why it sounded very much like I was dissing his home town. 'What I meant is, a DPhil's pretty full on. I don't have much time to travel. Plus my mom – well, let's just say her relationship with Minna wasn't the only complicated one.'

'It must've been hard losing a sister that young,' Ted said. 'To not know what happened.' We watched a couple cross the road in front of us, enter the laundrette.

He had a point. Who would I have become if Em had gone missing when I was growing up? How would her disappearance have affected me? 'What about you?' I asked.

'Me?'

'Yeah. I mean, it must be pretty lonely, a cop's life. Long shifts, antisocial hours.'

Ted side-eyed me, gave me a goofy grin. 'Maggie Elmore, either you're keen to change the subject, or you're trying to find out if I'm single.'

I snorted with laughter. 'Don't flatter yourself.'

'Touché.' He nodded, stared out the window. 'But for the record, I am. Single.'

I smiled to myself.

Almost an hour passed. Just as I was thinking I could do with using the bathroom, a middle-aged man exited the laundrette carrying a box. He certainly hadn't entered while we'd been sitting there, nor, I thought, was he doing his laundry when we went in. Had he been out the back all that time? He moved swiftly, round the corner and up the metal staircase. Before I could speak, Ted was out of the truck, jogging across the road. I scurried after him.

At the sound of footsteps clanging up the staircase behind him, the man turned, fumbling with a set of keys. A cigarette dangled from his mouth, the box at his feet on the platform.

'Hey,' said Ted. 'Wonder if you can help us?'

The man raised an eyebrow, and it suddenly occurred to me this mightn't have been the smartest idea: he was tall and stocky up close, none too friendly-looking either.

The door was open now, propped ajar with his foot. 'Depends,' he said, cigarette bobbing between his lips.

'We're trying to trace someone who lived here,' Ted told him. 'Back in the early seventies?'

'You a cop?'

Ted sighed. 'Off-duty count?'

I expected the man to be angry, but instead he smiled, took the cigarette from his lips and ground it out on the brick wall. Then, pushing the door wide, he nudged the box the rest of the way inside with his foot. 'Better come in,' he said.

He stood aside to let us pass, then picked up the box and kicked the door shut behind him. Ted stayed near the door, and although he didn't seem unduly worried, I stuck by him as my eyes adjusted to the light. The man walked over to a kitchen area and dropped the box unceremoniously onto the floor, sending up a puff of dust.

The place was stifling, airless and musty, not helped by the strong smell of stale cigarettes. My T-shirt stuck to my skin. The man turned, ran a tap, filled himself a glass of water and took a long swig. I looked around. The apartment appeared to be a studio: a tiny living-cum-sleeping area with a kitchenette in one corner. There was a single window, which I figured overlooked the laundrette, though any view was obscured by a layer of grime and a scrap of net curtain pinned haphazardly across it. There was no furniture, just more boxes and a dismantled metal bed frame propped against one wall. A bare light bulb hung from the ceiling, a thin film of cobwebs wafting from it. Other than the entrance, there was only one other door, on the opposite wall. It stood ajar, revealing a tiny bathroom – pale pink tiles, avocado-coloured suite; looked like it hadn't changed since the seventies. Even by convent standards, the place was hardly palatial. Who on earth did Sister Fran know who lived here? Was it someone in trouble, someone she was trying to help?

'So,' the man said, 'what's this about?' He leaned against the kitchen countertop, folding his arms over his ample belly. 'You wanna know about a tenant in the seventies, you gotta be more specific. Turnover was pretty high, if you know what I mean.'

'You were here in the seventies?' I asked, finding my voice at last.

He looked at me like he'd only just noticed me. He was unshaven and shiny, with a deep tan, the kind with an undertone of red that looks like it's gone through several layers of burn to get to.

'Uh-huh,' he said. 'I was a kid, though. It was my pops owned the building. He was the landlord. Owned the laundromat downstairs, too.'

Something he said rang a vague bell, yet I couldn't quite place what.

'Who exactly you looking for?' he asked.

'I don't know if you remember a case from '72?' Ted said. 'The murder of a nun, Sister Francesca Pepitone?'

'Jeez,' the man muttered, 'only forty years too late.' I shot Ted a look. 'Of course I remember. She rented this apartment.'

'Wait,' I said. 'Sister Fran – the nun murdered in '72 – rented *this* apartment?'

He threw back his head and laughed. 'You mean you didn't know?' He stopped laughing. 'You serious?' His face fell. 'Shit, lady, I thought that's why you were here?'

So that was why it rang a bell: the man standing before us was Travis Eavers, son of Leland Eavers, who'd owned the property in '72 and had gone to the police after recognising Sister Fran's photo in the local news.

'Whaddaya wanna know?' Travis asked, seemingly over his initial surprise.

'Just what happened,' I said. 'What you – your dad – told the police. Everything you know about the woman who rented the apartment.'

'Sister Fran, you mean?' He eyed me cynically, like he'd fought this battle before. 'Look,' he held up his hands, 'it don't matter to me if you believe me or not. All I know is that Pop told the cops everything at the time. She – the nun – moved in a few weeks before. We didn't have much to do with her, but we knew it was her. Pop's story didn't change till the day he died; mine neither.'

'It's not that we don't believe you, Mr Eavers,' Ted said. 'In fact, we've got information that corroborates your story – connects Sister Fran to this address, at least.'

'Oh yeah?' Travis thawed a little, rested his hands on the counter-top behind him. 'Like what?'

Ted told him about the letters, their return address. 'Plus my grandpa – Detective Ronald Hoppy? – he took the call from your dad all these years ago. From what he wrote down, and told my dad years later, I'm pretty sure he thought there was something in your father's story. And I've no reason to doubt his instincts.'

'No shit.' Travis raised an eyebrow. 'Well, I'm not sure how much I can help: we told your grandpa everything at the time.'

'Tell us anyhow,' Ted said.

'Like I say, my dad, Leland Eavers, he owned this whole building till he passed, few years ago. After that, it came to me.'

'So you know the area well,' Ted said. 'The people.'

'Too right, buddy. I was only twelve back in '72, but I was old enough to understand what went on around here; old enough – after my old man pointed it out to me – to read the story of the nun's mur-der for myself.'

'Old enough to recognise the photo?' Ted asked.

Travis Eavers nodded. 'It was her all right. Our tenant.'

'Your dad told Detective Hoppy he never knew the tenant's name,' I said.

'That's right. What you have to understand, lady, is that it wasn't unusual for tenants not to give their names – their real ones, at least.' He looked around the apartment. 'I mean, this ain't exactly the Four

Seasons, know what I'm sayin'? They paid cash up front, no questions asked.'

'But if you and your dad didn't know this lady well – he said you'd barely spoken to her; that she didn't dress like a nun – how could you be so sure it was Sister Fran just from the photos in the news?' I thought of the grainy black-and-white image in the *Boweridge Herald*. It wasn't much to go on.

'We hadn't spoken to her a bunch,' Travis said, 'but that don't mean we hadn't *seen* her plenty. 'Specially me. Pops had an office, back of the laundromat. After school was out, I'd come over, ride my bike up and down the sidewalk till home-time. Sometimes I'd sit on the kerb, talk to the customers. I seen her – Sister Fran – come and go from the apartment pretty regular. She'd always give me a wave. She seemed nice, real pretty, the perfect tenant, really – quiet, kept to herself, paid her rent on time.'

'So what happened?' Ted asked.

'So, like, must a' been a few days after school was out for summer, Pop sees this article in the *Herald*. "That's the woman who's renting our apartment," he says. "Look!" An' he shows me the article with her photo.'

'And that's when he went to the police?'

'Yeah,' Travis said; then, 'Wait, no. First, like right then, he goes up, knocks on the apartment door. You know? Just to be sure? But there's no reply. So he leaves it like, I dunno, till the next day? Day after? But there's still no sign of her, so he takes his key and lets himself in.'

'And?'

'An' she was gone. Someone'd cleared out all her stuff. Place was empty, just the furniture. No garbage, no belongings – nothin' but a month's rent left on the countertop. *That's* when Pops called the cops.'

'What did they do?'

Travis screwed up his face. 'Your grandfather, the detective, well he comes out, has a look round, asks a few questions. Pops told him the same as what I'm telling you: that it was this Sister Fran renting the apartment.'

'And you think my grandpa didn't believe him?'

'No, see, that was the weird thing.' Travis shook his head. 'Pops thought your grandpa took it seriously, 'cept no one ever got back to him. He tried calling the precinct a couple times after, but guess they just kept giving him the runaround – said someone'd get back to him. But no one ever did.'

'Do you believe him?' I asked Ted once we were back in his truck.

'Do I believe him about this mystery tenant being Sister Fran?' Ted replied. 'Do I think she was renting that apartment from them? Yeah, I guess I do. You?'

'I believe *he* believes it,' I said, buckling my seat belt. 'That his father did, too. But wouldn't other people have seen Sister Fran there?'

'Maybe.' Ted shrugged as he started the engine. 'But this isn't a part of town where people call the cops about stuff like that.' He checked his mirrors, pulled away.

'Fair point,' I said. 'Plus, if it wasn't Sister Fran, how do you explain the letters?' I'd been sceptical at first, before Joy gave us the address, but it all added up now. 'It seems a little too coincidental for it not to have been her. I mean, what are the chances that the address Joy gave us – the one she saw all those years ago, on the back of an envelope – takes us to the very building where a landlord rented an apartment to a woman he swears is Sister Fran?'

'But we still haven't figured out why she would rent an apartment there in the first place. Why she was receiving letters from that same address. What, she was writing them to herself?'

'God,' I said, rubbing my forehead. It felt like we'd taken one step forward, two back. 'It's all so confusing. Nothing makes any sense.'

'What if,' Ted said, eyes firmly on the road, 'there was some truth in the rumours about Sister Fran and Father Gil?'

I rolled down the passenger window, leaned my arm on the sill, head turned towards the breeze, eyes closed. 'What . . .' I opened my eyes, turned to Ted, 'that Sister Fran was pregnant?'

'No, not that.' He continued to look ahead. 'We know she wasn't pregnant from the medical examiner's report. But that doesn't mean there wasn't some truth to the gossip that she and Father Gil were more than just good friends. And what if Sister Fran *had* found something out – something bad about Father Brennan, about Minna, the girls at St Tom's . . .'

'You think they were going to run away together? Fran and Gil? That the apartment was – what? – a sort of love nest? Somewhere they could meet?'

Ted nodded. 'Why not? Think about it. Maybe not so much of a love nest, more, I don't know, a safe house?'

Safe house. The words echoed in my head. It all sounded so far-fetched, yet something in me felt that maybe, just maybe, Ted was on to something: the apartment, the letters, Sister Fran's relationship with Father Gil. It seemed to fit. Had Sister Fran been not so much planning to leave the convent as escape it? And if so, had Father Gil known? Were they planning to leave together, but then she was murdered? Was Father Gil the one who'd cleared her stuff from the apartment when he found out she was dead, paid the outstanding rent?

When I arrived home, I found Bob in the living room, watching TV.

'Oh, hey, Maggie,' he greeted me. 'You've been gone a beat. Been studying hard again?'

'Uh, yeah,' I said. 'Studying.'

'Now that's commitment. They're lucky to have you on that course.'

Lucky. For a moment, I was transported back to the UK, to Simon's office. 'I hope you realise how lucky you are to be here,' he'd told me, standing just a little too close. 'There's a lot of people would give their right arm to be in your position.'

Despite the crippling heat outside, I shivered. 'No Mom?' I asked, eager to change the subject.

'Migraine.'

A look passed between us. One of Mom's many afflictions was her frequent migraines. I'd always doubted they were even headaches, more an excuse to take to her bed when she wished to avoid something – or someone – just like she'd been avoiding me since she told me about that day with Minna and the photograph. Like she'd regretted it afterwards.

Bob gave a rueful smile. 'Help yourself to something to eat,' he said, gesturing to the kitchen. 'There's leftover takeout on the counter. And hey, I almost forgot. You got mail.' He pointed to a pile of letters on the sideboard, on the top of which sat a white envelope addressed to me.

'Uh, really?' I picked it up. 'Thanks.'

It was the typewritten address on the envelope that caught my eye. Not computer-typed, but typewriter-typed. Desperate to rip it open then and there, but not trusting Mom wouldn't make an appearance, I folded the envelope, slipped it into my back pocket and headed downstairs.

Closing the door to my basement suite, I took out the letter. I stared at it a moment, then ran my nail along the top of the envelope and slipped the folded piece of paper from inside. Though I was half expecting it, the words, stark before me, still made me recoil.

Minna didn't lie.
Father Brennan killed Sister Fran.

The same words as the letters Iris had received since 1972, every year but one. Except that this wasn't the anniversary of Sister Fran's death. But there was another difference too: an extra sentence. Three simple words:

Ask Flora Peterson.

And beneath that, something else. A phone number.

20

The next morning, with Ted still at work, Gretchen and I pulled up outside a quaint-looking house in a leafy suburb of Bower Cove. The house was a new-build, one of those little American doll's houses, as compact inside as the outside suggested, but beautifully furnished and neat as a pin.

Given that we'd only phoned that morning, had driven straight over, Flora Peterson was remarkably welcoming. As she fixed us drinks, my eyes wandered round her small living room. There were photos everywhere: a daughter, I assumed – she looked like Flora – plus what I guessed was a son-in-law and a couple of grandchildren.

'I hope you like iced tea,' she said, placing a tray with a jug and three glasses on the coffee table, her eyes lingering on me as she took her seat.

'It's good of you to see us,' Gretchen said. 'Our call must have been a bit of a surprise.'

Flora didn't respond, just poured the iced tea. A petite lady, older than middle-aged but youthful-looking, with shoulder-length fair hair, she wore silver jewellery and was dressed in pale linens – a daintier, catalogue version of Gretchen.

'To be honest,' she said, as she handed us our glasses, 'I'm not sure what I can tell you. You said on the phone you were looking into Sister Francesca's murder?'

'You know the case?'

'Of course.' She sat beautifully straight, poised and elegant like a ballet dancer. 'She was a teacher back when I was a St Tom's student. I graduated in . . . let me see now . . .' she counted on her fingers, ''69? But Sister Fran was young. She can't have been working there all that long when I left, so I wouldn't say I knew her well.'

So Flora Peterson had graduated a good four years before Minna would have done, had she been around.

'But let me ask *you* something,' Flora said.

'Go ahead.'

'Why me? Who gave you my name, my number?'

I didn't reply, just dug the letter from my pocket and handed it to her. Her jawline tightened ever so slightly as she read it.

'We don't know who wrote it,' I told her, 'but a journalist who covered Sister Fran's case at the time received similar letters. One a year since her murder.'

'Well,' Flora said, passing it back, 'perhaps this isn't so much to do with what I can tell you about Sister Fran, more what I can tell you about Minna.'

I swallowed. 'You knew my aunt?'

She tilted her head, smiling sadly at me. 'I should have guessed,' she said. 'You'll have to forgive me if I was staring. You see, you look so much like her. I bet you get that a lot.'

I swallowed. 'Only these past few days.'

'Well, to answer your question, yes, I knew your aunt. You see, although I was a few years Minna's senior, we were both members of the school's press pack. *The St Thomas Aquinas Gazette*?'

Gretchen nodded. 'I remember it well.'

I nodded too. 'There was an article on it in Minna's old yearbook.'

'Minna and I weren't close,' Flora said, 'didn't know each other for long, but I guess what I remember about her most is how much she loved to write. She had a talent for it – wanted to be a journalist.'

Minna loved to write. Even though I'd guessed as much from her school report and yearbook, now I knew for sure. It was the kind of detail you'd expect to hear from friends, family – Mom, Uncle JJ – but here I was being told it by a complete stranger. It made my heart ache.

'So if you weren't close friends,' I said, 'why you?'

'I'm sorry?'

'Why does the letter-writer think you have information on Minna?'

'I think,' Flora began slowly, 'that it may have something to do with an incident the summer she vanished. I was attending local community college by that time, working nights at a gas station outside of town, and early one morning – like two, three a.m. – I'd clocked off from my shift, was pulling out onto the highway, when I saw this figure up ahead. It was a young girl, her back to me, weaving along the roadside. I was pretty leery, as you can imagine . . .' she widened her eyes as though to emphasise this, 'like maybe it was some kind of ambush – the type you only heard of back then in big cities. But this was Boweridge. So I pull my car alongside, slow right down, open my window, go, "Hey, you okay?" and the girl – she's still a couple steps ahead – stops and turns.'

I could guess what was coming next. 'It was Minna,' I said.

Flora nodded. 'It'd been a good couple years since I'd seen her, but there she was, standing in the headlights of my car, face dirty and tear-streaked.'

'Did she recognise you?'

'I don't think so. Not right away. I called to her from the car, "Minna? Minna Larson?" but she looked blank, so I go, "It's me, Flora. We were at St Tom's together?" For a while she just stared – her eyes looked so hollow and it was clear something wasn't right. I'm not ashamed to admit that I was scared. The whole thing was very unsettling. I was still young myself and it was late, dark, but I knew Minna needed my help. She looked like a frightened deer – I thought she'd bolt any second.'

'So what did you do?' Gretchen asked.

'I put on my cheeriest voice, called something like, "Hey, jump in, I'll give you a ride." Minna hesitated – it felt like for ever – but then she got in. We were a good few miles from home. I tried talking to her, asking her questions – where have you been; how come you're out so late; what happened to you – but she didn't answer, just sat slumped in the passenger seat, staring out the window. It was obvious she'd been drinking.'

'Oh?'

'I could smell it. But you see, not only was she obviously intoxicated, she was thinner than I'd ever seen her. I didn't know her parents but I knew *of* them, that they were strict. I decided I couldn't drop her home in her current state – Lord knows what they would have done with her – so I stopped at a roadside diner, hoping to sober her up.'

'And did you?'

'I guess. She went to the bathroom to freshen up, and I ordered food – burger and fries. When it arrived, she picked at it like a bird while I drank my coffee and watched her. She'd throw me these looks now and then, like she didn't wholly trust me, but after a while she seemed to forget herself, wolfed into her food like she hadn't eaten in goodness knows how long.' Flora stopped, shook her head. 'When she finished, she pushed her plate to one side, drank her soda till there was nothing left but that slurping sound. Even then she didn't stop, wouldn't take her eyes from it, like she was afraid that if she did, I'd ask more questions. I thought, Oh honey, what on earth's happened to you? Why won't you tell me?'

'So what happened?'

'Well, we leave the diner, get back in the car – Minna still clinging to that blessed soda cup like her life depends on it – and I go, "Minna, please, won't you tell me what happened?" She doesn't answer, not right away, and we're still in the parking lot and I'm worried she's going to make a run for it. But she doesn't. Instead she says, so quiet I can barely hear her, "There's nothing anyone can do." I ask her what she means and she starts crying, shaking her head, says, "Sister Fran said she'd help, and look what happened to her."'

Gretchen gasped.

'I know, right?' Flora said. 'My blood ran cold. I mean, everyone knew about Sister Fran's murder – it was the talk of the town, all over the news. But the police said it was a robbery: wrong place, wrong time.'

'Did you ask Minna what she meant?'

'Of course. I asked her if she knew something about Sister Fran's murder, and that's when she told me.' Flora paused, collected herself. 'She told me that for three years, Father Brennan had been doing stuff to her, to other girls too. I asked why she hadn't gone to the police, but she just sort of laughed, said the cops would never believe her, that it'd be her word against Father Brennan's. She was a troubled seventeen-year-old girl; Father Brennan a beloved priest, pillar of the community – his brother police chief.' Her voice quivered. 'Makes me sick to my stomach just thinking about it.'

'Minna must've told Sister Fran what was going on.'

Flora didn't answer right away. 'I've heard since that in certain circles the abuse was an open secret, that high-up people in high-up places were protecting Father Brennan. Minna told me she'd tried telling her parents but they wouldn't listen. Her mom had called her wicked, a liar. Her dad – and this just broke my heart – well, he hadn't said a thing, just turned his back and left the room. Her school grades were suffering, she told me. She'd dropped out of book club; no longer worked on the school paper. She was absent a lot. Sister Fran must've noticed, because Minna told me that one day she'd sat her down, asked her outright. Minna had broken down, told her everything.'

Beside me, I knew what Gretchen was thinking: though we'd suspected it, now we knew for sure that Sister Fran had been aware of the abuse.

'I've always thought it was the promise Sister Fran made Minna that day that sealed her fate,' Flora said.

My stomach tightened. 'What promise?'

'That she'd deal with Father Brennan; that Minna no longer had to fear him.'

'Hello, motive,' Gretchen whispered.

'We sat outside the diner talking for goodness knows how long,' Flora continued. 'By the time we left, Minna had sobered up, but she'd clammed up too, didn't say another word the whole ride. I wondered if dropping her home was the right thing – she was clearly unhappy there – but I didn't know what else to do. I'll never forget the look on her face as she climbed out the car. It was like a switch flipped. She stopped, turned, leaned back in, thanked me for the ride. *Thanked* me, like nothing had happened. She was so calm, so normal-acting, it hit me like a smack in the face. As she turned to leave, I took her arm, told her one last time that she should go to the police.'

'What did she say?'

'Nothing.' I could see from Flora's eyes that she was reliving it. 'She just looks at me, then, before I know it, she's off, running down the pathway into the darkness of the porch. Then she was gone.'

21

After stepping out to use the bathroom, Gretchen stopped by a sideboard inside the living room door, admiring an array of photos.

'You have a beautiful family,' she told Flora.

Flora stood, crossed to join her. 'I thank the Lord for my daughter every day,' she said, and it reminded me of Joy, her feeling blessed by everything. 'She was very sick when she was younger. It was touch and go for a while.' She picked up a silver-framed photo. 'But look at her now: happy, healthy, all grown up, a teacher, like me, kids of her own . . .'

'You teach?' Gretchen asked.

'Used to.' Flora sighed. 'High school. Retired a few years ago.'

Gretchen pulled a sympathetic face. 'Leaves a void that's hard to fill.'

'Sure does,' Flora agreed, 'but I keep busy, do some volunteering, visit with family.'

'Your grandchildren?' Gretchen pointed to a photo of two toddlers, a smiling boy and girl with fair hair and cute dimples.

Flora nodded – 'Twins' – then laughed, made a joke about double the trouble, and Gretchen said something about her cousin – how twins ran in their family. 'They'll be twelve this year,' Flora was saying, though I was barely listening. 'It's crazy how fast time runs away.'

My ears pricked up. Those last two words. Gretchen began to reply, but I interrupted. 'Do you think that's what happened?'

Flora turned, looked confused. 'Excuse me?'

'To Minna,' I said. 'That she ran away.'

Flora crossed the room, sat back down, looked at me sympathetically. 'Truthfully?' She considered. 'I think she was unhappy enough to have wanted to, but I don't think so. She was too close to her little sister.'

'My mom,' I said quietly.

'Of course.' Flora nodded. 'She talked a lot about your mom that night. It was the only time I saw her smile. I could see she felt protective of her, that she wouldn't have just abandoned her.'

'Did Minna tell you she knew for sure who'd killed Sister Fran?'

'Not in so many words, but it was clear she thought Father Brennan had something to do with it. I heard she'd been telling other people as much, too.'

'Did you believe her?'

'That she was being abused by Father Brennan? That he abused other girls? Absolutely. That she had the evidence to prove he murdered Sister Fran?' She shook her head. 'I'm not so sure.'

'Did you go to the police?'

'I'm ashamed to say I didn't. I beat myself up about it for years. If only I had done, Minna might still be here.'

'So who knew?'

Flora looked nonplussed. 'Who knew what?'

'What Minna told you that night. Who wrote me the letter telling me to ask you? Whoever it was, they knew she'd confided in you. If Minna didn't go to the police, and you didn't tell anyone . . .'

'Ah,' Flora said. 'I didn't *go* to the police, that much is true. But after Minna vanished, well, I guess you could say the police came to me.'

'Huh?'

'There was a girl who worked at the same gas station as me – can't remember her name, but she was in Minna's year at St Tom's. She was one of the ones Minna had supposedly said stuff to about the Sister Fran thing – that she knew who'd killed her. Well, anyway, this detective – Hoppy, I think his name was – comes into the gas station one night looking to speak to her, but she wasn't there.'

'So he spoke to you instead? You told him?'

'We just got talking. I don't know why, but I trusted him. Before I knew it, I'd told him what happened with Minna that night.'

My brow knitted. 'I don't remember anything in Detective Hoppy's notes.'

'I asked him not to tell anyone. I was afraid. He gave me his word he'd keep it off the record.'

'And apart from Detective Hoppy, you didn't tell anyone else?'

Flora shook her head.

'Well someone must've known,' I said. 'Detective Hoppy's dead, so he can't have sent me that letter.'

'Maybe he told someone after all?' Gretchen suggested. 'Maybe he ran it by a colleague, a friend?'

'I don't know,' said Flora. 'He swore he wouldn't tell anyone. I believed him.'

'Me too,' I said. 'I mean, we've got copies of his notes. If he didn't keep a record of your meeting, there must've been a good reason: he didn't want to put you in danger. It's obvious there were cops on the force he didn't trust – his boss was Father Brennan's brother, for God's sake. I just don't think he'd've risked it.'

'Could *Minna* have told someone about your meeting,' Gretchen suggested, 'before she vanished?'

I looked at Flora.

'I guess,' Flora said, though she sounded doubtful.

So who was the mystery letter-writer, and how had they known about Flora Peterson? It seemed there were only two options: a mystery third party who'd spoken to Ron Hoppy or Minna; or Minna herself. Could it have been Minna who'd been sending the letters to Iris Hillenberg all these years? Minna who'd pointed me in the direction of Flora Peterson?

Was this the proof we'd been looking for all along that she was alive?

22

I have these memories of my mom, ones I find confusing because they're happy. They jar with the memories I have of the manipulative, neurotic, frequently shrieking woman who raised me, the woman I'd sworn all my life I was nothing like, the woman I swore I'd never become.

'You know your mum's, like, totally personality-disordered?' Tabby told me one day as we lay on her bed poring over a copy of *Smash Hits* magazine.

I was coming to the end of my first year of school in the UK, had just had a particularly fraught phone conversation with Mom, during which I'd broken the news that I wouldn't be returning to the States for summer vacation. Tabby's family had invited me to go with them to France and, having spent most of my free time with Tabby already, it seemed like the natural next step.

'Mum says you've got to check with your dad first, 'kay?' Tabby had said when she broached the idea, the two of us giddy with excitement.

I did, but Dad didn't mind. He was so laid-back about everything. If another family wanted to pseudo-adopt me, he couldn't see a problem. Mom, on the other hand – well, that was a different story. The ensuing phone call had deteriorated into a shrieking match (both of us), before descending into violent bouts of sobbing (Mom).

'Whatever,' I told Tabby, rolling my eyes the way I'd seen her do so many times, making a mental note to google *personality disorder* when I got home. 'I just don't get why she's so bothered. I mean, she's got this new *bloke*.' I emphasised the word, one I'd picked up since living in England. 'It's not like she *wants* to spend time with me anyway; it's only 'cos I *don't* want to go back that she's got a problem. She's so controlling.'

'God,' Tabby said. 'It's a wonder you're not more fucked up.' And we'd fallen about laughing.

Thing was, I wasn't sure Mom had always been that way. Em insists she was, that it was always there – this needy, clingy, manipulative creature – but we just didn't recognise it as children. I guess while we were little, we were like Mom's pets, giving her unconditional love, never questioning her. When, aged two or three, I went through a stage of night terrors, she'd sit patiently with me, whatever the hour, rock me back to sleep. When, aged four, I rolled Plasticine into my hair (emulating the Velcro rollers Mom wore) and it got stuck, it was Mom who – after patiently trying to remove it – much to my dismay had gently cut it free. Little could be done to disguise the stumpy chunks of hair left all over my head.

'Don't worry, baby,' she'd soothed as I cried. 'It'll grow back just as pretty.'

Contrast that with when, shortly before I moved to live with Dad, I had my hair cut in a pixie crop. Mom was so mad.

'It's ugly,' she said. 'You look like a boy.'

Though I didn't really like my new hairstyle myself, I kept it like that just to spite her, only growing it out once I was safely in the UK.

I often wonder why Mom changed towards us as Em and I grew older. I always assumed it was a vanity thing – that while we were growing into our looks, Mom feared she was losing hers. We became too much competition. What she had once loved most about us – being able to take credit for these beautiful little beings – she grew to resent, and because I was much more like her than Em was, life was more difficult for me.

'Just ignore her,' Em would tell me for the umpteenth time on the other end of the phone, her in England, me in Boweridge.

'But you don't understand,' I'd cry, and she didn't. How could she? I'd never told Em that Mom had once confided in me, quite matter-of-factly, that when she was pregnant with me, she'd thrown herself down a flight of stairs in the hope she'd miscarry (it happened after an argument with my father, she explained, as if this made it entirely acceptable); or how, when I was a baby, she'd left me unattended in my stroller, hoping she'd return to find me gone, taken by a stranger.

Yes, for Em it had always been different. Em, with Dad's dark hair, his pale complexion and bright blue eyes. His cool temperament.

'You're nothing like her,' she'd tell me, calmly, when I complained about people comparing me to Mom. 'Not like *that*, anyhow. I don't know why you let it bother you.'

Em was closer to Dad, too. Despite the fact that I was the one who spent the remainder of my teens living with him – Em moved to the UK and went straight off to uni – it was Em he doted on, Em I was sure he loved that little bit more, and while Dad and Em's relationship had only strengthened with age, the older I grew, the more strained mine with Mom became. My leaving for the UK – choosing Dad, as Mom saw it, over her – was the final nail in the coffin.

But all this time, I'd thought Mom hated me as I grew older because I was a reminder of what she once was. Now I wondered if she hated me because I reminded her of Minna.

*

Back at Mom and Bob's, I spent the first part of the afternoon in my room, trying to figure out what everything meant and where to go next. My conviction that Minna was behind the letters – the hope they'd sparked in me that she was alive – had diminished since we left Flora's. By the time Gretchen dropped me home, my sensible self had decided it was far more likely someone else had known about Minna's encounter with Flora Peterson, and that this mystery person was the anonymous letter-writer.

Flora said she'd only told Detective Hoppy about her encounter with Minna, so assuming he'd kept his word, that only left Minna as the possible source. The fact that Flora's name hadn't cropped up earlier, though, suggested that, if Minna had told someone, she hadn't told multiple people. Whoever she had told had kept the secret – until they wrote to me. So who might she have confided in? Someone close to her, most likely, and since she didn't seem to have any girlfriends, the most obvious candidate was Mom.

Minna and her little sister were close, despite the age gap. They'd shared a room – Minna regularly crying herself to sleep in Barb's arms – so it was possible they'd shared other things, too. Secrets. Maybe, all along, despite what Mom said, how she acted, she'd always known Minna hadn't just run away. Perhaps she believed there was a connection between Sister Fran's murder and Minna's disappearance; that that connection was Father Brennan. Could my own mom have been writing the anonymous letters to Iris Hillenberg all these years? If so, did it follow that she'd written an almost identical letter to me, telling me to find Flora Peterson?

And then there was Minna's boyfriend, Mike. How much had he known? Mom told me Mike and Minna had spent a lot of time together, that her ten-year-old self had resented him because of it. Could Minna have told Mike about Flora Peterson? Could *he* be behind the letters? Was it a male thing to do, anonymous letter-writing?

I wasn't sure, but I guessed I shouldn't count him out, not without knowing more about him.

Which was why, a little later, I found myself knocking at Mom's bedroom door.

'Yes?' came a languid voice from the other side.

I pushed the door open, realising as I hovered on the threshold that I'd never seen Mom's bedroom before. I'd always wondered what she did in there for hours, when she was *resting*, but here she was, sitting up in bed, full face of make-up and immaculate hair, watching TV.

'Migraine, darling,' she said, raising the back of her hand to her forehead.

So that's why you're sitting in bed, lights blazing, watching TV? I wanted to say, but I didn't dare. 'Got a minute?' I asked instead.

'Of course, darling. You know I've always got time for you.' She patted the bed. 'Come. Sit with Mommy.'

I did as I was told, perching awkwardly at her side, twisting uncomfortably to make eye contact so I could read her response.

'I went to see Flora Peterson today,' I said. I thought it best to get straight to the point. No preamble. No small talk. The less chance Mom had to see what was coming, the less chance she had to prepare. To lie.

But all she said was, 'Who, darling?' as she reached across her nightstand for an emery board.

'Flora Peterson.' I repeated it calmly. 'She was a St Tom's student, four years above Minna. I thought maybe you'd know her?'

Mom looked genuinely puzzled. 'Why would I know her, darling? If she was four years older than Minna, she'd be ten, eleven years older than me.'

Her reply sounded truthful enough, but if Mom told me it was raining, I'd look outside to check. Lying came so naturally to her, I sometimes wondered if it hadn't just become a habit, like brushing your teeth, or drinking coffee in the morning.

Still, I was undeterred. I'd planned for this, had already moved on. 'And Mike?'

The mention of his name made something shift in her, and though she asked, 'Mike who?' perfectly innocently, it was too late. There were some things even she couldn't disguise.

'Minna's old boyfriend, Mom. You know where he is these days?'

'Mike Freleng? No idea. Haven't seen him in years,' she said; then, typical Mom, unable to resist a dig, added, 'We hardly move in the same circles.' Though her recovery was remarkable, I knew I'd rattled her, so I said nothing more, let the silence hang between us until she bit. 'I just don't know why you feel the need to do this, Maggie.'

'Do what, Mom?' Now I was the one adopting an air of faux-innocence. I felt a twinge of satisfaction.

'Rake all this up,' she snapped. 'Talk to that man.'

'Because you've barely told me anything about Minna, Mom. I mean, God . . .' I gave a laugh of disbelief, 'you must've known what was going on?'

At this point I'd hoped she would crumble, tell me everything, but instead she threw back her head with all the melodrama of those tele-novelas she so loved to watch, though she spoke not a word of Spanish or Portuguese. 'Darling,' she said wearily, 'I thought you'd come to talk to Mommy about nice things. You've hardly given me a moment this whole trip, and now you want to bring up Minna again?'

'I've hardly seen you this trip, Mom,' I said, hands balled into fists beside me, nails digging into my palms, 'because you've been in your room the whole time.'

'How can you be so unsympathetic, darling? I've the *worst* migraine. Can we not do this now?'

'When exactly would you like to do it, Mom?' I stood, turning to look at her. 'When *would* be a good time to discuss your sister? Your sister who was being abused?'

'I've told you, Maggie,' she said, perfectly calmly. She was filing her nails now, avoiding my eye. I wanted to smack the emery board right out of her hand. 'I'm not doing this now.'

'No, Mom, no, of course you're not. But for goodness' sake,' I threw up my hands, 'you must've known! All of you! It was an open secret.'

'I think you should go,' was all she said.

I did as she asked, left the room before I said something I'd regret, something there'd be no going back from. Every time I argued with her, I swore it would be the last, that I wouldn't let her bait me, draw me in again, yet here I was, feeling like shit. Why did I keep letting it happen? I closed my eyes, counted silently to ten. There was one positive, I realised, opening them again: the fact Mom had shut me down meant I was on to something, I was sure, like when she'd refused to discuss Minna at the wake.

My phone vibrated in my pocket. I took it out, swiped to answer it with a trembling thumb.

'Hello?'

'Hey, this Maggie?' said a vaguely familiar voice on the other end.

'Who's this?'

'It's Trav,' the voice said. 'Travis Eavers?'

It took me a moment to place the voice, the name, but then I remembered: the landlord from the east side apartment. I'd given him my number before we left. 'Uh, Mr Eavers. Hi.'

'You said to call if I thought of anything?'

There was an awkward pause. I waited. 'Yes?'

'So, like, I dunno if it means anything, but I remembered something after you'd gone. Actually, it was something my dad found, after whoever it was cleared the apartment. Maybe you should come see for yourself.'

*

I'd called Ted once I got off the phone and he'd picked me up, driven us back across town to the laundrette. When we arrived, there was no sign of the surly woman from before, just Travis, who led us into the back room.

'It could be nothing,' he said, almost apologetically, 'but after she moved out of the apartment – the nun – Pops found this.'

He handed it to Ted. The room we were in was even smaller and dingier than the apartment above, and I craned my neck to see: a photograph. Ted turned it over, turned it back, passed it to me. It was a black-and-white shot of a baby, but as I peered at it, I realised it wasn't a whole photo: the neat but not quite straight line down the left-hand side suggested it had been cropped, so that whoever or what-ever else had originally been in the shot no longer remained. Like Ted, I turned it over, hoping for more, but there was nothing.

'I told you before, right? Someone came and cleared the apartment after she was killed. Nothing left but the bed frame, the mattress and a chest of drawers,' Travis explained.

'So where'd the photo come from?' I asked.

'Pops found it stuck behind a bit of baseboard. Must've slipped down there. He kept it; dunno why. It's been pinned to the notice-board in the office ever since. One of those things you mean to get rid of but never do?'

'But you don't actually know it belonged to Sister Fran,' I said. 'It could've belonged to another tenant, been there years before your dad found it.'

Travis looked deflated and I felt bad.

'Right,' he said. 'I can't be sure.'

My heart sank. The photo could have belonged to anyone.

23

No matter which way I turned it, how closely I held it to my face, squinted my eyes or wrinkled my nose at it, the photo was still the same. I'd hoped that in the bright light of day I'd be able to discern something more – a clue perhaps, some detail not obviously apparent in the laundrette's dingy back office – but it was still just a photo of a generic-looking baby: chubby-cheeked with a dimpled smile, wearing a knitted cardigan and matching bonnet. Impossible to tell if it was even a boy or a girl.

'I've been thinking,' I said, looking up as Ted joined me, his tall figure silhouetted against the sun. He'd hung back chatting to Travis while I'd gone out, sat kerb-side, knees hugged to my chest, much as I imagined a young Travis doing all those years ago – bike lying next to him – so much so I half expected Sister Fran to materialise. 'What if Travis and his dad were right and Sister Fran *was* their tenant? What if the photo *did* belong to her?'

'I'm listening,' Ted said. He sat down next to me, made an *oof* sound, the kind people make when they're relieved to take the weight off at the end of a long day, though he couldn't have been all that comfortable, long legs stretched out awkwardly into the street.

'Well, if we could speak to someone who knew her – her parents, say? – get them to confirm the photo's hers, it'd link her conclusively to the apartment. Do you know if her parents are still alive?'

'Her dad died almost twenty years ago,' Ted said. 'Far as I know, though, her mom's still alive. The Pepitones were older first-time parents – for those days, anyhow – so she's getting on. Last I heard, she'd moved to a nursing home. Place called Shady Nook?'

Shady Nook. The mere name evoked the feeling of Grandma Ida's papery skin against mine, making me shudder. Boweridge didn't have an infinite number of nursing homes, so it should have come as no surprise that the home in which Sister Fran's mother now lived was, unfortunately for me, the same one in which Grandma Ida had spent her last two years.

'I've been wondering about Minna's old boyfriend, Mike,' I said. It was the following afternoon, and Ted and I were in his truck, bound for Shady Nook.

'What about him?' Ted tapped a finger on the steering wheel in time to some tune on the radio.

'It'd be good to talk to him, find out what he knows. I asked my mom about him, but she says she's no idea where he is, hasn't seen him in years.'

Ted's brow furrowed. 'Weird.' I was about to ask what he meant, when he announced, 'Oh, hey, here we are.'

Shady Nook was an ugly one-storey building forming three sides of a square, a barren-looking courtyard in the middle. Inside was no better, with the same anaemic colour scheme and dated decor I remembered – the only discernible difference some leftover Fourth of July bunting – the same sickly sweet old-people-home smell of death and decay. I wondered how long Edith Pepitone had lived at Shady Nook; whether she'd been there on my last visit; whether she'd known Grandma Ida (I hoped for her sake not).

The room Edith called home was a carbon copy of Grandma Ida's, down to the brown-veneer furniture and hospital-style bed that gave it an impersonal feel despite being dotted with Edith's belongings. There was a statue of the Virgin Mary on a chest of drawers, a crucifix on the wall above and a Bible beside the bed, a string of rosary beads draped across it. Apart from that, there was little to speak of Edith's life, just a couple of framed photos on the chest: a black-and-white one of a man – presumably her late husband – and a colour shot of Sister Fran. With her grey-blue eyes and glimpse of fair hair peeping from beneath her veil, it brought her to life far more than the copy I'd seen replicated so many times in grainy monotones.

The woman sitting before us in her high-backed chair could have been Grandma Ida. She was tiny, wizened and stooped, with long grey hair in a bun, and clothes I guessed must once have fitted her but that now threatened to swallow her whole.

'One hundred and one years young,' the nurse informed us, with a wink. 'Isn't that right, Edith?'

Edith didn't respond, but I could have sworn she gave the faintest of eye rolls, though her eyes were milky-white.

'She can't see well,' the nurse whispered as she left the room. 'You'll have to move closer.'

Reluctantly I stepped forward, leaned down. 'Mrs Pepitone?' I placed my hand on her wrist, flinching at how fragile it felt through the sleeve of her cardigan, like the bones of a baby bird beneath feathers.

I thought again of Grandma Ida and the last time I saw her. There'd been no hugs or kisses, no hand on her arm, just the coldness of her fingers, her surprisingly strong grip when she grabbed my face.

At my touch, Edith turned slowly, her pale eyes on mine.

'Mrs Pepitone,' I began again. 'My name's Maggie. And this' – I gestured behind me – 'is Ted. We wondered if we could talk to you about your daughter, Francesca?'

'What do you want to know?' Her voice was weary, like a sigh, though clear enough.

I glanced back at Ted. *Go for it*, he mouthed.

'My aunt was Minna Larson. Your daughter was Minna's teacher at St Tom's. Minna disappeared a few days after your daughter was . . . after she . . .'

'Was murdered?'

The words surprised me. Blunt, emotionless.

'I know it must be difficult to have it raked up after all this time, but I was wondering—'

'You think I don't remember it every day?' Edith snapped.

I shrank back. 'Of course,' I said. 'You must do. I'm sorry.'

I looked round, widened my eyes at Ted. *Help me out here.*

'We're trying to find out what happened to Maggie's aunt.' At the sound of Ted's voice, Edith lifted her head ever so slightly, trying to place him. 'As I'm sure you'll know, Mrs Pepitone, Minna disappeared over forty years ago. No one's heard from her since. But there are rumours – you might have heard them – that your daughter's death and Minna's disappearance were connected.'

'Do *you* think they're connected?' I asked her.

'No.'

'Did you – do you – have any theories about who killed your daughter?'

'It was a robbery.' A shrug of her bony shoulders. 'Wrong place, wrong time.'

Just like Boweridge PD had said.

'So you've no idea who she went to meet that night,' Ted chipped in, 'at the diner?'

'What does it matter?' the old woman snapped.

'And St Tom's,' I said. 'Your daughter was happy there?'

'Yes.' Then, 'Well, she loved the girls.'

'There were parts of school life she didn't love?'

'Not at first. At first she was very happy.'

'But something changed?'

'Yes.'

'Do you know what?'

'No.'

'Did Francesca ever mention any of her students by name?'

'You mean the girl, Minna?'

'Yes.'

'No.'

This was going nowhere. I slipped the photo Travis Eavers had given us from my pocket, handed it to Edith.

'Does this mean anything to you?'

Edith held it up, peered at it so closely it almost touched her nose. Lowering it, she traced a thumb over its surface, like my mom with the photo of Minna, but then said curtly, 'Should it?'

'It was given to us by someone who knew Francesca,' I said. I supposed this was sort of true. 'He thought it maybe belonged to her. We wondered if Francesca might be the baby in the picture – that if it *is* her, you might want to keep it.'

She thrust the photo back at me. 'Well, it isn't.'

I hesitated. 'Perhaps you'd like another look . . .'

'You don't think I'd recognise my only child?' She made a shooing gesture with her hands. 'I'm old, dear, short-sighted, but I'm not stupid.'

Outside, I leaned against the wall, pressed burning brick into my back. The heat out here was searing, but at least I could breathe. Inside had been suffocating.

'So?' said Ted, joining me. He'd been signing us out, charming the nurses like a good detective while I made a dash for the exit. 'What d'you think?'

I shielded my eyes with my hand, squinted up at him. 'I think for someone who lost their only child, she doesn't seem particularly cut up about it. You?'

'I think that people grieve in different ways, that maybe that's just her way of dealing with it.'

Who was he trying to convince – himself or me? I pushed off from the wall and we headed for his truck.

'There was just something about her,' I said. 'She was so cold.'

'Families who've lost loved ones – they can come across defensive, angry. I've seen it before. Besides,' he opened the truck and I was hit by a wall of heat, 'Edith clearly has strong religious beliefs. Maybe her daughter's death is easier to accept if she thinks it's all part of God's plan.'

'You don't think it's odd that of all the people we've spoken to, Sister Fran's own mom is the only one – apart from Boweridge PD – who's adamant her daughter's death was a robbery gone wrong? I mean, she must have heard the rumours, yet she's still clinging to this wrong-place-wrong-time stuff.'

Ted shrugged, buckling his seat belt, turning the engine on, the air con up.

'And the photo,' I went on, 'I'm sure she recognised it.'

He looked doubtful. 'She might've done if she could actually see, but the woman's almost blind: I doubt she'd recognise her own hand in front of her face.'

'Well, it meant *something* to her,' I said. 'Till that point she'd been all one-word answers – yes, no to everything. The photo provoked more of a reaction than all our other questions put together.'

Ted didn't answer. I could tell he wasn't sold.

I leaned back and closed my eyes, let the cold air blast my face. 'By the way,' I said, opening one eye, 'what did you mean before?'

'When?'

'When I asked you about Mike, you said, "Weird." '

'Oh, that. I guess I was just surprised, that's all.'

'Surprised at what?'

'At your mom saying she doesn't know where he is. Everyone round town knows Mike – everyone who's lived here as long as your mom, anyhow.'

'Doesn't mean she knows where he *is*, where he's actually living.' But as the words left my mouth, I had the same sinking feeling I got every time I was misguided enough to fall for anything Mom said.

'Mike's lived in the same house all his life.' Ted laughed. 'I'd put good money on your mom knowing *exactly* where he lives.'

24

After Shady Nook, I couldn't face spending the evening at home, so Ted dropped me at Uncle JJ's. Greg wasn't home yet, but had told us to go ahead and eat, so we were preparing dinner in the kitchen.

'How's things with your mom?' JJ asked.

'Difficult,' I replied. 'So no different to normal.'

'You know,' he said, chopping tomatoes, 'your mom was the only one in the family to accept me when I came out, the only one to accept Greg, our relationship.'

I'm not sure what exactly he said that riled me, but something did. Maybe I was sick of people making excuses for Mom; sick of being told to cut her a break. *That's just how she is*, they'd say. Or, *Well, you know what she's like.*

'Of course she accepted you and Greg,' I snapped. 'She got free babysitting out of it.' I regretted the words as soon as they left my mouth. JJ looked stung, but I couldn't stop. 'I mean,' I went on, 'you live, what, a few miles apart? After I moved to the UK, how often did you see her then? She didn't bother with you after that, did she?'

There was an unbearable pause, then JJ said quietly, 'You're right, Mags. After you left, your mom didn't look near me. I guess you could say neither of you bothered after that.' He put down the knife and left the room.

I found him on the balcony, leaning on the railing smoking a cigarette, his back to me. He didn't look round as I slid open the door and joined him. We stood for a moment, side by side. I touched his arm.

'Uncle J?' He didn't move, just stared straight ahead. 'I'm sorry,' I told him. 'I shouldn't have said that. It was cruel. God, I'm so like her sometimes it frightens me.'

JJ shook his head. 'You're nothing like her.'

'Really?' Em was always telling me the same thing. So why did I find it so hard to believe?

'Really.' He put his hand over mine, gave a tired smile. 'You actually apologise for a start. Your mom never says sorry.'

We stood in silence for a few minutes, JJ puffing on his cigarette.

'God, Mags,' he said at last, tipping his head back, sighing. He smiled again, properly this time, the skin around his eyes dissolved into more lines than I could count, and I could see Mom, and Minna, and all the years in between. 'Maybe you're right. Maybe it was just the free babysitting.'

Despite hugging it out, both apologising some more – though JJ had nothing to apologise for – dinner was awkward. It was my fault, I knew, and as if I didn't already feel guilty enough, I felt even more so at the wave of relief that swept over me when Greg eventually arrived home.

Though neither JJ nor I mentioned it, I knew Greg could sense something had happened, but in true Greg style, he eased the tension, telling us about his day, funny stories about his students and tales from the courtroom. As he settled onto the sofa with his freshly microwaved leftovers and a glass of wine, I decided to fill him and JJ in on everything I'd discovered over the last few days. Admittedly, hearing myself say it out loud, it didn't seem like much, so when I finished, I was surprised to see a look of concern on Greg's face.

'You should tread carefully, Maggie,' he said, looking to JJ for backup.

JJ, industriously clearing the dinner table over the other side of the room, avoided Greg's gaze.

I half laughed. 'Aren't you being a tad melodramatic?'

I expected Greg to laugh in return, but he didn't. 'Take it from an outsider; this town doesn't welcome strangers coming in, shaking things up.'

I knew what he meant. Unlike JJ, Greg wasn't Boweridge born and bred. Also unlike JJ, he came from a loving family. After graduating from law school, tall, fair, cool-looking JJ – who'd long-since ditched his jam-jar glasses – and short, dark, bespectacled Greg moved back to Boweridge. Though nowadays attitudes had progressed somewhat, being gay was still taboo back then, even more so in the small, predominantly Catholic town of Boweridge. In Grandma Ida's eyes, that Greg was Jewish only added insult to injury. The fact that JJ's relationship outlasted all his siblings' marriages cut no ice with her – JJ once told me he thought his mother would have been more accepting of him had he been a serial killer.

I felt a fresh wave of guilt for disillusioning him, making him question Mom's loyalty.

'I don't get why people would have a problem with me wanting to know more about my aunt.'

'What you've got to remember,' Greg explained, 'is that Boweridge has a long memory. People here don't like the past being raked up, 'specially if it makes them look bad.'

'People?'

'The police,' he said. He twirled the stem of his wine glass. 'Local DA.'

'You're saying there was a cover-up?'

He didn't answer.

'Clearly Sister Fran's death wasn't investigated properly at the time,' I said, 'Minna's disappearance not taken seriously. But that's no reflection on the police now, surely?'

JJ raised an eyebrow but kept his mouth shut.

'I wouldn't be so sure,' Greg said. 'There are things they'd much prefer to sweep under the rug.'

'What do you think, Uncle J?' I asked.

'I think your Uncle Greg's had too much wine,' JJ said.

Later that night, back home, I lay in bed turning things over in my mind: my cruel comments to JJ; Greg's reaction to what I'd told them about Minna and Sister Fran. Was Greg overreacting, or was his concern justified? He was an intelligent man: thoughtful, logical. Rational. Not the type to get easily ruffled. But tonight, tonight he'd seemed, well, serious. *There are things they'd much prefer to sweep under the rug.* The words ticked over and over. Hadn't Ted said something similar? And then there was what Greg had said about the town not letting go: *Boweridge has a long memory . . .*

But what did it so desperately want to forget?

I thought of Edith Pepitone, her belief in the robbery narrative. Was her conviction not so much about her belief in God as her loyalty to the Church? Had someone got to her, warned her not to talk? Did the police, the Catholic Church, have such a hold over Boweridge that Sister Fran's own mother would rather bury the truth along with her daughter than risk speaking out? Would a grieving mother really collude with a cover-up instead of seeking justice for her only child? Maybe. But perhaps the truth was simpler. Perhaps, after four decades, like Susan Turner's family, Edith had had enough. She must have known the chances of getting justice for her daughter were slim.

If she hadn't let go, moved on at least somewhat, how could she live with the loss of her child? Maybe she was just tired of decades of questions, speculation and gossip, her coldness nothing more than a defence mechanism. Maybe all she longed for was her daughter's memory to be allowed to rest in peace.

After tossing and turning for hours, I got up to fetch a drink. The house was in darkness as I crept up to the kitchen, moonlight spilling in from outside, lighting my way. I was reaching on tiptoe to get a glass from the cupboard when the kitchen light flicked on.

'*Jesus!*' I nearly dropped the glass, turned to see Mom in the doorway. 'You almost gave me a heart attack, Mom.'

'I almost gave *you* a heart attack, darling?' Mom wore a silk nightgown and matching robe; slippers with marabou feathers – what else? – pink-painted toenails peeping from them. (I curled my own toes, nails unpainted, self-consciously into the floor.) 'I'm not the one sneaking round in the dark.'

'Couldn't sleep.' I held the glass up. 'Want one?'

She shook her head.

I ran the tap, filled my glass slowly. 'You know, it's funny,' I said, shutting off the water, turning to face her, 'but I found out today that Mike Freleng lives in Boweridge.'

'Oh?'

I took a sip, wiped my sleeve-end across my mouth, something Mom hated. 'But I guess you already know that.'

She pulled her *Who, me?* face. 'Why would I know that, darling?'

'Oh, I don't know, let's see – because he's lived in the same house all his life? Because, according to the person who told me, and I'm paraphrasing here, "everyone in Boweridge knows where Mike lives"?'

'Well, darling, I don't know who told you that, but if you will take the word of strangers over your own mother—'

'I have to, Mom!' I slammed my glass down so hard it took us both by surprise. 'I have to because you won't tell me anything. I've learned more about Minna from strangers these past few days than I have from you in a lifetime.'

She tilted her head at me, the look of someone addressing a toddler mid tantrum. 'Are you quite done?'

'No, Mom,' I said, quieter. 'I'm not. I need to know.'

'You *need* to know? You need to know what, Maggie? That my sister abandoned me? That I cried myself to sleep every night after, wishing she'd come home, wondering what I'd done wrong, why she'd left?'

'Yes! I need to know all of it: that you actually cared. Anyone would think it was a relief for you that Minna disappeared, the way you act. No one talks about her! It's like you just erased her from your lives.' I shoved my glass away. 'Like she never existed. No photos, no memories. It was easier for you to tell me she upped and left, ran away, than—'

'Than what?' Mom gave a brittle laugh. 'Easier than telling you I think something happened to her? Something bad?'

I didn't know what to say. Perhaps it *was* easier, less painful. Maybe I'd have reacted the same.

'Mom, *please*,' I begged. 'Do you know what happened to her?'

She shook her head.

'You've got your suspicions, though? You think her disappearance and Sister Fran's murder are connected?'

'Not think, know.'

'You don't know what happened to Minna, but you know that whatever did, it's connected to Sister Fran?'

'I know because . . .' Mom stopped, and for a moment there was nothing but the hum of the refrigerator, the drip-drip-drip of the tap. She closed her eyes, put her hands to her ears like a child trying to block out the world, but I wondered if she was trying to block out memories, memories she was afraid of letting in.

I took a tentative step forward, covered her hands with my own. 'Because what, Mom?' I asked gently. 'How do you know?'

She opened her eyes, looked up into mine. 'Because,' she exhaled shakily, 'on Sister Fran's last night, she came to see Minna.'

For a few moments I stood frozen, the implication of what she'd just confessed sinking in. *The missing fifty minutes.*

'What are you saying?' I said at last. I let go of her hands, took a step back. 'That the night Sister Fran was murdered, *before* she went to the diner, she was with Minna?'

Mom nodded.

'And you've never told anyone this?'

A single shake of the head.

I wanted to shake her, shout, *Oh my God, Mom!*, throw up my hands. All this time people had wondered where Sister Fran was that night, before she went to the diner. My mom had known, for over forty years she'd known, but she'd said nothing.

It was like she could read my mind, for she said, 'Don't you dare. Don't you dare judge me.' Her voice was quiet but dangerous, and for a horrible moment I saw Grandma Ida.

'I'm not judging you, Mom,' I pleaded. 'Honest. But help me. Help me understand. Why didn't you tell anyone?'

'Because Minna told me not to,' she spat. 'Because a few days later, my sister disappeared. Because for over forty years, I've been afraid. Afraid that if I told somebody, the same would happen to me.'

25

Barbara, summer 1972

It was a little before 9.30 p.m., the first Saturday of summer vacation, and Barb was in her favourite spot, the top step of the porch. The day had been hot – too hot – but the sun was low now, the worn wood of the porch pleasantly warm. It was past her bedtime, so every now and then she'd start, imagining Mommy was calling her: *Come wash up before bed!* But Mommy wasn't home, she was visiting with the old lady up the street – the one she didn't like – because her ancient, ratty old cat (which Mommy didn't like either – it pooped in everyone's yards) just died. The boys were still down at the lake, but Daddy was home. He'd been out back all day, pretending to do yard work when really he'd been smoking cigarettes and dozing in the sun, drinking from the bottle he kept hidden amongst his tools, the one he didn't think anyone knew was there, though everyone did. Now he was asleep indoors, pink and shiny, the sunburn he'd gotten during the day disguising the red nose from too much liquor, his low, grumbling snores wafting from the open window overlooking the porch.

Minna was home too, which was rare these days. She was sitting alone on the swing set, pushing herself half-heartedly back and forth.

Earlier that day, Barb had made her big sister a daisy chain, fastened it carefully round her slim, tan wrist before Minna had held it up, turning it this way and that, admiring it.

'Little Barb,' she'd exclaimed, 'you're so clever. It's just the prettiest!' and Barb had beamed.

But Minna couldn't have meant it – it must have been another of her lies – for now Barb watched her sister pick wilting petals from her precious bracelet, dropping them to the ground one by one, grinding them into the dirt with the toe of her tennis shoe. *He loves me, he loves me not; loves me, loves me not . . .*

Barb didn't think Minna *tried* to be mean and thoughtless, but it hurt all the same. Why couldn't she be caring all the time, like Barb knew she could, like that time a few weeks ago when those boys were picking on JJ? They'd been playing out front, five or six of them, had come all the way to the end of the street to seek out JJ – minding his business in the front yard – taunting him from the sidewalk, calling him a stupid dork, a nerd, a nancy boy, even, whatever that was. After JJ retreated indoors upset and Minna had gotten out of him what was wrong, she'd marched right out front – Barb and JJ following, though only as far as the porch – and given those boys a piece of her mind. Though Barb couldn't hear what her big sister said, it must have been good: all those stupid boys could do was gawp up at her like little cry-babies.

'Dude, that your sister?' one of them – the only one who'd regained the power of speech – called over the fence to JJ in awe once Minna had marched off, leaving them agape on the sidewalk. *Course it is, you dumb-ass!* Barb had had the sudden impulse to yell (but she didn't, because she was a young lady, and Mommy always said young ladies should act like young ladies *all* of the time), and JJ had said, 'Uh, yeah.' The boys didn't bother him again after that.

However thoughtless Minna could be, Barb supposed she should just be grateful that for the past few days her sister had been spending more time at home and less with that awful boyfriend. Maybe that meant things were cooling between them? She hoped so.

It was twilight now. From somewhere out on the street came the purr of an engine, the gentle squeak of brakes. Barb looked up as a car pulled into sight, coming to a stop at the end of the garden, just beyond the leaning picket fence. The Larson home was the last house on a dead-end street. It was set apart from the rest of its neighbours, a little further back, too, as though, Barb thought, it knew its residents were trouble. So when a car came this far along the street, there were usually only two explanations: either someone was lost, or the Larsons had a visitor. This time, it appeared to be the latter.

Barb blinked, did a double-take at the figure climbing from the car: wasn't that Minna's teacher, Sister Fran? Other than what she'd heard from Minna, and seeing her from afar at school fetes and parent–teacher evenings she'd been dragged along to, Barb didn't really know Sister Fran. She did know, however, that she was different from other nuns, the ones she herself was used to. She sounded nice for starters, kind and gentle. Another thing Barb knew was that Sister Fran rarely wore nun clothes – the habit the sisters at Sunday school wore, the ones who'd spank the back of your legs with a wooden rule if they caught you daydreaming.

As Sister Fran approached, it struck Barb just how pretty she was. It had never occurred to her that nuns could be pretty. Sister Fran wasn't pretty in that impossibly glamorous way Miss Quinn at the doctor's office was – Miss Quinn whose hair was always set just so, who had impossibly long eyelashes and wore scarlet lipstick that, in Barb's opinion, was the reddest red there could be; who walked with quick legs, seamed stockings on show, high heels clacking over the office floor as she moved from desk to filing cabinet and back again.

No, Sister Fran wasn't pretty like Miss Quinn. Nor was she pretty like Minna – there was no one in the whole entire planet as pretty as Minna! – who had an out-of-this-world beauty, like an angel, Barb thought. Sister Fran was pretty in a 'girl-next-door-type' type way, the type of way that didn't need blush, or lipstick, or nail lacquer; the type of way that made young boys sweet on you, made mommies trust you with their children, little girls follow you around, hang on your every word.

At the creak of the garden gate – yet another thing Mommy was always on at Daddy to fix – Minna looked up, something on her face, other than surprise, that Barb couldn't read. Though Sister Fran was headed for Minna and the swing set, when she noticed Barb, she smiled – a real pretty smile – and waved. Barb frowned in return, shrank back, scuttling up onto the porch proper, peering from between the wooden rails, a fistful of daisies smooshed inside her hot little hand. Sister Fran didn't seem to notice, however – she was too focused on Minna, who was still seated but no longer swinging, perched instead on tiptoe in what seemed like gravity-defying suspended animation.

Sister Fran stayed for some time, seated on the swing next to Minna. They talked together in low, hushed tones, so Barb could only catch snippets of conversation – 'don't have to worry' . . . 'no, not any more' . . . 'the weekend, that's all' – nothing that told her anything. A couple times, Sister Fran looked like she might get up and leave, but she didn't, and the conversation continued. At one point, from the shuddering of Minna's shoulders, the way she lowered her head, Barb was sure her sister was crying. She felt annoyed at Sister Fran for upsetting her so. Minna cried a lot these days, though never publicly.

At last – not much shy of an hour later, Barb reckoned – Sister Fran got up from her swing. The sun had slipped away and the porch light was now on. As she turned to face Minna, she caught sight of Barbara, still watching through the rail. For a second, she looked surprised, like maybe she'd forgotten Barb was there, but then she smiled – a forced smile, Barb thought – waved again. Barb didn't wave back, just sat, scowling, arms wrapped tight round her knees.

Minna stood too, and Barb was shocked to see her throw her arms around Sister Fran, hugging her tight, tighter than Barb had seen her hug anyone. She felt a pang of jealousy. Minna didn't like to be touched. Not these days.

'It'll be okay,' Barb thought she heard Sister Fran say, then, 'Promise,' though Barb didn't know what it all meant.

Barb also didn't know yet that next day, Sunday, the town would be abuzz with news of Sister Fran's murder. Nor did she know yet that when she asked Minna innocently, 'Why'd she come see you last night? The nun?' her sister would tell her to think no more of it, not to mention Sister Fran's visit to anyone. If Barb did that, Minna would say, then everything would be fine.

What Barb also didn't know yet was that just a few days later, Minna would be gone.

But it wasn't a few days later yet, or even the next day, so Barb didn't know any of it. All she knew, as she watched Sister Fran leave, was that darkness had crept up on them; and for some strange reason, it brought with it something she'd never felt before, something she could neither explain nor articulate. If she'd had to, it would have been a feeling of dread, like things would never be the same again. Then she wondered if she'd felt it at all, for the feeling was gone as quickly as it had come, swallowed up by the night.

26

'Holy crap,' exclaimed Ted, 'the missing fifty minutes. Sister Fran was with Minna? Your mom knew all this time?'

I nodded. We were at Wally's Wafflehouse – *the* Wally's Wafflehouse, the one that a few days ago I couldn't believe still existed; the one that when I was younger, still living Stateside, not a week would go by without a visit to, whether with my teenybopper friends, or Uncle JJ and Greg when they had me for the weekend.

The place was deserted but for a stick-thin man seated on a bar stool at the counter, devouring an enormous stack of pancakes. The decor was pretty much as you'd expect; what I remembered, too, from back in the day: linoleum flooring, Formica countertops and faux-leather upholstered seats, wipe-clean gingham tablecloths and chrome napkin dispensers. A bored-looking, gum-chewing waitress leaned on the counter, her attention mostly on her phone, but every now and then she'd throw us sidelong glances, in a way that made me wonder what her deal was.

'Does Gretchen know?' Ted asked.

'She does now.' It'd been too early to call, so I'd Facebook-messaged her, filled her in before texting Ted.

'But why didn't your mom say anything? After Minna disappeared, why not tell someone what she knew?'

I shrugged. 'Minna told her not to. Mom worried that if she said anything, she'd disappear next. I mean, I get it: she was ten, scared, didn't know what was going on but knew it was something bad.'

For the first time in my life, I understood where Mom was coming from.

'So I guess all this means Grandpa Ron was wrong,' Ted said.

'About what?'

'The four questions,' he reminded me. 'The ones he thought held the key. One of them was where Sister Fran spent the missing fifty minutes.'

'True,' I said, 'but it doesn't mean the other questions aren't still valid, just that we've gotta go back to the drawing board for now.'

'God, I'm starved.' Ted looked round, called to the waitress. 'Hey, yeah – can we order?'

I'd no appetite after a night of Mom's tale playing on an endless loop in my head, but I ordered anyway.

'So,' said Ted once the waitress departed, 'what do we have so far?'

I sighed. Where to start. 'We've got Minna: still missing, still no closer to finding out what happened to her. We've got a dead nun, Sister Fran: we don't know who killed her, or why. We've got Sister Fran's mom, Edith Pepitone, barely affected by her daughter's death; and a photo of a baby, but we don't know whose – the baby *or* the photo.'

Ted laughed. 'When you put it like that . . .'

'We've got letters, too,' I said, 'lots of them: the ones Sister Fran was receiving at the convent, mailed from the apartment Travis Eavers insists she rented; and the anonymous ones sent to Iris and me.'

'The letters,' Ted said. 'Yours and Iris's. They're almost identical, so I think we can safely assume they were written by the same person.'

That much was a given. I made a face. 'But who? It can only be someone who knows that Minna confided in Flora. I wondered about my mom, but she claims she's never heard of Flora Peterson.'

'And you believe her?'

'As much as I ever do.' It wasn't a ringing endorsement. 'I take everything Mom says with a pinch of . . .'

I broke off as the food arrived – eggs, bacon and coffee for Ted; French toast and orange juice for me.

'Get you guys anything else?' the waitress asked Ted, ignoring me completely.

'Uh, we're good, thanks.' He waited till she'd gone. 'So who does that leave?'

'Minna's boyfriend, Mike? Someone else entirely, someone we don't even know yet?' I prodded my French toast with my fork, pushed it around the plate.

'What about Flora herself?'

'She swears she didn't tell anyone. Well, apart from your grandpa.'

Ted's eyebrows shot up. 'She told Grandpa Ron?'

I nodded. Somehow, when I'd filled Ted in on Flora, I'd missed that bit.

'But there was nothing in his notes about it.'

'She asked him not to tell anyone. She was afraid. Your grandpa gave her his word he'd keep it off the record.'

Ted lifted his baseball cap, rubbed his forehead. 'I dunno . . .'

'What?'

'Well, I'm sure Grandpa would've kept his word, but I'm also sure he'd've made *some* kind of note of it. He was meticulous like that. Is Flora sure it was him she spoke with?'

Ted had a point. Had Flora definitely said it was Hoppy, or did Gretchen and I *ask* her if it was – put his name in her mind? I couldn't remember. 'You think she's mistaken?'

'Maybe,' Ted said slowly, 'or maybe she genuinely believes she spoke to my grandpa.'

'What, like, someone pretending to be him?'

'It's gotta be a possibility, right? I mean, if it wasn't Grandpa, God only knows who it was, *or* who else they told, which could also explain how the letter-writer knows.'

The thought made me shiver. But would someone really do that? Elicit information from Flora, find out what she knew about Minna under the guise of the trustworthy Detective Hoppy? And what would be the point?

'Ugh . . .' I pushed my plate away, shaking my head, 'it's all so confusing. Is there *anything* we know for sure?'

'Where Sister Fran spent those missing fifty minutes,' Ted said helpfully, then, pointing to my barely touched breakfast, 'You gonna eat that?'

I smiled, slid my plate towards him. 'We still don't know who killed her, though, or why.'

Ted stuck the French toast with his fork and took a bite. 'We also don't know *why* Sister Fran went to see Minna that night.'

'Well, we can probably assume it was about Father Brennan,' I said, ''specially since Minna told my mom not to tell anyone – she was obviously trying to protect her. We also know from Flora that Sister Fran knew about the abuse, that around that time she'd promised Minna she'd deal with Father Brennan. That's motive right there. And let's not forget, Minna was telling people she had evidence that Father Brennan murdered Sister Fran. Sure, we don't know what that evidence was – if it even existed – but if he *did* kill her . . .'

'Right: the threat of Minna exposing him was motive enough for getting rid of her.'

Getting rid of her. I shivered, wrapped my arms round myself. 'But none of this matters because we've got no proof, and because Father

Brennan has an alibi. I mean, if the letter-writer's so convinced he murdered Sister Fran, why not come forward? Because *they've* got no evidence either, that's why.' I rubbed my neck. My head hurt.

'Look . . .' Ted lowered his gaze, met my eyes, 'it's not easy, but we're getting close, I can feel it.'

'I know.' I swallowed, looked away. 'It's just frustrating. I mean, we've got all these snippets of information, but nothing concrete.'

'So,' he said, folding his arms, fixing me with a look that made me want to roll my eyes and smile all at once. 'Come on, Maggie. Who do we still need to speak to?'

'Father Gil, for one,' I said, 'but Gretchen's been trying his number every day, no luck.'

'Who else?'

'Well, now that we can account for the missing fifty minutes, I'd like to check Sister Fran's timeline out some more – maybe speak to the diner witnesses, see if anything in their accounts could blow a hole in Father Brennan's alibi.'

'Slight problem,' Ted said. 'The diner's owner, Don, died years ago. His patrons – the ones there that night – well, I'm guessing they'll be long gone too. Our best bet would be Dewey.'

Dewey: Don's son. He'd been there that night. 'We'll start with him, then.'

'Ah, right, second problem. See, no one knows exactly where Dewey is. He moved outta state after his dad died. Had a sister, though.'

'Oh?'

'Yeah. A Deirdra Hinkle. She was a St Tom's student too, couple years below Minna? Hinkle would've been her maiden name, though.'

Deirdra Hinkle. Why did that name sound familiar? 'And Mike,' I said. 'Minna's old boyfriend. It'd be good to speak to him. You know where he lives.'

'Sure do.' Ted dug in his pocket for his wallet. 'We could go visit him this morning if you like?'

'What, now? Shouldn't we, I don't know, call first?'

'No need.'

'But how'd do you know he'll be home?'

'Oh,' Ted laughed drily, 'he'll be home.' He signalled to the waitress. 'Mike was discharged from the hospital at five o'clock this morning. One of my buddies from the precinct gave him a ride.'

27

My mom tried to kill herself three times that I know of. I say *tried*, because obviously she wasn't successful. I also say *tried*, because I realise now they weren't serious attempts. I say *that I know of*, because I'm pretty certain it's a tactic she pulls with alarming frequency, though I guess I'd have to ask Dad, or Bob, or possibly JJ about that.

The first time it happened, I was kindergarten age. Mom and Dad had been out at some work thing, a dinner party at the house of one of Dad's colleagues. Dad was working away more and more, so by this time him being home was a novelty in itself, much less him and Mom going out together. Em and I had been left with a sitter. When they arrived home, though I was tucked up in bed, it was clear all was not well. Dad left to take the sitter home and I thought Mom had gone to bed, but when Dad arrived back, they started arguing. I went into Em's room – she was sitting up in bed, headphones on – and by the time we plucked up courage to sneak down, positioning ourselves at the optimum vantage point on the stairs, an eerie silence had descended. I felt relieved, but I realise now it was the eye of the storm. Mom and Dad were nowhere to be seen, then the doorbell rang, and Em and I jumped. Dad rushed through the hallway looking stricken, catching sight of us on the stair as he went.

'What's wrong?' Em asked.

'Your mom's not feeling well,' he said. 'I have to get her to the hospital.'

I began to cry.

'She'll be just fine, sweetie,' Dad assured me, opening the front door.

'Uncle JJ!' I cried, seeing Mom's brother in the doorway. I rushed to him and clung to his legs.

'Hey, you!' JJ said.

'Uncle JJ's going to look after you till your mom and I get back.' Dad stroked my hair, kissed the top of my head, grabbed his keys.

JJ picked me up and I wrapped my arms tight around his neck. 'You wanna watch a movie, Mags? Make waffles?'

I was confused. It was well after bedtime. A school night. 'Uh, yeah?' I said, unsure, like it was a test.

Em hadn't shifted from the stairs. 'But what's *wrong* with Mom?' she demanded, her young brow furrowed with suspicion.

'Oh, nothing to worry about,' Dad said. A look passed between him and JJ, a look I'd grow used to over the years. 'We might be back late, though, so don't wait up.' He disappeared into the lounge.

As Uncle JJ shepherded us through to the kitchen, I turned just in time to see Dad leading Mom towards the front door, an arm round her shoulders. She was walking kind of funny, still in her evening wear, Dad's dinner jacket slung around her shoulders. Her hair was a mess, and her face looked funny too, make-up all smudged, mascara running in tracks down her cheeks. She was holding her arms weirdly, straight out from the elbows, palms up. And that's what made me notice the bloodied bandages wrapped tight around her wrists.

The second time it happened, I was eleven. Em had not long moved to join Dad in England, so it was just me and Mom. I can't remember what precipitated the whole thing, but I came home from school to find her lying on the sofa, apparently unconscious, a liquor bottle on the floor, an open bottle of pills next to her, a handful scattered artfully around. Frantic, I shook her, begging her to wake up. When I eventually roused her, I half dragged, half pushed her to the bathroom, where she slumped by the toilet, face over the bowl, me grasping the back of her head like she was a naughty dog who'd got hold of something forbidden, all the time pleading with her to stay conscious, stay alive. I didn't know how many pills she'd swallowed and I wasn't able to get any sense out of her, so with shaking hands I dialled 911, then called Uncle JJ. Greg arrived first, just in time to watch Mom being wheeled to the ambulance. He stood hugging me to him until JJ joined us, then we all followed the ambulance in JJ's car.

Mom got off lightly, it seemed. At the hospital, after a myriad of tests, we were told that, although drunk as a skunk, she didn't appear to have actually swallowed any tablets – not enough to be harmful, anyhow. Other than an almighty hangover, there'd be no lasting damage. Back home, with a concerned JJ and Greg hovering, she wept, promised us she'd never do it again. For some reason, I believed her.

The third and final time, I was fourteen. School was out for summer, and after a particularly tense week – we'd argued about me visiting Dad: I wanted to go, Mom didn't want me to; she was convinced I wouldn't come back – I'd stormed out, called JJ to come pick me up. It was a rookie mistake. When I returned later that night, the house was in darkness. It was unusually quiet too – no sound of the TV from Mom's room – though for some reason, it still didn't dawn on me that something wasn't right. It was only when I heard a noise from the bathroom – not Mom's en suite, but the ground-floor cloakroom – that something clicked. With mounting dread, I knocked gently on the door, then, with no answer, tried the handle. The door wasn't locked, of course, and it swung inward to reveal Mom slumped on the floor in front of the toilet, pill bottle in hand. Her face was a mess, her make-up clown-like, and I had a sudden flashback to the night Dad had rushed her to the hospital with her slashed wrists and bloodied bandages. Through smeared, kohl-rimmed eyes, she raised her head to look at me with what I can only describe as a barely concealed expression of triumph. She opened her mouth to say something, but before she had the chance, I turned and left the room, closing the door quietly behind me.

That night, I'd called Dad, had him book me a one-way plane ticket to the UK.

'He drove straight at a tree,' Ted was saying. 'Tried to kill himself.'

We were in his truck en route to Mike's, and all I could think of was my mom's pitiful attempts.

'God,' I said. 'Why?'

'Guess you'll have to ask him that.'

'Was he hurt?'

'Well, according to witnesses who watched him weaving along the highway, he wasn't going all that fast. Still, it's a miracle he didn't kill someone. Guy's a walking disaster, but worst he'll get out of it is a DUI.' He raised an eyebrow. 'If we're lucky.'

I didn't have a chance to ask him what he meant, for we'd pulled onto a long, tree-lined dead-end street of large Victorian-looking houses. *Cemetery Avenue*, the sign read. The Freleng property was the end house, backing onto Holy Cross Cemetery, which, Ted told me, the Freleng family had been keepers of for generations. Mike had lived there all his life, sharing the house with his mother for most of it until her death a few years ago. Minna used to come here, I thought.

As we made our way up the flagstone path to the porch, the front door flew open and a woman burst out, hurtling so fast she almost ran into us. She was an alarming eighties throwback: stick-thin and over-bronzed, with pearl-pink lipstick, bright blue eyeshadow and a frizzy blonde perm. The double-denim combo – a short skirt and jean jacket – wouldn't have looked out of place with a pair of leg warmers.

'What?' she snarled, her face contorted in a look of aggression, though we'd said nothing.

She was so close, I could smell the peppermint gum on her breath. I grimaced, drew my head back.

Ted flashed his police badge. 'Mike about?' he asked.

The woman didn't reply, just pushed past us, then turned, shouted back at the house, 'Fuckin' a-hole! Rot in hell!'

We watched her disappear, a tornado whirling into the distance.

Ted pulled an overly melodramatic face, like *Jeez*. 'She seemed nice.'

I laughed. 'I wouldn't wanna cross her, that's for sure.'

I was glad he seemed so relaxed, particularly since I wasn't. As we drew nearer to the still-open front door, the knot in my stomach tightened. On the porch steps, I stopped. *Minna would have climbed these steps.*

Ted opened the screen door the rest of the way, then rapped gently on the frame.

'Mike?' he called. 'You home?'

No answer. Holding the door for me, Ted stepped inside and took off down the dingy hallway. I followed. At the end was a door leading into what looked like a living room, though Ted's silhouette was blocking the entrance. I hovered uncomfortably behind him. Through the gap between him and the door frame, I could see the figure of a man on a sofa, trying to light a cigarette, apparently oblivious to our presence.

'Hey, Mike,' Ted said.

'Shit!' Mike looked up, dropping the cigarette, and I realised it was the man from the funeral – the one who'd been staring at me. 'Man,' he said, 'you scared me.'

Though he hadn't exactly looked great the first time I'd laid eyes on him, up close he looked even worse. It was hard to believe that this could be the same man from the photo with Minna – the confident, tanned, all-American beefcake, his arm slung so coolly around her shoulder. This man was painfully thin, his fingers long and spindly, skin so waxen it had a yellow tinge. He had blue, blue eyes, but the whites were yellow too, and one arm was in a sling – the reason he'd been struggling to light the cigarette.

'The fuck are you?' he asked.

'You don't remember?' Ted replied in mock disappointment. 'Detective Hoppy, Boweridge PD. We've met before, Mike, remember?'

'Aww, shit, man,' Mike said. He leaned forward, retrieved his cigarette. 'I told the cops last night. I swear I hadn't been drinking. It's these meds I'm on.' He began flicking his lighter, hands trembling uncontrollably. 'They only let me outta hospital a few hours ago. Can't you come back later?'

'It's not about last night, Mike.' Ted stepped forward, took the lighter gently. 'Here.' He lit the cigarette. Mike took a long drag, exhaled a shaky sigh of relief. 'Sounds like you had a lucky escape, though. What were you thinking, buddy?'

'I dunno, man.' Mike's anger had melted into self-pity. 'I jus' . . . I jus' . . .' He began gesticulating wildly with his uninjured arm, the one holding the cigarette.

'Mike, buddy, calm down. So you've got a little trouble in your love life . . .'

'Naw, it ain't that.' He hung his head. 'You wouldn't understand.' He looked up at Ted, but instead caught sight of me, leaping up with such ferocity I took an involuntary step back. 'Fuck,' he said, arm flailing, pointing the cigarette at me, ash flying. 'What's she doing here?'

'Sit down, Mike.' Ted took a step towards him, gently but firmly pushing him back into his seat.

My heart was hammering, but Mike didn't protest. Though it hardly seemed possible, he'd grown even paler. He looked like he'd seen a ghost. He opened and closed his mouth a few times before saying, 'You was at the funeral. You ain't . . .' he stuttered, 'ain't . . .'

'This is Maggie, Mike, Minna's niece.'

I took a step into the room.

'Jesus.' Mike was shaking his head. 'I mean, Jesus.' He took another shaky drag on his cigarette, then flicked it into an ashtray on a coffee table in front of him, littered with mail, old newspapers and magazines, an assortment of pill bottles and a half-empty bottle of whisky. He gave a tremulous laugh. 'You look just like her. Anyone ever tell you that?'

I didn't realise I'd been holding my breath. 'Funnily enough,' I said, my voice as shaky as his hands, 'not until these last few days.'

He didn't take his eyes from mine.

Ted looked at me, then at Mike. 'Mike, buddy, okay with you if we take a seat?'

'Oh, yeah, sure, go ahead.' Mike waved at a couple of threadbare armchairs opposite him.

I perched on the edge of one, while Ted sank unperturbed into the other. I guessed he was used to this kind of stuff.

As Mike balanced his cigarette on the edge of the ashtray, only taking his eyes from me long enough to reach for the whisky bottle – which he opened and poured one-handed with surprising dexterity – I let my gaze wander around the room. It had an air of faded gentility: crocheted cushion covers, velvet upholstery, polished hardwood floors. A woman's touch, I thought, a sort of Miss Havisham quality, if Miss Havisham had been a chain-smoking, whisky-downing alcoholic. I jumped when Mike broke into a gravelly-sounding coughing fit.

'Jeez, bud,' Ted remarked. 'That doesn't sound too good.'

Mike ignored him, downed his whisky in one as though it was

medicine, took a final drag on his cigarette before stubbing it out. 'Jus' what exactly is it you're wanting?' He squinted at Ted through narrowed eyes.

'We're here about Minna,' Ted told him.

'No,' Mike said quietly.

'I'm sorry?'

'I said no,' Mike repeated. 'No, no, no, no, no-no-no.' He ground the heel of his good hand into his forehead. 'I ain't goin' through this again.' He began rooting around on the table.

Ted stood, searched the detritus, found Mike's pack of cigarettes. 'This what you looking for?' He slid one from the pack, handed it to Mike – who shoved it hungrily into his mouth – then lit it for him with all the tenderness and patience one would afford an elderly relative.

'Look,' I said, leaning forward, 'I'm not here to cause trouble. I just want to find out about my aunt.'

A couple more puffs on his cigarette and Mike seemed calmer again. 'She was the love of my life.'

'The night she vanished, she was supposed to be coming here?'

'Uh-huh.' He fidgeted, absently running the thumb of his good hand over the underside of a silver pinkie ring he wore on the same hand. 'I waited, but she didn't show.'

'And you weren't concerned?'

'Fuck, yeah, course I was,' he snapped, then, dropping his head, added, 'But, like, I guess I was more pissed. Kinda jus' thought she'd changed her mind. She was like that?' He said it as if I should know.

'Were you alone here that night?' I asked. Ron Hoppy's notes had said Mike's mom was home, but it wouldn't hurt to check.

'Huh? No. My mom was here. Look, man, come on,' he appealed to Ted. 'I told the cops everything at the time.'

'We just wanna find out what happened to Minna,' Ted said calmly. 'You must want to know, Mike.'

'Fuck, yeah,' Mike said. 'Course I do. I think about what happened to her all the fuckin' time.' He looked up at us, eyes brimming with tears. 'I fuckin' loved her, man. The summer she vanished? Fuckin' haunts me. I jus' don't understand why people have to keep raking this shit up.'

'To get to the truth,' Ted said.

'What do *you* think happened to her, Mike?' I asked.

His eyes snapped up to mine. 'I know what *didn't* happen,' he said defiantly. 'I know she di'n't run away.'

I swallowed. 'How do you know?'

''Cos that night,' he took another shaky drag on his cigarette, 'the night she vanished, it was *me*' – he stabbed at his own chest with the index finger of his good hand, ash flying – '*me* she was supposed to be runnin' away with. We were s'pposed to be leaving. Together.'

Then, the cigarette still burning between his fingers, he buried his head in his arm and sobbed like a child.

28

'I wasn't always like this, y'know,' Mike said.

I nodded sympathetically, like it was easy to believe he'd once been something other than the complete mess before us. At least he'd stopped crying. He reached for the whisky bottle, poured himself another glass. I glanced at my watch – not even midday – tried not to judge.

'I was a good student, won a college football scholarship.' He gulped his whisky down. 'Then I got injured and, well, that put an end to it. I was real fucked up for a while: partyin' hard, drinkin' heavy . . .'

'Then you met Minna,' Ted said.

'Yeah.' The tremor in Mike's hand had settled, I noticed. The whisky, maybe? 'She was a couple years younger, most beautiful girl I ever seen. Nothin' else mattered after that.'

'What did the Larsons make of your relationship?' Ted asked.

'Reckon they hoped I'd be a good influence on her. I was from a respectable Catholic family, see?' Mike laughed, quickly descending into another violent bout of coughing.

'You must've got along with them okay,' I said. 'I mean, you were at Grandma Ida's funeral.'

He snorted, tipped the last cigarette from the pack, fumbled with it, lit up again. 'Only went to make sure that ol' bitch really was dead.'

Ted shot him a look that told him he was on thin ice, said, '*Mike . . .*' a hint of warning in his voice I'd never heard before.

Mike heeded the caution, looked at me apologetically. 'Shit, like, no offence.'

I almost wanted to laugh, tell him, *No worries, no one liked Grandma Ida anyway*, but instead I asked, 'You didn't see eye to eye with my grandparents?'

He shrugged his good shoulder. 'Di'n't really know 'em.'

'Then why dislike them so much?'

Another shrug. ''Cos of the way they treated her.'

'Is that why you were running away together?' Ted asked.

Mike nodded, sniffed. 'She wasn't happy at home.'

'*Just* at home?'

He looked at Ted. *Huh?*

'She never mentioned Father Brennan?'

'Who?'

'Father Todd Brennan, a teacher at St Tom's.'

He shook his head weakly, looked down, mumbled, 'Never heard of him.' But his tremor had returned.

I sensed that to push further would be a mistake, so I asked, 'Where were you and Minna planning on running away to?'

'Canada,' Mike said, like it was obvious.

'And your mom wouldn't've minded? I mean, she was home the night you were planning to leave.'

He looked surprised. 'We was gonna wait till she was in bed, leave after that.'

'And when Minna didn't show,' Ted asked, 'you didn't think to report her missing?'

Mike shook his head, flicked his cigarette in the direction of the ashtray. 'Didn't reckon she *was* missing.'

'But once you knew she was, you still didn't say anything?'

'What, that we was running away?' He gave a rattly laugh. 'What good would it've done? She was gone. I mean, *shit*, if my mom'd found out, she'd've flipped, made my life—'

Ted's phone rang. He rose from his chair. 'Excuse me.'

I waited till he'd stepped out into the hallway, turned back to Mike. 'Does the name Flora Peterson mean anything to you?'

'Nuh-uh.'

'She was a school friend of Minna's.'

'Minna didn't have no friends. Girlfriends, anyhow.'

'And you're *sure*,' I said, just as he reached for the whisky again, 'she never mentioned Father Brennan?'

He slammed the bottle down so hard I almost jumped out of my chair.

Ted appeared in the doorway, still on the phone, one hand covering the mouthpiece. 'Everything okay in here?'

My heart was hammering. I nodded weakly.

'You should go,' Mike said. His tremor was worse than ever.

Before we left, I scribbled my mobile number on the back of an envelope for Mike. Ted stood with his arms crossed while I wrote, raised his eyebrows in a way that said, *Not a good idea, Maggie*, while Mike sat and glowered, refusing to meet my eye. You could have cut the tension with a knife.

'What was all that about?' Ted asked, back in the safety of his truck. It felt a world away from Mike's sad home.

'Dunno,' I said casually, trying to pretend that Mike's reaction hadn't scared me, even though my heart rate still hadn't returned to normal. 'I asked him about Father Brennan again and he just lost it.'

'You wanna be careful. Guy's probably harmless enough, but he's not playing with a full deck, if you know what I mean.'

'Do you believe him?'

'About not knowing Father Brennan?' Ted pulled a face. 'It's unlikely he hasn't at least *heard* of him, but even if he has, it doesn't necessarily mean he knew about the abuse.'

'But why not just be honest? Why not admit it if he did?'

'Maybe, for whatever reason, he doesn't want to acknowledge that he knew what was happening to Minna. Maybe he feels guilty that he did nothing, or maybe he's just in denial. We may never know.'

'And the rest? His story about the night Minna disappeared?'

'Guess there's no reason to doubt it,' Ted said. 'His mom and neighbour backed him up. His story's been consistent for over forty years.'

'Apart from the fact that he never mentioned before that he and Minna were planning on running away that night. That's a pretty major thing to leave out.'

'I guess,' said Ted, tugging on his trusty baseball cap. I wondered if he ever left home without it. 'I'm not saying he did the right thing by not telling anyone, but the way he saw it, it would've only stirred up a shit storm. Plus, it's obvious he loved Minna, knew she was having a hard time at home. What if, deep down – though he won't admit it – he really *does* think she left, is just happy she got away from her family?'

'I suppose,' I agreed. 'And if he *is* telling the truth – that they had planned on running away – it would explain why some of Minna's stuff was missing: her clothes, Walt's rucksack. So do we think she just decided to leave without Mike? That she went it alone?'

'I dunno . . .' Ted wound his window down, rested his arm on the sill. 'Doesn't make much sense if you've made plans to go with someone. I mean, single girl, travelling alone, hitching? Would've been safer for them to go together.'

I had a sudden image of Minna alone on a remote highway, thumb out, some random car slowing to a stop, Minna running to catch up, climbing gratefully into the passenger seat . . . It gave me chills.

When we reached the end of Mom's street and I climbed from the truck, I stopped, leaned back in. 'Hey,' I said, 'before you go. What did you mean when you said Mike might get a DUI if he was lucky?'

'A DUI,' Ted said. 'Means driving under the influence.'

'I know what it means,' I said. 'It was how you said it, like, he *might* get one. Seems an odd thing to say.'

'Ah, well,' said Ted, 'let's just say that over the years I've had my fair share of run-ins with Mike Freleng – domestic disturbances, bar fights, a handful of DUIs. Misdemeanours mostly, but still . . .'

'So he's got a record.'

'Should have,' he agreed. 'Funny thing is, nothing seems to stick.'

'Meaning?'

'Meaning no charges ever get brought. I looked at his record. He's got a couple of misdemeanours from out of state, but nothing before or since. Nothing from his home state, nothing from the county. Certainly nothing from Boweridge.'

'So you're saying what?' I leaned further into the truck. 'Someone's protecting him?'

'I'm not saying anything.' Ted smiled. 'It's just what I've observed over the years. I told you his family own the cemetery, right? Generations of 'em. The Frelengs were a big deal in Boweridge back in the day. Mike's dad was well respected. Guess some things don't change much.'

Guess not, I thought, as I lingered on the kerb, watching Ted pull away. The more I became reacquainted with this town, the more I wondered if anything had changed at all.

29

With Ted at work and Gretchen also unavailable, I spent the first part of the afternoon holed up in my bedroom, mainly to steer clear of Mom. I was still rattled by the meeting with Mike, so another message from Simon, this time through Facebook, didn't exactly help.

Maggie, *please*, was all it said.

I'd been taken aback by the matter-of-factness of his earlier emails, but this one threw me for different reasons. The tone appeared contrite, no trace of angry bluster, and he'd italicised the word *please*, which made it sound so desperate that for a moment I actually felt sorry for him. Had I blown the whole thing out of proportion?

I should have been thankful for Simon's message, though, for it was logging onto Facebook that sparked the realisation. Deirdra Hinkle – that was why I recognised the name! Back on the Sister Fran Facebook page, I scrolled until I found the right post – the fortieth anniversary one – then scrolled some more till I reached the comment by Deirdra Hinkle-Schroeder: *Fckn armchair detectives*. Surely Deirdra Hinkle-Schroeder was the Deirdra Hinkle Ted had mentioned, daughter of diner owner Don, sister of Dewey? I clicked on her profile. *Location: Boweridge*, it read, but other than that, nothing – no recent updates, no albums, only a cover photo of an ice cream sundae, a profile picture of a couple of kids (her children, grandchildren?); no education or work history, no relationship status, birth date or visible photos; and among her ninety-seven friends, no other Hinkles. Still, I shot her a message anyway:

> Hi, sorry to contact you out of the blue, but I saw your comment on the Sister Fran FB page. My mom and aunt went to St Tom's in the early seventies. I'm trying to track down anyone with a connection to Don's Diner around that time. I wondered if you might be Don Hinkle's daughter/Dewey's sister? If so, can explain more later if you'd like to chat. Thanks for your time. Maggie

I watched the screen for a couple of minutes, hoping for an instant reply, then logged out, turning my attention to other things. It still bugged me that we hadn't tracked Father Brennan down yet, so I decided to see what I could find online, but as I'd half expected, there was nothing. Other than establishing that there was a Father Brennan in *The Omen*, the only thing I learned after extensive googling was that as priests' surnames went, Brennan was pretty common. On the plus side, I found no obituaries, though I did find one for Father Brennan's brother, police chief Jim Brennan, who, as Gretchen had said, died ten years ago. However, although the obituary mentioned his wife, children and grandchildren, along with a surviving older sister, Mary-Anne, there was no mention of a younger brother. No reference at all to Father Brennan. Strange, given that Detective Jim Brennan had been close enough to him to risk his career protecting him.

I considered where else to find records of where priests ended up after they retired, before remembering something someone had said about St Tom's school adjoining the site of the Catholic church of the same name. The school site had been bulldozed long ago to make way for a new housing development – the one Lo was supposed to write the article on when she dug up the story on Susan Turner – but was the church still standing? A quick Google search revealed it was.

The 2006 article – the one Lo should have written – wasn't available, as it pre-dated the *Herald*'s online days. Like most newspapers, however, the *Herald* now had a strong internet presence, and there were a number of follow-up pieces, charting progress from the school's demolition, through construction and the official opening of the aptly named St Thomas Courts. Although the school had closed for good in '94, the new complex – 'a vibrant but tranquil development of over fifty high-end condos and apartments, set within lush landscaped grounds' – hadn't been completed until a couple of years ago, but despite all the change going on around it, St Thomas Aquinas Catholic Church stood untouched.

Site of Beloved Boweridge School Unrecognizable After Transformation, a headline from summer 2017 read.

There were celebrations today after work was completed on St Thomas Courts, the newly developed complex on the site of the former St Thomas Aquinas Catholic High School. The once-popular all-girls school closed two decades ago and was demolished soon after, but after problems with permits for the proposed new site arose, construction didn't begin until the fall of 2011.

'Some lucky residents were able to move in earlier this year after the first phase of the development was completed ahead of schedule, but most arrived within the last couple weeks,' said site manager Al Schneider.

It seems serendipitous then that the last resident to move into the complex is also a former graduate of St Tom's High. Retired secretary Pamela Christie, 68, who took possession of a two-bed condo last week, said, 'I've been here less than two weeks, but already I love it. The place is just beautiful, the neighbors all so welcoming.'

Asked how the site compared with how it was in her high school days, Pam replied, 'A complete transformation. Unrecognizable. The only thing left is the church. It's nice that it's still standing.'

History of the Site

St Thomas Aquinas Catholic Church was built in 1930, with the school of the same name opening on the adjoining site in 1959. Taught mainly by nuns, the school had a strong emphasis on religious studies – with students regularly attending mass at the neighboring St Tom's church – and English. 'A large proportion of our girls go on to secretarial college,' Sister Patricia Kinkel, school principal, said in an interview with the *Boweridge Herald* in 1979, shortly after the school celebrated its twentieth anniversary. 'Many go on to become teachers themselves,' she added. 'The tutelage of St Thomas Aquinas High School stands them in great stead.'

However, after student numbers began dwindling, with many parents choosing to send their children either to Boweridge High or schools outside of town, St Tom's finally closed its doors in 1994.

'The population of Boweridge shot up in the mid nineties,' town historian Harvey Bryant said, 'yet at schools like St Tom's, student numbers started to decline.' There are myriad reasons for this, Bryant says, including single-sex Catholic schools being seen as outdated. 'Add in the dramatic increase in Boweridge's population, urban sprawl, plus improved transport links – highways, better public transportation – and you've got yourself more choice when it comes to schooling, say, in the nearest city. Boweridge is now a bedroom town. Distances that were once not commutable now are, and this is the case for where you send your kids to school too, not just for where you work.'

*

After lunch, I borrowed Bob's bike and, with the help of Google Maps, arrived huffing and puffing at St Thomas Aquinas Catholic Church.

It looked pretty much as it had online, except that it was now surrounded by swanky new-builds. The only other difference was the large contemporary-style glass and wood porch, which according to the plaque beside the door had been gifted to the church by the St Thomas Courts developers. I left Bob's bike propped by the entrance (who'd steal a bike from a church, right?) and stepped inside. The porch was cool and bright, empty but for a table stacked with leaflets and flyers advertising various parish events, along with some religious trinkets for sale – wooden crucifixes, rosary beads, prayer cards – an honesty box for payment.

Inside the church, which was larger than it appeared from the outside, I stood for a moment taking it all in: row upon row of wooden pews, their varnished surfaces worn smooth from decades of use; the marble pillars that flanked the church either side, veins like huge cracks that might cleave apart at any second; the impossibly high ceiling and towering stained-glass windows. Though the place was deserted, the air silent and still, I imagined it full of girls attending mass, Minna among them. I could hear the creaking of pews, the whispering and shuffling and fidgeting. A stifled giggle.

Back in the present, and reluctant for some reason to make my way down the central aisle, I turned left and wound my way along one side. I'd almost reached the altar when the sound of a door closing somewhere echoed round the church, shattering the silence. A moment later, at the top of the plush green-carpeted altar steps, I spied the figure of a kneeling nun, her back to me, tending to a flower display.

I cleared my throat.

She twisted, got to her feet. 'Good morning,' she said without warmth, her eyes settling on me. 'Welcome to St Thomas's.'

The sleeves of the white blouse under her habit were rolled up, her hands damp from the flowers. She was petite and slim, older, but her face was remarkably unlined, and she moved lithely down the steps.

'Can I help you?' she asked, drawing closer. She had that look I was now both wary and weary of, somewhere between vague and startled recognition.

'I'm visiting,' I said, 'from out of town.'

'Out of country.'

She said it without humour, but still I laughed. 'Yes.' My accent again. 'From the UK. My aunt used to go to St Tom's High, so I thought I'd drop by, see the site, but of course the school's no longer here.'

On the bottom step was a bunch of flower-arranging stuff – scissors, a couple of vases, some of those foam blocks – from which the nun plucked a towel and wiped her hands, watching me all the while, mind ticking over, trying to figure me out.

'Have you been here long?' I asked. It sounded odd, but I didn't know how else to phrase it.

'Here? The church?' She placed the towel down. 'Longer than most.'

'You were here when the school was still open?'

'I taught at St Thomas's for close on thirty years.'

My stomach lurched. 'So you knew the girls?'

'Some of them.'

'Maybe you knew my aunt?'

A pause. 'When was she a student?'

'Umm . . .' I pretended to think, like the date of Minna's disappearance wasn't seared into my mind. 'Like, late sixties, early seventies?'

'A long time ago.'

'Yes.'

'I doubt I'd remember that far back.'

Try, I thought, but I said, 'Her name was Minna. Minna Larson.' The nun's face sharpened.

'You knew her?'

'Everyone knew Minna.'

There was something in her tone that riled me in a way only my mom usually could. 'Meaning?'

She drew a sharp breath, one that said, *You'll be sorry*. 'Far be it from me to speak ill of people,' she said, 'but if you must know, Minna Larson was a troubled young lady.'

'Troubled how?'

'That girl had a wicked tongue.' She said it with unmistakable relish. 'She told stories, lied—'

'*That girl*,' I interrupted, unable to listen any longer, 'was being abused by one of the teachers, the priest at this very church, Father Brennan.'

The nun's cheeks flushed like rosy apples. 'Father Brennan,' she said haughtily, 'is a good man.'

'*Is?*' I said. 'So he's still alive?'

She didn't answer, just looked shocked and furious all at once. From somewhere nearby, I was vaguely aware of the sound of a door opening and closing.

'Father Brennan *was*,' she hissed, deliberately exaggerating the past tense, 'a dear, dear man. He only wanted the best for those girls.'

'He was a predator. He preyed on vulnerable girls. People at the school knew, yet they did nothing. Except Sister Fran.'

At the mention of Sister Fran's name, the nun pursed her lips, turned, and began ascending the altar steps.

'Did *you* know, Sister?' I called after her. 'About the abuse?'

She didn't answer. She was gathering up flowers, her bony little arms working nineteen to the dozen.

'Where is he?' I asked, louder now. 'Tell me where he is and I'll leave you alone.'

She stopped, whipped round. 'Even if I knew where he was,' she said, 'I wouldn't tell you. I refuse to see that good, kind man's reputation tarnished by the lies of a wicked little—'

Someone coughed, and she froze. I turned, following her gaze, and saw a priest standing a little way away. The nun's face was stony, her mouth half open.

'Sister Martha,' the priest said. His tone was perfectly calm. 'Mrs Keller is here about the flowers. She's waiting in the vestry. Perhaps you'd be so kind as to . . .' He didn't have to finish.

'Yes, Father,' the nun said, practically bowing in deference, then scurried off without another word.

Only then did I realise I was shaking.

'Come,' the priest said, 'sit a moment.' He put out an arm, his hand hovering uncertainly, guiding me to the nearest pew. 'I must apologise for Sister Martha,' he said. I waited for a *but*. 'There's no excuse for what she said.'

'How much did you hear?' I asked.

'Enough.'

He sat down beside me, a couple of persons' width between us, and I studied him from the corner of my eye. He was perhaps late forties – not old enough to have known St Tom's school, not in Minna's day, anyhow – and completely bald, with thick-rimmed round spectacles.

'Do *you* know Father Brennan?' I asked at last.

'No,' he said quietly, 'though I know of him.'

'Is he still alive?'

'He is.'

'Do you know where he is?'

'That I can't say.'

'Can't or won't?' I felt the anger rising in me again, but I was also tired. I rubbed my temples. 'Why won't anyone help?'

'Have you asked Our Lord for guidance?'

For fuck's sake, I thought, but all I could muster was a weary eye-roll.

'You've lost your faith,' the priest said simply, as though it were a medical diagnosis.

'I never had any.' It came out harsher than I'd intended. In truth, part of me envied people of faith.

But he was unruffled. He smiled – *touché* – then held out a book. 'Perhaps this will help.'

It was a New Testament, the type bound in wipe-clean plastic with tracing-paper pages, the ones you find in cheap motel rooms where people go to top themselves. When I failed to take it from his outstretched hand, he placed it on the pew between us.

'Sometimes all we need is a little guidance,' he said.

Too exhausted to argue and not wanting to offend him – I could see he meant well – I picked it up. The priest rose, made to leave, then paused, resting a hand on the back of the pew in front.

'I hope you find what you're looking for,' he said, and then he was gone.

I want to find Minna, I thought. Or at least what happened to her. Some closure. Was that too much to ask?

30

I was in a foul mood when I got back, not to mention sweating from my cycle ride. As I approached the house, I could see Bob's car was gone; inside, the muffled sound of the TV came from Mom's room. I slipped downstairs unnoticed, not registering that the door to my basement suite was ajar, until I entered my bedroom and found Mom standing over the bed.

'Darling,' she greeted me, smiling innocently. 'I wasn't expecting you home.'

'Clearly,' I muttered, just loud enough for her to hear. 'Otherwise you wouldn't have been snooping.'

'I don't know what you're talking about.' She put a hand to her chest, wounded. 'I brought fresh towels, see?'

She pointed to the pile of neatly folded towels on my bed. Beyond it sat my laptop, open. I watched Mom follow my gaze, notice I'd noticed. What had she been looking for? Whatever it was, I doubted she'd have got far: my laptop was password-protected, Mom computer-illiterate. I snuck a glance around, breathed a silent sigh of relief: there in the corner of the room where I'd left it, hemmed in by my suitcase, concealed by clothing, sat Detective Hoppy's box. Untouched.

'Whatever, Mom,' I said. I was too tired for her games. I slung my bag and the Bible onto the bed. 'If there's something you want to know, just ask.'

'Well I would, darling, but I've hardly had the chance.'

'I've been catching up with people,' I told her. 'Uncle JJ, Greg.' I might be too tired for games, yet I couldn't help but point-score. 'Mike.'

Mom's expression faltered, just for a millisecond, but it was enough.

'You know, it's funny.' I folded my arms, leaned against the wall. 'Mike was at Grandma Ida's funeral, yet you claimed you haven't seen him in years.'

'He was?' She patted my bed covers, smoothing the wrinkles. 'I don't remember.'

'Did you know he and Minna were planning on running away together?'

'Mike told you that?' Then, not waiting for my reply, 'Well, I guess it doesn't surprise me. He was controlling like that.'

'The impression I got was that Minna was as keen to leave as he was.'

'So why didn't they then?'

'Because the night they were supposed to go, Minna disappeared.'

Mom made a little noise – *hmph* – muttered, 'Convenient.'

'Excuse me?'

'I said *convenient*. I mean, I presume you only have *Mike's* word that he and Minna hatched this supposed plan?'

I rolled my eyes, didn't even try and hide it. 'Uh, well, yes,' I said, in the insolent teenage tone she hated.

'Well if I were you, I'd take anything that man says with a grain of salt.'

'And why's that, Mom?'

'Because he's a liar, darling.'

'What reason would he have to lie?' I asked. 'Besides, it fits with what Grandma Ida told the police – she thought Minna took stuff with her that night: Walt's rucksack, a change of clothes . . .'

'Mm-hmm.'

'God, Mom, what?' By letting my frustration show, I'd lost control, but I couldn't help it. 'There's obviously something you're not telling me. Or is it that you want me to *think* there's something you're not telling me, when actually you know nothing at all?'

'Don't you get it?' She gave a small, pitying laugh. 'Mike lied about what happened that night.'

'How would you know?'

'Maggie, *darling*,' she said, in the tone one might use to break it to a close friend that her husband's cheating on her, 'do you honestly think that Minna left for Mike's that night and disappeared somewhere en route?'

'But the neighbour across the road,' I said, suddenly uncertain. 'The police spoke to him. He was on his porch all evening. He said Minna didn't arrive.'

Mom shot me a withering look.

'Christ, Mom.' I threw up my hands. This was her all over: she'd plant a seed, refuse to elaborate. 'If there's something you've got to say, tell me!'

There was a pause, and I could see her debating: should she tell me what she knew, revel in the glory of being able to impart information I wouldn't otherwise have known, or torture me some more by keeping it to herself?

'When Minna used to go see Mike,' she began, relishing every word, 'she didn't always use the front door. Sometimes she'd take a longer route round back, cut through the graveyard.'

'So you're saying she *could* have been at Mike's that evening, but the neighbour wouldn't necessarily have seen her?'

'That's exactly what I'm saying.'

'But why would she go a longer route?'

'Because Mike wasn't supposed to have company when his mom wasn't home, and that nosy old neighbour was a tattletale.'

'But Mike's mom *was* home that evening, so Minna would've had no need to go the back route.'

'Huh,' Mom said, 'that deluded woman would've done anything to protect that no-good son of hers.'

'Including lying about being home that night, about Minna not turning up?'

She shrugged. 'Guess you'd have to ask Mike.'

'But it doesn't make any sense. Mike's heartbroken by Minna's disappearance. He admitted she wasn't happy, that they were planning on running away together. Why would he lie?'

'Oh, I don't know. Because he's a violent bully? Because he hit Minna?'

Her words struck me as hard as if she'd hit me herself.

'What?' A slow smile spread across her face. 'Poor heartbroken Mike didn't tell you that?'

'Did Minna tell you?'

'She didn't have to. I saw the marks.'

'But if it was that obvious, how come no one did anything?'

'Because it wasn't obvious,' Mom said coldly. 'Mike was cleverer than that. He did it where no one would see – except me. I'd see when she got undressed at night: huge bruises across her back, the tops of her arms, all hidden, except for that last one. She must've done something to make him real mad that day.'

The black eye, I thought, the one Minna's classmates mentioned; the one Mom did, too, the faint trace that lingered the day of the photo. 'And you didn't think to tell anyone? I mean, God, Mom, first Sister Fran's missing fifty minutes, now this?'

Mom laughed – actually laughed – and I wanted to slap her.

'You think this is funny?'

'What I think is *funny* is that you think anyone would've listened. What I think is *funny*' – she spat the word – 'is that you take Mike's word as gospel.'

'What am I supposed to do when you won't tell me anything?' I yelled. We'd been here before. 'I need the truth, Mom, all of it, not just the bits you want to tell me when it suits you!'

'You want the truth? What – that Minna was being abused by a priest? That the school knew, the teachers, other girls – *God*, practically the whole town! – yet no one did anything? Is that what you want to hear? *Is it?*' And with that, she stormed out of the room, slamming the door behind her.

I let out a stifled roar, grabbed the nearest object – the Bible – and flung it with such force it hit the closed door with a thwack and dropped like a stone to the floor. Then I flopped back onto the bed and covered my face. How did Mom keep doing this to me? When we'd talked the other night, about Sister Fran's last evening, for once in my life I'd felt I understood her – had even told Ted as much. I'd actually felt sorry for her. God, I was such an idiot.

I breathed deeply. *Think rationally.*

I was missing the bigger picture: if Mom *was* telling the truth about Mike, it changed everything. It meant Minna *could* have made it to Mike's that night, and if she had, why would he lie about it unless he had something to hide? I'd seen his reaction for myself, the flash of anger when I pushed about Father Brennan. If Mike *was* violent, if he had hit Minna, then who knew what else he'd be capable of. But was his reaction proof of a violent temper, or just of a man tired of living, as he saw it, under the shadow of suspicion? Just because, technically, Minna *could* have made it to the Freleng home unseen that night didn't mean she had. Had what Mom told me actually lent *more* credence to the theory that Minna had run away, but on her own? She was unhappy at home and school, after all, had gone from being controlled by her parents to – if Mom was telling the truth – being controlled by Mike. Perhaps she'd had enough, so had told Mike what he wanted to hear and made plans to run away with him, then ditched him last minute.

Was I gullible for falling for Mike's story, or a fool for believing anything Mom said? Did what I'd just learned add weight to my theory that Minna might still be out there somewhere; or did I want her to be alive so badly I was only seeing what I wanted to see?

My head ached. I uncovered my eyes, blinking in the light as I sat up. Catching sight of the sorry Bible on the floor – face down, pages fanned out – I immediately felt guilty (what kind of person used a Bible as a missile?). There was something quite beautiful about it, like a dove's wings, but something else too . . . I stood and crossed to the door, frowning as I picked it up. A scrap of paper was sticking out from between the pages, with a handwritten address:

St Joseph's Villa, West Lake View Road, Cape West.

Had the address been all there was, I might not have thought much of it, but written above it, in the same crisp, neat handwriting, was a name:

Father Todd Brennan.

31

'Now that's what I call divine intervention,' Gretchen said when I told her about the address.

I'd googled it straight away, found St Joseph's Villa was a retirement home for priests, in a small coastal town north of Boweridge. The next morning, Ted still at work, I'd biked over to Gretchen's and filled her in on the events of the last couple of days. But while Ted and I had been busy doing our investigations, Gretchen had made a breakthrough of her own: she'd finally got hold of Father Gil, had arranged for us to Skype with him that morning.

Half an hour later, we were squashed together in front of my laptop, Gil Griffin filling the screen before us.

Now in his mid seventies, he resembled a kind of Santa-Claus-cum-surfer-dude: broad and tanned, silver hair and beard, a gaudy Hawaiian shirt, glasses perched on the end of his nose. Around his neck there was no dog collar, just a leather thong with a silver cross pendant.

'You were lucky to get hold of me at all,' he said. 'Guess I'm a bit of a Luddite when it comes to technology. I forget to charge my cell all the time; rarely use it.'

'Gretchen tells me you're still in Florida?'

'That's right. Moved around a bunch after . . . well, what happened with Francesca. Settled here in '75 and never left.'

'You're no longer in the priesthood?'

'What gave it away?' He glanced down at his attire, chuckled, then turned serious. 'It was hard, y'know. Guess you could say I lost my faith.'

'Did you continue teaching?'

He nodded. 'Right after I moved here, I took a job at the local community college, met my wife, Cathleen. We had a daughter, Stephanie. Life was good. But in 1979, when Stephanie was two, she and Cathleen died in a car accident.'

Next to me, Gretchen sucked in a breath, whispered, 'Jesus.'

'That's a lot of loss to suffer,' I said.

Gil nodded again, rocked in his chair. 'I took time out from teaching after that, never returned. I've done a bit of everything since – welder, grocery store clerk, surf shop manager, barber – but never remarried.'

'You said you're living at a retirement complex?' Gretchen asked.

'Uh-huh, right. I'm officially retired, but I work here as a cook, take our more senior residents on day trips.'

As we spoke, it struck me that Gil was the only person we'd connected with so far who hadn't been drawn back to Boweridge. Was that a sign of a guilty conscience, or just painful memories? He certainly didn't look like a cold-blooded killer, but then what exactly did cold-blooded killers look like? Young killers grow old, I reminded myself, and Gil had left Boweridge pretty quickly after Sister Fran's death.

'So,' Gretchen said, perhaps sensing we were getting off topic. 'When we spoke earlier, I filled you in on why we're so keen to talk to you.'

Gil's face seemed to fold in on itself, like a turtle retreating into its shell. 'I'm not sure how I can help, but I'll do my best.'

'You mentioned Sister Fran,' I said. 'You were close to her?'

'I was, yes.' He smiled, a twinkle in his eye. He had a habit of leaning in when he spoke, like he thought he needed to for the mic to pick him up. I wondered whether to tell him he needn't bother, but decided not to. I didn't want to interrupt the flow, but also, in a funny way, it was kind of endearing. 'I'm guessing you've heard the rumours?'

'That you were more than friends?' I ventured. 'Were you?'

'You could say that.' He was still smiling, but it was a sad smile now. 'We were in love.'

I was taken aback – had been expecting him to deny it – but tried not to let my surprise show. 'She would confide in you, then?'

'We talked all the time. I knew she wasn't happy. Not at school, anyhow.'

'In what way?'

'I'm guessing you'll have heard this too – most people have – but there was bad stuff going on at St Tom's. Stuff involving . . .' He stopped, looked down, shook his head, angry. 'Stuff that involved the girls.'

'You mean the abuse.'

'Right.'

'And Sister Fran knew?'

'Not at first, no. But she found out. There was this priest there, you see, Father Brennan. He was at the heart of it.'

'You know for sure?'

He nodded. 'In certain circles it was what you'd call an open secret. But Francesca didn't find out till one of the girls confided in her.'

'Minna Larson.'

'Minna, right. I never met her, but Fran told me about her and I saw the stuff in the papers after she disappeared. That was why it was so hard to believe it wasn't all connected. You see, about a week before school was out for summer, Minna told Francesca everything.'

Gretchen nudged me: this was the second person who'd confirmed Sister Fran knew about the abuse.

'What did she tell her?'

'Francesca spared me much of the detail, but she said it was bad, and it wasn't just Minna, either – there were others.'

'So what did she do?'

'She confronted Brennan.'

'She told you this?'

'Afterward, yes. I would've stopped her otherwise. The morning of the day she died, Saturday, we met for brunch and she told me everything. I wanted to go confront the bastard then and there, but it was already too late: Francesca had gone to his office the day before, last day of term, had it out with him.'

The day before her murder.

'How did he react?'

Gil shrugged. 'She'd given him an ultimatum: either he went to the archdiocese and confessed, or she would. Father Brennan agreed, said he'd go, but asked for some time first.'

'Some time?'

'Oh, just a couple days,' Gil clarified, then, seeing the look on my face, said, 'I know, I know. In hindsight, it wasn't the best decision. The fact he took it so well should've been a warning sign, but Francesca saw the best in everyone. Brennan told her he needed time to put his affairs in order, to pray for guidance and strength, so she took him at his word, said she'd give him the weekend. There's not a day goes by I don't wish I'd told her not to wait – that she should go straight away; that I'd go with her, *for* her.' He sighed. 'If I'd thought for one second that he'd . . . that it'd end the way it did . . .'

'So you don't believe the police's version, that Sister Fran's murder was a robbery gone wrong?'

He shook his head, looked down.

'And you've no idea who she was going to meet that night at the diner?'

Another head shake. 'We were together that morning and she never even mentioned it. All I've ever been certain of is that Todd Brennan had a hand in her murder, but the bastard had an alibi. Ironclad, apparently, which made it all a little *too* convenient if you ask me. Not that it matters – in that town they could have caught him red-handed and he still wouldn't't've been arrested.'

'You mean because of his brother?'

'Exactly.'

'But the police looked at you, right?'

'Course they did. That would have been perfect for them – pin it on me.'

'I hope you don't mind me asking,' I said, 'but there were rumours you were angry with Sister Fran – something along the lines that you'd confessed your love for her, asked her to leave with you; that she'd rejected you.'

Gil laughed. 'I'm sorry,' he said, 'it's not funny.' There were tears in his eyes. 'But it couldn't be further from the truth. Fran and I were truly in love. Whether you believe me or not, though, it doesn't matter: that bastard Brennan wasn't the only one with an alibi. I was home with five other priests.'

'*Were* you and Sister Fran planning to leave together?'

'We were thinking about it.' He welled up again, took his glasses off, wiped his eyes. 'Look, I've never told anyone this before . . .' Another pause. 'I'd asked Francesca to marry me.'

Gretchen's mouth dropped open.

'What did she say?'

'She wanted to, but it wasn't that simple. She was worried about her parents. She was all they had and she didn't want to let them down. I suppose she thought it would disappoint them.'

'So . . .' I said, wary of sounding too blunt, 'she didn't exactly turn you down, but it wasn't a yes either.'

Gil cleared his throat, dabbed his eyes some more. 'There was so much going on, you know. Fran was dealing with Minna, Father

Brennan. We'd been talking about leaving, starting a life together, having a family, but I didn't want to put any pressure on her. I could tell she had a lot on her mind. I thought she just needed a few days to come to a decision, but before she had the chance . . .'

Worried he'd start crying again, I said quickly, 'I know this must be hard, but we've got just a couple more questions.'

'Go ahead.' He sniffed loudly. 'Shoot.'

'Minna's disappearance,' I said. 'You believe it was linked to Sister Fran's murder?'

Gil nodded. 'Had to've been.' He replaced his glasses on the end of his nose, leaned in. 'I heard Minna was going round saying she knew who'd killed Francesca. Big mistake in a place like Boweridge.'

'And you didn't think to go to the police?' Gretchen asked. 'Tell them what Sister Fran had told you, about the abuse?'

'What good would it have done?' Gil said. 'The police already knew what was going on. They were in on it – protecting that bastard.'

Not all of them, I thought. Not Ron Hoppy. But Gil was right – Father Brennan was being protected, that much was clear.

'You've been really helpful,' I said, 'but there's one last thing.'

'Sure,' he said, 'anything.'

'When you met up with Sister Fran, where would you go?'

His brow furrowed. 'The movie theatre, the mall sometimes . . . usual places.'

'But if you wanted to be . . . alone. Together. You know, if you wanted to go somewhere you wouldn't be seen. Was there somewhere special?'

Gil looked genuinely surprised. 'Like a love nest?'

That was exactly what I meant.

'No,' he said, 'no, we didn't have anywhere.'

I'd pretty much assumed he was involved with the apartment above the laundrette – it seemed like the only plausible explanation – so it came as something of a surprise to hear him deny it. But why would he lie when he'd been so candid about everything else?

'So this doesn't mean anything to you?' I fumbled with the piece of paper on which Joy had written the apartment address, held it up to the camera.

Gil leaned closer still, pushed his glasses further up his nose, squinted at the screen. 'Nope.' He looked blank. 'Should it?'

'So, I'm not sure if you know this – if Sister Fran mentioned it – but in the weeks before her death, we've been told she was receiving mail from someone at that address.'

'Huh?'

'I suppose we were wondering if it was an apartment you rented together – you know, somewhere the two of you could escape.'

'Look,' Gil chuckled, 'I don't know how much you know about that part of town, but let's just say it's not somewhere you'd want to spend a lot of time – not then, anyhow. It wouldn't exactly have been conducive to romance, if you know what I mean.'

I nodded. 'I've been there. So you're saying the letters Sister Fran was receiving weren't from you?'

'Why would I be writing to her? I saw her pretty much every day.'

Fair point. 'And you've no idea who they could have been from?'

'Nuh-uh,' he said. He sounded genuine. 'But I'll tell you who might know: Fran's best friend. They shared a room at the convent.'

Best friend? I glanced at Gretchen, then back at the screen. 'Sister Joy?' I asked.

'That's right,' Gil said, 'Joy Greenway. Or Snelling, as she is now. When Gretchen called, she mentioned you'd been in contact with her – I kinda just assumed it was Joy put you in touch with me. Well, anyways, I guess you'll already know this, but Joy and Fran were close. *Real* close. They had a lot in common – both only children, both close to their parents, both living away from home. They told each other everything.'

32

'Cape West?' Ted raised an eyebrow. 'That's a good couple hours' drive away.'

We were waiting outside Joy Snelling's house in his truck. Gretchen was tied up all afternoon, so after we'd Skyped Gil Griffin, an off-duty Ted picked me up. We'd decided to return to Joy's, press her about what Gil had said, but we'd arrived to find – according to whoever answered the intercom at the enormous electric gates – she wasn't home.

'You sure you want to go?'

'A hundred per cent,' I said, surprised at how underwhelmed he seemed by the discovery. Whatever the truth of the whole sordid story, Father Brennan was at the heart of it. Now we knew where he was.

'So,' Ted yawned, stretching back in his seat, 'the basics. What do we know for sure now?'

I'd given him a slightly garbled account of events on the drive to Joy's: my trip to St Tom's; the retired priest home address; what Mom had told me about Mike; and everything Gretchen and I had learned from Gil Griffin. 'Well, we've now got two people who've confirmed Sister Fran knew about the abuse: Flora Peterson and Gil Griffin.

And we know from Gil that Sister Fran confronted Father Brennan about it.'

'We also know now that the rumours were true,' Ted added. 'Sister Fran and Gil *were* an item.'

'So I suppose the question is, does that make Gil more or less likely as a suspect? He admitted Fran didn't exactly rush to accept his marriage proposal, but if his alibi's to be believed, he's in the clear.'

'But then so's Father Brennan,' Ted reminded me, devil's advocate. 'Cast iron, remember.'

'A little too cast iron.'

'Same could be said of Father Gil's.' He raised that eyebrow again. 'Plus, either one of 'em could've hired someone to do it for them.'

'I dunno,' I said. 'Father Brennan, yes, but after speaking to Gil, I just don't believe *he* had anything to do with it. It's obvious her death devastated him.'

'I'm not saying Gil's guilty, but it's the oldest story in the book: guy meets girl, falls in love; girl rejects guy, guy feels humiliated. If the police believed every murder suspect who claimed they didn't do it 'cos they loved the victim . . .'

'*I'm* not saying Gil's not a suspect,' I countered, 'I just think there's a stronger one. Sister Fran was threatening to out Father Brennan as a molester of girls; he stood to lose everything. We know he had a temper, too. The fact that he apparently took it so well when she confronted him is suspicious in itself.'

'What about Flora Peterson?'

'What about her?'

'Gil know the name?'

'I didn't ask, but assuming it was Minna who told the letter-writer about her encounter with Flora, it has to be someone she came into contact with. Father Gil never met Minna, so he can't be our mystery letter-writer.'

A big, shiny car turned in front of us, pausing for a moment to allow the metal gates to open, and I caught a glimpse of Joy behind the wheel.

'Then there's Joy Snelling.'

'Yup. Why'd she lie about her friendship with Sister Fran?'

'Well,' said Ted, 'I guess we're about to find out.'

Joy Snelling greeted us with the same cheery disposition as on our first visit, but her smile fell when she saw our sombre faces.

'You lied to us,' said Ted. No *hi*, or *good day*. He wore that expression parents so often use when scolding their children, the I'm-not-angry-I'm-just-disappointed one.

Joy looked about, as though afraid we'd be overheard, but she seemed resigned, like she'd been expecting this moment all her life. 'You'd better come in.'

'We spoke to Gil Griffin,' I said gently, once we were back in her beautiful living room. No coffees or drinks this time, no polite chit-chat, just straight down to business.

Joy had looked close to crying from the start, but at the mention of Gil's name, her eyes widened and a single tear slid down her face.

'We know you weren't truthful with us, Joy,' Ted said. 'About Sister Fran – how close you were.'

She nodded glumly.

'We just want to know why,' I told her. 'Why say you barely knew her when you were so close?'

'I don't know,' she said, voice barely audible. 'I guess I was trying to protect her. There were so many secrets.'

'About Father Brennan?'

She shook her head.

'Father Gil then?'

She swallowed. Ted and I exchanged glances.

'You think Father Gil had something to do with Sister Fran's murder?' Ted asked.

'Oh, goodness, no,' said Joy, alarmed. 'That's not what I meant. I never knew exactly what their relationship was – Fran honestly didn't tell me – but Gil loved her, that was obvious. He'd never have harmed her. But there were rumours swirling about. I worried that if I told the police what I knew, about the letters' return address . . .'

'It might lead to Father Gil,' Ted finished, 'uncover his relationship with Sister Fran.'

She nodded. 'Fran's parents had endured enough, lost their only child. A scandal like that would have broken them. I didn't lie, you understand, I just didn't tell them everything.'

'Sorry – *them*?'

'The detectives – the ones who came, asked questions.'

'You mean Detective Hoppy?'

'Hoppy, yes, but there were others, too.' Another omission. Joy looked guilty. 'A pair of them came, a couple days after Hoppy. They asked me the same questions, but their manner was different. I felt uneasy, intimidated, so I just told them what I told Detective Hoppy: that I'd never seen the letters' contents.'

'Do you know who they were, these detectives?' Ted asked.

'Not at the time, but I found out who one of them was after, saw his photo in the *Herald*.'

'Let me guess,' I said. 'Jim Brennan.'

She looked surprised, nodded.

'So *did* you see the letters' contents?' Ted asked.

'Oh no,' Joy insisted. 'I didn't lie about that. I only ever saw the return address. Fran never told me what was in them, either,' she added, 'or who they were from. That much was true.'

She sounded sincere, but she'd lied to us before. 'But if you were best friends, why wouldn't she have confided in you?' I asked.

'You'd have to have asked her that,' Joy said, kneading a balled-up tissue between her fingers. 'All I know is that the two of us were close from the moment we met. We had so much in common, you see: both only children, both adopted . . .'

I glanced at Ted. That Joy and Fran were adopted, his expression told me, was news to him too.

'Go on,' I said.

The situation felt fragile, like an overinflated balloon. Joy hesitated, nodded. 'I'm not sure if you know this,' she said, her expression brightening, 'but the convent used to be the Boweridge orphanage. Fran and I were there as babies, at the same time – can you believe! – raised by nuns the first few months of our lives. Of course, neither of us could remember it, we were so young,' she added, in case we'd thought otherwise, 'and both of us were blessed to be adopted quickly, by loving families. That was what we bonded over, you see: when we met later through our shared vocation, realised our connection – well, you can only imagine!'

'I can see why you'd be close,' I said.

'But that's just it,' Joy went on. 'Something changed. Remember you asked me about what I'd said to Detective Hoppy – that I thought something had been on Sister Fran's mind in the weeks before her death?'

Ted and I both nodded.

'Well, it was more than that. Those last few weeks, there was a distance between us there'd never been before. At the time, I was hurt. I knew something had changed, I just couldn't figure out what. When I look back, I think she was protecting me from whatever was going on.' She stopped, kneaded the tissue. 'Which is why I'm so ashamed of what I did.'

Before we had a chance to ask any more, Joy got up, left the room. I looked at Ted, mouthed, *What the . . .?* He held up his hands: *Don't ask me*. After what felt like hours, but was probably only a couple of minutes, she returned holding a book.

'The night Sister Fran was murdered,' she said breathlessly, 'I knew she was going to meet someone. I just didn't know who.'

She passed me the book, already open, and I saw it was a diary, the pages closely handwritten.

'I've never told anyone what happened that night,' she said. She suddenly looked very small, everything that had previously been so shiny about her now dulled. 'Couldn't bear to. But I did write it down. It's all in there.'

I began to read.

06.17.72

Sister Fran asked me to keep a secret tonight, but how can I keep a secret when I don't know what that secret is? She whispered to me during evening prayer, said she had to go out, asked me to cover for her. She said she'd explain everything later, but I doubt it. We used to tell each other everything, but something's changed these past few weeks. I've no proof, of course, it's just a feeling, but there's something on her mind, I'm certain of that. Whatever it is, it's weighing heavy. Except tonight. Tonight, she seems lighter, happy. Excited, even? I wonder if it's got anything to do with Father Gil. I shouldn't say this, but he is very handsome, and Sister Fran's so pretty, and they do spend a lot of time together. They share a closeness that, if I'm honest (and Reverend Mother does like to remind us how honesty is a virtue), I can't help but envy. Not that I like to pry (although Sister Fran teases me good-naturedly me that I do), but I did ask her one day if there was something between them. She told me no. I'm not sure if I believe her.

But back to tonight. She left the convent right after evening prayer, though she didn't say where she was going or who she was going to meet. (I had no proof she was meeting someone, only suspected she was, though why else would she be going?) So here I was, expected to cover for her at the risk of getting into trouble myself, when she doesn't even trust me enough to tell me the truth! I feel guilty for thinking such un-Christian thoughts (for writing them down, anyhow), but there, it's done. Maybe that's why (because I was feeling out of sorts), when I returned to our room and found the piece of paper on Sister Fran's nightstand, I took a peek. I mean, who knows what she might have gotten herself into, sneaking off like that late at night?

It's not like the paper revealed much. It just had *10 p.m. Don's Diner* scribbled on it in Sister Fran's hand. Don's Diner? Wasn't that somewhere outside of town? What would Sister Fran be doing all the way out there at this time of evening? I was pondering this when there was a knock at the door: Sister Greta. She was flushed and out of breath, which isn't unusual (she's a plump little thing), so I wasn't entirely alarmed, not until, still puffing and panting, she said, 'Sister Joy – Reverend Mother wishes to speak to Sister Fran straight away.'

My heart sank, for nothing good comes of being summoned by Reverend Mother, and then it sank still further, for of course Sister Fran wasn't there. What would I say? I've never been good at thinking on the spot (Sister Fran teases me about that, too), and before I could stop myself, I blurted, 'Sister Fran had to go out' (how I cursed myself silently for being so indiscreet, then cursed myself for cursing). Sister Greta looked stricken, said, 'But what shall I tell Reverend Mother? She said she must speak with Sister Fran; that there's someone on the telephone for her,' and I felt bad for Sister Greta, because none of this was her fault, so I said, 'I shall go to Reverend Mother, Sister Greta. I shall go speak with her.'

By the time I reached her office, Reverend Mother was no longer on the telephone. I hadn't really considered what I might tell her, which seems silly now, but before I could even greet her, she said, 'Sister Joy. I asked Sister Greta to fetch Sister Fran. Father Brennan has been on the telephone. He must speak with her as a matter of urgency.' I think that's what threw me: Father Brennan? Why would he call to speak with Sister Fran (they disliked one another, I was sure)? I hesitated, think I may have opened and closed my mouth a few times, but because I'm a terrible liar, I could think of nothing to say. I just stood there feeling myself turn red as a tomato, before a thought occurred to me: what if it's an emergency? What if it's about one of the girls? And that was when I suddenly realised I was still holding the piece of paper from the nightstand.

I knew as soon as I did it that it was a terrible mistake. After Reverend Mother squinted at the paper, after her brow furrowed in puzzlement, she looked back up at me, said coolly, 'You may go now, Sister,' and as I turned to leave, I heard the ping of the telephone receiver.

The entry ended. I flicked forward a few pages, but the diary, it seemed, ended there too: the remaining pages were blank. I closed it slowly and looked up. Joy met my eye, lip quivering. Ted watched expectantly.

'You told Reverend Mother where Sister Fran was going that night,' I said.

Ted, confused, looked between us like he was watching a ping-pong game.

'As good as,' Joy admitted. 'I gave her the piece of paper. Reverend Mother must have phoned Father Brennan back and told him.' She dissolved into tears. 'Don't you see?' she said, through ragged sobs. 'If it hadn't been for me, Father Brennan wouldn't have known where she was that night. Sister Fran would still be alive.'

33

The next morning, Ted picked Gretchen and me up for our road trip to St Joseph's Villa, the retired priests' home.

'So Joy kept it to herself all this time?' Gretchen asked, incredulous, after we told her about our second trip to the Snelling home.

'Yeah.' I was in the back seat, Gretchen riding shotgun. 'I can't help but feel sorry for her. I mean, she knows she made a mistake giving the Reverend Mother the piece of paper, but she'd no idea it would end in murder.'

'She should've fessed up before now, though,' Gretchen said. 'What she told you changes everything, proves Father Brennan knew where Sister Fran was going that night – links him to the diner.'

I didn't disagree. 'I'm not saying she did the right thing, but Joy coming forward wouldn't've changed the fact that Father Brennan has an alibi. Plus, the police were clearly protecting him.'

'Some of them,' Ted added, from behind the wheel.

We broke our journey at a gas station, and while Gretchen used the restroom, Ted and I got out and stretched our legs.

'Doesn't this adoption thing bug you?' I asked. We were standing side by side, leaning against the hot truck.

'Only in the sense I'm surprised we didn't know about it till now,' Ted replied.

'Can you access that stuff?'

'Adoption records?' He looked doubtful. 'You think it's worth it?'

'God, I don't know.' I laced my fingers on top of my head, tipped my face skyward. It was all too much. 'Maybe we're just chasing shadows.'

'Maybe.' He pushed off from the truck, turned to face me. 'But we're not giving up.'

For a moment, I wondered why he even cared. Then I remembered his grandpa, the cases that haunted him for so long, the image I'd conjured of him lifeless on the floor, blood pooling round his head . . .

'You know,' I said, through an exhale, 'until Joy told us what she did, I was convinced it *was* Father Brennan Sister Fran went to meet that night at the diner. At least that he'd arranged the meeting, that she *thought* that's who she was going to meet.'

'You don't think it was?'

'I don't know, but if it was, why call the convent when he knew she'd probably've already left?'

'But if not Father Brennan, then who?'

'I don't know that either, but I feel like there's only three options. One, we're wrong and Father Brennan is innocent – of murder, at least. Sister Fran was murdered by whoever she went to meet that night, or it *was* just a random attack. Father Brennan phoning the convent was just coincidence. Sister Fran had confronted him the day before, don't forget – maybe he just wanted to talk.'

'Okay . . .' said Ted, unconvinced. 'Option two?'

'Father Brennan had no idea about the diner meeting – Sister Fran went there to meet someone else – but after he phoned the convent and found out where she was going to be, he seized his chance. We know he can't have gone there himself – he has an alibi – but he *could* have had someone kill her for him.'

'Seems unlikely.' Ted tipped his baseball cap, rubbed his brow. It was hot as hell. 'He might've had the connections to order a hit, but how easy would it've been for him to do it at such short notice? And what about the mystery person Sister Fran was really going to meet? Who was it? What happened to them?'

I didn't have answers.

'Option three?'

'Joy's blamed herself all these years,' I said, 'but what if what she did made no difference? What if Father Brennan already knew where Sister Fran would be, because he *had* arranged the meeting? Sister Fran thought she was going to meet Father Brennan – maybe he told her he wanted to talk, something like that – when really she was going to meet her killer, whoever Father Brennan had got to do his dirty work.'

'But we're back to the same question: why did Father Brennan phone the convent that night?'

'He might've wanted to make sure she'd left for their assignation, or maybe he had an attack of conscience – changed his mind, panicked, whatever – and tried to call in the hope he'd catch her before she left, stop her from going?'

'Maybe . . .' Ted said, as Gretchen reappeared.

'I got snacks!' she called across the forecourt. 'You guys hungry?'

St Joseph's Villa was much like any other retirement home, except its residents were priests, and it was staffed mainly by nuns. Gretchen had phoned ahead, though we needn't have worried; we were greeted warmly by a short, round nun with a smiley face and an annoyingly sunny disposition.

'We're here to visit with Father Brennan,' Gretchen announced.

We'd gone over our cover story on the journey: Gretchen was my aunt, Ted her son, my cousin.

The nun beamed. 'You're the lady who phoned. The one whose niece is over from England.' She turned to me. 'And you must be Maggie.'

I channelled my mom, smiling my sweetest smile, prayed she wouldn't go in for a hug (she looked like a hugger).

'Maggie's mom,' Ted said, resting a paw on my shoulder, relishing his character, 'my aunt, was a pupil at St Tom's when Father Brennan taught there.'

'Why, yes, your mom said.' The nun was leading us along a corridor, painted much like all the other old-people-home corridors I'd seen in a sickly shade of peach. She turned to me as we walked. 'He'll be so pleased you've come,' she said. 'He has such fond memories of his teaching days.'

I felt myself blanch.

The nun stopped at the door to what was apparently a communal day room, full of men. Most wore dog collars. Some sat reading, others played chess or Scrabble, a few sat in a horseshoe of armchairs round a TV. This room was painted sunshine yellow and had the most gaudily patterned carpet I'd ever seen. There was the obligatory crucifix on the wall, along with a couple of vases of artificial flowers and some bookshelves.

Ted and Gretchen eyed the group.

'Oh,' said the nun, 'of course. That's Father Brennan, right over there.'

She pointed to an old man alone in a wheelchair, his back to us. Stationed in front of some French doors, facing out onto a garden, head bowed, he was so perfectly still, I thought he must be asleep.

'I'll leave you all to get acquainted,' the nun said. 'I'll be just down the hallway if you need anything.'

I weaved my way over to the window, Ted and Gretchen following, priests nodding in greeting as we passed. I paused for a second behind the figure in the wheelchair, took a deep breath, stepped round to the front and looked down at the man before me.

It wasn't until he raised his head that I realised he wasn't asleep. I wish I could say he looked like a monster, but he didn't. *It was the eyes*, people always say of criminals afterwards. *He had these evil-looking eyes*. But Father Brennan's eyes weren't evil-looking, just rheumy and blue, familiar, somehow, the only recognisable trace of the younger man I'd seen in the photo – that and his height. Although seated, I could see he was tall, but where he'd once been fit and lithe-looking, now he was frail, stick-insect-like, his long legs doubled back on themselves like paper clips, feet resting awkwardly, hen-toed, on the wheelchair's footrests. He looked every one and more of his eighty-something years.

I took a deep breath and kneeled down beside him, my hands on the wheelchair's armrest, Father Brennan's own clasped loosely in his lap.

'Father Brennan?' I said, my face inches from his.

His skin was pale, foxed like old paper, his white hair thinning, a fine shock sticking up on the top of his head like cockatoo feathers. For a second he looked confused, and I had a sudden wave of doubt: could this benign-looking old man have been capable of doing what we thought he had?

'You taught my aunt Margaret at St Tom's,' I said, leaning ever so closer.

Nothing. Not a flicker.

'You may have known her as Minna.'

I could have sworn the faintest glimmer passed over Father Brennan's face, that I saw a barely perceptible tightening of his jaw. Then it was gone. The man clearly wasn't all there.

Still crouched, I turned to Ted and Gretchen. 'This is a waste of time.'

The room felt suddenly stuffy and hot. Too hot. Someone needed to open a window. Why were the French doors closed? I stood up quickly and everything began to spin. I had to get out.

I don't remember anything after that until all of a sudden I was outside, leaning against a wall, palms against rough stone, eyes closed, breathing deeply.

'Are you all right, dear?' came a voice.

I opened my eyes, blinking in the bright sunlight. It was a nun, not the plump one who'd greeted us, but a tiny thing, barely taller than a child.

'Thank you, yes,' I managed, hoping she'd go away.

'Are you visiting?'

I nodded dumbly.

'It can be a bit of a shock when you haven't seen someone in a while.' She gave a sympathetic tilt of her head.

'Oh,' I said. 'No. We'd never met before.'

The nun looked confused.

'I was visiting Father Brennan,' I explained. 'He taught my mom at high school. My aunt, too.'

I wondered if she'd detect the hint of bitterness in my voice, but apparently not, for her face lit up. 'Oh, well, I'm sure he'd have loved that,' she said. 'It's hard for him, you know. Physically he's not in good health, can't get about like he used to. But up here' – she tapped the side of her head and smiled – 'sharp as a tack.'

I opened my mouth, closed it again. Were we talking about the same man?

'Still,' she went on, oblivious, 'it's nice for him to get visitors – not many people come see him these days, except for his nephew.'

'Nephew?' I managed.

'Yes. Lives a couple hours away. Boweridge, I think.'

'Oh,' I said. Did Father Brennan's brother, Jim Brennan, the police chief, have a son? I remembered his online obituary. It had mentioned children, I thought. 'His brother's son?' I asked, unsure why it even mattered.

'No,' the nun said. 'Sister's, I think. Comes maybe once month? Was here just yesterday, actually.'

There was a visitors' book on a table inside the home's main entrance. We'd signed in when we'd arrived. I waited till the friendly nun had left, then, against my better judgement, went back inside.

I found the visitors' book still open at the page we'd signed in on, and flipped to the previous page – yesterday's visitors – hoping I was wrong, that somehow my instinct, which was based on little more than a feeling, was mistaken.

With a shaking finger, I traced down the page, through that morning's entries – *10:47*, *11:06*, *11:31*, and on into the afternoon. Nothing. If only I could get through the rest of yesterday's visitors without recognising a name . . .

I kept going – *12:56*, *13:02*, *13:15* – and then there it was, at 14:02, a name that, when I drew my finger over it, sent a jolt through me like an electric shock.

Mike Freleng.

34

So that was it, I thought, those blue eyes. Mike's mother was Todd and Jim Brennan's sister, the Mary-Anne in the obituary. Father Brennan was Mike's uncle. Why hadn't Mom told me? Why hadn't anyone?

Gretchen and Ted found me leaning against the truck, the hot metal burning my back.

'Christ, Maggie,' Ted said, when I rounded on him. 'You think if I'd known I wouldn't have told you?'

'Honestly?' I crossed my arms. 'I don't know. It's a pretty major thing, though, don't you think? Minna just happened to be dating Father Brennan's nephew. Father Brennan's brother just happened to be heading up the investigation into Sister Fran's death – Minna's disappearance, too.'

Ted appealed to Gretchen. 'Help me out here.'

'He's telling the truth, honey,' Gretchen said. 'None of us knew. Father Brennan and Mike have different surnames, no reason we'd link them.'

'There wasn't even anything in Grandpa's notes about it,' Ted said. 'You've seen them yourself.'

'But isn't that suspicious in itself?' I asked. 'The fact your grandfather *didn't* make a note of it? Why not even mention it?'

'Jeez, Maggie, I don't know.' Ted took off his baseball cap, put it on again. 'Because he didn't feel the need to write it down? Because it was a given that everyone already knew?'

'Ted's right,' Gretchen said. 'Why would his grandpa make a note of something that was common knowledge back then?'

'Besides,' Ted was pacing now, 'Mike wasn't considered a suspect in either case – my grandpa barely spoke with him.'

'But that's just it!' I shouted. 'Mike *should've* been a suspect. I mean, for fuck's sake' – Gretchen flinched – 'couldn't anyone see it? Minna was dating her abuser's nephew. I mean, God! That's not motive?'

'I don't disagree.' Ted puffed out his cheeks. 'But seriously, you think I knew all this time and didn't tell you?'

'Well, you weren't exactly keen on coming here . . .'

'You're joking, right?' He laughed in disbelief. 'I wasn't trying to hide something, Maggie. I was worried about what coming here would do to *you*! I mean, Christ,' he threw up his hands, 'it's unhealthy how obsessed you are with these cases!'

I could tell as soon as he said it that he regretted it, but the words stung all the same. Hadn't Ted been the one who'd said we wouldn't give up? That the clues were out there, we just had to find them? I swallowed the lump in my throat.

'I'm sorry, Maggie, really,' Ted said, shaking his head. 'But you thought coming here would achieve what, exactly? That Father Brennan would take one look at you, see Minna, break down and confess?'

'Of course not,' I snapped, though part of me *had* hoped that. 'But if we hadn't . . . I thought that if we could just . . .' Tears stung my eyes.

Gretchen cleared her throat. 'If we hadn't come here,' she pointed out calmly, 'we wouldn't have discovered that Father Brennan is Mike's uncle.'

I sniffed. '*Or* that he's a manipulative liar.'

Ted and Gretchen looked at me.

'One of the nuns told me,' I said, and suddenly I knew what it was like to be my mom, that thrill of smug satisfaction. '*Physically*, she said, Father Brennan's frail. But up here' – I tapped the side of my head just like the nun had – 'sharp as a tack.' I blinked my tears away, looked directly at Ted. 'Funny, that.'

Ted looked genuinely stunned. 'You think I knew that, too?'

I didn't, not really. Deep down, I knew he was telling the truth. Even so, I shook my head, turned away.

'I don't know what I think any more.'

It was evening by the time we arrived back in Boweridge. The drive had passed in excruciating silence, Gretchen having insisted I ride up front in a failed attempt to force Ted and me to clear the air. I'd left Bob's bike at Gretchen's that morning, so Ted dropped us there. He was due back on shift in less than an hour, but even if he hadn't been, I doubt he'd have hung around.

As I climbed from the car, he leaned across the seat, touched my arm. 'For God's sakes, Maggie, I swear I didn't know any of it.' His voice was soft, pleading. 'You were there. You asked Mike about Father Brennan yourself. Dude lied to our faces – said he'd never heard of him.'

My shoulders dropped. I couldn't make Ted suffer any longer. It felt horrible. 'I know,' I admitted.

Mike Freleng was a liar, just like his uncle.

'I can promise you Ted's telling the truth, honey,' Gretchen said as we watched him drive off. 'I've run that Facebook group for years and it's never come up.' She shook her head. 'Sure would've explained a few things if it had done, though.'

'Yeah,' I said. 'Like how Mike's got away with so much over the years. I mean, it changes everything. We already know he lied about Minna, when he said she'd have been seen by his neighbour if she had been at his that last night: Mom said Minna sometimes took a back route, to avoid being seen. And he failed to mention that he hit her. What if he's a chip off the old block, just like his uncle?'

'So where do we go from here?' Gretchen asked, though I'd no idea if she was talking about Mike, or Father Brennan, or me and Ted.

'Honestly?' I sighed. 'I don't know.'

I climbed onto Bob's bike, but Gretchen stopped me, a hand on the handlebars. 'Please,' she said. 'Take the evening to think things through. Promise you won't do anything you'll regret.'

'Promise,' I said, not meeting her eye.

By the time I reached the end of Mike's street, the air had shifted. It was eerily still. I glanced up at the sky. Looked like rain. At the gate to the Frelengs' front yard, I climbed from Bob's bike and wheeled it up the path, leaving it propped against the porch.

Unlike last time, the front door was shut, so I climbed the steps, opened the screen door and knocked. A minute passed. No answer. I moved to the nearest window, put a hand to the glass and peered inside. It was hard to see, but it looked like another living room, a more formal one. No signs of life, though. I went back down the porch steps and round the side of the house, following a narrow flagstone path that led into a small but surprisingly well-kept back garden. Here the path split in two, one trail leading to the back door, which stood ajar, the other to a gate that opened into the cemetery. I approached the back door first.

'Hello?' I called out, pushing the door inward, peering into the kitchen beyond. 'Mike?'

There were dirty dishes in the sink, empty bottles by the bin. I stood for a minute, listening, then heard a burst of noise, the tinny, high-pitched buzzing of garden equipment, coming from somewhere inside the vast cemetery. I took off down the path and through the gate.

I'd half expected the cemetery to be as neglected as the house, but it was pristine, green and leafy despite the heat, with rows of gravestones – dotted with mausoleums – as far as the eye could see. The noise had stopped, but there was still no sign of Mike, so I left the gravel pathway and crossed between the headstones. Some were laid with flowers, now wilting in the heat, but most had nothing at all. The first mausoleum I came to resembled a tiny stone church, its facade blackened, its once-sharp edges rounded with age. A carved stone cross stood at the apex of the moss-covered roof, beneath which the name *Freleng* was engraved above a metal door, flanked by stone columns. Despite the structure's aged appearance, it looked like it had been lovingly tended: not a weed in sight, grass trimmed neatly on all sides.

It wasn't until I made my way around the other side of the Freleng tomb that I spotted Mike in the distance, working among some gravestones. The sky had turned deep purple, bathing the graveyard in a dusky pink light. As I drew nearer, I coughed, so as not to startle him. He straightened up, looked round. When he saw me, he froze.

'Mike,' I called, 'hi.'

He nodded brusquely at the sky. 'Going to be a storm,' he said, just as the first rumble of thunder rolled in.

He began gathering his tools. There was no sign of the sling from the other day, but his wrist was still bandaged.

'You weren't truthful with us, Mike,' I said.

''Scuse me?' he replied, not stopping, still gathering.

Another rumble of thunder.

'I said,' I said, a little louder, 'you weren't honest with us when we came to see you. You lied about Minna, her last night.'

At the mention of Minna's name, Mike hesitated, then continued flinging tools into an old work bag on the ground.

'You said she didn't show. That your neighbour would've seen her if she had.'

He appeared not to hear me. He was wearing overalls, the top part of which he'd unbuttoned, arms tied round his waist, to reveal a white wife-beater and sinewy tattooed arms. He glanced at the sky, hefted his bag onto his shoulder.

'You not hear me?' he said, as the first fat droplets of rain began to fall. 'There's a storm coming.'

I ignored him. 'Minna used to sneak through the graveyard,' I continued, 'so's not to be seen by the very neighbour who backed your version of events. She was here that last night, wasn't she?'

I wasn't sure what I'd expected – a confession, perhaps – but Mike simply turned and set off, striding so swiftly I struggled to keep up. The rain was heavy now, bouncing off the gravestones, the saturated grass soaking my ankles and feet, and by the time we reached the house, I was dripping wet. Mike pushed through the back door, dropping his bag on the kitchen floor with a heavy clunk. I followed, unsure he was even aware of my presence until he tossed me a towel over his shoulder.

I stood with it in my hands, not moving.

'What d'you want from me?' He took a pack of cigarettes from the worktop and drew one out, cupped his hand around it as he lit it. 'I answered all your questions already.' He inhaled, blew smoke from the side of his mouth. 'Ain't nothing more to say.'

There was an almighty thunderclap, and I jumped. The storm was right overhead, the rain so torrential it reminded me of camping holidays back home, of being in a caravan with Tabby, raindrops pounding the roof like a tin can.

'You hit her, Mike,' I said. I had to raise my voice to be heard over the noise. 'More than once.'

'I loved her,' he responded, like the two things were related.

'Did she tell you she was leaving without you?' A crack of lightning, the kitchen lit up. 'Is that why you killed her?' I was shouting. 'Did you do it alone, or did someone help you? Like your uncle, Mike. Like Father Brennan.'

Without warning, he lunged. I stumbled backwards, landing heavily, cold, wet tile beneath me, Mike above me, his hands round my throat, rough, calloused fingers pressing into my neck. I swallowed and kicked and flailed and tried to call out, but he had me pinned down, was squeezing too tight. There was a humming in my ears, and my vision began to fray at the edges as the world closed in on me. As it did, as I balanced on that fine line between consciousness and unconsciousness – that same delicious one you traverse on the cusp of sleep – the only thing I could think was, *Is this how Sister Fran felt?* Then everything went silent, and that was when I heard it, a little voice in my head: *No!* At least, I thought it was in my head, for it couldn't have been aloud – I was physically incapable – yet at that very moment, like he heard it too, Mike's grip loosened, and I was able to take an almighty gasping breath, and the darkness that until that point had threatened to swallow me receded.

Mike's face, inches from mine, came into sharp focus, an expression on it I couldn't compute – fear? shock? – and with a strength I didn't know I possessed, I shoved him in the chest, hard, and he flew backwards. I heard the thwack of him landing as I scrambled to my feet, slipping and stumbling, but I didn't pause – didn't even look – I just ran, out the back door and through the rain to where Bob's bike, soaking wet, was still propped against the porch. My legs were too jelly-like to even climb on, so I grabbed the handlebars and continued running, pushing it alongside me, weaving like a madwoman along the street, as far away from the Freleng house as possible, not slowing or stopping to draw breath.

It wasn't until three, maybe four blocks later that, panting and soaked, I finally allowed myself to slow to a walk, but still I didn't look back.

35

Adrenaline carried me home. Other than my shaking legs, I hadn't felt a thing, not at first, but now my whole body ached and I was exhausted in a way I'd never been before. I'd snuck through the house and down to the basement, inspected my neck in the bathroom mirror, lifting my chin, tipping my head side to side, to see the lurid pink marks branded across my throat. Eventually, unable to look any longer, I'd gone to the laundry room, found one of Bob's old hoodies to put on. I'd drawn the strings at the neck as tight as I could bear and, though it wasn't even 9 p.m. yet, had fallen into bed fully clothed, curled up beside my mobile. I'd hoped that Ted would call, but he hadn't. I wanted desperately to call him, tell him what had happened, but the thought of him scolding me for going to Mike's – *You did what?!* – or, worse, not picking up at all, was too much to bear. I lost count of the number of texts I started composing to him but was too cowardly to send.

The storm continued into the night. In what felt like an endless cycle, I drifted in and out of sleep: I'd jolt awake, check my phone, listen to the thunder and rain, think about Mike. I went over and over it in my head – what exactly had triggered his reaction? Everything had happened so fast, it was hard to know for certain, but the more I thought about it, the more I was sure the catalyst was not my accusation that he had killed Minna, but the revelation that I knew Father Brennan was his uncle. But what did that mean? Was he simply angry at my discovery, or was it something more? Did he have such a deep hatred of his uncle he could hardly bear to hear his name? If so, why continue to visit him? And *did* Mike have anything to do with Minna's disappearance?

At one point, still before midnight, I awoke, groggy and delirious, and logged into Facebook in case Ted had messaged (he hadn't), only to find another message from Simon:

> You are aware you have a deadline? You can't keep doing this, you know, not when you're in your write-up year. There are only so many strings I can pull for you, Maggie. You do know that, don't you?

After that, every time I closed my eyes, began to drift off, I'd see Mike's face bearing down on me, feel his hands around my throat. The darkness would close in, then I'd hear the voice – *No!* – and my vision would return, but this time it was Simon's face before me in sharp focus, Simon bearing down on me, Simon's hands around my neck . . .

I awoke the next morning in yesterday's clothes to find a missed call on my mobile and the voicemail symbol blinking. I'd hoped it might be Ted, but it was an unknown number, and all I could hear of the message was crackle and white noise. A butt dial, most likely.

In front of the bathroom mirror, I pulled down the neck of Bob's hoodie and winced. The finger marks were turning purple, my neck puffy and swollen. Unable to stomach even the thought of food, I was in the kitchen making coffee when the doorbell made me jump. Bob wasn't around – his car was gone – and Mom was nowhere to be seen, though I could hear the TV in her room. I called to her, waited to see if she'd materialise, and when she didn't, I answered the door.

I was surprised to see two uniformed policemen standing there. The older one looked exactly like I'd expected Ted to: middle-aged, balding, moustachioed and paunchy. All that was missing was the doughnut.

'Ms Elmore?' he said. 'Maggie Elmore?'

'Yes,' I said. I felt suddenly self-conscious. My hand went involuntarily to my throat, brushed against the tender skin, pulled the neck of Bob's hoodie tighter.

'Can we come in?'

'Would you mind telling me what it's about first?' It was a question I'd only ever heard people ask cops in films.

'I think it'd be better if we come inside,' he said.

I looked from him to the younger cop, but the younger one glanced away. My stomach knotted, but I stood aside and let them in. Both wore Boweridge PD baseball caps like Ted's, the older one removing his as he stepped through the door. Wiping his brow, he handed his cap to his younger counterpart, then produced a notebook and pen from his shirt pocket.

'You, uh, you know Mike Freleng?' he asked.

The knot in my stomach tightened. Had Mike reported me for turning up uninvited yesterday, for accusing him of killing Minna?

'Yes,' I admitted. There was no point in lying if they already knew. 'At least, sort of.' Were they going to warn me off, tell me not to go near him? *Just get it over with.*

'How do you know him, ma'am?'

'He knows – knew – my aunt. I don't know him well, though. I mean, he was at my grandma's funeral, but . . .'

The cop scribbled something in his notepad, then, without looking up, said, 'So that was the last time you seen him, the funeral?'

'I saw him yesterday, actually, at his house. But look, if you could just tell me—'

'May I ask what the nature of your visit was, ma'am?'

I squirmed a little. 'Just a catch-up, I guess.'

'And about what time was that? Morning? Afternoon? Evening?'

'Evening.' I considered. 'I think I got there, maybe, like seven, seven fifteen?'

'And how long were you there? What time did you leave?'

'I'm not sure.' Wait. I remembered checking my phone when I got back, seeing the time. 'Eight thirty,' I said confidently. 'I was back here just before eight thirty.'

The older cop nodded, kept scribbling. Then he stopped, looked up, eyebrows question marks. 'And how did Mr Freleng seem to you, ma'am?'

'Like, his mood, you mean?'

He didn't answer.

'Well, uh, okay, I guess . . .'

'Uh-huh, uh-huh.' He dropped his gaze, scribbled some more.

This was unbearable. Did they know what had happened? Was this all a test to see what I'd confess? I'd done nothing wrong, though – Mike had attacked *me*. But what if the police were protecting him, like they'd protected his uncle? I was beginning to wish I'd phoned Ted.

The cop looked up again. 'And you've not spoken to Mr Freleng since?'

'Nope.'

He narrowed his eyes. 'You sure about that?'

'Course I'm sure.'

His gaze dropped to his notebook again. 'So,' he said, without looking back up, 'we've got Mr Freleng's phone records for last night . . .'

Huh? I wrinkled my nose. Why would they have Mike's phone records?

'Says here' – he licked his finger, flicked back a couple of pages – 'Mr Freleng placed three calls after you left last night. First was to a number in Cape West, around nine p.m. Second, a little after that, his girlfriend, Cindy. And the third, well, the third was to a UK cell, just before two a.m.'

'No.' I shook my head, confused. 'No, he didn't call me. I've not spoken to him since—'

The cop cut across me, 'His phone records say otherwise, ma'am.' He proceeded to read out a long number. My mobile number. 'You sayin' that's not your cell?'

'Oh God, yes,' I said, suddenly remembering. The missed call. The nonsensical voicemail. 'Someone called me during the night. I only realised when I woke up this morning. I didn't have Mike's number, though, so I'd no idea it was him.'

'You sayin' you didn't speak with Mr Freleng?'

'No.' I shook my head again. 'Not when he called.'

'Funny . . .' The cop chewed the end of his pen. 'Log showed the call lasted forty-two seconds.'

'Oh,' I said again, feeling silly. 'Right. There was a voicemail. I listened to it this morning, but it was just a load of noise, so I deleted it.' *Lying to the cops, Maggie*, I scolded myself. *Nice one.* 'My phone's downstairs.' That was a lie too. It was in my pocket. I shifted, feeling its weight against my leg, a guilty secret. 'I can get it if you want to check?' I said a silent prayer the policeman wouldn't call my bluff.

'Thank you, ma'am,' he made another note, 'that won't be necessary.'

I breathed a quiet sigh of relief. 'Look,' I said, 'if you can just tell me what this is about, then maybe I can—'

'Mike Freleng was found dead this morning,' the cop said bluntly.

I let out an involuntary gasp. 'Mike's dead?' My mind scrambled to remember – the thwack after I'd pushed him as he'd – what? Fallen? Hit his head? *Oh my God, he hit his head. I killed him!*

'Suicide,' said the cop. Behind him, the younger officer shifted nervously, removed his cap like a belated sign of respect.

'Suicide?' I felt so sick with relief that my legs almost buckled, then I felt guilty for feeling relieved. Mike was dead. Shit. 'How . . . how did he . . .?' The question wouldn't form.

'Looks like he took a loada pills. Washed 'em down with a bottle of cleanin' fluid and some Scotch.'

My blood ran cold.

'We'll know more when the medical examiner finishes up.'

'And this was last night?'

'Uh-huh.' The older cop took his cap from his colleague, pulled it back on. 'Girlfriend found him this morning, called it in. Reckon it happened sometime between two and four a.m.' He narrowed his eyes at me again, my face burning under the weight of his scrutiny. 'Right around the time he called you.' He arched an eyebrow. 'So you can see why we wanted to check.'

'Uh, of course,' I said. Everything seemed to narrow in front of me, like I was looking through a pinhole, and for a moment I felt Mike's hands around my neck again. 'Did he . . . uh, did he leave a note?'

'Not that we've been able to find. Not everybody does. Mr Freleng had liver cancer, you know?' The cop's voice sounded far away, like I was underwater.

'Uh, no, no, I didn't,' I barely managed.

'Yeah. Seems his days were numbered.' He clicked his tongue, shook his head. 'Still, real nasty way to go.'

I managed to hold it together until the cops left, but after I closed the door behind them, I leaned against it, slowly slid to the floor. I felt dizzy, so I rested my head on my knees, tried to process everything I'd just learned. *Mike had killed himself.*

In the safety of my basement room, I took out my phone. I should call Gretchen, I thought, let her know. But first I had to swallow my pride and call Ted. I swiped a shaky finger across the screen, but before I could dial, something stopped me: the tiny symbol still blinking in the top corner. I hesitated, my finger hovering over the keypad; then, against my better judgement, I dialled voicemail.

'You have one new message,' the robotic voice stuttered. 'First new message sent yesterday at one fifty-seven a.m.'

Then, just as I'd thought: nothing. I strained to hear. Some rustling, background noise, the sound of the storm. Thank God. A butt dial after all.

But then I heard it, and I almost stopped breathing. About thirty seconds in, through the crackling and the static, the sound of heavy, ragged sobs. Then, barely audible, two small words, full of pain and anguish. Full of regret.

'I'm sorry.'

36

I'm sorry.

The words haunted me. I'd listened to them over and over; sat on the bed for almost half an hour replaying the message, hoping every time that I might make out something else, something that would convince me I'd misheard, that Mike's words weren't what they appeared to be. But I couldn't. Instead, the more I listened, the clearer they became.

I'm sorry.

After that, I'd called Ted and Gretchen. Ted had picked up on the first ring, come straight over. The news about Mike was all round the precinct. 'Jesus,' was all he said when I told him about the voicemail.

I couldn't remember the last time I'd eaten, and Ted had just come off shift, so we went for breakfast and I told him what had happened at Mike's.

'That son of a . . .' he muttered through a clenched jaw when, gingerly, I pulled down the neck of Bob's hoodie, showed him the marks. He reached out as if to touch them, then thought better of it, drew his hand away.

'I should've been there, Maggie,' he said, shaking his head. 'I wish you'd called me.'

'I know,' I said. 'Me too.'

'What I said yesterday, about you being obsessed with the cases—'

I held up a hand. 'We both said stuff we didn't mean,' I said; then, desperate to change the subject, 'You know, despite what he did, I feel bad. I can't help thinking that if I hadn't gone there . . .'

'You can't blame yourself,' Ted said. 'Guy had issues. You know he had cancer, right?'

I nodded.

'He was on borrowed time, had probably just had enough, wanted to go on his own terms.'

'I guess,' I said. 'But what if his suicide *was* linked to my visit?' Ted opened his mouth to reassure me some more, but I stopped him. 'No, hear me out. I don't mean I'm blaming myself, though I kind of am. What I mean is, Mike called a Cape West number after I left last night. It must've been Father Brennan. Then, later on, he phoned me, left the voicemail. What if my visit *did* precipitate his suicide, because he *did* have a guilty conscience?'

Ted made a face. 'I'm listening . . .'

'What if we've got it the wrong way round?'

'Got what the wrong way round?'

'Well, what if it was Mike who killed Sister Fran? What if he knew about the abuse, so he killed her to protect his uncle, stop it from coming out? And what if Minna knew that he'd killed Sister Fran – she was his girlfriend, after all, they'd've talked – so Father Brennan got rid of *her* to protect Mike? Minna had been going round town telling people she knew who killed Sister Fran. We've assumed all along she meant Father Brennan, but maybe she didn't – maybe she meant his nephew. After all, Mike was never looked at for Sister Fran's murder, and vice versa: no one thought of Father Brennan for Minna's disappearance because there were never really any suspects – everyone just accepted she'd run away.'

I stopped, waiting for Ted to respond, dismiss my theory outright, but instead he rubbed his chin, said, 'I guess it's possible . . .' and I felt a fresh spark of hope. He sipped his coffee. 'Far as I know,' he said, 'Mike was never interviewed about Sister Fran, so we've no idea if he had an alibi for her murder. Same with Father Brennan and Minna. But a no-body homicide charge is almost impossible. How do we prove it? That's the problem.'

'I don't know,' I said. 'But I do know where we go next. Look.' I passed him my phone, showed him the Facebook message I'd received that morning from Deirdra Hinkle-Schroeder:

Hey Maggie, yeah that's me. My dad owned Don's Diner in '72.

Want to meet after I finish up at work today? DeeDee

Work, it turned out, was DeeDee's Ice Cream Parlor, the place Ted and I had visited on our first evening together, the one on the former site of Don's Diner. How hadn't I made the link? I wondered, as we pulled up outside a little after 7 p.m. It had the look of somewhere getting ready to close for the day, but there were more signs of life than last time: blinds drawn but slatted open, lights still on. Inside was empty and quiet: no customers, no music playing, just the hum of fridges – the largest, a long glass and chrome display counter, full of rows of colourful ice creams – and at the far end, a woman sweeping the black-and-white chequerboard floor. She looked up as we entered.

'Hi,' I said. 'We're looking for DeeDee?'

'That's me, hun,' she said, straightening up, propping her brush against the counter. 'You must be Maggie. I saw your post in the Sister Fran Facebook group after you messaged me. You're Minna Larson's niece, right?'

I nodded. 'Did you know her?'

'Most people knew Minna, hun.' It was said without malice. 'But no, not personally. She was a couple years older than me. Summer she vanished, I was only fifteen.'

That made DeeDee early sixties. She was petite, with a shiny mahogany-coloured bob and a deep smoker's voice that belied her size. Though not in a bad way, there was something about her – her small frame, her lined face – that reminded me of Mom, which would have horrified Mom but was probably more an insult to DeeDee.

'We'll talk out back,' she told us after I'd introduced Ted and she'd offered us coffees. 'I could do with some fresh air and a smoke.' She said it without a hint of irony.

We followed her behind the counter, through the kitchen and out a back door into a small yard, the one we'd glimpsed the first time we came here. Despite the heat, I felt a chill at the thought that the space in which we now stood had once formed part of the parking lot in which Sister Fran's body was found. But there was no parking lot now; to even call it a yard was generous. It was a strip of tarmac really, bordered by a tall fence and rows of giant wheelie bins. A couple of diner chairs stood by the open kitchen door, which DeeDee eschewed in favour of standing, despite complaining, 'God, my feet are killin' me.' One chair held an ashtray. DeeDee slung her server's apron onto the other, untying it from round her waist with all the relief of someone released from a corset, but not before removing a lighter and pack of cigarettes.

After the *Fckn armchair detective* comment on Facebook, I'd been a bit wary about meeting her – I was, after all, an armchair detective myself – but as so often with Facebook, appearances can be deceptive: just as DeeDee's voice belied her small stature, the don't-mess-with-me impression created by her Facebook post belied a more genial nature.

'You own this place?' Ted asked as she lit up, took her first drag.

She nodded, lips puckered round her cigarette, the tiny vertical lines surrounding them deepening. 'I know, right?' she said through an exhale. 'Miracle it wasn't razed to the ground decades ago. I'm tellin' you right now, if there was a nuclear war, there'd be roaches and this place left.'

'You inherited it from your dad?' I asked.

'God, no. Dad sold up in '73. Guess the sucker who bought it struggled on till all this . . .' She tipped her head at the houses beyond the fence, blew a trail of smoke in their direction. 'Been everything in the years since: nail salon, coffee house, dentist's office . . .'

'How come you got it back?'

'Dewey – my brother – he owned a trailer park up north. Left it to me when he passed.'

She stopped, took another drag, and I shot Ted a look: *Dewey's dead.*

'Anyways,' DeeDee went on, 'this place was up for sale, so I sold the trailer park, used some of the money to buy it.' Her eyes narrowed at me through a haze of cigarette smoke. 'Your message said you're looking to track people down from the diner back in the seventies?'

'Seventy-two,' I clarified, then added slowly, 'June 17th specifically.'

'Ah.' She wrapped an arm around her middle, rested the elbow of her cigarette-holding hand on it. 'The Sister Fran case.'

'We'd been hoping to speak with Dewey,' I said, 'but obviously . . .'

'Yeah, you're a couple years too late, hun.' DeeDee smiled sympathetically.

'And the other customers that night?'

'Too late for all of 'em, God rest their souls.'

My heart sank. '*All* of them?' I pictured the list of names in Detective Hoppy's notebook: *Don, Dewey, Joe, Old Joe, Earl, Burt, Lonnie.*

DeeDee nodded matter-of-factly. 'Cancer,' she replied. 'The lot of 'em. 'Part from Lonnie, the cook. He had a whaddya call it – brain aneurysm? And Burt,' she added. 'Burt died in a yachting accident. That's what his folks liked to call it, anyhow.'

Ted, leaning against the wall, looked doubtful. 'A yachting accident?'

'Yeah.' DeeDee laughed her gravelly laugh. 'Came outta a 7-Eleven one night, drunk as a skunk. Was crossing the street. Got hit by a truck towing a yacht.'

I pictured the list of names again, imagined a pen strike through each of them. 'There's no one left from that night?'

'Nope,' DeeDee said, flicking her cigarette into the ashtray. 'No one 'part from me, that is.'

'What?' I thought I'd misheard, looked at Ted, could tell I hadn't. 'You were there – *here* – the night Sister Fran was murdered?' I asked. 'At the diner?'

Ted gave a sceptical eyebrow-raise, said to DeeDee, 'There's no record of it.'

'Wouldn't be,' DeeDee replied, with a shrug that said she didn't really care whether Ted believed her or not. 'I was home before the police arrived.'

'Wait,' I said. 'Rewind. How? Why?'

'School was out for summer,' said DeeDee. 'My mom was out of town that Saturday, visitin' with family, so I'd gone to the diner with Dad and Dewey.'

'You were there when Sister Fran came in?'

'Sure was. It was twenty before eleven. Door flies open, in she barrels, looking kinda harassed, y'know? Like maybe she was running late? She looked around like she was expectin' someone, then left again, not a word to anyone.'

'She didn't say hi?' DeeDee went to St Tom's, after all. 'I mean, you knew her, right?'

She nodded. 'Taught me high school English.' She shrugged again.

'But she was in such a rush, so wrapped up in . . . well, whatever, doubt she even noticed me.'

'Did you see where she went when she left?'

'Back out to her car, I guessed, but you couldn't see the parking lot from inside the diner.'

'Did you see a car leaving?' Whoever killed Sister Fran must have fled the scene somehow.

'Don't think so.' DeeDee thought, tapped her cigarette on the ashtray. 'The parking lot was pretty huge, though, a big ol' piece of scrubland. You could access it from either side of the diner, so you *could* see cars as they turned in from – or out onto – the road, but you'd have to be payin' attention, lookin' for 'em, 'specially at night.'

'And Sister Fran's body was found at what time?' Ted asked, just checking.

'Quarter after eleven. That's when all hell broke loose.'

'You didn't hang around, speak to the police?'

Another shrug. 'Wasn't really my choice. I was supposed to've been home by ten, but Dad forgot. He knew he was gonna be in all kinds of trouble letting me stay out so late, but now there's a dead body involved?' She shook her head. 'I was real shaken up, too. I mean, my favourite teacher, dead, in the parking lot?'

'How'd you get home?'

'We didn't live far, so Dad drove me. Police took time getting here, so he was back before they arrived.'

'And afterwards, no one thought to mention that you'd been there?'

'Dad didn't want me involved. I was fifteen. A girl. Things were like that back then. Besides, wasn't like I saw anythin' the rest of 'em didn't.'

'The timings that night,' I said. 'How can you be so sure of them?'

'Burt – he found Sister Fran's body – was a creature of habit, left the diner same time every night. Plus, I guess they knew what time the call was placed to the cops. As for the time Sister Fran showed up . . .'

DeeDee stopped, sighed. 'Well, business wasn't good since the new highway opened, routed traffic round the other side of town. Dad had just looked at the clock, said he was shutting the kitchen for the night, when Sister Fran blows in like a hurricane. It was ten forty exactly.'

It sounded pretty concrete.

'You said you thought she was meeting someone,' I said.

DeeDee nodded. 'Sure looked like it.'

'Any idea who?'

'Nope. There was no one else in that whole evenin' – not apart from the regulars.'

'And other than being in a rush, how did she seem?'

'Normal, I guess. Not, like, frightened or anything. Stressed, maybe. It was all jus' so weird. Like, you know when you're only used to seein' someone one place, so when you see 'em somewhere else, outta context, it's kinda strange?'

'Maybe it was because she wasn't wearing her habit?' I suggested.

She shook her head. 'Sister Fran didn't wear her habit much – not at school, anyhow – so it wasn't that. I guess it was more just, I dunno, like it looked like she'd made more of an effort – had on this long skirt and button-down shirt, a flowery one, all pinks and reds. Skirt had buttons down the front, too. Yeah, she looked real pretty.'

'That's a lot of detail,' Ted said.

'It's not every day your favourite teacher's murdered,' DeeDee pointed out. 'Dewey used to tease me, say I never stopped talking about her, that I was all *Sister Fran this, Sister Fran that*. But *all* the girls loved her. She was special, y'know? What happened to her jus' wasn't right.' She stopped, sighed. 'I think about it all the time, that night. Like, what would've happened if Sister Fran had seen me? If I'd said something – *anything* – when she came in? I keep thinking that if she *had* seen me, stopped to chat, she might still be alive.'

*

Later that evening, after Ted dropped me home, I found Mom in the living room pretending to read. Though I hadn't mentioned it to Ted, there was something niggling me about our conversation with Dee-Dee; I just couldn't work out what.

'What was Sister Fran wearing that night?' I asked Mom.

She looked up from her book. 'Good evening to you too, darling.'

'The night Sister Fran came by the house to speak to Minna. That last night. Do you remember what she was wearing or not?'

I wasn't sure why I was bothering – Mom gave nothing away for free – so I was surprised when she put her book down, looked like she was genuinely considering. Maybe she was just tired of the endless games and petty bullshit; or maybe she sensed it was important, bigger than both of us.

She closed her eyes. 'Definitely a skirt,' she said, opening them again. 'And a shirt, a button-down one, patterned. Flowers, maybe?'

Back in my room, I rooted in Detective Hoppy's box until I found the ME's report with its inventory of Sister Fran's clothing and belongings. I reread it. There was her purse, with her driver's licence, pocket book and a small amount of cash, and her car key. Then there was her clothing: sneakers, socks and underwear, shirt and pants. I stopped, reversed, skim-read the list again, pausing when I hit the bit that read: *plain blue shirt, tan pants*. No mention of a patterned shirt in pinks and reds. No skirt. Come to think of it, Ted had said something about Sister Fran's trousers – something about dirt or grit stuck to the leg.

To double-check, I dug out the crime-scene photos – the ones showing Sister Fran's body. She was definitely wearing trousers; a shirt, too, but a plain one. No flowers. Could DeeDee have been mistaken? Possibly. But my mom, unprompted, had said the same thing. Could she and DeeDee both be wrong? And if they weren't, what did it mean? Was it possible that in the time between entering the diner and her body being found, Sister Fran had somehow changed her clothes? But where? Why? And if she hadn't, did that mean the killer had done it? Some kind of ritual, perhaps? A sick game? And all in a thirty-five minute window, in a dark, dusty parking lot.

I wanted to quiz Mom some more, but it was late, and by the time I went back upstairs, she'd gone, the living room in darkness and the house so quiet that at the sound of the doorbell I jumped. Afraid that it was the police again, I tiptoed across the room and peeped through the window, but there was no cop car, just a beaten-up old truck, driver's door open, headlights on, idling at the end of the driveway. I moved to the front door, took a deep breath and opened it. Standing before me was a woman, gruesome-looking in the porch light. It took me a second to place her, but I realised it was the same woman Ted and I had almost collided with as she stormed from the Freleng home the first time we visited Mike. Was this Cindy, the girlfriend the cop had mentioned? She stank of alcohol, her hair was askew and her make-up looked like she'd slept in it.

Before I had a chance to speak, she shoved an envelope into my hand. 'Mike phoned last night,' she said. 'Asked me to make sure you get this.'

Then she was gone.

I closed the door and stared down at it. *Maggie* was scrawled across the front. I hurried back down to the basement and, with shaking hands, ripped open the flimsy envelope. Inside was a bundle of papers – a letter – pages and pages of lined A4, handwritten on both sides. There was no return address, just the previous day's date. The day Mike killed himself.

Maggie, the letter began. *I'm so sorry*.

And in that instant, I knew Minna was gone.

37

Maggie,

I'm so sorry. There's no easy way to tell you this. I've started to write this letter a thousand times. Not to you. Not to anyone especially. But maybe it was always meant for you, and maybe this is how it was always meant to end, for me.

It's hard to know where to begin, but I should probably start by saying that what I told you about me and Minna – that we were planning on running away together that last night – was true. See, earlier that day, Minna had packed a rucksack, thrown it from her bedroom window into the bushes by the front door to collect after she left, so she wouldn't be seen leaving with it. What your grandparents told the cops – that she left home around 7 p.m., never returned – was also true. So was your mom's description, the one she gave the cops of Minna's clothing. Only thing she missed was the claddagh ring I gave her, the one I'd had engraved: *Mike & Minna always.* You know what a claddagh ring is, right? Two hands holding a little heart with a crown on top? If you're single, you wear it with the point of the heart facing outward. But if you're taken – like

Minna was – you wear it with the point facing inwards. Towards your heart.

Back to that last night, and maybe you've already worked this out, but my mom wasn't home that evening. She lied to the cops after, to protect me. I lied too: Minna did show that night – cut through the graveyard so our nosy old neighbor never seen her, just like your mom said. Plan was we'd get our stuff together and jump in my car, leave town for good. But things went south pretty quick after Minna arrived, and we'd gotten into it. It wasn't nothing physical – honest – just shouting and arguing, some pushing and shoving. I mean, hands up, yeah, I'd hit her before – a bunch a times – the last time given her a black eye. But that was an accident really. Well, not an accident, but you know what I mean – just a slap across the face, but harder than I'd meant. I felt bad, obviously – hitting girls is wrong, I know that. And I'm not trying to make excuses – I hated when my dad hit my mom – but what you have to understand is that Minna knew how to push my buttons. And this isn't me trying to jus-tify shit, but honestly? I think she liked to make me mad. See, I'm not a violent person, but push anyone enough and they'll react. You know that thing they say about not poking the bear? Well, that was me – the bear – and Minna would prod and poke and pick till she got a reaction.

But however bad things had gotten in the past, that last night there was just this tension between us there'd never been before. Gasoline vapor, waiting for a match to ignite it. Minna said something about Barb, like how it killed her abandoning her little sister without telling her, like we hadn't already been over that shit a hundred million times, like I'd not already promised her Barb could come live with us once we were settled, just so Minna would agree to go. And then I brought my mom up – like, I hate the thought of leaving her too, but we both gotta make sacrifices, right? Well, that was a red rag to a bull.

See, my mom and Minna had never gotten along. 'Your mom thinks the sun shines outta your ass,' Minna would say, rolling her eyes. 'She thinks you can do better than me.' I'd tell her not to take it so personal – that's just moms and their sons' girlfriends, right? I mean, Mom hadn't liked my brothers' girlfriends either – hated their wives. And you understand, I'm not trying to make excuses for my mom. But she hadn't had it easy. Like, when my dad was around, everything was okay. Sure, he had a temper, drank too much, cheated on her, but he took care of shit. Then one night he was out driving and his car veered into the path of a truck. He died instantly. After that, Mom wasn't the same. The melancholy spells she'd always suffered from got worse. My brothers didn't stick around, so all the anger Mom previously focused on them and my dad? Well, I was all she had left – she directed it at me. She blamed me for all her shit, would tell me I should never've have been born; that I was just like my no-good father; that it was my fault he was dead, that my brothers left . . . I could go on, but you get the picture. Despite everything, though, I loved her. I mean, that's my blood – you know how it is. But shit like that can really screw a person up.

For a time, life was hard to bear, but seven years after Dad passed, Minna came along, an angel from heaven. But ever since we'd come up with our plan to leave, I'd lain awake at night worrying how Mom would cope on her own. I mean, I seen the way she went to pieces over Dad, but back then, she still had me. Who'd keep the cemetery once I was gone? Who'd keep an eye on the bills, the finances in check? Yet I knew there was no other way, and even if Mom didn't understand – and she wouldn't – in time she'd come to see it had all been for the best. See, thing was, Minna was becoming more vocal about my uncle – not Uncle Jim, the police chief, but Uncle Todd, the priest. You know him as Father Brennan. I guess you'll have figured it out by now – what people said was happening at St Tom's, what my uncle was supposedly doing to Minna, those other girls – but Minna was threatening to tell.

At first I'd thought that if we could just leave Boweridge, start afresh, everything would be okay. But then Minna announced she'd been thinking about shit, like what would happen when Barb started at St Tom's. Just the thought of my uncle coming into contact with her little sister paralysed her with fear, which is why I'd caved over Barb in the first place, promised she could join us. But that wasn't enough, and I began to wonder if the whole thing wasn't just a test, another of Minna's games, like whose side would I pick if it came down to it – hers or my mom's? Was it less to do with my uncle and more to do with my mom? In the end, I decided to let her think whatever she wanted, long as it meant she'd keep her mouth shut. Not that I was happy about what she said my uncle did to her, you understand, nor that I didn't believe her – not exactly – but with Minna it was hard to know how much of it was true. All I knew was if any of it came out, it'd destroy both my uncles and my mom. Yes, end of the day, the choice was clear: leaving would be hard on Mom for a while, but if we stayed and the truth about Uncle Todd came out – well, it just didn't bear thinking about. So I guess what I'm trying to say is that Minna thought we were leaving to spite my mom, when really it was to protect her.

Anyways. Back to that night, and Minna had gone to cool off while I loaded the car. I'm packing some extra stuff in her backpack when I feel this little rectangle of plastic, like a cassette tape. I take it out. It *is* a cassette tape. There's this strip of paper wrapped round it, and when I open it out, it's got IRIS HILLENBERG written on it – just like that, all caps – in Minna's writing, and I'm like, huh? But then I seen what's written on the label on the tape – FATHER TODD BRENNAN – and I'm all, wait, what the . . .?

Right then, Minna comes back into the room, sees me with the tape, and her face just falls. She's trying to act all normal, like everything's fine, but we both know it isn't. She asks what I'm doing – why I'm going through her stuff – and I thrust the tape at her, say something like 'The fuck's this?', more aggressive-sounding than I mean, and Minna – probably more defensive than she means – says, 'What's it look like, dummy? It's a cassette tape.' I take a deep breath, try to keep my cool. 'I can see it's a cassette tape,' I say. 'But what's it for? It's got my uncle's name on it.'

And that's when I know, right, 'cos soon as I mention my uncle, Minna turns white as a sheet. She must've forgot about the label, forgot she'd wrote his name on it, 'cos she holds her hands up, like, okay, okay, don't get mad, smiles at me, the smile she knows I find hard to resist, tells me: 'Your uncle murdered Sister Fran.' Says the words like they're poison. 'That tape has the evidence.'

Well, I'm blindsided, but Minna just shrugs it off, swears she was gonna tell me, that she's just been waiting for the right time – after we'd left . . . once we'd crossed the border into Canada . . . she isn't sure. Reason she hasn't told me before now, she says, is 'cos she knew I'd react like this – unreasonable, angry. 'Can you blame me?' she asks.

But I'm not really listening. *Your uncle murdered Sister Fran.* I'm stuck on those five words. And that's when Minna makes her first mistake: she laughs at me. Actually laughs. Scornfully. At least, I thought she was laughing at me and I thought it was scornful, but now, when I think back, I'm not sure. Maybe it was just a nervous laugh. Problem was, then and there, I didn't have time to think – couldn't think – 'cos Minna won't let me, won't shut up, is saying, 'Mikey, baby,' in that tone she always uses to get her way, the one I'm powerless against but perversely love, the one that now gives me the sudden urge to smack her in the face. 'You must've known?' She tilts her head, pouts. 'I mean, like, everyone in town does.'

I shake my head. No! Like, sure, my uncle's done stuff, awful stuff. But murder? I look at the tape again, then at Minna, feel so dumb. Is she bluffing? After all, everyone knows Minna lies. Is this just another of her tales? And then it comes to me. 'My uncle's got an alibi.' I say it all triumphant, but Minna only shrugs, says, 'Apparently not,' pulls this whatcha-gonna-do-about-it face. I ask what she means – stuttering like an idiot – but she kinda just shrugs again, says something about witnesses and cops screwing up the timeline – 'Your uncle even says so.' I ask her exactly what my uncle said – whether he actually admitted murdering Sister Fran – if she knows for sure it's him on the tape, and she looks at me like I'm stupid. 'Listen for yourself,' she says, so I fetch my own cassette player, put the tape in – it's all the way at the end – press rewind.

It's agony waiting for that tape to rewind, Minna talking the whole time, telling me in detail about the stuff my uncle done to her. I mean, deep down I guess I'd always known, but hearing the words come out of her mouth, well, no one wants to hear that about their girlfriend – it's a real sucker punch.

From the start, she tells me, she's been convinced my uncle murdered Sister Fran. Just the week before, she'd confided in her about my uncle, the abuse. Now Sister Fran's dead. But Minna wasn't dumb: she knew her suspicions alone weren't enough. Who'd believe her? Minna lies, right? Plus my uncle had an alibi. So she hatched a plan.

Sister Fran was murdered on the Saturday. By Sunday, word was all round town; papers full of it Monday. My uncle was running summer school gym classes at St Tom's, so that same Monday, Minna had snuck into school, hidden in his office. It wasn't hard, she said: school was out, deserted. I'm not sure she even knew what she hoped to get outta it – overhear a confession, I guess, or something incriminating – but just like she knew her suspicions alone weren't enough, her overhearing something wouldn't be neither. She needed proof. Something watertight. And that was where your mom came in, Maggie. See, your mom had gotten one of these cassette players. Guess it'd be kinda old-fashioned now, but back then, it was pretty ace. What was really neat about it, Minna said, was that it could record stuff. She'd borrowed it a couple weeks before, like she so often borrowed stuff – just because. Now she'd found its purpose.

My uncle had a closet in his office. I guess it was for gym clothes, school shit, but Minna told me he also used it for the girls – he'd shut them in it after he was done with them. A place for contemplation, she said he called it: somewhere they could think about how wicked and sinful they were. And that was how she knew there were others, that closet – some of them had scratched their names inside the back of it. When my uncle left Minna there, she'd sit tracing her finger over the letters till she knew them by heart.

So that Monday, Minna hid in that damn closet with the tape recorder, sat there till her butt went numb. In her mind, I guess she expected it to play out like some Hitchcock movie: the plan, the sting, the smoking gun. Bad guy gets caught. Goes to jail. But real life ain't like that, and that first day nothing happened. My uncle was in and out the office, sure, but there was no one else about, no idle chit-chat or gossip to overhear. No confession. So next day she snuck back into school, this time with a copy of the *Herald* from the day before, made sure to leave it front and centre on my uncle's desk, headline blaring: BOWERIDGE NUN SLAIN IN DINER PARKING LOT. But, see, Minna figured the newspaper alone wasn't enough, so she done a little editing to it, borrowed one of your mom's crayons – bright red – scrawled, WE KNOW!, just like that, big old capital letters above the headline, wrote *we*, not *I*, to fox my uncle – make him think more than one person was involved, so he wouldn't suspect her.

So there she is, back in the dumb old closet, listening to the sounds of the gym class through the open window. It's real warm and stuffy, the cupboard door only open a crack, and she must've nodded off, 'cos when she woke, the noise from outside had stopped – the sports class had finished – and she only just had time to press record before the office door opened.

Remember Minna's telling me all this as I'm waiting for the tape to rewind? Well, just as she finishes, right that second, the cassette player clicks off – rewind done – and I look at her, and she looks at me, asks, 'What are you waiting for?' And I press play.

At first there's a whole lotta nothing. Well, not nothing. Noise. A door opening and closing. Shoes squeaking across a floor. The clink of a glass – a whisky glass, probably – a chair scraping back. The flick-flick of a lighter. Then paper rustling, and I reckon this musta been when my uncle seen the newspaper. Then silence – I pictured him staring down at it, wondering what to do, finishing his cigarette – followed by the noise of a telephone receiver being lifted, the whir of the dial. In my mind I seen him sitting at his desk, whisky glass in one hand, telephone receiver in the other. Ashtray in front of him, stubbed-out cigarette still smoking. Like I was there. That's how, I guess, I remember the telephone conversation that followed on the recording so well.

It was my uncle spoke first: 'Sister Loretta? Yes, yes, Father Brennan here.' A pause, then, hissed, 'You don't understand – I'm telling you, someone knows!'

Silence while the person on the other end of the phone – Sister Loretta – spoke.

Then, 'Yes.' My uncle again. 'I did have an alibi – do have one.' Another pause. 'I don't know either!' A loud thud, probably my uncle slamming the desk with his fist. 'The witnesses – they must've got the timing wrong.' More silence – Sister Loretta speaking; another thud – my uncle slamming the desk again. 'I know! I was just so angry. Sister Francesca threatened me. I went to the diner to have it out with her, got there a little before ten, saw her across the parking lot. Something just came over me. It all happened so fast. I lost control. I . . . I . . . I hit her, then . . . then I strangled her.'

I shut off the tape. Felt sick. If this came out, it would all be over. My family would be destroyed. It'd kill my mom. But Minna didn't care. Like a dog with a bone, she won't let up, says, 'Now d'you believe me?' I don't answer. My mind's spinning. 'So you're planning on, what – blackmailing him?' I say at last, and she claps back, 'Jesus, Mike, don't be so dumb!' She must know she's pushing her luck, yet she goes on, says she's going to mail the tape to a journalist, the one whose name's on the piece of paper, the one who wrote the *Herald* articles. I ask her why she has to send the tape at all – we're leaving, she doesn't have to deal with Father Brennan anymore; Sister Fran's dead, mailing no stupid tape won't bring her back! But she says it's about right and wrong, says Father Brennan oughtta pay for what he's done; that he's still abusing other girls. That he won't stop. Besides, she says, she's gone to too much trouble getting the confession not to use it.

Well, I've heard enough, tell her she can't send the tape, that's an end of it, but she just cocks her head, says, 'Uh, excuse me?' I repeat – still calm, still reasonable – 'You can't send it,' and she throws up her hands, goes, 'Oh my God! This is about your fucking mother, isn't it?' And I swear I ignore the bait – swear – just keep repeating, 'You can't send it. I won't let you.' But me and Minna are as stubborn as each other and neither of us is backing down, and she shouts, 'You won't let me?' and lunges at me, shrieks, 'Give me that!', grabs the tape right outta my hand. So I tell her – I warn her – say, 'You're not listening,' but she can't just drop it, says, 'Oh yeah? Maybe *you're* not listening!' and I says, 'I mean it, Minna. I won't let you destroy my family.'

That's when she looks right at me, like suddenly she knows, and for the first time I seen fear in her eyes. She takes a step back, and I take one forward, and that's her second mistake: showing weakness. But it's a good thing, really: means she's backing down, makes me think I can reason with her, make her see sense. So I tell her, 'You win.' I say it calmly, hold up my hands. 'I picked you,' I say. 'We're leaving. Together.'

But instead of agreeing, she hesitates, takes another step back, reaches the bottom of the stairs. There's nowhere to go. She looks at me, pleading, says, 'Mike, don't you see? This isn't about me. It's not about you, either, or your mom. It's your uncle.

What he did to me – to us, the other girls. Those who came before. The ones who'll come after.' She's almost crying now. 'Barb . . .' she whispers, right as I step forward, reach for the tape. 'Give me it,' I say, and if she only had, everything would've been fine. But she doesn't. Instead she looks at me with absolute hatred, spits, 'You're just like him.'

Her third and final mistake.

I didn't mean it. I need you to know that. It was an accident, really. I don't know what came over me. I mean, like I said, I'd hit her before. Sure. But this time was different. This time it was like people describe – a switch flipping, the red mist descending. You have to understand: Minna was threatening my uncle – my whole family. Everyone has a breaking point, right? Well, Minna found mine, was prepared to ruin everything. I couldn't've stayed with her if it had all come out. You get that, don't you, Maggie? Like, why couldn't she just be satisfied? Why did she always have to push?

In the split second I lunged at her, her words rang in my ears. *You're just like him*, she'd sneered, or I was pretty sure she'd sneered, but now, when I lie in bed unable to sleep, haunted by her face, replay it in my mind – like that damn tape in the cassette player – I'm not so sure. Maybe she didn't sneer at all. God, I don't know. Perhaps it was only fear, that twisted look on her face, and all I done was prove her point. I *was* just like my uncle.

I don't remember much else. I think I blacked out. In the months after, bits started coming back to me in flashes. I'd grabbed Minna, hit her – that was one. She'd fought – another. She'd scratched me – I remembered that, too – but I'd only gripped her tighter, shook her, grabbed her by the throat. At some point she'd fallen awkwardly – another flash – head striking the edge of the wooden stair with a sickening crack, snapping backwards like she'd been hit by a car. Then she was completely still. I tried to help her – you have to understand. I begged her to come back, shook her some more, prayed she'd wake up – you've no idea how I prayed. But it was no use.

Afterward, I'd covered her beautiful face with a towel to give her some dignity. Then I drunk some whisky from the stash in my room, to make me feel better, but all that did was make me hate myself more, made me think of my mom, how she'd tell me I was a no-good drunk, just like my father. Still, I'd sat on that bottom step, drunk the best part of the bottle before passing out. I'd come round, gotten sick, passed out again. And I guess that was how Mom found me when she'd gotten home late that night, slumped at the bottom of the stairs next to Minna.

Mom took control, of course. She'd slapped me round the face to wake me, marched me to the kitchen sink, forced my head under the cold faucet till I begged her to stop. Next she took the whisky – what was left of it – emptied it down the plug hole. Then she sorta half carried half dragged me into the par-lour, sat me on a chair. She'd kneeled in front of me and I'd flinched, sure she was gonna hit me, but she'd taken my face in her hands, said, 'My baby,' over and over, shaking her head. 'What did she make you do?' I'd broken down right then, fallen sobbing into her arms, but she'd shaken me off, prized my hands away. She never was one for self-pity. She was furious now – her temper always could turn on a dime – furious at the position I'd gotten her into; furious I'd been so weak and stupid. I'd gotten that from my father, she'd told me, as I cried. He was weak and stupid. I didn't know what to do – didn't know what Mom wanted me to do – so I told her I'd go to the police, but that only made her more mad. Was I going to throw my life away all because of that little madam? Minna was bad news from the start, Mom said. She'd tried to tell me, but I wouldn't listen. That came from my father, too.

Mom never did ask what happened that night. Guess she didn't want to know. End of the day, it didn't make no difference – Minna was dead. Far as Mom was concerned, she knew everything she needed to: it was Minna's fault. After I was done crying, she'd wiped my face, kissed my forehead tenderly. What would she do without me? she'd asked. If I confessed to killing Minna, I'd go to jail. It'd bring shame on the family, destroy our good name. But more than that, it would leave Mom on her own. She'd have no one. How would she look after the cemetery?

And so I agreed, and together we fixed it. We fixed it so there was no trace of Minna left: cleaned the hallway – the vomit, the spilled whisky, Minna's blood – wrapped Minna in a sheet, cleaned more blood from the stair. After dark, we carried her through the graveyard to our family's mausoleum, heaved her into a sarcophagus, stuffed her rucksack in after her, me whimpering like a baby the whole time, Mom tutting in irritation. I remember the sheet we wrapped her in coming loose, flinching at the feeling of her cold skin, still tan in the moonlight. I remember her looking the same but different – that was almost unbearable – reaching out to brush her long blonde hair from her face, make her neater. I remember her beautiful brown eyes glinting dully in the dark, dried tears glassy in their corners. And then I remember leaving her all alone, sliding the heavy stone coffin lid closed so no one would ever know.

Outside, after it was all done, I got sick some more, this time into the long grass that edged the mausoleum. Mom looked on in disgust, then turned and headed back to the house.

You know, I desperately wanted to keep something of Minna's to remember her by, but Mom wouldn't let me. There couldn't be anything that'd raise suspicion, she said, nothing tying me to Minna that evening. Minna was flighty, unreliable, she kept reminding me (even though she was dead, Mom couldn't pass up an opportunity to insult her). It'd be no stretch of the imagination for people to think she'd skipped town. The fact she hadn't gotten along with her parents, Mom assured me, only added weight to that theory. She probably wouldn't even be missed.

If what happened that night affected my mom, I never seen it. Aside from what she told the police – that she'd been home with me all evening, that Minna didn't show – we never spoke of it again. I never told Mom what I knew about her brother, Uncle Todd, and in return – an unspoken pact – Mom would take my secret to the grave. I visited my uncle in his retirement home up till the last, but I never forgave him. I blame him for everything. Problem is, though I know all his secrets, he knows mine, too. See, turns out my mom didn't take my secret to the grave after all; my uncle's held it over me ever since.

I want you to know, Maggie, I'm not a monster. I loved Minna – maybe too much. What happened that night has haunted me my whole life. I've been running from it ever since. It finally caught up with me when I saw you that first time, at your grandmother's funeral. Maybe, if you hadn't've come along, things might've been different, though somehow I doubt it. You see, Boweridge is like a waterlogged sponge, soaked with secrets. And living with secrets takes its toll.

At some point, they always come seeping out.

Forgive me.
Mike

38

I realised I was still standing in the spot where I'd first opened the letter. I'd no idea how long I'd been there, how long it had taken me to read it. I looked up from Mike's words and the room shifted around me. I put a hand out to steady myself, the pages bunched between my fingers, the envelope still with them, and that was when I felt it: something else inside, tiny and light. I upended the envelope, tipping it into the palm of my hand; then, realising what it was, let it drop like it was scalding. It hit the floor and bounced, rolling in a spiral, coming to rest at my feet. It was a silver ring, which, although too small and dainty for a man, I recognised as the one I'd seen Mike fiddling with on his pinkie finger as we talked – a heart clasped between two hands, topped with a crown. A claddagh ring. *Mike & Minna always*, the inscription read.

So he had defied his mother and kept something after all.

After that, I called Ted. He, in turn, called Gretchen, and they came straight round. Mom and Bob appeared, awoken by the commotion, and reluctantly I told them everything. Mike's letter was taken and bagged – evidence – and the police were dispatched to the Freleng property. Ted put the call in himself. I wanted to go, to be there when they carried Minna from her resting place, but Ted wouldn't let me. He'd be there, he assured me, would make sure everything was done as it should be.

I stayed up all night. At a little after six in the morning, Ted called to say, unofficially, that they'd recovered Minna's remains from the Freleng tomb, just as Mike's letter had said. She still had to be identified, though I didn't ask how – DNA, dental records, I wasn't sure: her remains were little more than skeletal. She was still clothed, the arms of her plaid shirt tied loosely round what would have been her waist. Her rucksack was there too, though there was no sign of Mom's cassette player, the one Minna had borrowed but never returned. Who knows, perhaps she'd thrown it in a dumpster after she'd got Father Brennan's confession; maybe she'd sold it – money for her and Mike's trip?

But at the bottom of the rucksack was a cassette tape.

39

'I just remembered,' said Ted. We were on the phone, wrapping up our call, Ted still at the Freleng property, me in Mom's basement. 'I heard back from the adoption people.'

'Oh?' I'd forgotten I'd even asked. With everything going on those past few hours, it was the last thing on my mind. 'Anything useful?'

'Hang on a sec.' I heard muffled conversation, could tell he was speaking to someone, his hand over the mouthpiece. 'Sorry,' he said, back with me. 'Where was I? Right. So as we know, Boweridge's convent also housed the orphanage. The orphanage part closed before the convent did, in the sixties; records were turned over to the local adoption agency.'

'So?' I said.

'So, it took a couple calls, but I was able to get copies of the records. Turns out Sister Fran had a twin.'

'You're kidding. Boy or girl?'

'Girl. Identical.'

I was sitting cross-legged on my bed, Minna's yearbook open in front of me. As we talked, I flicked through the photos of the St Tom's teaching staff. I could barely look at Father Brennan's. Sister Fran's, a couple along, was the same one I'd seen so many times – the one from the news articles and Gretchen's Facebook group, the one from Ron Hoppy's notes and Edith Pepitone's room. She was beaming, her dimpled smile lighting up the page. It made me think of Joy – how different she'd looked as a young nun; how different she'd looked with her hair covered – and how I'd never actually seen a picture of Sister Fran without her veil. But, I realised with a start, I had. *She'd taken over the running of the student newspaper.* That was what Gretchen had said. I hurriedly flicked through the yearbook until I came to the page on the *St Thomas Aquinas Gazette* and its student press pack. And there she was, the picture captioned, *Students hard at work preparing the week's edition of the St Thomas Aquinas Gazette!*, the fair-haired young teacher helping the student journalists. Sister Fran. No habit or veil, wearing normal clothing.

'Maggie?' came Ted's voice at the other end of the line. 'You still there?'

'God, sorry,' I said. 'I was miles away. You were saying, about twins.'

'Sister Fran's twin,' he said. 'Her name was Flora. The family that adopted her . . .' he paused, took a breath, 'their name was Peterson.'

And that was when it dawned on me: the adoption; Edith Pepitone's apparent coldness at her daughter's death; the letters Sister Fran had been receiving; the late-night diner meeting; the missing crucifix; the discrepancy in the descriptions of Sister Fran's clothing that last night; the downtown apartment. The half-photo of the baby. The dimpled smile.

The letters to Iris every year.

40

When she opened the door and saw us, she looked surprised yet resigned.

'What should we call you?' I asked.

I was standing right in front of her, Gretchen behind me.

She almost looked relieved. 'You can call me Fran.' The woman we'd known as Flora Peterson stepped aside to let us in. 'How on earth did you work it out?'

It was, she told us, a relief to finally come clean after all this time. She'd lived with the burden of her secret – the guilt over her sister's death, Minna's disappearance – for almost fifty years. Unlike those who were convinced Minna had simply skipped town, Fran could only hope that was what she'd done.

'I prayed every day,' she told us, 'that Minna was happy, settled somewhere with a good job, a kind husband, children. I prayed she was loved.'

I swallowed the lump in my throat and glanced at Gretchen, who gave a single shake of her head. Now was not the time to disillusion her. That would come later.

'So I guess you've figured it all out,' Fran said once we'd settled back in her living room.

'Pretty much,' I agreed. Gretchen looked less certain, so I said, 'But tell us anyway.'

'It all started in '72,' Fran began. 'I'd known Minna a while – had taught her English, worked with her on the school newspaper – but that year, the year I was her form tutor, I'd gotten to know her better. At first, it was just little things that told me something wasn't right, like how easy she'd startle, how she'd flinch if anyone touched her. I got the feeling she wasn't happy at home – didn't get along with her parents – but when I asked her about it, she said everything was fine.' She paused. 'But then I began noticing the bruises. They were hidden for the most part – the tops of her legs, her arms – but I'd catch sight of them. Then, a couple weeks before school's out for summer, she shows up with a black eye. I kept her back after class that day, asked her about it – felt sure she'd tell me this time – but just as she was about to reply, the classroom door opens and *he* comes in – Father Brennan. This look passes between him and Minna, and suddenly – don't ask me how – I knew. I knew what he was doing to her. There was an awkward exchange – he asked if I could spare Minna to help him with something; I said no, made some excuse – and after he'd left, I asked her again if there anything she wanted to tell me, but the moment was lost. She clammed up.'

'So the story you told us,' I said, 'about finding Minna on the highway that night – her confiding in you about the abuse, you telling Hoppy – that wasn't true?'

'Yes and no,' Fran said. 'I never spoke with Detective Hoppy, never even met him.'

So that explained why there'd been nothing in Hoppy's notes, I thought. Ted's instincts were right.

'See,' she went on, 'I was the one who sent you the anonymous letter telling you to find me – well, Flora Peterson. The first time we met, when you asked me who I thought might have written it – and

I realised you knew about the letters to Iris – I had to make you think there was someone else out there who knew what Minna had confided in me, so you didn't suspect *I'd* written it. If you did, it would've been obvious I'd written the other letters – the ones to Iris – that there was more to my story. I wanted to help, to tell you what I knew – as much as I could, anyhow – without giving away my true identity.'

Gretchen's jaw dropped, but I just nodded. I'd figured as much.

'Me finding Minna on the highway, though,' Fran continued, 'well, that was true. I mean, obviously I wasn't a St Tom's alumnus working nights at a gas station; and it didn't happen after the murder – *my* murder – it happened a week before, before school was out.' Gretchen looked confused, so Fran said, 'I'm sorry. I'm not explaining myself very well. Look, I think maybe, in order that everything makes sense, I should tell you about my sister.'

'Your identical twin,' I said.

Fran nodded. 'Flora.' She smiled sadly. 'I guess for the time, our story wasn't all that unusual: born out of wedlock to a too-young Catholic mother. She had no choice but to give us up. Flora and I were raised by nuns for the first part of our lives, though I've no memory of it – I was adopted within a few months. But Flora – well, poor Flora, she remained in the orphanage until she was six. And when she eventually found a home, it wasn't a happy one.'

I thought of the half-photo of the baby that Travis Eavers had given us, the one his dad had found at the apartment. I slipped it from my bag, passed it to Fran. 'Is this your sister?' I asked.

Fran's mouth made an O shape. 'Flora's adoption photo,' she said. 'They pinned her half on her file, my half on mine. Other than the clothes on our backs, it was the only thing we left the orphanage with when we were adopted.'

'Hang on,' Gretchen said. She stood, crossed to the array of family photos she'd admired on our last visit, picked one up – a silver-framed black-and-white photo of a baby. She gasped. 'It matches this one.'

Fran joined her, held the half photo I'd just given her alongside. Apart from the fact that one was framed, they were mirror images: two identical babies, side by side, dressed in matching outfits.

'I was my adoptive parents' only child,' Fran said, sitting back down. 'I was very much loved. But Flora was never close to her parents. They had biological children of their own; Flora said she was made to feel different, an outsider.'

'So when did you discover you had a twin?' Gretchen asked. '*How* did you discover?'

'Spring '72,' Fran said. 'I received a letter from Flora. You can imagine what a surprise it was: I'd no idea I even had a sister, let alone a twin. I'd been so content with my life it'd never entered my head to look into my past, track down my birth family. Flora and I began corresponding. She lived out of state, but before long, she wrote saying she was moving back to Boweridge. I was thrilled, but . . .' she hesitated, uncertain, 'I also couldn't help but be leery. See, I hadn't told another soul about my sister's existence – not my friends, family. I couldn't wait to meet Flora – it wasn't that – but I knew from her letters that her life had been tough: she'd been estranged from her adoptive family for years, moved around a lot, struggled to put down roots, keep a job. Now she wanted to start afresh in Boweridge. She was looking for a job, had gotten herself a car, put down the deposit on an apartment, but still, I worried it'd all be too much for her – that she'd get cold feet – so I decided to wait till she was properly settled before I told anyone about her.'

'But that time never came,' I said.

She nodded. 'The night of the highway incident, I was driving to meet my sister for the first time when I came across Minna. She told me she'd been out with her boyfriend, that they'd argued, that she'd told him to stop the car, had gotten out. Well, I couldn't just leave her on the side of the road – she looked awful, was clearly intoxicated – so instead of going to meet my sister, I took Minna to a diner just like I said. She told me everything: about the abuse; the closet he'd make them sit in after he was done; the tennis shoes he'd leave outside his office door as a signal – the one I and the other sisters knew meant he wasn't to be disturbed.' She shuddered.

'So after that, you confronted Father Brennan?' I asked.

'Yes. What I told you the first time was true – Minna had tried telling her parents, but they wouldn't listen. I knew the police wouldn't do anything, so I slept on it a few nights then, on the last day of term, went to Father Brennan's office, made it clear to him that either he went to the archdiocese, told them everything, or I would.'

'And the following day,' I said, 'the night of the murder, you dropped by Minna's house to tell her.'

Fran looked surprised. 'Yes. How did you . . .?'

'My mom saw you, though she never told anyone.'

'I remember,' Fran said, as though it was all coming back to her. 'She was up on the porch.'

'That night,' I said, 'the night everything happened, you were on your way to the diner to meet your sister.'

Fran nodded wearily. 'After that first time – when I'd run into Minna on the highway, stood my sister up – we tried again,' she explained. 'There was a payphone near the convent, and one just by the laundrette where Flora was living, so we'd fix a date and time by letter to chat on the phone. It was during our last call that we arranged it –ten p.m. Saturday night, Don's Diner. It was kind of late to meet and a bit of a trek for me, but it seemed a good idea to go somewhere out of town. I left the convent right after evening prayer that night, but on the way, I detoured, stopped by Minna's to tell her the good news – that she didn't have to worry any more about Father Brennan.'

'But you stayed too long.'

'Minna was in the garden, so we sat on the swing set, talking. I meant to stay no more than five, ten minutes, but things got pretty intense, and by the time I left, it was more like forty-five. I knew I was going to be late. I drove across town as fast as I could, but it was twenty before eleven by the time I got there. Flora was nowhere to be seen inside. I guessed she'd just got fed up, thought maybe she'd be waiting in her car, so I ran back out into the parking lot to look for her.'

'And instead you found her body.'

'Yes.' Fran's eyes filled with tears. 'It was the first time I'd seen her since we were babies. It was so strange looking down at her body – *my* body – on the ground. She was . . .' she faltered, collecting herself, 'she was still warm. I checked to make sure that . . . that she wasn't breathing, but I could tell she was gone and somehow I just *knew* Father Brennan was to blame, that he must have mistaken my sister for me. Problem was – and I didn't know this till later – the fact that I'd been seen alive at the diner after ten thirty gave a false time of death, and Father Brennan a false alibi.'

'Right,' I said. 'Brennan was safely back in Boweridge by half ten.'

She nodded. 'The thing I couldn't work out was how he knew I was going to be at the diner in the first place.'

'You'd written it on a scrap of paper,' I explained, 'left it in your room. Sister Joy found it, gave it to the reverend mother, who must've told Father Brennan. He phoned the convent just after you'd left that evening, wanting to speak to you.'

If I'd thought Fran might be angry at Sister Joy's indiscretion, I was wrong. Instead she smiled fondly. 'It figures. Sister Joy always did have trouble keeping secrets.'

'So after you found your sister's body,' asked Gretchen, 'what did you do?'

'I made a decision,' Fran said, 'one that would change my life for ever.'

'You took Flora's identity,' I said.

'It sounds crazy, I know.' She shook her head. 'Sure, Flora was a little slimmer than me, her hair slightly longer, but we were identical in every other way. I worked quickly, swapped our purses, car keys, driver's licences – everything. The only thing I couldn't swap was our clothing – I just prayed no one would notice.'

No one did, I thought, except DeeDee. I nodded at Fran's shirt front. 'And your necklace?'

Her hand went instinctively to her neck, lifted a small silver cross from beneath her shirt. 'My parents gave it to me. I couldn't bear to part with it, so I kept it, figured if the police realised it was missing, they'd think it was lost or stolen.'

'And the letters from your sister? Detective Hoppy didn't find them when he searched your room.'

'I had them with me that night, so I kept them too,' Fran explained, 'switched them to Flora's purse. That was how I knew where to go – Flora's address was on the back of the envelopes. It was pretty simple, really: I left my car in the parking lot, took Flora's. I drove straight to her apartment, spent a couple hours just pacing, wondering what to do, then called my parents from the payphone.'

'Your parents *knew*?' Gretchen looked aghast. 'All this time?'

That explained Edith Pepitone's apparent indifference to her daughter's murder. Of course Edith didn't want the murder investigated properly, or feel the need to have the killer caught: she knew Fran was still alive, was protecting her.

'By the time I called, my dad had already identified the body, so when my parents heard my voice on the other end of the phone, well, they thought they were talking to a ghost. They had no clue I was a twin – the sisters at the orphanage hadn't told them. Once they'd calmed down, I told them everything. That was when we hatched a plan. Mom stayed home while Dad drove across town, met me at Flora's. It was early morning, still dark, so we cleared the apartment – destroyed all my letters to her – then loaded Flora's car with a few belongings, left some money for rent. And that was that: my father waved me off. I can still see his face in the rear-view mirror . . .' Fran stopped, blinked away tears. 'I drove as far from Boweridge as I could, and over the next few weeks, my mom and dad withdrew their savings bit by bit, sent the cash to me, wherever I was, till I got settled. It sounds paranoid now, but for the longest time I lived looking over my shoulder, afraid Father Brennan would somehow figure out what had happened, come looking for me. There were so many people helping him – protecting him – I didn't know how far that network extended, or who it involved. Every time I even *thought* about coming back to Boweridge, something pulled me to my senses – like when my parents told me Ron Hoppy had died. Everyone thought it was suicide, but, well, I just couldn't risk it.'

'So when did you learn about Minna going missing?'

'A few days after I left town, right after she vanished. I wasn't sure where I was headed, or when I'd see my parents again, so I phoned home and they told me. I felt guilty, of course, but I felt in my heart that Minna had run away because she thought I'd been murdered. You know,' she said, tears in her eyes again, 'I actually felt relieved. She was free.'

Gretchen and I looked at each other.

'So where did you go?' Gretchen asked.

'I continued north, but I never stayed in the same place too long. Not for the first few years, anyhow. I know what you're thinking,' Fran added. 'You think I was selfish, that I abandoned Minna, never looked back. You'd be right: if it had only been about me, I might have made a different decision that night; I might have stayed. But it wasn't just about me. There's something I haven't told you. Something I'd only just found out before that awful night, something that changed everything.'

'You were pregnant,' I said.

41

It was Uncle JJ who took me to the airport. Not my mom. Not even
Bob. Greg came as well, and Gretchen and Ted. We piled into two
cars, stopping by the cemetery on the way. Not Holy Cross, the one in
which Minna had lain for so long, but a different one: the one we
chose as her final resting place.

At the airport, I said my farewells to JJ, Greg and Gretchen outside the terminal, after they'd insisted – I got the impression it was
a done deal before we even got there – that Ted alone should see me
off inside. It was awkward, in a good way, saying goodbye to someone I'd got to know well over the past few weeks yet barely knew at
all. Ted was overdue some holiday, he told me as he waited with
me in the check-in line. He'd always wanted to visit England, see
the sights.

'I'd like that,' I told him, and I meant it. We left it at that.

I'd originally been due to fly home the day after Gretchen and I met
with Fran, but in the end, I'd stayed a few extra days. I wanted to be there
when they released Minna's body so I could attend her funeral, so I took
Uncle JJ up on his offer, uprooted part way through my extended stay
and went to his and Greg's. Mom took it surprisingly well.

But before I cancelled my flight, rebooked it, left for my uncles', there was something else I had to do. I logged into my uni email account and opened the drafts folder. It was Simon's last email that had cemented my decision.

Do you know how much I've done for you? No one will believe you.

No one will believe you. But for that one sentence, I probably wouldn't have even looked at it again, the email I'd written weeks ago, the one headed *Formal complaint*, beginning, *It is with regret . . .* But for that one sentence, I probably wouldn't have clicked send.

I'd hoped to see Fran again before I left, but it didn't pan out. She'd told us that day that she'd never married, never had another relationship. It was all just too complex. The summer Minna vanished, Fran had begun her life anew. A few months after leaving Boweridge, she gave birth to a baby girl.

'As my daughter grew older,' she said, 'she began to ask questions. I told her that her father died before she was born. Guess it was just easier that way.'

Fran and her daughter saw her parents sporadically over the years, though not as often as she'd have liked. Fran couldn't risk returning to Boweridge, so the Pepitones travelled to see her, wherever she was in the country. But as her parents grew older, it became increasingly difficult, and it was Edith's move to Shady Nook that finally cemented Fran's decision.

'I had to return,' she said simply.

Her daughter was grown, had children of her own: twins, it appeared, ran in the family.

'So it was Fran who wrote you the anonymous letter?' Uncle JJ had asked as we made our way to Minna's graveside.

'Yeah.' It was a beautiful afternoon. Bright blue sky, gulls circling high overhead. 'She saw my post in the Sister Fran Facebook group. Mom's address wasn't hard to find.'

'And she wrote the ones to Iris, too?'

I nodded. 'She was desperate to keep her sister's case alive. I mean, God, can you imagine? Writing to someone every year – almost – on the anniversary of the murder?'

'And the missing year?' Greg asked.

'Fran's daughter got ill – like, *really* ill. It was the only year she didn't write.'

'But why not just come forward?' he asked. 'Fran knew Father Brennan wasn't just an abuser, but a murderer too. She was the only one who could blow his alibi apart.'

'She was torn,' I explained. 'She wanted him to pay, didn't want her sister's case to go cold, but she'd started a new life. She had to stay safe for her daughter's sake.'

'And Gil Griffin?' said JJ. 'He's no idea he has a daughter, that Fran's still alive?'

I shook my head. Gil had no idea of either.

'Jeez.' He let out a low whistle.

'I guess she'll tell him when she's ready,' I said, though I knew Fran hadn't yet decided if – or how – she would. Having had no contact with him for over forty years, she was conflicted, and although he would eventually find out one way or another, Gretchen and I were sure, it wasn't our tale to tell. One tale we *did* have to tell, however, was to let Fran know what had become of Minna. That story was due to break imminently – the press were already sniffing around – so it was better that she heard it from us first. I say 'us', though I'm ashamed to admit I left Gretchen to shoulder that burden alone: when the time came, I couldn't bear it and had to leave the room.

*

Mom didn't come with us to the cemetery – hadn't attended Minna's funeral either – but that was okay. I spent the last night of my extended stay back at hers, out of a sense of duty more than anything, and we'd stayed up the whole night talking.

'You know the real reason I found it so hard to forgive Minna for leaving?' she'd asked.

I hadn't replied, though I was afraid I did know.

'Because it left me at *his* mercy,' Mom answered, and I knew then that she meant Father Brennan, that Minna's worst fears had been realised.

Even though I was half expecting it, it was still a bombshell. Once Mom started at St Tom's, the cycle began all over again. It continued, she said, till she was eighteen, when she'd met a dashing British man, had a shotgun wedding. Eight months later, my sister was born.

I never told Em, of course, as I never knew for sure; but even if I did, I still wouldn't have said anything. Now, though, every time I look at her bright blue eyes – the eyes I so envied, as I thought they came from Dad – I can't help but wonder. Although I still hate it, I've never again complained to her about being compared to Mom; never whined, *It's all right for you, you're nothing like her.* I no longer begrudge Dad loving Em that little bit more, either. Knowing what I know now, it would seem unfair.

The last thing I did before I left Mom was to give her a letter recovered from the bottom of Minna's rucksack and addressed to *Barbara*. I guess Minna had intended to post it once she and Mike reached Canada. I never asked Mom what the letter said and she didn't tell, though I hope whatever it was brought her comfort.

As for Father Brennan, the abuse happened too long ago. There's a statute of limitations on sex crimes; he would never be charged. But there's no statute of limitations on murder.

'What happens now?' I'd asked Ted.

'Father Brennan's been picked up. He'll be charged with Flora's murder. But he's old.' Ted shook his head. 'Whether he'll even make it to trial . . .'

In some ways, it didn't matter. What mattered was that Minna had told the truth. Soon, everyone would know. Iris had come out of retirement. Together she and Lo were writing a piece on the whole convoluted story: *The Summer She Vanished: how one girl told a truth her small town wasn't ready for. Almost fifty years later, the world is finally listening.*

Lo hadn't yet returned to New York, though she'd never been more in demand. She was finally writing the kind of pieces she'd always wanted to, the kind that mattered. Susan Turner's siblings had been in touch, asked her to tell their sister's story. This time, it would not be buried.

As for Iris, well, she was content to take a back seat. 'I'm too old for all that,' she'd said with a smile.

The cemetery we'd chosen as Minna's final resting place was on the coast.

'Minna loved the sea, did you know that?' Fran had said when I last saw her, and I'd shaken my head – something else I hadn't known about my aunt.

She was buried on a bluff overlooking the ocean, under the shade of a tree. Perfect, really. We laid fresh flowers and stood together – me, Gretchen, Ted, JJ and Greg – a motley crew at her graveside, the earth around it still freshly dug. Gretchen hugged me and I didn't protest. Minna would have liked it here, I thought. Framed by the sea, the place was so beautiful it needed little else but the simple headstone and inscription:

*Minna Lies
Here*

Epilogue

Barbara, 2019

Barb hadn't attended Minna's funeral – some people just weren't built for that kind of grief – but a few days after, the day after Maggie flew home, she found herself, supported by Bob, at her sister's graveside. Someone had laid flowers recently, probably Maggie, though they'd already wilted in the heat. It was nice here, Barb thought, the bluff under the shade of a tree, its view out over the ocean. Minna loved the sea.

There was a wooden bench nearby and, feeling a little overcome – the heat, probably, she thought – she took a seat. As Bob pottered nearby, hands in pockets, not quite sure what to do with himself, Barb opened her purse and took from it the envelope Maggie had given her, the one addressed to *Barbara* in Minna's hand, seven familiar little letters in neat cursive script that sent a jolt through her every time she looked at it. Though she'd had it in her possession a few days now, she hadn't opened it yet – hadn't been able to bring herself to. But as she sat there on the bench, she felt a sense of peace she'd rarely felt before, one that took her back to her childhood, to before Minna vanished, before Mike came on the scene. Before Father Brennan.

With a deep breath, she opened the envelope, slid the single piece of paper from inside and began to read.

June 22nd 1972

Little Barb,

By the time this letter reaches you, I'll be long gone. You'll probably have guessed, but me and Mike have left Boweridge. For good. One day I'll explain everything, but right now, all you need to know is that I'm safe, that I'm mailing this letter from wherever we've ended up. Who knows how long it'll take to reach you, but when it does, you have to swear you won't tell anyone – not Mommy (especially Mommy) or Daddy. Not even the boys.

I'm sorry I left without saying goodbye and I know it's tough right now, but one day, when all this is long behind us, you'll see it was for the best. I love you more than anything, which is why, in part, I had to do it, even though leaving you is the hardest thing I've ever done. Once we've found work and a place to stay, you can come live with us. Promise. I mean, I know you don't like Mike, but that's because you've never really gotten to know him. Sure, he has a temper, but he's smart and funny and kind (and real handsome). And he loves me.

You know what, Barb? I just remembered. I did borrow your cassette recorder. I meant to give it back before we left but forgot. Sorry. But when you come live with us, I'll get you an even better one! You probably won't need it, though, as – unlike Mommy – I'll let you listen to whatever you like on the radio (we'll have a swell radio!), even Donny Osmond. Promise.

Anyways, little Barb, I gotta go. Look after the boys (especially JJ), don't miss me too much, and remember, I'll see you someday soon . . .

Love always,
Your big sister Minna xoxo

As Bob looked on from a distance, concerned, though knowing it was best to allow his wife some space, Barb wiped a tear from her eye. So Minna had taken the cassette recorder after all. She smiled – typical Minna. That summer, the summer she vanished, had been a scar that never healed. But this, right now, maybe this helped. Just a little. Maybe that was enough.

A warm breeze sprang up, and Barb let go, watched Minna's letter soar upwards, over the bluff edge and out to sea, flitting and dancing with the gulls until it was no more than a speck in the distance.

Acknowledgements

I have to start with my agent, Marina. I know every writer thinks they have the best agent, but I really do. Thank you, Marina, for being supportive, perceptive, diplomatic and an all-round good egg. I'm not fatalistic at all(!), but the stars truly aligned when I found you.

To my wonderful editor, Bea, and the Headline team. I'm beyond thrilled to be part of the Headline family and so excited to find out what the future holds. Bea, thank you for not only being a great editor, but also for being patient (incredibly so), insightful and kind.

Thank you to Will and the team at New Writing North: your support and encouragement has been invaluable. After many years of writing without success, Northern Writers' Awards not only opened so many doors, but gave me a much needed confidence boost when I was close to giving up on my writing dream. Thank you Helen, Kathryn and the team at Cornerstones. Without your feedback on my first manuscript all those years ago, I'd never have had the confidence to start a second. Helen, you've been incredibly generous with your time and advice since then, sharing your knowledge of the industry. Likewise, to Aki, Joe, Nelima and the team at TLC: without the wisdom, support and encouragement of agencies like you, far fewer writers would make it. Thank you for everything.

Thank you to all the agents who took the time to give me advice and feedback over the years, even if most of it went hand in hand with rejection. Thank you also, Julia Silk. I'm not sure if you'll remember, but you kept me company while I waited at an agent-meet in 2016. I was so nervous, and your kindness that day meant a lot.

To my family. Thank you to my parents for fostering in me a love of reading – even if it took until my twenties for me to realise it! – for all the bedtime stories (and story tapes – how old school!), and for encouraging creativity. Thank you Mum and Fi for all the manuscript reads, and for telling me not to give up. Fi, you were right: no one gets their first novel published.

Thank you, Kristin, for being a great cousin and an even better friend. Our chats mean so much to me. Let's always make time for them.

Finally, to the Katie Kerr ladies: Katie, Ann, Marjorie, Karin, Deryn and Janet. I've never been surrounded by such a smart, strong, stylish group of women. Katie, thank you for taking a chance on me and making me laugh till I cry; Ann and Marjorie, I loved our 'shifts' (sorry, Ann!) together then, and our coffee dates now. The two and a half years I worked with you all were some of the happiest of my life. Without you, there would be no Minna.